THE BLOOD BRIDE

Other Books by Rae D. Magdon

Amendyr Series

The Second Sister - Book 1

Wolf's Eyes - Book 2

The Witch's Daughter - Book 3

Wolf Eyes – Book 4

Lucky Breaks Series

Lucky 7

Lucky 8

Death Wears Yellow Garters

Fur and Fangs

Tengoku

Song of Stars

And with Michelle Magly

All the Pretty Things

Dark Horizons Series

Dark Horizons – Book 1

Starless Night – Book 2

Eclipse – Book 3

THE BLOOD BRIDE

RAE D. MAGDON

Desert Palm Press

The Blood Bride

By Rae D. Magdon

©2023 Rae D. Magdon

ISBN (book): 9781954213739
ISBN (epub): 9781954213746

Desert Palm Press
1961 Main Street, Suite 220
Watsonville, California 95076
www.desertpalmpress.com

Editor: CK King
Cover Design: Rachel George Illustration

Printed in the United States of America
First Edition August 2023

Acknowledgments:

Toska, mintychocochoo, Rico D, Luna, and all my patrons on Patreon!

Dedication

To Tory and to Desert Palm Press

Chapter One

THE STORMY, RESTLESS AURA of magic filled the cavern. That Which Dwells Beneath the Ice was closer to waking than ever before. Valis descended the spiral staircase of thick, blue ice dusted with powdery snow to prevent slippage. The magic resisted, an invisible barrier attempting to push her back. It didn't appreciate her intrusion and it told her so with a biting blast of wind that whipped against her fur-lined robes.

She ignored the wind and continued. Down, down, down.

The daylight above faded, then disappeared. Valis' eyes, well-used to dim light, began to fail her so deep beneath the surface. She drew Aefbain from the scabbard strapped to her outer thigh. The dagger glowed red and dim like a dying candle, providing just enough light to see. Not that there was anything to see other than the fog of her own breath and more ghostly blue ice, tinted purple by Aefbain's light.

It stirs, Aefbain whispered in Valis' mind. Its voice was soft but frightened, like the thrum of her own heartbeat in her ears. *Don't you feel it?*

Valis scoffed. "Of course. What sort of question is that?"

Just checking. No need to get pissy.

Valis rolled her eyes and continued down the stairs. The blackness grew blacker and the cold grew colder, as though she'd dived, naked, into the deepest, darkest part of the northern ocean. Still she descended, following a path none but her bloodline had trod in centuries.

After a long time, Valis spotted a soft, white glow in the distance. She hurried down the last few steps to an enormous cavern, three times the size of her own palace on the glacier above. Huge icicles hung from the ceiling, refracting every bit of light, whose source was locked within the ground: a white orb, buried at least a hundred feet beneath the frozen floor. It too was massive, almost as large as her throne room.

Valis followed the only path, a shallow furrow that stopped just before the center of the light. At the end of the path, a frozen pillar held a much smaller orb of polished ice, three feet in diameter. At chest level, this orb looked exceptionally tiny compared to the cavern's vastness and the giant, white glow underfoot.

"Are you ready?" Valis asked Aefbain. Her voice sounded small and lonely in the depths of the large cavern.

1

Are you?

Without hesitation, Valis removed her right glove and drew Aefbain across her palm. Blood welled from the wound, but she felt no pain. She'd done this countless times since becoming Queen Valis Nyxera Aefbain. Placing her dripping hand upon the orb, she sang as her blood, her magic, her very essence, seeped into the ice.

"I am Aefbain, daughter of Aefbain.
Look upon my mother's blade.
That which dwells beneath the ice,
Tis I shall see your blood price paid.
Magic blood into the deep.
Magic blood to soothe your sleep.
I am Aefbain, daughter of Aefbain.
Through my blood, the compact keep."

Aefbain flared crimson in Valis' left hand. A moment later, so did the orb. Its surface grew cloudy, whorls of dark red spreading through the clear, blue ice. Far below, the giant sphere did the same. With painstaking slowness, red overtook white until the light shone a brilliant scarlet.

Valis hardly noticed. Dizziness struck hard and fast. She swayed, then collapsed to her knees. Aefbain clattered onto the ice as Valis caught herself on her hands—one bleeding, one clean. She panted, curtains of snow-white hair hanging limp on either side of her face. When she blinked, she saw three different Aefbain's blurring into one another.

Excuse you. Aefbain's voice dripped with reproach. *You dropped me! Aren't you going to apologize?*

Valis licked her cracked lips, trying to collect herself. Though she'd only sacrificed a small portion of her blood, she'd poured considerable power into the spell. She felt frozen in a way even a warm fire wouldn't soothe. Groaning, she groped for Aefbain, finding the grip with her unbloodied palm.

Trembling, weary, she pressed the blade flat across her wounded palm. Burning, the scent of sizzling flesh, then—nothing. The cut was closed. She felt no pain, only bone-deep exhaustion.

You're welcome, by the way.

"Oh, shut up." Valis shoved the dagger back into its sheath. It muttered its contempt, which she ignored, flipping onto her back and spreading her arms and legs as though she were a child making a snow hawk. The icicles above glittered like stars. Briefly, she wished one might snap free, fall, and pierce her heart.

But no.

No one else could fulfill the compact. No one else could protect her people. Only an Aefbain could keep That Which Dwells Beneath frozen in the depths where it belonged, and she was the last of her line. *Nothing but a worthless scion, drained of power faster than it can be replenished. What will happen next month, and the month after that?*

You needn't be the last, Aefbain pointed out. *You have options.*

Valis closed her eyes. She didn't want to consider those options, but with how exhausting the ritual had been this time, and all the times before, she had little choice. Perhaps it was time to admit that Ruith and Shalana were truly gone.

You never should have died for me, Mother. Sister. But since you have, I will do whatever is necessary to preserve what you and our ancestors built. What you entrusted into my care.

She opened her eyes, pushing herself into a seated position. Stray bits of snow clung to her cape and sleeves. "Very well, Aefbain. I will inform my advisers that I'm in need of a consort. If you speak another word to me about it before then, I'll put you in the nightstand and leave you there for a week."

* * * * *

Brynn trod softly through the forest, rolling the balls of her feet to silence each step. The damp leaves crunched less than usual, one of many reasons she preferred hunting after heavy rain. She held her bow loosely, but the line of her shoulders remained tense. While she trailed the deer she'd been hunting for the better part of the morning, something else was hunting her.

She spotted the deer first, a young buck whose branching antlers marked him as a fine specimen. Slipping behind a tree, she watched him. The buck turned his head, scanning for predators, but didn't see her hiding place. After a while, he lowered his head to graze on the weeds sprouting from the forest floor.

Brynn nocked an arrow to her bow. She hesitated. The presence that had stalked her for the last hour was close. She suspected it would make its move soon.

A black shadow leaped from the canopy of a neighboring tree, hurtling over her from above. No time to think. Brynn released her arrow, causing the shadow to yowl before its bulk crashed into her. Sharp pain snapped in her right side. The breath rushed from her lungs as she hit the ground.

But the creature wasn't dead, as it should have been after a direct hit, and she'd dropped her bow when she fell. She eyed the large, black panther. It was a treestalker—or it had been once. Now it was all wrong. Thorned vines sprouted from its back, and its yellow eyes gleamed with madness. A second, smaller mouth opened beneath the first as it roared, spraying Brynn's face with spittle. The Rot.

Brynn groped for her bow. Too late. The treestalker had knocked it well out of reach. As the creature's fangs flashed in her face, the world slowed. She felt a stab of terror, then sudden, eerie calm. Heat bloomed in her hands as she threw them up to shield her head.

Blue light flashed. The treestalker shrieked, thrashing as cold, hungry blue flames licked its patchwork hide. Brynn didn't waste her chance. She scrambled for her bow, firing another arrow right between the beast's eyes.

The treestalker dropped like a stone, dead the instant the arrow pierced its brain. Brynn remained where she was, panting. A surge of euphoria flooded her chest. *I'm alive!*

Fuck. I used magic again. Granted, it had been to save her own life, but she'd promised herself...

Darrow would call me an idiot. Brynn picked herself up. She winced at the pain in her ribs. Her shoulder bled where the treestalker's claws had gouged her flesh. This day was getting worse by the minute. She didn't even have a deer to show for her near-death experience, only the treestalker's carcass. Useless for eating, Rotted as it was, and she didn't have the necessary supplies to dispose of its body. It needed to be done soon.

Keenly disappointed but unwilling to admit defeat, Brynn made sure the magical flames she'd produced were well and truly gone before limping off through the forest and heading back toward her village. Hopefully her parents wouldn't ask too many questions about her injuries. She doubted she'd be so lucky.

The trek back to the village took longer than Brynn hoped. Her legs worked, at least to a degree, but the rest of her was in bad shape. She was staggering by the time she arrived, sweaty and exhausted. Greenglass village was tucked in a peaceful grove between the forest's edge and the eponymous river. Its silhouette was a welcome sight when she broke the tree line.

Several residents noticed her arrival, peeking out of vine-strewn huts and flower-adorned treehouses. A few folk of mixed elven and human heritage straightened up from their vegetable gardens and hurried over to support her. Brynn knew them all by name, as one did in a small community.

"Brynn?"

"By the Great Root, what happened?!"

"Are you all right?"

Brynn gave no reply other than, "I'm fine," which she mumbled over and over as half a dozen worried neighbors escorted her to the middle of the village. She was on her sixth I'm fine when she saw a familiar face. The old elf's skin was brown and wrinkled like the bark of a tree, but clear eyes caught and pinned her as though an arrow through her jerkin.

"*Sa'thalas,* Grandchild."

Brynn averted her eyes, staring shamefaced down at her boots. The ancient elf hobbled toward her with the aid of a gnarled walking stick. "I'm fine, Grandmother."

Grandmother was not actually her grandmother—more like her great-aunt once removed—but they were distantly related somehow. More importantly, Grandmother had done as much to raise her as her own parents, who scurried out of the same cottage with identical worried expressions.

"Brynn?" Her father, Galen, was mostly human but not entirely. A bushy, black beard covered the lower half of his pale face, and he had a round belly with tree trunks for limbs. Normally cheerful, he wasn't smiling at all.

"Oh, you're bleeding!" Her mother, Isuna, more obviously of elven blood with tapered ears and brown skin, looked just as upset. She hurried past Grandmother, taking Brynn's injured arm in gentle hands for closer examination.

Brynn's heart sank. Glad as she was to be alive, she'd hoped to avoid a scene. "A Rotted treestalker," she said before anyone could ask. "Its body lies two hours' walk to the southeast."

Grandmother nodded to some of the worried onlookers, young ones around Brynn's age. Three detached from the group, presumably to gather weapons and torches. Their people had learned, through trial and error, that ritualistic fire was the only way to cleanse the desecrated corpses before they spread the Rot to other living parts of the forest.

"Another?" Galen asked. "But we killed one near the village just last week."

Brynn sighed. "I know. Please, can I sit down?"

Isuna took charge, leading Brynn into Grandmother's hut by the elbow and fending off the remaining gawkers. "Let her be. Can't you see she's injured?"

Brynn disliked having that fact pointed out, but she submitted, allowing her mother to seat her in a wooden chair at Grandmother's table. She slumped, resting on her good arm as Galen returned with a medicine kit. Thankfully, the hut was dark and cool. Brynn allowed herself to relax amid the familiar smell of herbs and stew.

"Flush the wound well." Grandmother closed the door, following them into the kitchen at a slower pace. "The last thing we want is an infection."

"Of course, Grandmother," Isuna said from the fireplace, where she'd already replaced the stew with a kettle of water.

Brynn shuddered. She'd seen Rot wounds go bad. The results were nightmarish. These days, her people could protect themselves to a certain extent, but in previous years, the Rot hadn't been as well understood. There was still much they didn't know—like why it was spreading.

She didn't make a peep when Isuna brought over the kettle and bathed her injured shoulder with a steaming cloth, nor when she spread a poultice of bank moss and crushed moonflower root over the gashes. Isuna finished it off by wrapping the wound in clean bandages.

"Much better." Brynn winced only slightly as Isuna pulled the bandages tighter. "Thanks, Mom."

"You should have brought a hunting partner with you," Galen said. "You know how dangerous the forest is."

The furrow in his brow and the worry in his pale eyes made Brynn's stomach churn with guilt. She averted her eyes. "I know. I'm sorry." *It's just, Darrow used to be my hunting partner. My partner in everything. Going with someone else feels wrong.* Speaking that truth aloud to her parents would be needlessly painful for everyone.

Even so, her parents knew her well enough to read the heavy silence that followed. Brynn had lost a twin brother. They had lost a child.

"I'm glad you're home safe, Brynn," Grandmother said, ending the somber moment, "because an important message arrived today, from Winterwail."

At the mention of Winterwail, Brynn's spine stiffened. Fresh pain seized her ribs, but she hardly noticed. "The snow elves? Why? The only thing I have to say to them is with my arrows."

Grandmother's placid expression hardened, her eyes glittering like cut emeralds. "Circumstances have changed. Two years ago, in fact, but you were grieving and didn't want to hear it then. The snow elves haven't sent any hunting parties into our forest since."

"That we *know of*." Brynn sounded petulant even to her own ears.

Said ears drooped as she noted her parents' frowns. She realized how inappropriate her response had been, especially toward Grandmother. Shouting and contradicting elders simply wasn't done.

"Forgive me," she murmured, trying not to squirm in her seat like a sulking child. "I spoke out of turn."

"I see your pain," Grandmother said, with the same piercing stare. Brynn sometimes wondered whether Grandmother could see into her very soul. "We all mourn Darrow's loss, but the Rot continues to spread. There may come a time when we can no longer protect ourselves, even with the help of the neighboring villages."

"You want the snow elves to fight the Rot?" The idea made Brynn uncomfortable to her core, though there was a cold, calculating sense to it. She didn't want the snow elves anywhere near her home, but letting one rotten thing fight another was an elegant solution. While the other people in her village were wary of snow elves, not all carried the same grudge she did.

"It isn't that simple," Isuna said. "Alliances come at a cost." Exchanging a furtive look with Galen and Grandmother, she withdrew a scroll from beneath her cloak, unrolling it onto the table. The wax seal upon its edge had been broken. The paper was completely blank.

"An empty scroll?" Brynn's sensitivity to magic was hardly the most reliable, but she didn't notice anything odd.

Grandmother took the nearest empty chair, pulling it close beside Brynn. With some assistance from Galen, she sat, withdrawing a vegetable peeling knife from her belt. "Hold out your palm."

Expecting Grandmother to give her the knife, Brynn winced as the blade flicked across her palm. She retracted her hand, but it was too late. A thin trickle of blood oozed from the shallow cut.

"What was that for?" Brynn cradled her hand to her chest. Her heart hurt more than the cut itself. "We don't... we don't *do* that kind of magic."

Blood magic was the dangerous, degrading kind of magic snow

elves and their ilk used. Druidic magic was the pure, wild energy the forest provided in exchange for her people's stewardship. *Darrow's* magic.

"Magic is magic. Power is power." Grandmother took Brynn's bleeding hand. Reluctantly. Brynn allowed it. She watched, wide-eyed, as Grandmother pressed her bleeding palm over the scroll. Wet, crimson lines spread from her cut like vines growing along invisible tree limbs, or a spider's web of incomprehensible patterns.

Isuna and Galen gasped, but Brynn remained hypnotized by the sight of her own blood writhing across the paper. Gradually, the squirming lines solidified into something recognizable: a downward-pointing dagger with a six-pronged, stylized snowflake at its cross hilt.

Brynn's stomach sank like a stone. She recalled that symbol all too well. She snatched her hand back from the scroll, but the damage was done. The scarlet dagger remained, shimmering with fresh blood. "Why did it do that?"

Galen looked pointedly away. Isuna withdrew another bandage from the medicine kit and offered it wordlessly to Brynn so she could bind her own hand. Only Grandmother met her gaze, though her eyes had softened with sadness, perhaps even sympathy.

"It means your blood was tested and found satisfactory. You must go to Winterwail and present yourself to the queen."

Brynn's jaw dropped. Her mind shouted *No!* but she managed to bite her tongue. Another outburst wouldn't help her case. "But why?"

"The queen seeks a consort among those with powerful, willing blood. Fortunately for us, her needs are quite specific. The scroll was a test. You passed."

Brynn looked down at the scroll, then back at Grandmother, pushing her jaw forward in defiance. "My blood isn't willing and neither am I."

"The scroll says otherwise," Grandmother said. "I suspected it would. Though you've refused training, there is powerful magic in your blood."

"But I'm part human," Brynn protested. "We aren't usually magical—"

"And your brother, also part human, was the most talented young wildmage this village has ever seen. The same potential lies within you. You must go and present yourself at court. In exchange, Winterwail will cull the Rotted creatures within our forest and their Artificers will work with our Druids to find a permanent solution."

All of Brynn's instincts urged her to protest, but to her great displeasure, she understood Grandmother's point of view. The Rot had consumed more and more of the forest over the past few decades, starting before she was born. Year after year, it spread faster. If things didn't change, Greenglass might be overrun.

Winterwail had a proper army. Soldiers to cull the Rotted creatures. Even if all other villages loosely allied with Greenglass sent their finest warriors, wildmages, and Druids, they wouldn't have enough people to achieve such a daunting task.

"All I have to do is show up?" Brynn asked. "What if the queen doesn't pick me? Will she still help us?"

"I cannot be certain," Grandmother said, "but if you refuse to attend at all, it will severely hamper our request for aid. Either way, you must appeal to her. Convince her to help us."

Brynn shook her head. "Me? A diplomat? You must be joking."

"Unfortunately not," Isuna said. "Hopefully, she'll like you enough to help us, but not enough to marry you. Honestly, I doubt she'll choose you. We know aristocracy and bloodlines aren't important, but the snow elves are obsessed with ancestry."

Galen nodded. "Right. They'll probably pick someone from their own kingdom, a bloodline they know, but since you qualify, we need to use this opportunity to get an audience with her. It might be our only hope."

"What makes you think she'll listen to me?" Brynn said with a hint of pained laughter. "As far as she's concerned, I'm a bumpkin from the middle of the woods!"

"Exactly." Isuna placed her hand on Brynn's shoulder, and Brynn grudgingly accepted the touch. "But if we humor the queen, Winterwail might help us. And we need the help."

Brynn pressed her lips into a thin line. "I don't like it. At all. They're the ones who..." Her unfinished sentence hung in the air like a loose, frayed thread at the edge of a tapestry, a sign of damage deeper within the weave.

"I know," said Grandmother, "but our people and our way of life must be preserved before all is lost. Do you understand?"

Brynn thought of the Rotted treestalker. She allowed herself to feel the pain in her shoulder and ribs. She remembered the icy knife of terror that lodged in her gut as it snarled over her with its two mouths. And of course, she remembered Darrow. She tried to imagine him alive, rather than lying on the ground in a pool of his own blood, an arrow piercing the middle of his throat.

Can I live with myself if I don't do whatever I can to fight the Rot? What would Darrow do?

"Fine. I'll go, but I can't promise the queen will pick me. In fact, I'm going to do everything I can to convince her otherwise—without ruining our chances."

Grandmother smiled. "I expected nothing less."

Chapter Two

"WHAT DO YOU THINK, Kraal?" Valis stared at her reflection in the full-length mirror. She held two dresses before her, similar in design but dyed different shades. "Blue or violet?"

The frost giant stood at her post by the bedroom door, taller than the door frame itself. Her gray face remained fixed in a neutral expression. She blinked, then uttered one word in a gravelly alto. "Blue."

"Thank you. Let's see." Valis draped the violet dress over the adjacent vanity's chair and held the other in front of herself. The royal-blue ball gown fit tightly in the bodice and waist before flaring dramatically at midthigh. The white ermine fur trimming the neckline and hem was accented with sewn-in, black tail spots. She had yet to try it on but knew it would fit perfectly.

Though beautifully tailored, imagining herself in the dress brought Valis no spark of joy. The mere thought made her queasy. The gown had been her mother's, one of many things Valis had inherited from Queen Ruith in recent months. Her castle, her kingdom, and of course...

You should wear the purple one, Aefbain said from its resting place atop the vanity. Valis had removed it to change, but as usual, being sheathed in its scabbard didn't stop Aefbain from sharing its opinion.

"Are you saying that to be contrary, or because you actually think so?" Valis asked without turning.

Contrary? You wound me, Queen Valis.

"You are well aware how immensely I dislike being addressed as Queen in private," Valis said in her iciest voice. "I may have to hear it from my subjects and my advisers to keep up appearances, but I refuse to endure it from you."

She stepped into the royal-blue gown, pulling it up to her chest and sliding her arms through the sleeves. Kraal left her station by the door, standing behind Valis and doing up the laces with large but practiced fingers. Valis' shoulders sagged. She averted her eyes, avoiding her reflection.

It flatters you, Your Majesty. Aefbain's silky voice sounded almost sincere. Perhaps it might have been. Aefbain was occasionally kind, but liberal doses of sarcasm were to be expected. The dagger held pieces of her ancestors' souls, and the Aefbain dynasty had never been particularly humble.

Reluctantly, Valis glanced at herself in the mirror. The dress did flatter her, which was part of the problem. It made her look older, more like her sister Shalana, or perhaps a younger version of her mother. They shared the same periwinkle skin, the same long, white hair, the same slate-gray eyes. It wasn't a comparison Valis enjoyed, only serving to remind her that they were gone.

"Thank you," she said to Kraal, who had finished with the laces.

"You're welcome." Kraal stepped back, allowing Valis to finish observing herself. Begrudgingly, she admitted that she looked presentable. It was a good thing, too, or she'd surely get an earful from Naddox, one of her three advisers.

That reminded her of something else. "Will you please do something with my hair as well? Naddox won't give me a moment's peace if I leave it down."

Kraal went to the dresser, returning with a comb and hairpins. She worked with silent efficiency, pulling Valis' hair off her shoulders and weaving it into a crown of interlocking braids around her head.

In the span of a few minutes, Valis' hair was finished. The final touch was a longer, decorative hairpin, with a white rose on the end, which sat atop the crown of braids like the snow-capped peak of a mountain above the frosty tundra.

It looked lovely.

She looked lovely.

Valis felt horrible.

An eruption of cloying black smoke from the fireplace interrupted her gloomy thoughts. Rather than the normal scent of burning wood, the sweeter, spoiled smell reminded her of rotten fruit. The oily cloud billowed, then hung in the air without dispersing.

Naddox. Wonderful.

"Thank you, Kraal." Valis flashed her attendant a weak smile. "That will be all for now."

Kraal frowned around her tusks, but returned to her post, resembling a statue once more. Meanwhile, Valis turned to the fire. She took Aefbain from the vanity and drew the blade from its scabbard, cutting the back of her arm with the dagger's tip.

Your blood tastes bitter this morning, Aefbain casually informed her. *Does your adviser irk you so before he's even manifested?*

Valis refused to rise to the bait. She watched until drops of blood welled from the cut, then flicked them casually into the fireplace.

As soon as her blood touched the flames, the cloud of smoke took on a recognizable shape. The gloom condensed into a tall column, from which sprouted arms, legs, and a head. More details emerged—piercing blue eyes, a thin nose, flowing white hair—until a very lifelike version of a snow elf stood before her, carrying a bejeweled golden staff and wearing formal green robes.

"Your Majesty." The smoke shape of Naddox bowed at the waist, folding one arm beneath his torso and extending the other backward with an unnecessary flourish. "I trust you are well this morning?"

Valis pursed her lips, sheathing Aefbain. "Well enough, thank you. And yourself?"

"Very well, for I have the opportunity to serve—"

"Yes." Valis pretended she didn't realize Naddox wanted to continue. He *always* continued. She suspected it was because he disliked her and enjoyed needling her whenever possible. Naddox had been her mother's pick for adviser. Valis' position as queen was far too new to consider appointing her own.

Naddox straightened, standing a head taller than Valis. "The latest nine candidates who wish to become your consort are ready to be tested. Will you see them before lunch, Your Majesty?"

Valis fought a sigh. It was an order disguised as a request. She didn't relish her position as queen, but lately she'd received more 'orders' from Naddox than she gave herself. "Of course. See to it that they're fed and made comfortable. And be sure to ask if any might faint at the sight of blood." The last thing she wanted was a repeat of the previous week's disaster. The poor maiden had been hurried to the infirmary, and Valis still felt responsible for the unfortunate incident.

"As you command, Your Majesty."

It was difficult to prevent herself from pulling a face, but Valis managed. Years of tedious royal functions had to pay off somehow. "You are dismissed, Lord-Adviser Naddox. I will be ready within an hour."

Naddox gave a tight smile. "There is one more issue to discuss, Your Majesty. A fortnight has passed since you last descended beneath the palace. I must remind you that it would be prudent to select a consort before the next ritual."

Valis gritted her teeth. "I am well aware. However, none of the candidates have been strong enough for Aefbain. If you wish us to make our selection faster, bring us better candidates."

Naddox's smile faltered, but only for a moment. He was all honeyed words as he bowed one final time. "It is my sincerest hope that you'll find one among this next group."

"And my hope as well," Valis said.

"Then I shall leave you to your preparations, Your Majesty. Farewell."

Valis waved her hand. "You are dismissed."

Naddox disappeared in a final, dramatic puff of black smoke. Valis coughed, lifting her forearm to shield her mouth.

Naddox is warming up to you, Aefbain drawled. *Why, I've never seen the two of you more at ease with each other.*

Kraal had a blunter interpretation of events. "Dick," she muttered from her place by the door.

Valis laughed. She knew it was rude, but she couldn't help it. Naddox *was* a dick, with all his extra unnecessary bowing, scraping, and whining. He hadn't waited a minute after her mother died before attempting to insinuate himself into her good graces, when he'd hardly paid her the slightest bit of attention before—likely because he'd assumed Shalana would ascend to the throne.

Oh, how I wish that had happened.

Her laughter faded into a sigh as she pushed the sad thought from her mind. She already had enough to endure this morning, and she hadn't even gotten around to eating breakfast. "Thank you, Kraal. You always know what to say."

The slightest hint of a smile twitched around Kraal's tusks. "Yes, milady."

* * * * *

Standing amidst a throng of fur-clad city folk, Brynn gaped at Winterwail's tall, gleaming palace. Carved into the side of a ghostly blue glacier, its walls and parapets sparkled in the morning light. Three narrow spires thrust into the sky, casting the sprawling city below in an eerie glow that reminded Brynn of diving underwater.

"Isn't it beautiful?" Isuna clasped Brynn's hand.

"Yes," Brynn murmured, though she doubted she admired it the same way her mother did. The palace possessed an ethereal aura that left her as unsettled as she was awestruck. It wasn't a natural beauty like the forest or tundra, so she remained somewhat cold.

Cold. I've been cold nonstop for the past week.

Though she and her mother had packed their warmest furs, the bitter chill seeped into Brynn's bones even during the warmest parts of the day. The prospect, however unlikely, of living in such a climate was horrifying to consider.

Others had no such reservations. The city was bustling with merchants hawking their wares around the palace's walls. There were plenty of humans, as in every country, but fewer snow elves than Brynn expected considering it was the capital of their kingdom. Brynn only caught a few glimpses of them, blue or purple skinned, tall and slender, wrapped in luxurious furs with their ears tucked into warm caps.

Most common were the frost giants, sturdy folk of eight or nine feet. Their faces were various shades of gray and curved tusks jutted from their mouths. The tusks were often adorned with rings and other jewelry, which Brynn admired. Jewelry was rare in Greenglass, since it served little practical purpose.

Several more frost giants stood guard in front of the palace, carrying stone clubs which Brynn doubted two elves could lift together. "Um, hello." Brynn offered the guards a friendly wave. "We have an audience with the queen?" She glanced uncertainly at her mother.

"Right," Isuna said. "Here's our invitation." She unrolled the parchment, still covered in a sprawling spiderweb of dried blood.

The frost giants said nothing. They didn't even make eye contact. They stood still as statues without any kind of acknowledgment.

"Excuse me, please!" A high, fast voice said from behind the giants. A dark-skinned human pushed her way through. The woman from the southern deserts had large, beautiful brown eyes that took up more than their fair portion of her face. Even standing still, she seemed to vibrate with energy, or perhaps nervousness. Wrapped in furs as she was, Brynn could discern little else.

"Honored guests," the woman said, "please tell me that one of you is the last prospective candidate to be tested by Queen Aefbain this morning. We're missing a..." She drew a scroll from within her coat, studying it while mouthing the names in silence until she landed upon the correct one. "Brynn Woodwarden?"

"That would be me," Brynn said with forced cheer.

The woman sighed, smiling with relief. "Excellent. Only eight candidates simply wouldn't do. My name is Delia, Assistant Manager of Social Engagements in Winterwail." She said it all in a rush, smushing words together as though the title were part of her name.

"Nice to meet you, Delia," Brynn said. "So, there are nine candidates in all?"

Delia motioned Brynn and Isuna past the guards, who didn't spare them a glance. "Yes, there are nine in each group."

Groups? That made Brynn feel better. Surely the queen would find a consort more suitable than her. All that remained was to make herself as undesirable as possible while still being persuasive so Queen Aefbain would sympathize with their cause. A fine line to walk.

"Is there somewhere we can prepare for my daughter's audience?" Isuna asked, breathing heavily as she struggled to keep up with Delia's blistering pace. "Receive some instructions, perhaps? Brynn and I have never been to a royal court before."

"Goodness, no!" Delia cried. "There's no time. We must go straight to the throne room. Queen Aefbain is scheduled to arrive in five minutes."

"Five minutes?" Isuna repeated, sounding horrified.

Brynn barely stifled a laugh. Five minutes? She couldn't have planned this better if she'd tried. In no possible world would the queen select a scrubby, mixed-race elf fresh from two weeks of travel, no matter how powerful her magic was. No doubt she looked a mess and didn't smell much better. Once she'd been rejected, Isuna—far more diplomatic and refined—could make their case.

Delia hurried them through a pair of towering double doors. Like everything else, they were made of crystalline ice. Brynn wondered if the entire palace was magically preserved to prevent it from melting or if it really was that cold in Winterwail. Her breath came fast and hot past her chapped lips, forming clouds of mist.

The palace's interior boasted decorative ice columns and carved sculptures of northern animals, which looked incredibly lifelike from the quick glances Brynn stole. Club-wielding frost giants patrolled the hall, but none acknowledged their small trio as they rushed past.

Before Brynn had a chance to admire the vaulted ceilings or determine which chandeliers were made of ice or crystal, Delia stopped before another set of doors. "Here we are, with one and a half minutes to spare." She paused, looking Brynn up and down. "You look... fine. Nice. You look nice. Please excuse me." With an apologetic nod to Isuna, Delia grabbed Brynn by the elbow and hauled her through the doors.

Brynn found herself in an enormous throne room. Its interior possessed the same ghostly blue glow, which left her just as unsettled as her first sight of the palace from a distance. Before her, eight other women stood in a straight line. The majority were snow elves, who ranged from lilac to blue-gray in hue, but Brynn noticed two other wood elves—full-blooded, judging by their builds and the length of their ears—and a single fair-haired human.

Not all the women were stunning beauties. Half were conventionally lovely, perhaps snow elf nobles, but the others were what most would call plain. Two were even middle aged. Though they all wore clothes far finer than Brynn's ragged traveling cloak and snow-damp furs, they weren't what she'd expected.

"Stand here." Delia shoved Brynn toward the end of the line. The other women turned, examining her much as she'd examined them. Brynn's face burned. She'd relished the thought of looking a wild mess before, but it was still mildly embarrassing to be judged by so many strangers. Surely she resembled a drowned rat more than a prospective bride.

To avoid returning their stares, Brynn studied the rest of the room. Two symmetrical stairways of ice, dusted liberally with powdered snow, dominated the far wall. They curved up toward a shimmering throne of blue ice, with a stylized frozen waterfall in three tiers descending from its base. Upon the throne sat a slender figure, whom Brynn couldn't see well from a distance.

Is that Queen Aefbain? Of course it is. Who else would dare sit on the throne?

She swallowed, then whispered to Delia out the corner of her mouth. "Um, should I bow, or...?"

"When she approaches," Delia whispered before making good her escape. "Best of luck!" She slipped away faster than anyone should be able to move. In another life, she could have been a master thief—except for the loud voice.

Queen Aefbain rose from her throne, descending the left stairway with all the grace and poise one might expect of royalty. Brynn's heart hammered, leaping up into her throat. To her immense relief, the queen didn't approach her end of the line. She began on the other side, working left to right.

Brynn tried to observe without being obvious but forgot all subtlety as Queen Aefbain paused in front of the first candidate, who curtsied deeply. Queen Aefbain said something in a low voice Brynn couldn't hear, then drew a ruby-encrusted dagger from a scabbard strapped to her thigh. Sweat sprouted on the back of Brynn's neck. The slit in the queen's dress was much higher than she'd expected, and the pale-blue thigh that peeked out was slender but toned.

Don't stare at the queen's legs, idiot. Do you want to be thrown in the dungeon?!

She forgot all about ogling when Queen Aefbain sliced the dagger across the first candidate's hand. As soon as a thin trickle of blood touched its blade, the dagger flared red. Redder than a ripe apple fallen from its tree. Redder than holly berries. Red as the blood it had spilled. The queen murmured something, and the candidate curtsied again, taking a step back from the line.

The process was repeated with the next candidate. And the next. And the next.

Brynn's confidence wavered as Queen Aefbain approached her end of the line. The longer the queen went without selecting another candidate, the more agitated Brynn became. Her heart pounded and her stomach twisted into a nervous knot. The dagger glowed each time, sometimes bright, sometimes dim, but always a vivid red.

She doesn't seem to care who these women are or how they look. It's all about their blood.

It was an unpleasant realization. If the queen only cared about blood, Brynn's attempts to be off-putting wouldn't work. She could only hope the dagger wouldn't react to the magic in her blood. Magic had always been Darrow's domain, not hers.

Soon, only one other candidate remained. As Queen Aefbain sliced her neighbor's hand, Brynn watched with intense curiosity. Instead of staring at the dagger, she found herself studying the queen. She was the same height as Brynn—in other words, average—but very slender. Her royal-blue gown clung to her hips, flaring at the upper thigh. Lush white fur patterned with black spots lined the gown's hem, neckline, and sleeves. The neckline itself was low, showing off prominent collarbones and more than a hint of cleavage.

Stop it! If staring at her legs was bad, staring at her tits will probably get you a death sentence.

When Queen Aefbain turned, Brynn's mouth fell open. The queen's eyes were wide set and pale gray, like the sky on a rainy day. Her nose was long and regal, her dark, purple lips surprisingly full. She had what Isuna affectionately referred to as 'diamond cheeks', as in sharp enough to cut.

Oh no. She's beautiful. This is awful.

As Queen Aefbain glided to a stop in front of her, Brynn forgot how to breathe. She stared, stunned, until the queen tilted her head. Everything came rushing back in a flash of heat, unfreezing Brynn's body. She managed a clumsy curtsy, nearly tripping over her own feet. *Thank the seasons. The only thing that could make this moment worse is planting my face in the queen's cleavage.*

"Give me your hand," Queen Aefbain said in a soft, melodious voice.

Brynn nodded dumbly and stuck out her hand. Queen Aefbain's fingers were cool as they wrapped around hers.

"There will be no pain."

And, as Queen Aefbain sliced the dagger across Brynn's palm, there wasn't any. Brynn watched her own blood seep from the wound and onto the blade. A flash of crimson light burst between them, burning Brynn's eyes. She threw up her other hand to shield her face, but the light burned through her closed lids, as though she'd been staring directly into the midday sun.

Brynn's heart dropped straight through her stomach and down to her snow-crusted boots. Apparently, tripping and falling onto the queen wasn't the worst possible outcome after all.

* * * * *

Her. She's the one!

Valis squinted as Aefbain's brilliant glow dimmed. She withdrew the dagger from the wood elf's hand, examining the blade. Aefbain had absorbed her blood, leaving the blade shiny and clean.

Cautiously, Valis lifted her gaze to the candidate Aefbain had chosen. To her dismay, the wood elf wasn't much to look at. She had a handsome face, if such things mattered, but her overall appearance was dirty and disheveled thanks to her damp traveling furs and the bird's nest of brown hair beneath her cap.

I suppose none of that matters, so long as her blood is strong enough for the ritual.

Exactly, Aefbain whispered. *We need the strongest magic possible in order to quell That Which Dwells Beneath. This one possesses incredible power, although there is something... different about the taste of her blood. Something that puzzles me.*

Valis' eyes widened. Aefbain had tasted more blood than she could fathom over the centuries. If this wood elf's blood impressed it, confused it...

"Tell me," Valis said, focusing on the scruffy wood elf. She too had opened her eyes, which were a rich, honeyed shade of amber. "What is your name?"

The wood elf's mouth opened and closed like a stunned fish.

Valis sighed and took the wood elf's hand, placing Aefbain flat over the cut. It healed instantly, but she kept the wood elf's hand in hers afterward, surprised by the noticeable calluses. They were somewhat familiar. An archer? Ah, that was it. Shalana had carried a bow for situations when blood magic wouldn't suffice.

Upon being touched, the wood elf's face hardened. Her stare became visibly cold. "Brynn Woodwarden, Your Majesty."

"Brynn Woodwarden." Valis tested the name. An average name for someone who was, despite appearances, extraordinary—at least according to Aefbain. She had no choice but to trust its judgment. "In that case, Brynn Woodwarden, would you do me the honor of becoming my consort?"

"Me?! But—" Brynn gestured helplessly at the other candidates, who stared back at her with a mixture of envy and fascination.

"Aefbain has selected you." Valis had expected an immediate yes. Brynn Woodwarden's hesitation was becoming awkward, especially in front of all these people, some of whom were nobles in her own kingdom.

"You're letting a dagger choose who you'll marry?" Brynn blurted out, with no small amount of disdain in her voice.

"As is tradition." Valis' jaw tightened. "I will ask once more. Will you do me the honor of becoming my consort?"

Brynn fired back a question of her own. "Will you send your best warriors and Artificers to fight the Rot infecting my home forest?" She pinned Valis with a sharp, accusatory stare.

Valis blinked, not merely due to Brynn's inappropriately demanding tone. Naddox had suggested an offer of aid as a way to widen their pool of potential candidates beyond Winterwail's borders. She had agreed, though she'd doubted such incentive would be necessary. Apparently, she had been incorrect.

It reassured her, in a way. That meant their marriage would be a simple transaction. Better to marry someone with clear expectations rather than a scheming social climber who happened to possess powerful blood. "Yes," she told Brynn. "My adviser has already arranged it. You have my word as Queen of Winterwail."

That didn't seem to reassure Brynn. She squared her shoulders and jutted out her chin, bristling with barely suppressed hostility. Her brown eyes burned like wood upon a blazing hearth, and Valis was taken aback by their spiteful heat.

"No. I can't do this. Coming here was a mistake." Brynn turned and left without another word. Her heavy boots squeaked across the floor as she rushed out of the throne room. She burst through the doors and out into the hallway, leaving the entire throne room in shocked silence.

Valis stared as the doors swung shut. *No?* She could scarcely believe the rejection. She shoved Aefbain into its scabbard, uncomfortably aware of the other candidates' eyes on her. At least they weren't whispering amongst themselves... yet. What would happen when word of this reached her nobles?

You must have made a mistake, Aefbain. How dare you pick the only woman in this kingdom, or any other, who would reject a marriage proposal from a queen? Is this your idea of a joke?

No joke. Still, Aefbain's voice carried a hint of dry amusement. *Her blood is perfect for ritual spell casting. It's the strongest I've tasted in centuries. I've never been wrong before.*

Aefbain's tone stoked the flames of Valis' temper. *Enough! I will not stand for this humiliation. Select another candidate or keep your silence.*

No other even comes close, Aefbain said. *The only way you will avoid humiliation is to convince this Brynn Woodwarden to marry you. So, how are you at courting, Your Majesty?*

Valis balled her hands. "Delia," she snapped.

Delia scurried over and made a deep curtsey. "Yes, Your Majesty?" From Delia's look of shock, she'd witnessed the entire spectacle from the sidelines.

"Find her." Valis brandished a finger at the double doors through which Brynn had escaped. "Now."

Chapter Three

NO, NO, NO.NO! The word thumped in Brynn's head, in her ears, in the cage of her chest. *No. No. No.* The frantic drum throbbed faster with each frigid breath. *No* followed every pained pulse of her heart.

She burst through the throne room's double doors, skidding on the icy floor despite the dusting of snow beneath her boots. Steadying herself, she ran down the hallway, unsure where she was going except away. The frost giants standing guard made no move to stop her. She ignored them, hardly even seeing them.

No. She would not, *could* not, do this. She'd come to Winterwail with the best of intentions: present herself to Queen Aefbain; be rejected for a lengthy list of reasons; secure the snow elves' assistance and her people's future. Yet against all logic, the queen had chosen her. How had everything gone so wrong?

Brynn stopped, breathless, and sagged against one of the spiraling ice columns that lined the hallway. Tears burned in her eyes. The taste of copper rose in her mouth, the scent of red in her nose. *Blood, a bright crimson pool, gushing around the arrow embedded in...*

No. She had to leave this place and banish the cold that had lived in her bones these past two weeks. Forget the shudder that had crawled down her spine as Queen Aefbain's dagger bit into her flesh. Not hurting, but all the more horrifying for that. Brynn would have welcomed the normalcy of pain in that moment. Instead, she'd felt...

She couldn't name it. To name it would be to make it real. Not merely to acknowledge it but accept it. She refused.

"Brynn!"

Isuna. Her mother's voice should have been familiar, soothing. Instead, Brynn's gut churned with self-loathing. Isuna grasped her by the shoulders, pulling her away from the column.

Brynn closed her eyes, hot tears running down her cheeks. "I can't," she said through gritted teeth. "Queen Aefbain asked me to marry her, but I..." She'd already said no, but how could she refuse? How could she disappoint every single person she'd ever known? *Selfish, selfish, selfish.*

"Brynn." Isuna's voice struck, hammer upon anvil, sharp and demanding. "Look at me."

Brynn blinked back her tears. Isuna's face didn't burn with anger but pulled taut with pain. Her own eyes, brown like Brynn's, glistened with tears. "Queen Aefbain didn't kill your brother," Isuna said softly. "It wasn't her hand that drew the bow. The arrow didn't come from her quiver."

Fiery heat burned in Brynn's throat, a dragon of anger. "It did! Her hunters are her arrows, her kingdom her quiver. They invaded our lands for blood—"

"For game," Isuna said.

"They drained his body!"

That was the worst of it. The wound that would never heal. Above all, the thing Brynn couldn't forgive. The snow elves had come to poach unicorns, whose silver blood possessed strong magic, but the Rot had proven far more dangerous than they bargained for.

A frightened, exhausted scout had mistaken Darrow's shadow for a Rotted creature. Such monsters had dogged them for three days. None of the hunters had slept. Their captain told these things to Brynn as she knelt by her brother's crumpled form, silently weeping. Darrow lay still in a pool of his own blood—pale, so pale, except for the red stain on his throat and chest.

Despite profuse apologies, they'd opened up Darrow's body while it was still warm. As though he were merely a corpse and not a person. "We cannot waste," they'd told her. "You must understand."

They painted wards in his blood. Coated their arrows and blades. Their healer used it to cleanse an injured hunter's leg before the Rot took hold. They stole her dead brother's blood to sustain themselves.

Brynn had screamed at them to stop. She'd strung arrow to bow and declared she would put it between the eyes of anyone who defiled her twin's body. They took her weapon and bound her, dragged her to Greenglass like an impudent child. They handed her over, offered galling apologies to her parents, and left. Without punishment. Without *suffering* for the murder they'd committed.

"Would you rather they burned him?" Isuna's voice brought Brynn back to the present, replacing the hammer with a soft blanket which Brynn longed to wrap herself in. "You know our traditions. Unless they are Rotted, our bodies return to the forest. The forest gives to us, so we return her blessing."

Brynn sniffed, wiping her nose and eyes on her sleeve. "Darrow's body didn't return to the forest, not until after they stole his blood."

"Don't you think I grieve what happened?" Isuna cupped Brynn's cheek. Brynn's face was so numb from cold that she felt little more than gentle pressure. "Don't you think your father and I feel angry? Cheated? A mother should never outlive her children, but I remember that band of hunters—"

"Poaching murderers."

"They were young, Brynn." Isuna's eyes held an ocean's worth of grief. "Little more than children, some of them. A few were younger than the two of you were then. In the middle of the night, when the pain is unbearable, I wonder what would I say to their mothers. If their captain hadn't used Darrow's blood, what would I say to the mother of the hunter with the infected leg? My son is gone, so yours should die too?"

"They cut him open!"

"We do the same when we hunt," Isuna said, low and mournful like a night wind. "We respect their bodies by using them to sustain ourselves. That's exactly what the snow elves did, in a different way."

"That isn't... he wasn't..." Brynn faltered. She was a candle at the end of her wick, nearly burnt out. Had she only heard her mother's words, absent the weary look on her face and the weight of her touch, Brynn would have thought them cold. Instead, they were a warm glow. Isuna truly believed that Darrow's death, however tragic and unjust, had served a purpose. Perhaps she had to believe that, to make sense of a world without her son. How could she sleep thinking otherwise? How could she go on?

How will I sleep, knowing I put myself before everyone I know and love? Brynn knew she could do worse than to emulate her mother. Darrow was gone. Her people yet lived. So did the Rot, despite all efforts to quell its hunger. The living, not the dead, had to come first.

"Who knows if Queen Aefbain will even have me now?" Brynn said after a while, with a tired but resigned sigh. "I've ruined our chances."

Brynn's mother tucked a wisp of Brynn's curly hair beneath her fur cap, tugging it down over her ears. "There may still be time. She didn't choose you for your looks or personality, after all."

"Mother!" Despite the lingering ache in her chest, Brynn couldn't hold back a cracked laugh. She swatted Isuna's hand away and finished adjusting the cap herself.

Isuna smiled, a sad smile that nonetheless reached her cheeks and turned them into brown-gold chestnuts. "I mean to say, Her Majesty must have had another reason for selecting you. That reason hasn't changed in the past five minutes."

It seemed so. At that moment, Delia came hurrying toward them. Brynn recognized her high-pitched voice before she saw the woman's face. "Lady Woodwarden! Ah, there you are. Thank the ancestors. I've been searching everywhere."

Brynn offered Delia an apologetic bow. "Well, you've found me, but really, I'm no lady. Just Brynn."

Delia waved off Brynn's objection. "You must come with me, please. Queen Aefbain wishes a private audience." Her tone of voice made it clear that the queen's wishes weren't wishes at all, but decrees. Brynn didn't have a choice in the matter. She noticed two frost giants lumbering after Delia with heavy steps. They came to a stop, one at each of Delia's shoulders. Though their clubs remained in their belts, their looming postures alone were enough to ensure compliance.

With a heavy heart, Brynn straightened her spine and squared her shoulders. At only five and a half feet to their eight, she stood to her full height nonetheless. With her chin held high, she said to Delia, "Very well, but could I get cleaned up first?" If she was to apologize for her rashness and accept Queen Aefbain's proposal, surely it would be better to do so smelling like soap rather than damp fur, sweat, and horses. Without red-rimmed eyes and a runny nose.

Delia's dark face relaxed into a crescent-moon smile. She exhaled in audible relief. Perhaps, Brynn thought, the poor woman had expected more resistance. "Of course, Lady Woodwarden. If you'll come with me, I'll see to it at once."

"And my mother?" Brynn glanced hopefully toward Isuna, who reached out and rested a hand upon her shoulder.

"She may accompany you to your suite, if you wish," Delia said.

Brynn leaned into Isuna's touch, receiving a squeeze on the shoulder in return. "Good." It wasn't good, not really, but it was good enough. Though she might have to marry Queen Aefbain for her people's sake, she wouldn't have to bear the burden alone. Her mother was with her.

* * * * *

Valis scanned her private study, finding plenty of fault with its cluttered state but far too exhausted to care. There wasn't a speck of dust on the shelves of the large, wooden writing desk by the window—one of the few items of furniture in the palace made of neither ice nor stone—yet the space looked as though a blizzard had blown through.

Towers of books leaned against the desk and filled the armchairs by the fireplace. Rolls of parchment littered the floor, some blank, others scribbled upon in a hand that wasn't Valis' own. Whenever she found something of her mother's in the study, her instinct was to keep it on her desk, until it eventually migrated elsewhere in the room in her reluctance to throw anything away.

Valis preferred order in most aspects of her life. She had servants to keep things clean and organized while she went about the business of running a kingdom. However, the study was another matter. She had expressly instructed the cleaning staff to return all items they disturbed to their precise locations, lest she lose something irreplaceable.

Weariness lent extra weight to her steps as she dragged herself to one of the chairs and deposited the books and scrolls onto a clear patch of floor. She slumped into the seat, leaning her head back and staring at the glittering ceiling. It was only afternoon, but the morning had seemed to last a week, at least.

No. An untitled wood elf in dirty furs had actually told her no! Valis could scarcely believe it, but Aefbain had insisted that this Brynn Woodwarden possessed the most powerful blood among all the candidates, by far. If Aefbain's claims were to be believed, this wood elf was more powerful than many renowned snow elf Artificers. Aefbain often lied about trivial matters for its own amusement, but it would never deceive her about something so serious.

The dagger slept in its scabbard, but she suspected it would awaken when her future bride arrived. There was no other acceptable outcome. She had to convince Brynn to marry her, regardless of the scene she'd caused—in front of several nobles, no less! Surely the story had traveled halfway around the city by now.

A tentative knock made Valis lift her head. "Enter."

The door opened. "Queen Aefbain," Delia curtsied deeply.

"Enough of that," Valis said without rising from her chair. She saw Delia so often that she no longer held herself quite so formally around the human. Months of severe depression had seen to that. She had fuzzy memories of throwing a pillow at Delia in those early days, when she hadn't thought she possessed the fortitude for royal functions. There had been no choice but to find hidden reserves within herself, because her mother and sister were dead and Winterwail needed a queen.

"Lady Woodwarden awaits your invitation," Delia informed her. Judging from the wideness of her brown eyes and the subtle wringing of her hands, which she tried to hide within the fur of her skirt, Delia was either nervous or excited. Possibly both.

Valis closed her eyes, breathing through the bitter resentment in her stomach. To reject a queen! Just how arrogant was this strange wood elf? Valis knew that holding onto the morning's embarrassment would do her no good. She needed to be patient and straightforward in order to get what her kingdom needed. Her feelings of humiliation—her feelings in general—were irrelevant.

"Send her in, Delia."

"At once, Your Majesty."

Delia backed out of the room and into the hall, holding the door open. Another figure entered. Valis sat up straight. When her eyes settled upon Brynn Woodwarden for the second time that day, she was pleasantly surprised. A bath and some clean clothes could work wonders, it seemed.

Instead of the ragged fur cloak she'd worn that morning, the wood elf had donned a gray vest trimmed with wolf fur. Her breeches were similarly lined. Though the pieces were far from lavish, she no longer looked like a dejected pile of pelts in the back of a trapper's cart. A round cap sat atop her head, which she removed and held in front of her.

Only then did Valis note how short Brynn's ears were. Not fully of the blood, then. There was a sizable portion of human in this one. Not that it mattered, if her magic was potent enough. Still, people would talk...

Brynn seemed to decide that bowing was the appropriate thing to do. She bent forward, rising after a few moments with a nervous clearing of her throat. "Your Majesty." She took a deep breath and exhaled a swirl of white mist. "I sincerely apologize for this morning. Please forgive my terrible manners. I've never been around royalty before. I've never even been outside Greenglass, really. I scarcely know what to say or how to behave."

Valis rose from her chair but remained by the fireplace. She'd expected more arguments rather than an apology. Some of her stubbornness softened. Every second she spent alone with Brynn, the more certain she became: this was no haughty noble, so there was no point in treating her like one. A direct approach was best.

"Greenglass is your home?"

Brynn nodded, keeping a tight grip on her cap. "Yes."

A woman of few words, then. That was all right. In fact, Valis preferred it that way. Straightforwardness was most certainly an improvement on Naddox's ceaseless platitudes. Perhaps this was salvageable.

"This morning, you asked if I would send soldiers to the southern forest, to quell the plague there. Does this plague threaten Greenglass as well?"

Brynn nodded again. Her jaw bunched and her lips became a narrow line. Ah. *So she doesn't like speaking about her troubles, either. Ironic, since no came so quick to her lips.*

"It does."

"That is why you answered my invitation?" Valis asked.

"That is the *only* reason I answered your invitation." Each syllable sounded a jarring note in an otherwise pleasant voice.

Valis chose to overlook Brynn's simmering hostility in favor of her attempts at civility. This was not about feelings—it was about pacifying That Which Dwells Beneath. "In that case, why reject me and run away? I am in the perfect position to help you."

That question seemed to penetrate Brynn's guard. Her eyes, which had remained fixed on Valis the entire time, flicked down toward her feet. "I was in shock," she said after a long hesitation. "I didn't think you would actually select me. I hoped to ask for your aid, alongside my mother, after being rejected."

Valis waited. Brynn remained silent, but it seemed she desperately wanted to say something else. *She's holding something back.* This woman was no great liar. Her toes curled in her boots, and her mouth couldn't settle on one shape for more than a moment. She wrung her cap in her hands before realizing what she was doing and stuffing it in her pocket.

"Tell me plainly why you do not wish to marry me," Valis said, fascinated in spite of herself. Even standing still, Brynn was full of telling gestures. No, a liar this woman was not. "Perhaps I might alleviate your concerns?"

Something flashed in Brynn's eyes then, a fire that turned the dark brown of them into something more like amber. "Unless you can raise the dead, there's no point."

Valis tilted her head. The bitterness in Brynn's voice revealed she'd suffered a personal loss of some sort, yet Valis had no idea why Brynn should blame her. "Please, explain."

Brynn's shoulders stiffened into an even more defensive posture. Her fingers curled into her palms. "Your people murdered my brother."

That pronouncement was mildly alarming, but Valis kept her expression placid and calm. If there was one thing her mother had taught her, it was that others often followed the example of the most self-assured person in the room. Even rude, obviously stubborn people like Brynn.

"That seems highly unlikely. I have never ordered any of my subjects to slay wood elves. Neither did my mother, to my knowledge."

"But she did order them into our forest to poach unicorns. The Rot hunted them instead, until they saw enemies where there were none."

It was easy enough for Valis to piece together the rest. Intentionally or not, her hunters must have slain Brynn's brother. Likely by accident, or Brynn would have blamed the one who wielded blade or arrow against him, rather than snow elves as a whole. The wood elf reeked of a woman looking for somewhere to cast blame in an effort to ease her grief.

To her surprise, Valis realized she felt sorry for Brynn. She knew what it was like to lose a family member. Two, in her case. "I lost a sister recently. My mother as well. Words are inadequate."

For the flicker of a candle flame, Brynn's brow softened. Then the clenched jaw and stiff shoulders were back. "I don't want to talk about my brother anymore. So, am I allowed to change my mind about your proposal? Your Majesty." Brynn added the title at the last moment, a halfhearted attempt to seem less rude. Obviously, it had occurred to her that she needed Valis' cooperation as much as Valis needed hers.

"Allow me to state my offer in clear terms, in a manner I believe you will appreciate. I do not wish to marry anyone. However, there is a monthly ritual I must perform to ensure my kingdom's continued safety. That ritual requires blood. My own blood is exceptionally powerful, but insufficient for this. If you become my royal consort and allow me the use of your blood, I will provide you with anything you want. The full force of my soldiers and Artificers to protect your village and fight this Rot, wealth for you and your family, whatever you wish."

Brynn's brows rose, as though she were impressed. While she considered her response, Valis felt Aefbain stir. The dagger didn't move, but magical energy quivered around its scabbard, as though it were vibrating, or perhaps purring. *What a romantic proposal, Your Majesty. So full of feeling! No woman in her right mind could resist you.*

Valis ground the points of her teeth. Any further reaction would only encourage Aefbain's playful mood. She kept her gaze on Brynn, wondering what the wood elf's thoughts might be. Did she doubt Valis' honesty, or was she merely deciding which boons to ask for? Was she thinking about the life she would leave behind if she accepted? Surely no forest home, no matter how beautiful, was worth more than a queen's proposal.

"This ritual," Brynn said after an uncomfortable pause. "It won't kill me, right? How much does it hurt?"

Valis blinked. *Of course. Wood elves never use blood magic.* Brynn would have little reference. "You may find yourself exhausted afterward, but the ritual will not physically hurt. I certainly have no desire to kill you. Then I would have to find a new source of blood."

Brynn's brows rose even further.

And most people don't want to be murdered, Aefbain helpfully reminded her.

Valis was grateful only she could hear Aefbain. "I can promise your life here will be comfortable in every respect," she added, hoping to put Brynn at ease.

"If," Brynn said, weighing down the silence with her pause, "you agree to help us fight the Rot, allow me to go where I please within reason, and don't force me to participate in royal functions, I'll accept your offer." She ticked off each request on her fingers. "Oh, and I've never wanted to carry children myself, so if you need biological heirs, you'll have to do that yourself...Your Majesty."

The weight upon Valis lifted as quickly as it had settled. Brynn's hostility had given way to reason. Still, the nerve of her, to name so many concessions! Nevertheless, she let the rising heat of her anger frost over. She needed Brynn's cooperation. "You must attend at least some royal functions. Our wedding, for instance, will require your presence."

"Fine. Royal functions, only as needed. Do we have a deal?" Brynn stuck out her hand with such boldness that Valis was taken aback. While most people knelt and offered her their upturned palms in supplication, it seemed Brynn expected to shake. An egalitarian custom her own people did not practice, and Valis refused to engage in.

She'll have to get used to our ways sooner or later, Aefbain said.

Are you sure you aren't greedy for another taste of her blood, Aefbain? Nevertheless, Valis drew Aefbain from its jeweled scabbard. She stepped forward, closing the distance between them, She took Brynn's hand in hers. Instead of shaking, she turned Bryn's palm up. "Be warned." Valis examined Brynn's calluses, as she searched for the cutting line. "Bonds sealed in blood are unbreakable. You will not be able to change your mind."

Brynn's swallow was visible. "Just do it quickly."

Despite the note of doubt in Brynn's voice, Valis took her at her word. She cut Brynn first, allowing herself only a moment to watch the weeping line of red form a river in the crescent of Brynn's palm, before slicing her own hand. Not a single drop of blood marred Aefbain's gleaming edge.

Once her blood flowed freely, Valis clasped Brynn's hand in her own, lacing their fingers. Aefbain flashed in her other fist, bright enough to make Valis squint. A moment later, she was overcome by a wave of raw, roaring power.

Before, she hadn't felt anything. She'd merely listened to Aefbain's assessment. Now, feeling Brynn's blood mingle with her own, it was unmistakable.

This is why!

Her entire body hummed, trembling with excess energy. She flushed despite the temperature, sweat beading at the back of her neck and between her shoulders. Her head spun as though she'd downed several glasses of wine. Though she had years of experience in schooling her features, a smile broke across her face.

Brynn gasped, pulling her hand away.

Valis allowed it, albeit with a gut-deep reluctance she couldn't adequately explain. Brynn's blood was unlike any she'd ever encountered. It had none of its own insistence. Though Brynn was willful, her blood was not. It was pure power, waiting to be shaped into whatever Valis willed. Oh, what she could do with more...!

I told you, Aefbain said.

"Yes," Valis sighed, too dazed to realize she was speaking aloud. The motions with which she closed her own wound, using the flat of Aefbain's blade, were more ritualistic than anything.

"Yes, what?" Brynn cradled her bleeding hand protectively against her chest. Her brow furrowed with confusion and perhaps mistrust. "Did it work or not?"

Valis nodded. "You mean to say you felt nothing?"

"No. Your dagger glowed, but that's all." She hesitated, her ears pulling back into a worried position. "Was I supposed to feel something?"

Any magically inclined being should have felt power leaving their body, yet Brynn claimed to have felt nothing. Was she naturally numb in some way, or was her blood so potent that she scarcely noticed her magic being taken? A subject for further study. "Our pact was sealed," Valis said, ignoring Brynn's question.

"Good. Um..." Brynn rubbed the back of her injured hand. "Can you do that thing where you seal the cut again?"

"Of course." Mildly embarrassed not to have thought of it first, Valis took Brynn's hand and pressed Aefbain against her palm. Aefbain pulsed with a much softer white light. Brynn's wound sealed shut, leaving only unbroken skin. There was no longer any sign she'd been cut at all.

"Thank you." Brynn did not withdraw her hand.

Valis shaped her lips into what she hoped was a friendly smile instead of a forced one. The motion felt very awkward. "We can't have blood on my nice, shiny floors, can we?"

Brynn did not withdraw her hand.

"I suppose not."

Still, Brynn didn't withdraw her hand.

Valis looked down, noting that while Brynn's wound had closed and almost all the blood had been absorbed into Aefbain, a smear of red remained on her wrist. The droplets were shining rubies, twinkling in the faint afternoon light that filtered through the window.

In the grip of some otherworldly force, Valis drew Brynn's wrist closer. Closer. Inches away, now. The scent of copper coiled into her nose. Salt rose in her mouth. She ran her tongue along her upper lip, feeling a pang of hunger much lower than her stomach.

"What's wrong?" Brynn asked.

She did not withdraw her hand.

A string snapped somewhere behind Valis' eyes. Her sanity, perhaps. She leaned forward, pressing her lips to the smooth flesh of Brynn's wrist. Her tongue flicked out, so quick and light she could almost pretend it was merely a thought and not an action, but there it was—the taste of blood and magic on her tongue. Sweeter than the ripest fruit, fairly singing with power. She caught the last drop on her lower lip, hardly daring to breathe. She longed to sink her fangs into Brynn's wrist, roll her tongue over the blood that leaked from the punctures.

Then came mortification. What in the world had possessed her to do *that?* Suddenly, Valis wanted nothing more than to shove Brynn's hand away. She'd seized a red-hot iron, like a foolish child enthralled by its glow. Now, she felt the anguished burn of embarrassment. To drop Brynn's hand quickly, however, would be to admit her own mistake. Her own weakness. Queens do not make mistakes.

With an outward calm that in no way reflected the rapid thunder of her heart and the churning of her stomach, Valis casually released Brynn's hand, as if nothing strange had happened. She ignored the wood elf's blatantly curious look. "Delia awaits you outside." Valis sheathed Aefbain in the scabbard strapped to her thigh. "She will provide you with anything you might wish for during your stay. We will meet again in a day or two, to discuss the wedding ceremony itself. Is that agreeable?"

"Yes." Brynn's eyes darted down to her boots. She rubbed her wrist with the opposite thumb. "That sounds fine, Your Majesty. I'm, ah, glad we could come to an understanding." With a noticeable russet tinge to the burnished copper of her cheeks, she made a short bow and turned, marching from the room at a brisk pace.

Once the door closed, Valis breathed a sigh of relief. She sank into the armchair, moaning as she hid her face in her hands. *Oh my, oh my...and earlier, you compared her to a drowned rat and seethed at her impudence. How quickly your opinion changes, Your Majesty.*

Valis dragged her hand down her face and removed Aefbain's scabbard from her thigh. She had no patience for its taunting. Without a word, she rose from the chair and stomped to her desk, throwing open the top drawer and dropping Aefbain inside with a careless clatter.

What? How dare you! Retrieve me at once!

Whatever else Aefbain said was muffled. Valis closed the drawer and her mind, ignoring the psychic link between them. She returned to the armchair, sinking back with a contented sigh. She wouldn't leave Aefbain in there for long, just long enough to remind it that she didn't have to put up with its rudeness.

And long enough to catch her breath. What strange force had overcome her, to taste Brynn's blood before it was offered? A woman she hardly knew! But it had been intoxicating. Irresistible. As much as the idea of marriage displeased her, she wondered if certain other rituals she had been quietly dreading might not be so horrible.

Chapter Four

BRYNN STOPPED SHORT IN the doorway. "Great seasons!"

The circular room Delia had shepherded her and Isuna into overflowed with dresses. Dresses of every color and cut decorated the curved walls, except where they might block the room's numerous mirrors. Dresses hung on silver racks, a swaying rainbow of fabric. Dresses were fitted on mannequins, draped over chairs, and spread across worktables, some in the early stages of creation. It looked as though a storm had blown through twenty different tailor's shops and deposited the resulting debris in a single place.

Delia gave an airy laugh. "A little overwhelming? No need to worry. Shalure, the imperial tailor, is an absolute genius. You'll look nothing less than your best on your wedding day."

Brynn tensed, scanning the dress-strewn space as though something dangerous might leap out from behind one of the racks. The room's landscape was denser than the forest she called home and made her ten times as nervous. She feared she might accidentally rip something worth more than all the coin in her village.

Isuna was far less wary. "Oh my!" Her warm brown eyes shone with delight as she trailed her fingers along a nearby mannequin's skirt. "Is this caveworm silk? I thought it couldn't be dyed without damaging the fabric."

"It cannot," a crisp voice answered.

A slender snow elf of ambiguous gender emerged from a rear doorway that Brynn had overlooked. They wore sunny yellow robes trimmed in emerald green and tall, crimson heels that clacked across the ice. Brynn wondered how they kept their balance and walked with such grace in shoes like that. Their snow-white hair was pulled back into a series of interlocking braids and the long, curved points of their ears were heavily pierced.

"Hello, Shalure," Delia chirped. "As you can see, I brought guests. This is Lady Brynn Woodwarden, Her Majesty's future consort, as well as her mother, Isuna."

Shalure bowed, offering their palms. "An honor to meet you both."

"I'm pleased to be here," Brynn said, with less confidence than she would have liked. She wasn't sure what was expected of her, now that she was Queen Aefbain's betrothed. Who should she bow to, and who was supposed to bow to her? What was her status, exactly? She would have to ask Delia once they finished with Shalure. Brynn decided that doing nothing was probably best.

It seemed she had guessed right, because Delia gave her an approving nod. Shalure rose and went to stand beside Isuna. "You're right, this is caveworm silk, but the color comes from a specialized diet." They gestured at the mannequin and several shiny bracelets jangled at the motion. "One may achieve varying shades of blue, purple, and red that way."

Brynn scratched her neck beneath her cap. Something about this odd tailor made her skin prickle. Her discomfort grew as Shalure rounded on her, their gaze sharp as a sewing needle. Brynn suddenly felt like a pincushion.

"You dislike dresses, Lady Woodwarden." Shalure's long white eyebrows drew together in the middle of their forehead.

Brynn forced a smile. "How did you know?"

"You failed to fawn over my creations like your mother." Shalure glanced between the two of them, obviously searching for a familial resemblance.

Brynn wrinkled her nose. She and her mother looked different enough that few guessed their relationship unless informed. Her skin, though darker than a snow elf's, was lighter than her mother's, her ears only half as pointed, thanks to her father's human ancestry.

"Furthermore," Shalure continued, "mature wood elves rarely wear dresses or robes. I've been told your people find them *inconvenient."* From their tone, it was obvious they disagreed with this assessment.

"Loose clothing snags on branches." Brynn folded her arms across her chest. Something about Shalure's demeanor put her on the defensive.

Shalure's heavy-lidded eyes abandoned their penetrating stare. They scanned the chaos of the room. "I see no branches here, Lady."

"That's just Shalure's idea of a joke," Delia said with a nervous laugh.

As usual, Isuna took it upon herself to smooth over any awkwardness. "Are dresses common attire in Winterwail? We only arrived yesterday."

"With leggings underneath for warmth, yes," Shalure said. "Dresses are a popular choice among all genders. Of course, those with enough arcane power rarely worry about the cold. That allows them more flexibility in their dress."

Like Queen Aefbain.

Brynn flushed as she recalled the form-fitting, fur-lined, blue trumpet dress the queen had worn the previous day. The bodice had dipped low enough to show an ample amount of sharp collarbone and pale, purple cleavage. Surely the cold was of little concern to her. The mental image made Brynn feel warmer. Though she continued to dread her upcoming marriage, it was impossible to deny that Queen Aefbain was stunningly beautiful.

"You may stop scowling, Lady Woodwarden." Shalure fixed their gaze on Brynn once more. Brynn shuddered as the brief flare of warmth within her died. "No one looks breathtaking in outfits that leave them feeling uncomfortable or exposed. I have other plans for your wedding attire."

A note of excitement sounded in Shalure's voice, quivering like a plucked lute string. This odd elf, who took up far more space than their diminutive size suggested, was clearly passionate about their work. Still, the mention of her upcoming nuptials made Brynn's stomach roil.

"In that case, I'm looking forward to it," she lied.

"Good. Now, Lady Woodwarden, if you'll allow me to take your measurements?"

The process was just as uncomfortable and drawn-out as Brynn had feared. Shalure ushered them into an adjoining room and posed Brynn on a low platform, whipping out a roll of measuring tape. "Please, remove your outer garments."

Brynn was reluctant to do so, especially in Delia's presence, but the beaming human showed no signs of leaving. With a sigh, she took off her cloak and vest, then shucked her leggings. That left her in a loose undershirt and smallclothes. To her surprise, she wasn't as cold as she expected to be. The room's temperature was neutral, although the ice all around showed no signs of melting. Magic, most definitely.

While Brynn stood upon the platform, rubbing her bare arms to soothe the goosebumps that had risen there, Shalure threw open the drawer of a nearby worktable. The roll of measuring tape floated toward Brynn while Shalure scribbled on a sketchpad with a stick of charcoal.

Brynn gawked as the tape took her measurements all by itself, starting with her legs before moving on to her inseam. Eventually, it snaked beneath her arms to measure her bust as well. She wasn't sure whether she felt pleased to have avoided a stranger's hands upon her or annoyed by such casual use of magic. Back home, Druids never used their powers for such trivial things. Their skills were reserved for growing crops, healing wounds, and other necessities.

I suppose it's something I'll have to get used to if I'm going to live here.

She comforted herself by remembering the agreement she'd struck with Queen Aefbain. If she had her way, she'd make frequent visits to Greenglass, though they couldn't be long if the queen required her blood for the mysterious monthly ritual. Idly, Brynn wondered if stored blood was as good as fresh for spellwork. She doubted it.

The measuring tape finished its job, whipping back into Shalure's outstretched hand. It coiled into a circle, and Shalure placed it inside the drawer before returning their attention to their sketchpad. "Hmm." They rubbed their chin, leaving a smudged charcoal thumbprint on their pale skin. "Yes, that will do nicely."

"What will?" Brynn asked, hoping her nerves wouldn't bleed too much into her voice.

Shalure tilted their sketchpad toward Delia and Isuna. Their eyes widened above mouths making sounds of approval. Delia even clasped her hands over her mouth.

Brynn chewed her lip. "Mom, *what* will do nicely? Mom?!"

"Relax, dear." Isuna's sly grin did nothing to soothe Brynn's worries. "You'll like this. Trust me."

* * * * *

An hour later, Brynn had to admit that Shalure's work was beyond compare. Dressed in perfectly fitted sealskin leggings and a flowing shirt of blue caveworm silk, her outfit was as comfortable as it was stylish. After a few alterations, it moved with her like a second skin. At the very least, Brynn trusted Shalure not to put her in something utterly impractical for the wedding.

Right. The wedding.

Brynn could think of little else as Delia escorted them to her second private audience with Queen Aefbain. She'd been reasonable yesterday, but Brynn remained apprehensive. She shoved her hands in her pockets, willing herself not to remember the way Queen Aefbain's lips had brushed her inner wrist.

No, that never happened. It must have been some kind of strange daydream. She hadn't slept well the night before, tossing and turning in an overlarge bed. That was another question for Queen Aefbain. Would they share a bed? Personal quarters? How much time would she be required to spend with her new wife?

Delia cleared her throat, interrupting the worried spiral of Brynn's thoughts. They'd reached their destination, a pair of closed double doors which gave no hint as to what sort of room lay beyond.

Isuna took Brynn by the shoulders, fussing with her new shirt even though it didn't need adjustment. "Remember to kneel and offer your hands, palms up."

"Couldn't you have told me that yesterday?" Brynn protested, gently guiding her mother's hands away.

Isuna sighed. "I've told you six times this past week alone."

"Really?" Brynn couldn't recall, but it was likely true. She'd been so sure Queen Aefbain would never select her that she'd ignored all of her mother's advice during the journey to Winterwail.

"If you didn't know that, how did you greet Queen Aefbain yesterday?" Delia asked, twisting her hands.

Brynn didn't answer. No response she could give would inspire confidence. She was adrift in this strange country, rafting down a river without a paddle.

She was saved from further interrogation by the arrival of a tall snow elf draped in glimmering silver. His long, ornamental sleeves hung low, with intricate, white-fractal patterns woven throughout. His ears were even more heavily pierced than Shalure's, and so were his eyebrows, though their edges were plastered down with wet-looking gel. There wasn't a hair out of place in his long, white braid, nor on his clean-shaven face. He wore a jewel-studded scabbard at his hip, containing a ritualistic bloodletting dagger.

Behind him stood two sturdy frost giants—bodyguards, most likely—with furrowed brows and matching frowns. Each stood nine feet tall with dark, swirling tattoos on their bare chests and hefty stone clubs tucked into their waistbands.

Brynn half expected the gaudy elf and his guards to pass their group without a second glance. Instead, he stopped in front of the same unopened door.

"Oh!" Delia dropped to her knees, offering her hands with palms outstretched. "My sincerest apologies, Lord-Adviser Naddox. We were delayed by an appointment with the royal tailor."

Upon seeing Delia bow, Brynn decided she ought to do the same. She lowered her knees to the icy floor, offering her palms. Beside her, so did her mother. It chafed Brynn's pride, playing this stupid game, but she had no choice unless she wanted to insult a noble. Maybe she'd have to do less bowing and scraping once she and Queen Aefbain were officially married.

"You may rise." Lord-Adviser Naddox sounded almost bored. Brynn did so immediately, while Delia and her mother took more time to regain their footing. "Her Majesty will be here soon, ladies, so you ought to go in."

"You're attending the meeting?" Too late, Brynn realized she'd forgotten to include the Lord-Adviser's title.

Lord-Adviser Naddox lifted a waxed eyebrow. "It is my *honor* as well as my *duty* to ensure these negotiations are finalized, Lady Woodwarden."

Brynn decided she disliked this obvious sycophant and the judgmental emphasis he added to his words. She agreed that Lady was a strange title for someone with her background, but she hated the way it sounded in Naddox's mouth, as though she were unworthy. Nevertheless, she forced a polite smile. "After you then, Lord-Adviser." She reached for the door, opening it in a gesture of reconciliation.

Lord-Adviser Naddox's smug expression transformed into one of shock. His ears stood straight up, and he looked as though he'd swallowed his own tongue.

Confused, Brynn glanced at her mother, who gave a visible wince.

"Please forgive my daughter, Lord-Adviser," Isuna said. "In our culture, one holds the door for one's elders or those they respect. It is meant to be a helpful gesture."

Brynn's heart sank. Only now did she recall one of the many boring pieces of snow elf etiquette her mother had tried and failed to teach her. While holding the door was polite back home, snow elves were the opposite. With few exceptions, the highest-ranking person in attendance always entered last. No important business could start without them, after all, and it was considered rude to make them wait.

What must Queen Aefbain have thought of me, arriving in the throne room well after her and all the other candidates?

To his credit, Lord-Adviser Naddox did not rage or bluster. "Then we shall proceed the wood elf way this time," he said, his tone as soft as his glare was devastating. He passed Brynn with a swirl of his sleeves, entering through the open door without waiting to see whether she would follow.

The frost giants took up residence on either side of the door, positioning themselves like statues. Brynn studied them, feeling nauseous for more than one reason. Was club-wielding guard really the only job available to frost giants in the royal palace? It seemed unfair. Winterwail was their ancestral homeland, colonized by the snow elves. She'd seen frost giant merchants in the market as well, selling all sorts of wares. Would they have anything positive to say about Queen Aefbain's rule?

Brynn resolved to ask once she learned whom she could trust, but that was a problem for another time. She offered the frost giants a friendly smile. One cracked his stony expression and smiled back, showing large, square teeth that looked more human than elven. That made Brynn feel a little better, as she followed her mother and Delia through the door.

The room beyond was large and spacious, with a long, stone table as the centerpiece. A variety of animal pelts lined the walls, as did several silk tapestries, most of which depicted hunting scenes. A crystal chandelier hung from the ceiling, refracting the afternoon light that streamed in through the windows.

Lord-Adviser Naddox took a seat near, but not at, the far head of the table. His expression read annoyance, and Brynn wondered if it was because they were the first arrivals. If timing was so important to snow elves, perhaps an early entrance reflected poorly on him.

Brynn remained standing while she pondered which of the empty chairs to take. Delia made the decision for her, escorting her to the head of the table nearest the door, far away from the Lord-Adviser. Brynn sat, assuming her appointed guide to this strange new world would steer her right.

"It won't be a long wait, since we arrived so late." Delia shepherded Isuna into the chair on Brynn's left.

"Then why are we the first ones here?" Brynn asked, incredulous. "Does everything run constantly behind in Winterwail, because no one wants to be first?" What an inefficient way to conduct royal business! There was no time for that kind of nonsense back home, where everyone had a never-ending list of chores.

Lord-Adviser Naddox chuckled, a cold and unkind sound. "What a refreshing point of view, Lady Woodwarden. You should mention it to Queen Aefbain."

Brynn decided she most certainly would not mention it.

They were interrupted by the entrance of two more elves, dressed in similar finery to Lord-Adviser Naddox. One woman was tall and angular in the shoulders, the other short and full-figured. It was difficult to tell, but Brynn pegged them at late middle age. Like Lord-Adviser Naddox, they carried ornamental daggers at their hips, partially hidden by their long, flowing sleeves.

Delia knelt, offering her palms. "Lady-Adviser Fayeth. Lady-Adviser Galesha."

Advisers Galesha and Fayeth acknowledged Delia with brief glances, but both seemed far more interested in Brynn herself. They studied her openly, and their searching gazes made Brynn uncomfortably hot beneath her silk shirt. She'd always hated being a spectacle, and she feared the problem would only grow worse once she was married.

Since she'd bowed to Lord-Adviser Naddox and these people had the same title, Brynn rose from her chair and knelt again. Beside her, Isuna did likewise. When the advisers nodded, Delia stood and motioned for Brynn to do the same. "Lady-Advisers, I humbly present Lady Brynn Woodwarden, Her Majesty's future consort. This is her mother, Isuna Woodwarden."

The taller of the two elves clasped Brynn's hand with warm palms. One was perfectly smooth, while the other held a prominent scar that Brynn felt against the back of her hand. "Welcome to Winterwail, cousin. Galesha and I are overjoyed to meet you and your mother."

It was the friendliest greeting Brynn had received since leaving home. The ever-present weight in her chest lightened considerably. "The same to you, Lady-Adviser Fayeth," she said, holding the woman's eyes to convey her gratitude.

"I assume our Delia has taken good care of you both." Lady-Adviser Galesha's voice was softer, but no less welcoming. "Despite coming all the way from the Golden Sea, she knows everything there is to know about our fair city, even more than many of us who were born here. Ask her to show you the sights sometime."

"I highly doubt," Lord-Adviser Naddox drawled, "that Lady Woodwarden will have time for sightseeing. Wedding preparations must take precedence, you understand."

Galesha and Fayeth exchanged mildly exasperated looks, which only made Brynn like them more. Perhaps some Winterwail nobles had senses of humor after all.

"Cheer up, Naddox," Fayeth said. "The queen has finally chosen a consort! We've been waiting months for her selection. This is a happy day."

"Isn't the wedding mostly preplanned, anyway?" Galesha asked.

Brynn's brows rose. That sounded promising! The fewer decisions she had to make, the better. She just had to survive the inevitable spectacle the wedding would undoubtedly become.

Naddox frowned, looking as though he wished to protest. The door opened again, forcing him to swallow his words. He rose from his chair and fell to his knees, as did everyone else in the room. Everyone except Brynn. She stared, mouth agape, at the vision framed in the doorway.

Queen Aefbain resembled a cloud, walking with the same lightness. She wore a gray stole about her shoulders, trimmed with fluffy white fur. Her dress, also white, flared at the waist into voluminous skirts. Constellations of twinkling jewels—*Diamonds?*—were sewn into the tightly fitted bodice. Both dress and stole left the queen's pale, purple-blue shoulders bare, showing the sharp cut of her collarbone and the graceful column of her throat.

Brynn's head spun. She didn't necessarily like her fiancée, but it was impossible to deny that she was breathtaking. Queen Aefbain looked as though she'd stepped out of a painting or leaped from the pages of a fanciful storybook. People simply weren't supposed to look that lovely in reality. It was almost unfair.

Only when Queen Aefbain's eyes fixed upon her did Brynn realize she was gaping—and notice the dour-looking frost giant at the queen's left shoulder. *Great seasons, how did I miss someone so large?*

This frost giant was even taller than the guards Lord-Adviser Naddox had left outside, though narrower in the shoulders. Brynn assumed she was female, due to the slight flare of her hips and subtle blunting of her tusks, but there was little difference in height or muscle mass. Instead of a club, she carried a polished black staff that barely fit through the doorway. Her well-defined arms were heavily tattooed, and the shaggy, brown furs she wore must have come from an enormous beast.

Following the conventional wisdom of better late than never, Brynn knelt, lowering her gaze so she wouldn't have to look at the queen or her escort. Perhaps if she was lucky, her mistake would be forgiven.

A pair of fur-lined boots passed into her field of vision as Queen Aefbain stopped in front of her. "Rise and take your seat. We have much to discuss."

* * * * *

The meeting that followed wasn't the dullest Valis had suffered through since her coronation, but it came awfully close. Try as she might, she couldn't force herself to care about the proposed guests, the food, or any other ceremonial details. She cared deeply about her upcoming marriage, insomuch as it would save her kingdom, but the wedding ceremony itself? Far less so.

During Lord-Adviser Naddox's third attempt to expand the guest list, Valis nearly lost her temper. Instead, she took a deep breath and gave herself the gift of delegation. "Your intimate knowledge of the nobility astounds me, Lord-Adviser. Why, I had no idea that seating the Glendarks and the Persalors near each other might rekindle an ancient feud. Perhaps I should leave the guest list in your capable hands?"

The ploy worked. Lord-Adviser Naddox accepted her offer with all the smugness Valis expected. "It would be my honor to ease you of this burden, Your Majesty. Not a single detail, no matter how small, shall be overlooked." He took that as permission to steer the conversation a while, discussing potential invitees with Fayeth and Galesha.

Was that a wise decision? Aefbain whispered in Valis' head. *An insufferable planner makes for an insufferable wedding day, my dear.*

Valis kept a neutral smile while mentally rolling her eyes. *Anything is endurable for one day.*

I will remind you of that during your reception.

Valis ignored Aefbain's threat, allowing her attention to wander. She found herself studying Brynn. With an entire table between them, she couldn't make out every detail of the wood elf's expression, but she saw enough. Brynn looked as bored as Valis felt. Her eyelids drooped and her chin threatened to fall onto her chest.

Ah yes, Aefbain said. *Your blushing bride. She seems eager to marry you, doesn't she? Have you explained the bloodbinding ritual yet? I would hate to have missed that conversation.*

Valis' smile wavered. She fully intended to tell Brynn about the bloodbinding ritual before the ceremony, but it was a subject she dreaded broaching. Aefbain's goading only made the prospect seem worse.

One day, I shall find a way to silence you permanently. On that day, I shall finally know peace.

Aefbain merely laughed. *We'll see, Your Majesty. Others of your line have tried and failed to be rid of my counsel. None were successful.*

"Wait, what holdings?!" Brynn loudly blurted out. Startled, Valis detached from her mental bond with Aefbain and refocused on the meeting. Brynn's ears stood fully upright, her amber eyes wide.

"Queen Aefbain cannot marry a commoner," Lord-Adviser Naddox explained, "especially a foreigner." His smarmy tone reminded Valis of a teacher lecturing a slow pupil. "Therefore, she will generously bestow upon you the title of Lady, along with all accompanying lands and wealth. There is precedent for promoting new nobility when someone performs a great act of service for the kingdom of Winterwail or its royal family."

"But I haven't performed any great services," Brynn protested, "so why must I be given land?" She leaned back in her chair and folded her arms across her chest, as though bracing for an argument.

"You will soon enough." Valis cut off Lord-Adviser Naddox before he could reply. "The holdings my esteemed Lord-Adviser mentioned are in Sikah, a few days north of Winterwail. The lands were once my father's, but they are now yours to do with as you wish. For the most part, they are self-sustaining, so they should be easy to care for."

"Land isn't..." Brynn's voice trailed off as frustration furrowed her brow. She uncrossed her arms, gesturing as if that might make her audience understand. "You don't *own* land! It doesn't belong to individual people."

"Ah, wood elves," Lady-Adviser Fayeth sighed. "Your connection to nature is so charming, cousin. By all means, reintroduce the local wildlife and turn it into some kind of sanctuary, if that is your wish."

"Maybe I will." Brynn's voice rose with her emotion. "Or maybe I'll return it to the frost giants. I'm sure many still live there."

Gasps sounded around the table. Galesha paled. Fayeth pressed a hand to her heart. Naddox sputtered, managing only a hoarse, "What? But people live there!"

"Yes, the frost giants. They were there first, weren't they?"

Valis ignored her advisers and glanced at Kraal, who stood at her shoulder. The frost giant's normally impassive expression flickered with a brief smile, before settling into neutrality once more.

Perhaps Brynn speaks sense. The Aefbain legacy was not a peaceful one. That legacy had killed her mother and sister. Renouncing the snow elves' claim to Sikah would win her no allies among the nobility but might prove a valuable step toward peace between her people and the northernmost frost giants. It might even prevent another leader like Murta, the frost giant who had slain Ruith and Shalana, from coming into power.

Negotiating with frost giants? Aefbain scoffed. *Your mother would disapprove.*

Kindly shut up, you crooked, rusted nail underfoot, Valis snapped. *Mother is gone. Her approval is irrelevant.*

"We shall discuss the Sikah holdings later." Valis seized control of the room before her advisers could panic. "Since we have already made significant progress, we shall continue this meeting tomorrow. I wish to speak to Lady Woodwarden. Alone."

If her advisers were displeased, they gave few outward signs. Galesha seemed relieved to make her bows and leave, while Fayeth took a moment to bid Brynn and her mother farewell. Naddox lingered, as if he wished to say something more, but Valis sent him on his way with a sharp glare.

"Delia, please make sure Lady Woodwarden's mother is made comfortable. I promise to return her daughter shortly."

"Of course, Your Majesty," Delia said, taking Isuna with her.

Kraal slipped silently after them, securing a station outside the door. Though she was technically Valis' personal attendant, she was also a trained bodyguard. Her skills were many and her discretion invaluable. Valis didn't miss the brief, searching look Kraal shot in Brynn's direction before she disappeared.

"Did I really just empty an entire room by suggesting your people return stolen land?" Brynn asked, leaning back in her chair.

"I meant it when I said we would discuss it later," Valis said. "There are merits to your idea." It was somewhat bothersome, speaking to Brynn from across the entire length of the table, but it seemed neither of them were inclined to move closer. Valis wouldn't be the first to get up.

"What is there to discuss?" Brynn asked. "Either this Sikah place is mine to return, or it isn't. Either you believe in owning land or you don't."

Valis sighed. This conversation wasn't going anything like she had planned. "That is not why I asked the others to leave."

"Then why did you?"

Yes, Aefbain interjected. *Why did you, Your Majesty?*

Quiet, Valis thought. *No need for you to involve yourself with this.* To Brynn she said, "In addition to the monthly ritual that will preserve Winterwail, there is another ritual we must perform together... on our wedding night."

Brynn's eyebrows shot up toward her curly hairline. "What kind of ritual?" Her knee jiggled beneath the table and she wetted her lower lip.

Valis took note of all this with mild amusement. Brynn was painfully easy to read, but she supposed that made sense, given the wood elf's stubborn attitude and blunt nature. In this case, she seemed embarrassed. Twitchy.

"I know you appreciate straightforwardness, Lady Woodwarden, so you shall have it now. While we need not have an ongoing sexual relationship, it is necessary that you—"

Fuck me with my most valuable family heirloom? Aefbain vibrated gleefully within its scabbard.

Valis persevered, in spite of Aefbain's wry commentary. "...consummate the marriage with an instrument of my choosing. This will strengthen our bond when I use your blood for spellwork."

Brynn's jaw dropped. She gaped, her lips moving soundlessly for several seconds before she managed to say, "Wait, *what?*"

Valis sighed and began to repeat herself. "You will consummate the marriage with—"

"No, I heard you, but... I have to...?" Clearly at a loss for words, Brynn made a very inappropriate gesture with her hands, after which she gave a helpless shrug.

Valis' neutrality finally cracked. Her chin sank to her chest, and she pinched her forehead to ease the tension there. The motion had the added effect of blocking her eyes from Brynn's questioning gaze. "This is no base, lustful activity. It's an intensely powerful ritual that will bond me to... the instrument... and you. The blood of one's maidenhead, willingly given, is exceptionally potent."

"Willingly given?" Brynn's frown was so forceful that Valis felt it without raising her head to look. "You don't sound all that willing to me, if you'll forgive my saying so."

Valis lowered her hand from her forehead and lifted her chin, glaring across the table. "Consent for a ritual you see as sexual may be given for reasons other than mere pleasure: to produce an heir, to satisfy one's partner, or to unlock one's full magical potential. Do not insult me by implying that I, a queen, am incapable of making decisions regarding my own body."

Brynn flinched, the tips of her ears drooping slightly. "Fine, point taken. If this is what we have to do..."

"It is," Valis insisted.

Brynn's frown faded, though only a little. When she addressed Valis again, it was in the softest and most respectful tone the wood elf had used since their meeting yesterday. "All right. If it's necessary for your ritual, and you hold up your end of the bargain afterward, I consent. Is there anything else I can do for you, Your Majesty?"

"No, Lady Woodwarden. That will be all." Feeling something akin to pity in her breast, Valis forced a smile. "Spend time with your mother.

She is welcome to stay in my palace for as long as she likes, even after the ceremony. I hope she and your other relatives will be frequent visitors when it pleases them."

"Thank you," Brynn murmured. She rose from her chair, knelt with palms outstretched, then left without another word, dragging much of the air in the room through the door after her.

Valis slumped in her chair, adopting a most unrefined posture as she flopped her head back to stare at the ceiling. "Black Wolf's teeth, that was awful."

An utter disaster, Aefbain agreed, unrepentantly delighted.

"I have no idea why you feel the need to be smug," Valis muttered, "since you must be in a meditative state during the ritual anyway."

So you say.

Valis didn't dignify Aefbain with a response. She pushed her chair back with a loud scrape and stormed toward the door, preparing to collect Kraal and retire to her study. There was a drawer with Aefbain's name on it. She couldn't be rid of the cursed thing soon enough.

Chapter Five

BRYNN FIDGETED WITH HER golden gloves as she sat before one of the changing room's vanities, resisting the impulse to rip them off. Her nails were uneven from nervous chewing—a former bad habit she'd resumed in the past few weeks—and they snagged the silk fabric. Reluctantly, she kept them on while her mother put the finishing touches on her hair.

Though Brynn avoided her reflection, she had to admit that her outfit was stunning. Shalure had come through for her. The main piece was a fitted tunic of blood-red silk, offset by an asymmetrical white-gold cape covering only her right shoulder. Her white pants were embroidered in gold thread. They followed the shape of her legs, tucking into a pair of pliable sealskin boots.

Brynn would have been proud to wear the impressive ensemble, if it weren't for the important caveat that she would be married in a few minutes.

"Shalure went above and beyond with your wedding ensemble." Isuna was weaving snowdrops into Brynn's braids. Her mother had taken over from the three snow elf attendants assigned to do her hair. Brynn had never been more grateful for her interference.

"Yes." One syllable answers were all she could manage. Her heart boomed like thunder and her stomach roiled like rain-battered mud.

"There." Isuna finished adding the snowdrops and caressed Brynn's cheek. "You look so handsome, my love. I know this isn't what your heart wants, but I'm proud of you. More than words can say. You're saving your people. Never forget that."

"Thanks, Mom." Blushing at the compliments, Brynn checked herself in the mirror. Under her mother's skilled hands, her hair was perfect. Thin braids formed horizontal stripes on either side of her head, while the top gave way to a thicker, longer braid. It looped atop her head several times like a shiny serpent, if serpents were known for carrying snowdrops in their coils.

Isuna squeezed Brynn's shoulder, then busied herself brushing nonexistent dust from the white-gold cape. "I won't leave Winterwail until you're completely comfortable here, no matter how long it takes. Your father agrees."

Brynn snorted. "Right." Speaking felt like tugging a fishing line snagged on a log.

Isuna frowned, placing a hand on Brynn's shoulder. "I know how you feel, Brynn. You're afraid of marrying a stranger, living so far from home—"

"Please, Mom. I appreciate you, really, but I don't want to talk about it right now. Not today. Just help me get through the ceremony, okay? I need to focus on one thing at a time."

Isuna offered Brynn a sad smile but dipped her head in acknowledgment. "Of course."

Brynn stood, pushing her chair back. As she did, she stole one last glance at the mirror. Her mother was right. She did look handsome. Striking, in fact, but not at all like herself. She wondered whether every morning would be like this, whether she'd face Queen Aefbain's consort in the mirror instead of Brynn.

"Brynn..." Isuna's voice trailed off, her brows knitting with worry.

"Don't worry. I know what's expected of me." Brynn forced a tight-lipped smile.

A knock sounded on the chamber door. Isuna hurried to answer it. Brynn's spirits lifted when she saw Galen, dressed in a fine green tunic. "Dad!" She hurried to the door, throwing her arms around him.

"Brynn." He put a large hand on the back of her head and pulled her face into his shoulder. "See, darling? I told you I'd make it."

"Just in time to ruin our daughter's hair," Isuna quipped.

Brynn wept into her father's shirt, inhaling the familiar scent of sandalwood and earth. Though she remained in his embrace for a long time, she emerged with renewed strength. She took a deep breath, like a swimmer emerging from the surf.

Her family wasn't going anywhere. Her home wasn't going anywhere. Her life would change, but everything and everyone she loved was still there. Just further away.

"No tears." Galen brushed the hot streaks away with his thumb. "Here, I have something for you. A gift from Grandmother. Said she had a feeling you'd need it soon." He reached into his pocket and withdrew a flat, black stone. Its surface was unnaturally smooth, and it was just the right size to rest between thumb and forefinger.

Brynn blinked. "A worry stone? That's an ominous gift for a wedding."

"That's what I said," Galen protested. "But Grandmother gets these ideas..."

Isuna shook her head. "I'm sure she didn't mean to imply that your marriage would be full of worries, Brynn."

"No, it's all right," Brynn said. "I'm already a bunch of worries stacked on top of each other and wearing a fancy tunic."

Galen laughed. "Why not think of it as a little piece of home to carry with you? The stone came from the forest, after all."

A smile crept across Brynn's face. She took the stone and slipped it into her pocket. Even with her silk gloves, rubbing her thumb over the stone felt surprisingly soothing. "Thanks, Dad. Tell Grandmother I appreciate it."

* * * * *

Valis spent the morning in a state of muted awareness. She knew it was her wedding day. She knew the names of everyone who congratulated her before the ceremony. She knew precisely what to say and how to behave. Yet she felt untethered as she waited in the alcove offside her throne room, alone for the first time since sunrise; a restless, aimless ghost on a day that should have been full of life and joy.

Something had died, she supposed—the death of certain childhood dreams. As the younger of two daughters, Valis had been allowed more freedom than her elder sister. She'd been quite content to sacrifice queenship for this taste of freedom, one aspect of which was the hope that she might marry someone she loved, or at least liked.

How foolish of me. Even as the younger daughter, I should have known better.

Someone cleared their throat. She turned to see Kraal, dressed in a fine purple suit with gold trimmings, entering the alcove. The embroidery perfectly matched the shiny rings on her tusks and piercings in her ears. For the first time that day, Valis managed a genuine smile. "Good morning, Kraal. Did you find what I asked for?"

Kraal nodded instead of offering her palms. They were around each other so often, such formalities had become tiresome in private. Besides, frost giant blood was useless for spellcasting, so the gesture was pointless. "Yes. A fine specimen."

"Wonderful. Thank you." Valis hesitated. "Do you think it's a good idea?"

Kraal gave Valis a soft-eyed look. "Yes. Lady Woodwarden will agree."

"At least it will give us something to talk about during tomorrow's carriage ride through the city."

"Lady Woodwarden is never at a loss for words," Kraal said. "Though they aren't always flattering."

Valis laughed. "I'm inclined to agree."

As am I, Aefbain added from its jewel-encrusted scabbard at Valis' waist.

"No one asked for your opinion," she snapped.

"Dagger being smart again? I could fix that." Kraal made a motion as if bending an invisible Aefbain in half.

"Trust me, I've considered it," Valis said.

I don't recommend it, Aefbain said, *unless you wish to add an extra layer of complication to this evening's ritual.*

Valis rolled her eyes. She didn't appreciate Aefbain's goading, especially not today, nor the unwelcome reminder of the bloodbinding ritual. She focused on Kraal. "You look nothing short of wonderful. I see Shalure worked their magic on you."

"Thank you," Kraal said. However, her face read worry rather than pleasure. It was only a subtle tensing of her jaw and narrowing of her brows, but Valis had known Kraal for decades. The signals were practically a shout.

"Kraal, do you have any doubts about standing with me today?"

Kraal shook her head. "Of course not."

She's lying, Aefbain said.

Valis didn't respond right away. She pondered what to do, torn between warring instincts. Kraal probably felt the same. A child of two different frost giant clans, with wildly differing opinions of the Aefbain dynasty, Kraal had always been an outlier. Though Valis dearly wanted her only friend by her side during the ceremony—even if that friend was also technically an employee—she would never force the issue.

"If you would rather watch from here, I understand," Valis said carefully. "But for my part, I have no doubts. You are the one and only person I want by my side."

Kraal tilted her head. Her dark eyes widened. "Truly?"

"We've discussed this before," Valis reminded her. "I feel the same now as I did then."

Kraal sighed, but the crinkles on either side of her eyes deepened as she smiled. "Well, I already have the suit."

"Yes," Valis said. "Shalure's work deserves admiration."

Kraal gave Valis' own outfit a respectful but appreciative look. "My suit hardly compares to your dress."

Valis dipped her head modestly. It was a beautiful dress, one she would wear proudly despite her misgivings. The heart-shaped neckline flowed into straps that cascaded off the shoulder. Red crepe followed her shape in seamless lines, flaring into a trumpet above her knees. There was little fancy embroidery. That was reserved for the golden belt on her waist, from which Aefbain's scabbard hung.

"You've asked after me," Kraal said. "How do you feel? If you want me to arrange some kind of delay…" She gestured as if to encompass the entire throne room and the crowd that awaited them beyond the safety of the alcove.

Valis touched Kraal's arm. "I know you would, but I'm at peace with my decision. At least Lady Woodwarden has been reasonable so far, if somewhat stubborn and crude."

"Lord-Adviser Naddox disagrees," Kraal said.

"Of course he does."

The music drifting in from the throne room changed, transitioning from light and airy phrases led by the higher strings to a slower, more solemn marching tempo urged along by the bass. Valis took a deep breath, closing her eyes and searching within herself for calmness.

"My cue," she murmured.

Kraal picked up the bouquet Valis had set aside, a bundle of fiery calla lilies wrapped in gold ribbons and gauze. She said nothing more, but the tenderness with which she offered the flowers spoke volumes.

Valis took the flowers and squared her shoulders, preparing for her most regal and queenly walk. The eyes of an entire nation would be on her.

* * * * *

"Ready?" Isuna asked.

Brynn's mouth had gone dry. Her knees wobbled, but Galen was there to steady her, placing his forearm beneath hers. On the opposite side, Isuna did the same. Before Brynn knew it, the three of them were striding toward the same double doors she'd entered two weeks ago. The doors she'd escaped through in an effort to outrun an unfair choice, only to return with the weight of responsibility on her shoulders.

This time, the doors were open. A vast crowd waited in the throne room, snow elves swathed in silk, jewels, and all manner of finery. They stood as one when she crossed the threshold, craning their necks to catch a glimpse.

"Don't look at them," Galen whispered. "Just smile and stare straight ahead. Squeeze my arm if you need to."

Brynn's gut churned. She would have preferred to watch her feet so she wouldn't trip on the golden carpet that led to the curved staircases and tiered frozen waterfall. A bower bursting with wildflowers stood between the staircases—a lovely tradition from her home, which Brynn appreciated—and beneath it...

Suddenly, Brynn had no trouble looking ahead.

Queen Aefbain was a vision in red. Her silhouette made her seem taller than Brynn remembered, or perhaps she wore heels beneath her flared dress. Her periwinkle shoulders were bare, as was the graceful column of her throat. Her long white hair had been gathered into a loose braid, with stray ringlets to frame her face. A gold circlet rested atop her head, with a matching torque around her neck. Both were studded with rubies, but it was the brightness of her eyes that truly captured Brynn's attention. The pale-gray irises shone with an iridescent silver light that made it impossible to look away.

As Brynn stared in awe, Queen Aefbain extended her hand. Though reluctant to release her parents' arms, something in the queen's eyes compelled Brynn to reach out. She let go, taking Queen Aefbain's outstretched hand and joining her beneath the bower. Her own hands trembled, sweating inside her gloves.

Brynn brushed a kiss across Queen Aefbain's knuckles. She wore similar golden gloves, though hers reached all the way to her elbows. To Brynn's surprise, Queen Aefbain caught her eye, giving her hand a gentle squeeze. Brynn's stomach hitched. *What in the world does that mean? Is she trying to be kind? Encouraging?*

Brynn had no time to process. The officiant, an elderly snow elf sage with wrinkles around her mouth and hair even whiter than Queen Aefbain's, lifted her voice to address the crowd. It must have been magically amplified, because it echoed around the throne room despite her subdued inflections.

"On this joyous day, in this hallowed and historic place, we have come together to witness the binding of Queen Valis Nyxera Aefbain and Lady Brynnflor Woodwarden."

Brynn bit her cheek to keep from laughing. Despite her nerves, she couldn't help but find humor in the situation. Though somewhat ignorant of snow elf culture, she knew enough traditional elvhen to get by. *Valis Nyxera? Her name literally means Snow Snow. What was her mother thinking? Maybe it's a family name...*

Though Queen Aefbain didn't make a sound, her grip tightened around Brynn's hands. Her gray eyes narrowed in disapproval. Sheepishly, Brynn cast her own eyes down to the floor. Sometimes, it seemed like the cold, distant Queen of Winterwail could read her mind.

The officiant continued. "Know that, just as your blood is bound, so will you bind your lives together. Do you seek to enter the bond of marriage?"

Brynn's heart skipped. *Last chance to run.* A shudder coursed through her, seizing her gut in its iron grip. She swayed a moment before steadying herself.

Queen Aefbain's look shifted to one of concern. Still, she spoke. "Yes, I seek to enter."

The officiant's heavy-lidded eyes fixed on Brynn.

Summoning her courage, Brynn answered in the most confident voice she could muster. *For my home. For my people.* "Yes, I seek to enter."

"Look down at the hands that hold yours."

Obediently, Brynn looked at their hands, covered in the same golden silk. Queen Aefbain's were smaller than hers, with long, graceful fingers. Time slowed as the officiant's voice droned on in the background.

"These are the hands that will love and cherish you through the years. These are the hands that will countless times wipe tears from your eyes, tears of sorrow and joy. These are the hands that will support and uplift you every day of your lives."

Brynn swallowed. Her mouth was drier than before, but her eyes were strangely wet. She blinked rapidly. She didn't love this woman, so why did tears threaten to brim over? Was it feelings of longing? Of loss?

"The blade, Your Majesty."

Queen Aefbain withdrew one of her hands, letting the other remain with Brynn. She unsheathed the same dagger she'd tested Brynn's blood with and later used to seal their promise. Cold sweat prickled along Brynn's neck as pale red light pulsed around the blade.

As before, Queen Aefbain turned Brynn's palm upward. She didn't remove the glove, cutting into Brynn's hand without regard for the fabric. The shallow slice flashed hot, but Brynn couldn't say it was painful. She stared as crimson blood seeped from the wound, blossoming across the gold fabric.

Brynn blinked, remembering it was her turn as Queen Aefbain offered her the dagger. She took it with her uninjured hand, curling her fingers tight around the hilt. It was warmer than she anticipated, almost like a living thing. She pushed through her fears and doubts as Queen Aefbain offered her palm. Brynn sliced her hand with a single stroke, watching the rapid bloom of blood on silk.

Fingers laced, and they pressed their open palms together.

* * * * *

The officiant launched into the next part of the ceremony, expounding on the importance of blood and the life it sustained. Valis hardly heard the words. A surge of hungry, white-hot power coursed through her, pure enough to steal her breath away. She was blood-drunk within moments, head spinning, heart racing.

I told you so.

Valis barely registered Aefbain's opinion. She felt lighter than air, buoyed by a boundless ocean of blood magic.

By the Black Wolf, it's endless!

All the magic users Valis had drawn from in the past were rivers. Some were like small streams, others waterfalls, or rushing rapids. Everyone had their limits, even her mother and sister. Questing within Brynn, Valis felt no current. No banks or borders. Bathing in Brynn's magic was like basking in the warmth of the sun at the height of summer and awakened her much the same. She gave a low moan as red fog closed around the edges of her vision.

Only when the officiant cleared her throat did Valis remember where she was and what she was supposed to be doing. Brynn's face had drawn remarkably close to hers, though the look in the wood elf's amber eyes was hesitant, unsure.

Valis struggled to recall the words she was supposed to say. Eventually, Aefbain nudged her in the right direction. *Blood of my blood...*

"Brynnflor Woodwarden, you are the blood of my blood, the flesh of my flesh. I give you my blood and myself, that we two may be one, 'til our life shall be done. You are the blood of my blood, the heart of my heart."

Solemnly, Brynn repeated the same words back to her. "Valis Nyxera Aefbain, you are the blood of my blood, the flesh of my flesh..."

Magic swelled within Valis' breast, coursing from her bloodied hand straight to her heart. Once more, the dizzying rush threatened to overwhelm her.

"I give you my blood and myself, that we two may be one, 'til our life shall be done. You are the blood of my blood, the heart of my heart." Silence hung throughout the throne room as Brynn finished.

Kiss her, idiot, Aefbain demanded. *Everyone is watching.*

Under other circumstances, Valis might have hesitated. She'd never kissed anyone outside her immediate family, and dimly, she realized the significance of the moment. For some reason, it didn't matter. Brynn's lips were full, parted in anticipation. Her breath was warm, though it came fast and shallow. Valis suddenly, desperately wanted to kiss her.

So she did.

The kiss was more heat than flavor. Their lips brushed gently at first, a silent question. Several heartbeats passed, and Valis nearly drowned in the fathomless sea of Brynn's magic again. Unable to find an anchor point, she lost herself in Brynn's mouth much the same, opening wider without conscious thought.

Brynn's eyes widened, but she didn't pull away. Valis felt Brynn's fingers tighten around hers and the brief sweep of a tongue against her bottom lip before their kiss broke with a shared gasp.

Dazed, Valis stared at Brynn as the officiant concluded. "Before all those gathered here today, these two have become one. All hail Queen Valis Nyxera Aefbain, and Princess Consort Brynnflor Woodwarden!"

Chapter Six

BRYNN'S GAZE ROAMED THE spacious royal bedchamber. After an exhausting day, Queen Aefbain had stolen away to the adjoining washroom, leaving Brynn alone for the first time since dawn. Predictably, the room was larger and fancier than the guest suites. Winterwail couldn't allow its queen to sleep in anything less than total luxury.

An expansive four-poster bed with an overhanging canopy took up most of the left wall. Far too many fur blankets covered the mattress. Just in case those weren't enough to ward off the chill, a cheerful fire burned in the hearth opposite the foot of the bed.

Brynn felt decidedly uncheerful as she examined a long counter and its accompanying mirrors. Jars and bottles covered all available space. She wondered why Queen Aefbain required so much makeup and perfume. She was already hauntingly (or perhaps annoyingly) beautiful. Did she really need a whole counter's worth of cosmetics?

Her restless energy got the better of her. She picked up one of the bottles, tilting it this way and that. It contained some sort of watery pink liquid with a pump for spritzing. She squeezed. A puff of cloying floral scent sprayed in her face. She coughed, knocking over another jar with her elbow.

"Consort Woodwarden?"

Brynn whirled at the sound of Queen Aefbain's voice. The queen—my *wife,* she reminded herself, with no small amount of lingering disbelief—stood in the doorway. She still wore her blood-red wedding dress, but she'd let her hair down. Unbraided, the silky white waves fell several inches past her waist.

Brynn set the perfume down. "Sorry!" She straightened the other bottle and edged away from the counter, as if that small amount of distance would make her appear innocent.

Queen Aefbain crossed her arms. "If you wish to borrow my things, you need only ask, but I would prefer they remain unbroken."

Brynn's cheeks burned. There really was no excuse—she'd been caught snooping. "I got bored." Her eyes darted down. The toes of her boots had become extremely interesting.

"Bored? I thought you would appreciate a few moments to yourself after everything we endured."

Queen Aefbain's choice of words perked Brynn's ears, and a smile pulled at the corners of her mouth. The two of them agreed on one thing, at least. "It wasn't so bad. The wedding bower was beautiful."

"Yes, well, I fear our obligations are not yet finished." Queen Aefbain straightened to her full height. "We must perform the ritual we discussed."

Brynn's mouth went dry. Her heart hammered far too fast. "Right. The ritual. 'With an instrument of your choosing.' What instrument is that exactly, Your Majesty?"

Queen Aefbain drew her ruby-encrusted dagger from the sash at her waist. "Aefbain, of course. And please, call me Valis. If I cannot escape 'Your Majesty' even in my own bedchamber, I may go mad and throw myself from the window."

Brynn snorted. The thought of fucking someone with a dagger was so strange that it was easier to focus on Valis' second statement. "Please don't go throwing yourself from any windows, or I'll have to jump after you. I certainly don't want to be queen in your stead."

"You could never become queen, even should you want to," Valis said. "The title would pass to one of my many second cousins, although my death or abdication would cause considerable unrest amongst the noble houses."

"Thank the seasons for that. Me not having to be queen, I mean." Brynn hesitated, studying Valis more closely. Perhaps it was how her soft, white hair looked unbound, or the way the firelight danced on her pale blue skin, but the queen seemed less severe than usual. She appeared small and waifish, despite her ramrod posture. Not uncertain, but something like it. More of an individual and less of a figurehead.

She even asked me to use her first name. Maybe she needs someone to see her as a person instead of a queen? She acts as though the position is a burden rather than something she covets. I can respect that.

"We don't have to do this ritual tonight," Brynn said. "Why not wait 'til morning? It's been a long day…"

Valis' expression hardened. "I understand this may be awkward for you, but I will remind you that you promised."

Brynn winced. So much for that idea. "Fine. Just to clarify, I'm putting the hilt, uh..." She gestured clumsily. "Not the pointy end? Because that seems like a very, very bad idea—"

Valis pinched the bridge of her nose. "Of course, not the pointy end. This is a blood-magic ritual, not a murder. Here, take it." She thrust the dagger at Brynn.

Reluctantly, Brynn took the dagger. Its hilt was warm to the touch and fit comfortably in her hand. Lustrous rubies decorated the golden pommel and matching scabbard, but its surface was surprisingly smooth, despite the gemstones. She wondered how Valis intended to clean the gaudy thing afterward, or whether magic would take care of that as well. Aefbain absorbed blood easily enough. Perhaps it could absorb other fluids? She swallowed nervously.

"First, unsheathe Aefbain and cut off my dress," Valis commanded. Her voice was a high, taut thread. "One slice, directly down the middle."

Brynn's eyes widened. "But that will ruin it," she stammered.

"Shalure will repair it with golden thread, to show where the cut was made. Then it may be worn again. Nobles consider it an honor when the queen receives them in her wedding dress."

Brynn looked down at the dagger. At Valis, whose crimson dress clung to every curve. Back at the dagger. She hated to ruin Shalure's hard work, but she'd promised. She stepped forward, closing the gap between them. "If you're sure."

Valis pursed her lips. "I am."

Brynn resolved to keep her doubts to herself. Valis' discomfort was obvious, and Brynn didn't want to make it worse by objecting at every turn. She reminded herself of what Valis had told her, that people had sex for all kinds of reasons. *I'm going through with it for her people's sake, after all.* Could this ritual even be considered sex? It certainly wasn't like any kind of sex she'd had, though with only two previous partners, she was far from the most experienced elf of her age.

"Fine. Just don't move. I know my way around a knife, but I'd hate to cut you."

"You will not," Valis said. "Aefbain is no mere knife. It knows what to do."

Not for the first time, Brynn wondered how much power Aefbain possessed. "You talk about your dagger like it's alive."

"It is, after a fashion." Valis pulled her shoulders back as though bracing herself—a soldier standing on parade. "Now, cut."

Carefully, Brynn cut Valis' dress down the middle. Doing so caused her fingers to brush Valis' skin, though she tried her best to avoid contact. The queen's flesh was warm, without a single blemish. She resembled a topaz statue more than a living being.

That impression only grew as her dress fell to the floor, revealing the rest of her body. Completely naked, illuminated only by flickering firelight, Valis was a vision of loveliness. Her sharp facial features were offset by her softly rounded shoulders, the fullness of her breasts, and the generous swell of her hips. Her stomach had a slight curve, but her thighs were long and lean.

Brynn didn't miss the shiver that coursed through Valis' slender frame. Somehow, she doubted it was from cold.

"Come with me." Valis went to the bed, leaving her dress in a pile on the ground.

Brynn gaped. *I'm not aroused by this weird ritual.* Her eyes remained riveted by Valis' backside. *I'm not. It's just, seeing a naked woman…a stunningly beautiful naked woman, with gorgeous hair and perfect skin…and she smells like flowers, and I happen to be married to her…*

"Brynnflor?"

Brynn flinched. "Just Brynn. I hate Brynnflor."

Valis offered another tight-lipped smile. "Brynn, then. Come here."

Brynn stumbled forward. She was ashamed to admit the instinct urging her closer to Valis. Close enough to feel her body heat. Close enough to touch. Her hands clenched, one still wrapped around the dagger's hilt. Touching Valis except as instructed was a dangerous idea.

"Here." Valis held out a small, blue bottle.

Brynn blinked again. Where had Valis produced it from so quickly? *Was I really that distracted?* She took the bottle in her other hand and gave Valis a curious look. "What's this?"

"Lubrication," Valis said. "It should lessen my pain."

"Pain?" Brynn frowned. "Oh, no. We'll go through with this if you insist, but I'm not hurting you."

Valis' brow furrowed. "I have been informed that some discomfort is unavoidable."

Brynn rolled her eyes. "What idiot told you that?"

"My mother, thank you," Valis said.

Brynn cringed inwardly. "Well sorry, but that's a load of...never mind." She made to run a hand through her hair before remembering she still held Valis' dagger. Two previous partners wasn't anything to brag about, but it certainly gave her more experience than Valis.

And why should her first time be some stranger shoving a dagger in her, anyway? That sounds awful, even for a stuck-up queen. Maybe...

Her eyes roamed Valis' naked form, unable to deny her admiration.

"All right. We'll perform your ritual, but we're starting off my way." She set both dagger and bottle on the nightstand, then removed her jacket and shirt, dropping them beside Valis' ruined dress.

Valis blinked. "What are you doing?"

Brynn bent down to unlace her boots, shooting Valis what she hoped was a reassuring grin. "Sex works best without clothes, or so I've been told."

Valis' mouth opened and closed as though she were struggling for words. Eventually, she sat on the edge of the mattress, wrapping the topmost fur blanket around herself and settling in to watch Brynn strip. Doing so with an audience brought tingling heat to Brynn's skin, but she persevered.

"Look, I know this isn't ideal"—Brynn straightened with her hands on her hips—"but if we perform your ritual more like real sex, it should be a lot less painful and more pleasurable for both of us." Valis nodded, though Brynn didn't miss the purple blush that bloomed across her cheeks.

"I was planning to rip the bandage off, so to speak, but climaxing during the ritual is preferable anyway. We may as well attempt it."

Brynn sat on the bed beside Valis, extremely aware of the narrow gap between their thighs. Not an inch of their flesh touched, but she swore she felt Valis' body heat anyway. "Grandmother always says bandages aren't supposed to be ripped off. That means the wound isn't done healing."

Valis arched an eyebrow. "Grandmother?"

Brynn sighed. Perhaps bringing up Grandmother while naked in bed hadn't been the brightest idea. "I'm just saying, a little finesse might...ugh, you know what I mean."

Gathering her courage, she scooted closer, placing her hand above

Valis' knee. The skin was remarkably warm, and so soft that Brynn couldn't resist rubbing a circle with the pad of her thumb. "Stop me if you need, but at the very least, I can promise this won't hurt."

To Brynn's surprise, Valis placed a slender hand atop hers, lacing their fingers. "Very well. Proceed."

Brynn felt a flash of annoyance. *'Proceed?' Hmph. This isn't a favor she's doing me. If anything, I'm the one doing her a favor.* Nevertheless, she slid her hand higher on Valis' leg, squeezing as she bent to brush a kiss atop the ball of Valis' shoulder.

Valis sucked in a sharp breath. The muscle of her thigh tensed beneath Brynn's hand. Her jaw shifted, as though she were gritting her teeth against some sort of threat or bombardment of sensation. Brynn rested her forehead on Valis' shoulder, trying to ignore how good the crook of her throat smelled. Her job was to reassure, not be selfish.

Gently, Brynn tipped Valis onto her back, spreading her slender thighs and kneeling between them. Her new bride lay naked on the bedfurs, eyes wide and silky hair splayed behind her head like a fan. The sight affected Brynn more than she wanted to admit. A keen but familiar ache swelled between her legs, which she kept at bay by clenching her own thighs shut.

To Brynn's surprise, Valis' fingertips trailed along her forearms, over the muscles that stood out as she braced herself on her elbows. The feathery touch caused her to rock forward, and they both shuddered as their bodies met in a warm line.

* * * * *

Valis' hammering heart echoed in her ears. When was the last time someone had touched her so tenderly? Embraced her? Aside from Kraal fixing her hair or helping her into some of her more ornate outfits, she couldn't recall. Queens existed to look powerful and ethereal, not to make themselves vulnerable through physical contact. No one had so much as caressed her cheek since her mother and sister died.

A helpless moan escaped her lips as she savored the softness of Brynn's skin. Each breath Brynn took passed through her own body, pressed together as they were, breast to breast and belly to belly. When had she become so touch-starved? So skin-hungry? Why hadn't she realized it before now? Perhaps she had, when Brynn's blood had flowed freely with her own earlier that day, mingling between their sliced palms.

When Brynn nuzzled the base of her neck, hitting her pulse point with hot breaths, Valis reacted on instinct. She wrapped a knee around Brynn's thigh, running the sole of her foot along a firm calf and shifting her hips forward. Something deep within her pulled as she rocked against the firm plane of Brynn's stomach. Liquid warmth pooled low in her belly.

She hadn't expected it to feel this good, this fast. From the day she'd met Brynn to the moment they'd retired to her bedchamber, she had planned to perform the ritual and nothing more, but Brynn's idea was working. Too well, in fact. The warmth and weight of Brynn's body left Valis so dizzy that her trembling limbs slackened.

"There we go," Brynn murmured against her collarbone. "Relax."

The words made Valis melt. Maybe Brynn was right. Some bandages weren't meant to be ripped off. She wrapped her arms around Brynn's torso, running her hands over the wood elf's narrow, muscular back. "All right," she whispered.

Her toes curled as Brynn's warm breath moved lower, followed by the tentative flick of an even warmer tongue. It swept along the top of her breast before circling a stiff nipple.

"Oh!" Valis' hips jumped beneath Brynn. She couldn't tell which felt better, the cautious tug of Brynn's mouth or the heated satin strokes of her tongue.

Brynn spent a long time at Valis' breasts, sucking both nipples to straining points. The tips throbbed each time Brynn took one in her mouth, leaving the other to ache against the cool air. All the while, her hands stroked soothing lines along Valis' curves, occasionally dipping down to caress her bare legs.

Valis chewed her lip, completely overwhelmed. She hadn't known anyone could undo her this quickly or thoroughly. She resolved not to let Brynn know how good it felt. Allowing Brynn to get her sufficiently aroused for the ritual was one thing. Submitting to the wild thrum that threatened to overtake her body was quite another. And Brynn had barely touched her! Surely a mere mouth didn't possess the power to move her so, no matter how skilled that mouth was.

Brynn released Valis' nipple, blowing a cool stream of air across it. Valis tossed her head sideways on the pillow, avoiding Brynn's searching brown eyes. She wasn't entirely comfortable with the way they bored into her. It was easier not to look.

"Let's see how we're doing." Brynn's fingertips grazed Valis' inner thigh, a gentle warning before she cupped her hand higher. The press of her palm made Valis realize how wet she was. She hadn't noticed, focused as she'd been on Brynn's mouth, but there was no denying it now. She was uncomfortably swollen and slick. Her core clenched as Brynn's fingers coaxed her outer lips apart, seeking the source.

"You were right," Valis said, ashamed of the needful note in her voice. Better to hurry things along before she spun too far out of control. "I doubt the ritual will hurt now. You should be able to— ohhh…"

Her head lolled and her eyes rolled back as Brynn slid one finger past her entrance, curling forward and up. It was much too slender to cause any pain, but the pressure it applied to Valis' front wall made her voice trail off into a groan.

"Not yet." Brynn kissed one of Valis' nipples, sweeping her tongue across its pebbled surface. "I'll need to open you up more than this." She sucked in earnest, crooking her finger just so.

Valis keened. It wasn't fair! How was she supposed to withstand this sort of treatment? The blissful fire of Brynn's mouth and the gentle thrusting of her finger threatened to push her over a precipice she'd never reached with another person. She suspected all the orgasms she'd given herself in the past would pale in comparison. She was quietly mortified, but had no choice except to endure.

Such horrible torture, Your Majesty, Aefbain drawled from its place on the nightstand. *I can't bear to watch.*

Valis' embarrassed arousal blazed into anger. She fisted the sheets tighter and lifted her head, glaring at the nightstand. "Shut up," she snarled through gritted teeth. Allowing Brynn such liberties was awkward enough without Aefbain as a witness.

Only too late did she realize that, in her distraction, she'd spoken the words aloud.

Brynn made a concerned noise and released the nipple she'd been sucking, withdrawing her hand as well. The sensation of her finger sliding out made Valis' inner walls ripple. She barely stifled a sob as she rocked forward, seeking what she'd lost.

"Did you just tell me to shut up?" Brynn asked, frowning.

Valis blushed to the roots of her hair. "No! Not at all. I—" She fumbled for Aefbain on the nightstand, nearly knocking it onto the floor before grabbing hold of its scabbard. "My apologies. One moment." *Sleep,* she directed Aefbain, *so your thirst may be quenched.*

I think you are more concerned with quenching your own thirst. Nevertheless, Aefbain began to glow, pulsing with faint white light.

Valis breathed a sigh of relief. During certain rituals, Aefbain entered a receptive state that prevented it from speaking—a trait she was grateful for, particularly in this moment.

Once the dagger was dealt with, she passed it to Brynn, eager to be rid of the obnoxious thing. "Aefbain speaks to me," she explained when she saw that Brynn's eyes were still narrowed in reproach. "Suffice to say, I did not appreciate its commentary on our activities."

Brynn gave a startled laugh. "Your dagger speaks to you?" Her dark brows rose almost to her hairline. "Do I even want to know what it said?"

"No," Valis said. "Now please, continue."

Brynn's look of surprise shifted into one of hesitation. Her eyes darted to the sheathed dagger in her hand as she gave it a doubtful once-over. "It isn't going to start evaluating my technique, right?"

"Aefbain is asleep." Valis tried desperately to hide the hope in her voice. "Here." She passed the small blue bottle of lubricant to Brynn.

Brynn uncapped the bottle, drizzling a generous amount into her palm. Valis watched in fascination. Knowing one of those gleaming fingers had recently been inside her made them look all the more enticing. Brynn slathered Aefbain's hilt in the stuff, coating it liberally.

Valis spread her thighs wider, fighting the temptation to rock forward. Despite her insistence that they continue, she feared what Brynn might think if she appeared too eager. Even without Aefbain's metaphorical eyes upon her, she felt frighteningly exposed beneath Brynn's gaze.

I must remain calm. Even though I'm experiencing pleasure instead of pain, this is still a serious, somber ritual...

Then Brynn touched the rounded end of Aefbain's hilt between Valis' legs. Her thoughts melted like the last of winter's snow beneath the spring sun. The metal was warm and smooth as it rubbed against her, gliding back and forth rather than pushing inside.

"There," Brynn murmured, gazing down with half-lidded eyes. "How does that feel?"

Valis bit her cheek, uncomfortably aware of the fact that Brynn was watching everything that happened between their bodies. "Pleasant," she forced out when she realized Brynn was waiting for a response.

"Hmm. We'll see."

Valis stiffened as Brynn withdrew the hilt, only to whimper with relief as she replaced it with two warm, slippery fingers. They slid inside her as though they were meant to be there. She rolled her hips into Brynn's hand, unable to stop her spine from arching.

"And this?" Brynn asked, leaning over her.

Valis quivered. There was more of a stretch with two fingers, but they caused a wonderful pressure that pounded deep within. Her inner walls had never gripped and pulsed like this before, not even when she pleasured herself. When she tried to answer Brynn, all that came out was a high-pitched moan.

It transitioned into breathless whines as Brynn's fingers curled within her, hitting a spot that caused spots of white light to flash before her eyes. Her hips hovered, unsure whether to pull back or push forward. Brynn made the decision by sliding even deeper, sweeping her thumb over the swollen point of Valis' clit.

Stars spun around Valis' head. Her body bowed beneath Brynn's and she dug her heels into the mattress, squeezing her eyes shut. She pulsed with living fire as she fluttered around Brynn's fingers, utterly helpless in the face of her own pleasure. She gasped something that might have been Brynn's name as a warm mouth sealed back around her nipple, sucking the stiff bud in time with each curling thrust.

The first gush of wetness took Valis by surprise, but she couldn't have held back if she tried. All her cool composure went up in flames. She clutched Brynn's shoulders, clenching around the fingers buried deep inside her.

Brynn didn't seem to mind the mess. She moaned and swirled her tongue, as if quite pleased with herself. Valis spilled harder as Brynn's thumb rubbed slow circles on her clit. "Good. That's good. Come if you need to."

Valis went limp. Her arms fell by her sides as the powerful waves of her peak receded into rippling eddies. Brynn's soft encouragement brought on a few more aftershocks, but she kept her eyes closed, unwilling to look at Brynn's face. The uncertainty of what she might find there terrified her more than the prospect of the ritual.

She lay perfectly still and silent for a short time afterward, breathing shallowly, unable or unwilling to move. *What happened to me?* The intensity of her release, the loss of control—it had all been so unexpected. Her heart began to race again and her limbs trembled. *Enough, Valis. You must regain control!*

She mustered the most neutral expression she possibly could, then forced her eyes open. Brynn was staring down at her with a look of mild concern. Valis felt a stab of guilt. Brynn had been so kind about the whole ordeal and here she was, ruining everything.

"I am ready for the ritual now," she said, summoning what little regality remained to her while she lay naked in post-orgasmic shambles.

Chapter Seven

"I AM READY FOR the ritual now."

Brynn stared down at Valis, fighting a frown. The queen's face was blank—not merely neutral, but entirely empty. Aside from a faint purple flush on her prominent cheekbones, there was no sign that Valis had peaked moments ago. She lay still, her shallow breaths having already evened out.

There was no doubt in Brynn's mind that Valis had come. She remembered the rush of heat and rippling contractions around her fingers. Yet all Valis had to say for herself afterward was, "I am ready for the ritual now." Not so much as a "Thank you," or "That was nice."

Perhaps it was her own fault for attempting to turn a somber ritual into something pleasurable, but great seasons! Despite the slippery heat on her hand, Brynn decided Valis was colder than the kingdom she ruled.

If that was true, though, why had Valis been so responsive before? Why had she cried out, quivering like a bowstring after loosing its arrow? The arch of Valis' pale, blue body, head thrown back, snow-white hair spilling onto the pillow like a frozen waterfall, was already emblazoned upon Brynn's memory. Such a strong reaction had to be real.

Her mixed emotions—puzzlement, annoyance, and uncomfortable arousal among them—solidified into petulant stubbornness. She would thaw this ice queen if it ruined every tendon in her wrist, but first, she had to be sure. "You're certain?" she asked, searching Valis for signs of doubt.

Briefly, Brynn thought she spied some emotion returning to Valis' face. An encouraging smile, perhaps? Alas, no. Her plum-colored lips were merely moving to speak. "The ritual is our sole objective," Valis insisted, her tone polite and passionless. "Again, I must remind you that you promised."

Brynn set her jaw. Valis' frosty demeanor was a constant annoyance, like a prickling itch she couldn't reach, only in her brain rather than the middle of her back. "Fine. But make no mistake, Your Majesty. You're about to get more than you bargained for."

She kissed down Valis' body, sucking both nipples back to straining points. She delighted in the hitch of Valis' breath and the way the queen's slender fingers clutched the fur sheets, relishing each sign as a small triumph. Her confidence swelled as she rolled her tongue around Valis' hip bone, causing her thighs to flex.

"The ritual requires Aefbain," Valis said, her voice still frustratingly steady. "Not your mouth."

Brynn pulled back to admire the landscape of Valis' body. So lovely was the view that she almost forgot her goal. Valis' breasts rose and fell with each breath, her gray eyes inscrutable. She was too beautiful, too perfect to be real—and the more distant and aloof her behavior, the more determined Brynn became.

"I know." Brynn groped across the nightstand for Aefbain. Once she found the hilt, she ducked beneath Valis' knees, guiding both long, graceful legs over her shoulders. "Give me a moment."

A moment was all Brynn needed to make sure Valis was ready. Valis' body said everything she could not. Her pale outer lips were puffy and parted, while the inner ones were flushed a dark, shimmering purple. Her clit strained beneath its hood, pleading to be sucked.

"Beautiful," Brynn murmured.

Valis gasped. "What?"

Brynn blushed. Perhaps that was too affectionate a compliment for such bizarre circumstances. She moved past the awkwardness by sucking Valis' clit, flicking her tongue across its tip. Valis tasted warm and faintly of salt. The scent of sex swelled in Brynn's nose.

"Oh..."

Valis gripped the furs tighter, calves tensing against Brynn's back. Brynn smirked around her prize, petting Valis' thighs with open palms. The queen's heart might be frozen, but her skin was warm, smooth, and inviting. Touching it made Brynn recall how wonderfully silky Valis had felt wrapped around her fingers. She almost wished she didn't need to use the dagger...

"Aefbain," Valis said, with the subtlest of tremors. Her heels dug in behind Brynn's shoulders. "You must use Aefbain."

If Brynn hadn't been paying such close attention, she might have mistaken Valis' words for an order. Instead, she heard a plea. Triumph glowed within her chest. Her plan was working.

She brought Aefbain's rounded hilt to Valis' entrance, grateful for the dagger's scabbard. The last thing she wanted to do was cut her chin or her own hand. Rather than push the hilt inside, she rubbed up and down, timing each stroke with a pull of her lips.

Soon, Valis' hips rocked in time. They thrust forward and down, trying to sink onto Aefbain's hilt, but Brynn held it out of reach. She removed her mouth with a wet pop. "Relax. Hold still and breathe out."

Brynn half expected an objection. To her surprise, Valis obeyed. She exhaled shakily, relaxing her thighs. As she did so, Brynn brought the hilt to her entrance, pushing forward with gentle pressure.

Aefbain slid home without a hint of resistance. Valis' muscles squeezed tight around the pommel, but their grip was more than welcoming. Brynn felt a telltale tug along the scabbard, as though Valis were trying to draw Aefbain's hilt deeper.

"All right?" Brynn asked.

Valis drew her lower lip between sharpened teeth and nodded yes, remaining utterly silent.

Brynn's brow furrowed. That wouldn't do. She gave Aefbain a soft push, watching for any sort of reaction. Her reward was a gasp and the subtle stirring of Valis' hips. Taking that as a positive sign, she withdrew Aefbain about half an inch before sliding it back in.

Valis tightened her knees over Brynn's shoulders. She turned her head and closed her eyes, swallowing visibly, but her clit turned an even brighter shade of purple. Aefbain's hilt glimmered in the low light.

Encouraged, Brynn adopted a slow thrusting motion. She angled the pommel upward, noting the way Valis trembled whenever she nudged a sensitive spot. Valis' eyes stayed shut, but her lips parted with a whimper. To Brynn, that whimper was the first ray of spring sunshine after a long, dark winter. She wanted to hear it again, so she pressed harder.

Valis drew an unsteady breath between gritted teeth. "Please."

A bolt of lightning struck between Brynn's legs. She hadn't intended to seek pleasure herself—it was a side benefit, if anything, but she couldn't ignore the ache pounding deep within her core. She slid her free hand between her own legs, surprised to find her clit stiff and sensitive.

Brynn had already known she was aroused. How could she not be with a beautiful, naked woman beneath her? What she hadn't accounted for was the strength of her eagerness. Her core clenched and she twitched beneath her own fingertips. A few perfunctory circles had her on the verge of coming.

To distract herself, Brynn focused on thrusting Aefbain. For something that had seemed so off-putting at first, claiming Valis with the dagger made for a strangely beautiful sight. As she stared, the golden scabbard began to glow, making Valis' parted lips seem darker and shinier in comparison.

Brynn's eyes widened. No noticeable aura emanated from Aefbain, so far as she could tell, but the glow was clearly magical. Was this part of the ritual? Brynn had no idea. She'd never been sensitive to magical energy, not even when she used her own unwanted powers.

Valis remained unconcerned by the light radiating from Aefbain. She unfurled a desperate hand from the furs and reached for Brynn's head, grasping her hair. "Keep going," she whispered with a gentle tightening of her fingers.

Since Valis wasn't worried, Brynn decided she had no reason to be, either. She sucked Valis' clit, withdrawing Aefbain a few inches before sliding it home again.

They soon established a rhythm. The scent of sex grew stronger, and the soft, slippery sound of each thrust mingled with Valis' heavy breathing. Brynn's chin occasionally bumped Aefbain's scabbard, due to the position of her mouth, but it was only a small nuisance. She swirled her tongue, bucking into her own hand whenever Valis rolled her hips.

Suddenly, Valis threw her forearm across her face as though to hide herself away. She arched off from the mattress, murmuring something in elvhen that Brynn couldn't catch. Brynn drew back in time to watch Valis tighten around Aefbain's hilt, spilling rivers of slickness around its shining scabbard.

Before Brynn sought her own release, she smirked with silent pride. There was no mistake. Valis had definitely come. Hard, if her fluttering abdomen and flexing thighs were any indication. Brynn slid two fingers inside herself, curling at a well-learned angle. *A reward for a job well-done.* She ground her clit into the heel of her hand. *Less awkward than getting myself off in the bathroom later, anyway.*

* * * * *

Blood.

Valis craved blood.

Its richness. Its sweetness. Its power.

She yearned for it, the phantom taste of copper tingling upon her tongue.

As Valis came, rippling hard around Aefbain's hilt, she knew only hunger. Brynn's magic churned nearby, a vast ocean of energy hovering somewhere beyond reach. No amount of thrashing, groping, or pleading brought it any closer. All the while, Aefbain's need blazed bright within her. Always starving, never satisfied.

She snapped at empty air, growling when she failed to find a proper bite-hold. Where was the flesh beneath her fangs? The heady rush of power flowing over her tongue and down her throat? This was wrong! All wrong. In desperation, she threw an arm over her face— partially to hide her expression, but mostly so she could sink her teeth into her own wrist.

Ah! There it was. The familiar taste of her own blood flooded her mouth, bringing some measure of relief. Magic raced through her veins, beating alongside her heart, eating its way to her core. Warmth coated her throat, feeding the growing fire in the pit of her stomach.

Aefbain pulsed, its hilt like burning ice within the grasp of her inner walls. Though it didn't speak, it was clearly pleased. Only then did Valis feel the tug of its will, the siphoning of her newfound power. Aefbain absorbed everything she possessed—magic, energy, emotions—just as it drank blood, leaving her limbs tingling with invisible weight.

Valis collapsed, panting heavily, but still Aefbain drank. She weakened as the dagger gorged itself, but echoes of intense pleasure radiated through her body with each pull of Brynn's lips. She sighed, shuddering as all her tension melted away. It was one of the most blissful sensations she'd felt in her life. She never wanted it to stop.

Her vision blurred at the edges, becoming foggy at first, then cool and dark. The chill spread, wrapping her in its icy embrace as the sight of Brynn's head between her legs grew fainter. Unable to resist the heaviness of her lashes any longer, Valis closed her eyes, sinking into numbness. It was a relief compared to the wild flames that had threatened to consume her.

"Your Majesty? Valis? Are you all right?"

Valis blinked at the distant sound of her name. "Hmm?"

Brynn's face hovered above hers, a knot of concern between her dark brows. Her dimpled chin shone with wetness, a lurid image that brought unexpected heat to Valis' cheeks. "You look like you're about to pass out. That's not supposed to happen, is it?"

A stray thought wandered through Valis' mind. *Brynn looks rather handsome when she's upset...*

With considerable effort, Valis dragged herself out of the restful cold and into the persistent warmth of reality. "I am awake," she insisted, though she sounded like someone disturbed from slumber even to her own ears.

"Under other circumstances, I'd take that as an insult," Brynn said. "Women don't usually fall asleep on me during sex."

Valis thought the humor in Brynn's voice sounded forced, as though concealing genuine worry. It was... strange. She was unsure how to feel about Brynn's concern. Unsure whether it was wise to feel anything at all. Her mind whirled in a futile effort to process what they'd done, so she pushed all emotion aside and focused on presenting Brynn with a distant, unaffected persona.

"Aefbain's appetite is sated for now. You may withdraw it."

"Ah. Right. Breathe out for me?" Carefully, Brynn withdrew Aefbain's hilt. "There."

Valis winced as the hilt dragged along her inner walls. Earlier, physical pleasure had drowned out any discomfort, just as Brynn had promised. Now, she felt sore and stretched in an unfamiliar way. It would take some getting used to.

To her dismay, Brynn noticed when she flinched. "Sorry. Um, here." She passed Aefbain over, held between two fingers as though she were reluctant to grasp it. *Silly, considering what those fingers were doing moments ago.* Nevertheless, she reclaimed Aefbain without regard for the wetness coating its hilt. *Awaken,* she commanded, *and purify yourself.*

Pale-blue flames erupted from within Aefbain's scabbard, swallowing both dagger and hilt. The fire didn't burn, but some residual warmth seeped into Valis' palm, causing her flesh to tingle.

Ahhh. Aefbain's voice dripped with sweet satisfaction. *It's been ages since I feasted so well. My thanks, Your Majesty.*

Before Valis could chastise Aefbain for addressing her as Your

Majesty, Brynn yelped. The mattress bounced as she retreated to the foot of the bed, brown eyes wide with alarm. "Fuck! At least warn me next time before you set something on fire right next to my face."

Valis fought a smile. She hadn't intended to frighten Brynn, but the sight of the wood elf scrambling to safety like a startled cat was completely unexpected—and amusing. Such body language completely contradicted Brynn's brash personality.

"My apologies." Valis lowered Aefbain and quenched its flame with a thought. "I had no idea you were so skittish around magic."

Brynn scowled, pulling the furs beneath her arms as though to protect herself. "I'm not skittish." Her short ears flattened, her upper lip peeling back to reveal subtly sharpened teeth, until she no longer resembled a startled cat so much as an irritated one. "Normal people don't appreciate fire exploding into being right next to them."

Valis pressed her lips into a thin line. "Implying that I am abnormal?" It was hardly the first time someone had described her thus, but coming from Brynn, it stung more than anticipated. *Why? Her opinion should hardly matter more because we were briefly intimate...*

Brynn huffed, casting her irritated gaze toward the fire. She pulled the furs tighter around her torso. "You're a queen. That's one point against you already. And using blood magic doesn't exactly project an air of normalcy either, sorry to say."

Valis frowned. It was true enough. She had been different by virtue of her birth for her entire life. Why then, was she so concerned what Brynn thought of her? Their marriage was one of political necessity, and the ritual had only taken on sexual elements because Brynn had claimed it would cause less discomfort.

"What about you?" Valis fixed Brynn with an unwavering stare. "If you were normal, you would be of no use to me as a consort."

Brynn turned back from the fire, her expression hard and defensive. "My magic is nothing special. I can barely use it except when my life's in danger. My brother was the special one. If he was still alive, you'd have married him."

"Highly unlikely," Valis said, "considering I only invited women to participate in the selection process. I allowed myself at least that one personal preference."

Brynn rolled her eyes. "You know what I mean. I'm a rain-damp torch, barely able to light when needed. So, I guess you're right, Your Majesty. I'm not normal either way. Regular folk see my magic as strange, and magic users see me as defective."

Once more, Valis considered objecting to the use of Your Majesty, but decided the argument wasn't worth the effort. "You are far from defective," she said, rolling out of bed and attempting to bring the top blanket along with her.

After a brief but silent struggle, during which they both tugged on their respective ends, Brynn surrendered her half of the fur blanket, allowing Valis to wrap it around her shoulders as she went in search of a nightgown. "Your blood contains raw power the likes of which I have never before encountered," she continued without turning around. "With proper instruction, I see no reason you could not learn to harness it."

A soft gasp sounded from behind her as she opened the bureau. Valis didn't need to turn to sense Brynn's look of surprise. "Really? With training, could I use my magic to destroy the monsters back home?"

"I doubt killing them off one by one is the permanent solution you seek, but yes. Why not?" She selected a white nightgown embroidered in purple, its delicate stitchwork enchanted to ward off cold despite the relatively thin material. Her skin warmed up as soon as she slipped it on. She did her best to ignore the lingering heat between her thighs, which had never completely left.

When Valis turned, she found Brynn staring at her with undisguised hope. "Teach me."

Valis arched a brow. "I thought you considered your magic a burden?"

"Not if it can get rid of those awful things. Teach me."

"Please might be appropriate in this situation." Valis returned to the bureau for another nightgown. Selecting the largest one in hopes it would fit Brynn's broader shoulders and wider hips, she returned to bed and handed it over.

Brynn pulled the nightgown over her head. "Thanks. And...please."

To her surprise, Valis found the disappearance of Brynn's naked flesh disappointing. She managed a small smile. "You might fare better with a different tutor. Adviser Naddox could—"

Brynn groaned, flopping back onto the bed. "Seasons, not him!"

Valis almost laughed. For all that Brynn annoyed her, the two of them agreed on some matters. "Very well. I have never taken a student before, so you may find my methods...trying."

"I don't care," Brynn said. "I already find you trying."

From the grin that crept across Brynn's face, Valis could tell the statement was meant as a joke. She decided to treat it as such. "The feeling is mutual. Nevertheless, I will attempt to teach you the basics."

"Really?" Brynn gave a small, excited bounce on the mattress as she shifted back onto her knees. "Excellent. As much as I love archery and distrust magic, my bow wasn't getting the job done."

"That distrust may be why your magic is so inflexible," Valis said. "I must admit, I find your perspective difficult to understand. Magic is simply part of me. I cannot deny something so entwined with my very essence."

Another wrinkle of frustration formed between Brynn's brows, and Valis realized the wood elf's expressions were already becoming familiar despite their relatively short acquaintanceship. "I guess that's as good a starting point as any. I'll try thinking of magic as...me...instead of this strange thing that happens to me."

"Precisely," Valis said. "But your education must wait until tomorrow. I find myself weary." She returned to bed, allowing Brynn to stand up and help her return the fur blanket she had taken. Even after Valis climbed beneath the covers, Brynn remained standing, shifting awkwardly from foot to foot.

"So, should I go back to my room, or...?"

Valis sighed. "You will share my bed, at least for tonight. Imagine if one of the servants saw you sneaking back to the guest rooms on our wedding night?"

The corners of Brynn's mouth twitched into a smirk. "Would that be considered a scandal here?"

"Perhaps," Valis said. "Everyone knows our marriage is a political union, but for the sake of politeness and tradition, we should maintain the illusion that we are fond of each other."

Brynn scoffed, folding her arms across her chest. "So, everyone knows the obvious, but we have to pretend they don't? That's stupid."

"It is how things are done," Valis said.

"But why? No, don't bother. I already know I won't like your answer." Brynn climbed into bed, snuggling beneath the covers and pulling them all the way up to her chin. Only her bright, brown eyes, curly black hair, and slightly rounded ears poked out. "At least the bed is more than big enough. Hey, it's pretty warm under here."

Valis allowed herself a small chuckle. "Thanks to magic. Your nightgown will keep away the worst of the cold, as will the fire."

"Hmm. Guess magic isn't all terrible."

"I sense a shift in your perspective already. Good night."

"Um. Goodnight."

Valis turned onto her side, facing away from Brynn and toward her nightstand. She closed her eyes and slowed her breaths, but it was a futile effort. Sleep wouldn't claim her for a while yet, if at all. Her body buzzed with strange energy. Not magic, but something far more physical and primal.

She suspected it had something to do with what she and Brynn had done. Not the ritual itself, but the sexual aspect. She was no longer a virgin. The last thing she wanted to do was sort through her feelings about that, but she couldn't deny that she *had* feelings in need of sorting. She could do that later, alone. Not now, with her new bride and the source of her angst attempting to sleep mere inches away.

As usual, Aefbain was no help. *What a generous offer, Your Majesty,* it drawled from the nightstand, inserting itself into her thoughts where it most definitely was not welcome. *How selfless to volunteer as her magic tutor. It will require a lot of hands-on instruction, of course. Surely you have no other motivations, such as a repeat of tonight's activities.*

Valis chose not to dignify Aefbain with a response. She pretended to be asleep even though she knew Aefbain wouldn't be fooled. It was a long time before she actually managed to find slumber. Her last thought before surrendering to her dreams was that her bed felt much warmer than usual.

Chapter Eight

MM. WARM.

BRYNN WOKE to an arm draped over her waist, light breaths upon her neck, and silky hair tickling her cheek. She yawned, scooting toward the source of warmth. The warmth cuddled closer, soft breasts pressing above her shoulders. A sleepy smile spread across Brynn's face. This was the first morning since leaving home she hadn't woken up shivering...

Oh. Oh no!

Brynn went rigid, scarcely daring to breathe. Sometime during the night, Valis had snuggled up against her. Sweat sprouted on the back of her neck. Her face burned. She needed to escape Valis' embrace, but what if the queen noticed?

Valis moaned, nuzzling Brynn's hair. Her arm tightened around Brynn's waist. Brynn's borrowed nightgown suddenly felt very flimsy indeed as Valis' body heat bled through the fabric. Brynn chewed her lip, desperately trying to ignore the growing ache between her legs.

Stupid, stupid, stupid! The previous night's ritual had meant nothing—merely one of many obligations her new role as consort required. Yet thoughts of Valis' smooth periwinkle skin, of the lovely sounds the queen had made, of her salty-sweet taste, left Brynn reeling. Not only was she afraid to move, part of her didn't want to.

She didn't have a choice. She and Valis didn't have an ongoing sexual relationship. She'd only stayed the night to avoid any appearance of impropriety. To stop the servants' tongues from wagging...

Valis' hand slid up Brynn's stomach, causing her abdominal muscles to twitch. She held perfectly still, but her eyes widened when that same hand cupped her left breast, not precisely squeezing, but peacefully resting there.

Brynn's heartbeat hammered so loud she feared it would wake Valis, but the queen slumbered on, blissfully unaware. Gathering her courage, Brynn prepared to remove Valis' hand and arm as stealthily as possible. Maybe she could escape without jostling the mattress.

The steady breathing behind her changed, becoming faster and more alert. In a panic, Brynn snapped her eyes shut and slowed her own breaths. Perhaps she could fake sleep until the awkward situation resolved itself. She held perfectly still. Valis stirred, then gasped. She snatched her hand away as though it had been burned.

Instead of relief, Brynn felt an unexpected pang of disappointment. Was she really so unpleasant to touch? Not that she *wanted* Valis to touch her...

Brynn kept up the act as Valis slipped from the bed and escaped, tiptoeing away on quiet feet. Only when Brynn heard the door to the adjoining washroom close did she open her eyes. She rolled onto her back, staring at the purple silk canopy and exhaling a long sigh. That had been far too close for comfort.

Realizing she couldn't lie in Valis' bed forever, Brynn abandoned the warm, cozy furs and retrieved her clothes from the night before. They carried the scent of Valis' perfume. Brynn wrinkled her nose, though not from distaste. The smell brought back a flood of memories from the previous night.

No. Don't think about how smooth her skin was. Don't think about how good her hair smelled, how soft her breasts were, or how warm and tight she felt around my fingers.

A polite knock startled Brynn out of her unwilling recollections. She whirled, clutching the bundle of clothes to her chest. "One moment!" She didn't know much about snow elf manners, but surely it would be improper to greet someone in nothing but a borrowed nightgown.

The door cracked open anyway and Delia's head poked inside. The plump, dark-skinned woman wore her usual excitable, almost manic smile. Brynn fought the urge to flinch at its fixed brightness.

"Good morning, Consort Woodwarden!" Delia slipped into the room and closed the door behind her. "How did you sleep?"

Brynn flushed. It would be rude to demand Delia leave now, nightgown or no. "I slept well, but as you can see, I haven't had time to dress."

"No need to worry," Delia said. "Shalure and I have already outfitted the wardrobe behind you...no pun intended."

"Really?" Brynn asked. When had Delia found the time? Then again, the woman never seemed to stop moving.

"Have a look."

Hesitantly, Brynn opened the door of a wardrobe full of fine clothes, shirts, breeches, robes, and several fancy vests and jackets. Though they were undeniably exquisite, Brynn's brow furrowed. "What about Valis' clothes? There's no room left."

Delia giggled. "Oh. The queen's clothes wouldn't fit in a single wardrobe. Most are in her dressing room."

Brynn worked her mouth in silence for a moment. "Queen Aefbain has a whole room... *just* for clothes?"

"It comes with the position, I'm afraid," said Valis in an airy and detached voice. Brynn turned to see her emerge from the washroom, wearing a robe of blue silk over the same nightgown. Trying to avoid staring, particularly since the robe was cinched tight around Valis' narrow waist, Brynn recalled there was another door leading out of the washroom on the opposite side. Perhaps that was the entrance to this mysterious dressing room?

"My wardrobe also recently tripled in size due to circumstances beyond my control," Valis added as she circled the bed.

It took Brynn a moment to understand. When she did, her heart clenched in sympathy. How often had she worn Darrow's old jackets the past several years, even though they were too big? The faint remnants of his scent were a comfort. She could still imagine them long after they'd faded.

"I wasn't judging," Brynn said. "Queens need fancy clothes to make people respect them, I suppose."

"Precisely. Now, what shall we put you in?" She glided over to the wardrobe, pushing Brynn aside with her aura alone, and ran her fingers along the material of several shirts.

"Oh, Your Majesty, if you intend to select the consort's outfit, may I please assist?" Delia clasped her hands in hope. Her warm, brown eyes glittered and shone with anticipation.

Valis gave Delia a sidelong look. Perhaps it was Brynn's imagination, but she thought she saw a brief smile tug at the corners of Valis' lips. "Why not?"

Delia looked like she might squeal, but she managed to maintain proper composure. She hurried to join Valis by the wardrobe.

Brynn hung back, frowning. "I'm not some doll for the two of you to play dress up with, you know." Neither Valis nor Delia showed any sign of having heard her. They rifled through the wardrobe, withdrawing clothes and laying them out on the bed. Brynn's stomach sank. *Oh no. What have I gotten myself into?*

Fifteen minutes later, Brynn studied herself in the full-length mirror, surprised and pleased by what she saw. Her new outfit began with a royal-blue half cape and snow-white cravat, which fell over a loose, shirt of dark gray, with two lines of shiny silver buttons. Her breeches, the same blue as the cape, tucked neatly into her sealskin boots. The material was light and breathable but still managed to keep her warm.

"I'm impressed," she said to Valis and Delia. "I'll admit, I had some misgivings, but this looks snappy."

Delia bowed and extended her palms. "Why thank you, Consort Woodwarden. I'm thrilled it meets with your approval."

Valis said nothing, but the edges of her full lips curled into a ghost of a smile. Her sharp chin rose in a subtle gesture of endorsement.

Brynn's heart skipped a beat. Though she liked her outfit, it felt strange and a bit embarrassing to fall under such intense scrutiny. What did Valis think of her appearance now that she was dressed? She scrounged for something to say, struggling to fill the silence.

Salvation came as the door opened without the forewarning of a knock. A large frame filled the doorway, casting a long shadow upon the floor. Brynn recognized Kraal from her first meeting with the royal advisers, as well as the wedding ceremony. At the time, she'd thought it strange, but rather sweet, that Kraal had stood with Valis.

"Milady," Kraal rumbled, bowing deeply.

"Good morning, Kraal."

Brynn was sure she heard a hint of warmth in Valis' tone.

"Shall I help you dress for breakfast now?" Kraal didn't use Valis' title.

Valis left the wardrobe, heading for the washroom without a backward glance. "Yes. Hair up this morning, I think..."

Kraal followed in silence. She and Valis disappeared, leaving Brynn with Delia and a lingering whiff of Valis' perfume. To her embarrassment, Brynn remained dazed by the floral scent until Delia gave a polite cough.

"Shall I send for some servants to style your hair and help you finish dressing, Consort Woodwarden? Tomorrow, as one of the first orders of business, I shall see about selecting an appropriate attendant from among the palace staff."

"Do you have to?" Brynn asked. "Having my own attendant seems like more trouble than it's worth."

Delia blinked several times in rapid succession. "You...don't want a personal attendant?" she asked, clearly bewildered.

Brynn shrugged. "I've bathed, fed, and dressed myself just fine until now, so...no. Not really."

"But..."

"We have that breakfast thing soon, right? Why don't I get ready for that," Brynn said, eager to move the conversation along before Delia could actually say no.

"Of course." Delia looked somewhat flabbergasted. "May I help with your hair, at least?"

Brynn eyed the braided locs arranged atop Delia's head. The human's hair was even more tightly curled than her own, and seemed in good health, so she relented. "Thanks. That would be helpful."

* * * * *

Breakfast was a busy, bustling affair which allowed scant time for the consumption of food. Valis spent the meal forcing a clench-jawed smile, because Black Wolf take her if she ever chewed in front of an audience. Royalty must give the appearance of subsisting on air alone, lest they be judged for everything from food choice to the size of their plate.

Unfortunately, Brynn, who was seated beside her at table, had not received the same upbringing. The wood elf kept her mouth closed while chewing, much to Valis' relief, but tucked into her loaded breakfast plate with unbridled enthusiasm. She was far more interested in the mountain of jam-filled pastries than conversation. She ate heartily, without concern for what Valis, her advisers, or the high-ranking nobles in attendance might think.

Valis paused in speaking to Lord Verdigris of Crystal Pass, only to catch sight of Brynn licking a glob of jelly from the corner of her mouth. Valis swallowed, struggling not to remember how that same tongue had felt between her legs. She tore her gaze away, unsure whether the fluttery feeling in her stomach was arousal or revulsion.

"I see your new consort is enjoying palace fare," Lord Verdigris chuckled. "As she should. The marvelous cuisine from your palace kitchens is unmatched anywhere."

Valis offered Lord Verdigris a thin smile. "You are welcome to as much as you would like. This is a celebration, after all."

Lord Verdigris' smile never faltered, but he tilted his head slightly, causing some of his snow-white braids to fall across his shoulders. "Indeed, Your Majesty. A glorious day."

Before he could reply with a sufficiently subtle barb, a chorus of handbells rang out. Everyone turned to the front of the room, where Lord-Adviser Naddox, alongside Lady-Advisers Galesha and Fayeth, stood at attention. They wore their finest magenta robes, with sleeves nearly down to the floor.

"If I may have everyone's attention," Lord-Adviser Naddox drawled, his voice expanding to fill the dining hall. "Her Majesty, Queen Valis Nyxera Aefbain, will now present her wedding gift to her new wife, Lady-Consort Brynnflor Woodwarden!"

Valis sat with a straight spine and raised chin as all eyes in the dining hall landed upon her. The gaze she was most aware of was Brynn's. The wood elf stared at her with wide-eyed uncertainty, perhaps some alarm.

The dining hall doors swung open to reveal Kraal, dressed in a fine velvet suit of forest green. Upon her arm was a large leather falconer's glove, and upon the glove perched a giant snow eagle.

Gasps and murmurs swirled around the room, and Valis smiled with satisfaction. Trained and domesticated snow eagles were rare enough, but this specimen was pure white, without a single brown feather to be found.

Kraal strode through the hall, approaching the platform upon which the royal table stood. She climbed the short steps and easily balanced the raptor as she dropped to her knees before Valis and Brynn.

The snow eagle tossed its hooded head, flapping its giant white wings before tucking them back into its body. The awesome creature was three and a half feet tall from head to toe, with a wingspan twice as

forearm was large and thick, but the eagle's sharp, black

cled the frost giant's wrist.

in her chair and gaped, her plate of food all but

s a present for me?"

aid. "A snow eagle, one of our most treasured native

species. This one is female. She is trained to hunt medium to large game, as well as carry messages over long distances. It occurred to me that you might wish to communicate with your family in Greenglass."

Brynn's wide brown eyes softened in an instant. Her lower lip trembled slightly, as though she were overcome with emotion. "I... *thank you.*"

Polite applause filled the hall, enthusiastic enough to let Valis know that she'd chosen well, and Brynn looked positively touched by the gesture. Valis made eye contact with the kneeling Kraal, communicating a silent *thank you.* The snow eagle had been her attendant's idea, for which Valis was grateful.

"Now"—Lord-Adviser Naddox raised his voice over scattered murmurs from the courtiers—"Lady-Consort Woodwarden will present her gift to the queen." He made a grand gesture in Brynn's direction, his long sleeves fluttering in the air.

Brynn suddenly looked like she'd swallowed her own tongue. Her bronze skin became a shade paler, and she worked her lips nervously. When Valis peered into Brynn's eyes, she saw pure panic.

What? Did no one inform her that she was meant to find a post-wedding gift? Someone will definitely be punished for this!

Future punishment couldn't prevent the current disaster. Her mind raced as she tried to think of a solution. Everyone in the hall was staring at them, waiting with palpable curiosity. For one terrifying moment, Valis found herself at a loss. What could she do? Something, anything...

"Er. All right, then."

Brynn pushed back her chair, the sound of its feet scraping the floor unnaturally loud in the anticipatory silence. She stood, swaying for a moment. She found her footing by briefly gripping the back of the chair.

"Her Royal Majesty is a queen." Brynn's voice grew steadier as she continued along. "She has all the gold and diamonds and such anyone could want. So, I...ah..." She paused, rummaging in the pocket of her breeches. "I decided on this."

She withdrew a small black stone, holding it up between two fingers. "A worry stone. These are sacred to my people, the wood elves. They're often passed down in families. This one has been in mine for generations. With it, I hope that Her Majesty's own worries will disappear, and all of Winterwail will prosper in turn."

Valis' mouth formed a small o as she processed everything Brynn was saying. When Brynn knelt before her, offering the smooth black stone in an outstretched palm, she clasped a hand to her chest—more from relief than emotion, but it was good enough.

Kraal, who had risen to her feet during Brynn's speech, clapped first by slapping her palm against her thigh. After a moment, the rest of the room followed suit, applauding Brynn's gift.

"How charming and sentimental, Your Majesty," Lord Verdigris whispered. "Just what I would expect from a wood elf."

Valis didn't bother replying. Verdigris and a few of the haughtiest nobles might sneer, but Brynn had cleverly saved them both from social disaster. Valis would gladly take a stone, whether smooth or sharp, or even poisonous, rather than the embarrassment of no gift at all.

"Beautiful." Valis offered a genuine smile. "Thank you very much, Brynnflor."

Some of the color returned to Brynn's cheeks. "Ah. You're welcome." She lowered her voice and whispered, "It really has been in my family for generations...although all those generations were spent with one eccentric grandmother." She winked, then returned to her seat.

Finally, Valis allowed herself to exhale in relief. Disaster averted. One more public obligation met. Besides, it *had* been rather nice to witness Brynn's reaction to the snow eagle. She reminded herself to think of some extra reward for Kraal in addition to her weekly pay. The frost giant had proven herself invaluable, yet again.

Chapter Nine

AFTER BREAKFAST CAME THE celebratory carriage ride through the city, an obligation Valis simultaneously anticipated and dreaded. It was an excellent excuse to escape the insincere simpering of her wedding guests for a few hours, but she would be stuck in an enclosed space with Brynn the entire time.

Not that Brynn was horrible. She'd presented herself well at breakfast, better than Valis had anticipated (in spite of her overeager eating habits). She'd also been surprisingly gentle the night before.

Valis forced those particular memories from her mind swiftly and decisively. She would have preferred to ride alone, in order to let down the public mask she wore and process her feelings. Unfortunately, she and Brynn needed to present a united front and convince her subjects they were happy, even though their marriage was nothing more than a political contract.

She floated down the palace steps toward the waiting carriage, wearing her best fake smile and waving to the nobles who had gathered to see her off. Brynn walked beside her, supporting Valis' forearm with her own. She neither floated nor turned to wave. Her eyes remained fixed on the carriage until the time came to lift Valis inside.

Valis felt a flash of warmth in her belly as Brynn's hands came to rest upon her waist, but her expression never faltered. Her lips remained frozen in their usual distant smile, in case any of the royal guards commissioned to march alongside the carriage were watching.

She maintained the charade until she was seated comfortably with her door shut. Only then did Valis close her eyes and rest her chin upon her chest. She lifted her head as the opposite door opened for Brynn, assisted by Kraal. "Please drive the horses at a slow pace. I plan to make the most of this ride."

Kraal smiled, showing more of her blunt tusks and causing her cheeks to dimple. "Of course." She closed the door behind Brynn, then circled the carriage to climb up on the driver's box.

"I thought Kraal was your attendant?" Brynn fidgeted in her seat. "Why is she driving us?"

"Kraal's role is flexible," Valis said. "She is my attendant, bodyguard, and one of the few people I trust in my kingdom."

Brynn blinked as though surprised, then frowned. "That doesn't bode well for your rule, does it? Should I be worried about coups or assassination attempts?"

"Unlikely, but always possible for one in my position," Valis said. "Rest assured, as long as you are in my presence or Kraal's, you are as safe as can be."

Brynn lifted a brow. "Your presence?"

Valis didn't answer. She waved goodbye to the nobles on the steps through the lightly frosted windowpane. It was designed to allow a partial view, but not the clearest one possible. Asking for this particular carriage had been a selfish act, which Lord-Adviser Naddox would surely berate her for later—in the politest, most deferential, yet demeaning language possible, of course.

The carriage lurched into movement, rumbling and bouncing only slightly as they headed for the palace gates. Two parallel lines of guards marched in formation on either side, shoulders stiff and heads held high.

"So. That snow eagle was a lovely and thoughtful present," Brynn offered. "Writing to my family will make me a lot less homesick. Thanks."

Valis dipped her head, a gracious nod she had perfected in childhood. "You are most welcome. I know this marriage is not ideal for either of us, but if there is anything I can do to make you more comfortable here, do not hesitate to ask. I wish for your new life in my kingdom to be as happy as possible, given the circumstances."

"Thanks," Brynn said. "I'm getting used to it, I think. Sort of."

Awkward silence stretched between them. Valis glanced out the window. They'd left the palace grounds and were about to turn onto the main thoroughfare, the center of Winterwail's marketplace. A large crowd had gathered on either side of the street. Mostly snow elves, but a few humans and elves of other varieties as well. The tall heads of frost giants stood over them all.

"By the Great Root." Brynn waved a little too eagerly out her own window. "I've never seen so many people in my entire life. Do they all live here in the city?"

"Most of them, yes," Valis said. "Perhaps some have come from the outlying villages to shop at market and catch a glimpse of the royal carriage, but the population of Winterwail is large. It is the biggest city in my kingdom."

"A lot to explore, I suppose," said Brynn.

"You may," Valis said, "provided you bring the appropriate attendants."

"Could I bring Delia?" Brynn asked. "I like her a lot, although her enthusiasm is…"

Valis laughed as she waved through her own window. "Delia has energy and excitement to spare. Not a bad thing, for a woman in her position. Yes, you may bring her, provided she agrees."

"What about my magic lessons?" Brynn asked. "When do we start those?"

Valis turned from the window, looking at Brynn with an expression of mild surprise. "You seem eager. Excellent. I wondered if you might put it off, considering your loud and frequently stated distrust of magic."

"If it helps me kill Rotted things, I want to learn as soon as possible." A shadow passed over Brynn's face. She rubbed her upper arm, scratching through her shirt as though massaging some old wound. "We could start right now, in fact."

"In the carriage?" Valis shook her head in mild disbelief. Spite-fueled or not, Brynn's determination would serve her well if she truly wished to harness her powers.

"Why not?" Brynn said.

Valis angled her knees, turning fully toward Brynn. Brynn's own knees jiggled as her toes bounced upon the carriage floor. Her dark eyes shone with something almost like hunger.

Heat bloomed on Valis' cheeks. She forced herself to hold Brynn's gaze, as though she were most definitely not thinking of how Brynn's eyes had looked staring up from between her legs the night before. "None, I suppose. Sit straight forward. Plant your feet. Hold out your dominant hand."

Brynn did so. "Now what?"

"Close your eyes."

Brynn obeyed.

"As you inhale through your nose, concentrate on the center of your chest, where your breath lives. Do you feel any sort of energy there? A warm light, or perhaps pressure?"

"Pressure," Brynn said, without opening her eyes. "A lot of pressure, actually."

"Inhale again. As you exhale the same breath, guide that pressure out of your chest and up along your arm, gathering it in your palm."

Brynn inhaled, held her breath a moment, then exhaled. Her lips pursed as she blew out and the fingers of her hand twitched. Valis waited, watching the center of Brynn's palm. At first, there was nothing, no sign of magic emanating from within.

Light. Blinding. Bright. So bright that Valis threw up a hand to shield her eyes. Heat washed over her, like steam from within a lively furnace. She pulled back against the window, still covering her face. "Black Wolf's teeth!"

"Fuck! Fucking fuck!" Brynn shouted from the opposite end of the carriage. "Put it out!"

Valis waved her hand, summoning her own will and pressing in upon the blinding light from all sides. It fought her at every step, so strong she could scarcely believe it. *Such power!* It reminded Valis of her mother and Shalana's most grueling magic lessons, and all from a wood elf born in the middle of nowhere.

Nevertheless, she persisted. She shrank the light, squeezing it into a small globe. The orb that had nearly filled the carriage shrank to the size of a fist. Finally, a marble, before it disappeared with one last twinkle. Valis sighed with relief, summoning the firmest voice she could muster through a slightly raspy throat.

"No more magic lessons in the carriage. I must admit, I fail to see what you meant by comparing yourself to a rain-damp torch. That doesn't seem an apt description of your abilities at all."

* * * * *

Brynn stared at her own hand in slack-jawed shock. *Was that really me? Did I do that? How?!* Cautiously, she lowered her hand into her lap. "Maybe I should have mentioned I have a tendency to explode things and set them on fire."

"That information might have been helpful."

Brynn looked at Valis. Her polite, unreadable expression had been replaced by perhaps the most honest emotions Brynn had seen on her lovely face: surprise, relief, delight...hope?

"Sorry." Brynn felt the heat of Valis' inquisitive stare. "I—well, I guess I got you back for startling me in bed last night, right?" She forced a weak chuckle that faded into tense silence.

Valis laughed. Not the airy, crystalline laugh Brynn had heard during the reception while Valis charmed various nobles, but a deep, honest belly laugh. She threw her head back, letting it loll upon the carriage seat. Even when her laughter began to die out, she swiped the corners of her eyes with her hand as though brushing away tears.

"Oh Brynn, I think I might grow a bit fond of you after all," she said with a hint of a giggle. "I can help with your problem, but in an open space next time. I shudder to think what precious family heirlooms or architecture you might destroy."

A grin crept across Brynn's face. "Fair enough. By the way, how did you get rid of—whoa!" She pitched forward in her seat as the carriage slammed to a stop. The sound of shuffling boots and gruff voices floated in through the window, followed by frightened whinnies from the horses. Instinctively, Brynn reached over her shoulder for an arrow, only to realize she had neither quiver nor her trusty bow.

Valis, who had maintained her balance better, leaned forward to speak through the small gap between the carriage interior and the driver's box. "Kraal, what is going on?"

"Duck!" Kraal bellowed.

Brynn ducked. She threw her hands overhead as a large rock crashed through her window. Glass exploded, raining shards onto her back and shoulders. She shook the worst of it out of her hair and cautiously lifted her head, heart pounding. Through the broken window, she saw several frost giants barreling toward the carriage, but they weren't dressed in royal uniforms. Some wore patchwork leather armor, but most had none at all.

The frost giants threw themselves upon the guards. Stone and wood clubs crashed together, angry shouts rising into a fierce din. Brynn reached for the carriage door. Even without her bow, she still had her fists.

"Stay down!" Valis climbed past Brynn through the partially open door with surprising speed.

Brynn tried to follow Valis, but a whirlwind of fury grabbed her attention. Kraal held three giant foes at bay all on her own. She dodged one enemy's club, ramming her shoulder into another's stomach. The first tipped off balance, stumbling into a snowbank. The second gave a pained grunt. Brynn recoiled as Kraal's club crashed down upon his head. He slumped to the ground, his caved-in skull blooming dark crimson across the snow.

Kraal dispatched the third enemy with fierce efficiency. The handle of her club jabbed up into his face, shattering his nose with a sharp crack. She swept his legs out from beneath him, sending him sprawling atop the dead body already at her feet.

She'd failed to notice a fourth, smaller enemy creeping up behind her, club raised to strike. Disregarding Valis' orders, Brynn leaped from the carriage. She started toward Kraal, a warning in her throat.

"Enough!" Valis cried.

A glowing red wave rose from the snow, reaching high above the frost giants' heads before crashing down upon them. The royal guards stood unharmed, but the frost giants who had besieged their carriage floated in midair, frozen in contorted positions.

Remembering how to move, Brynn turned in the direction from which the wave had come. There stood Valis, both hands raised. One held Aefbain aloft. The dagger pulsed with eerie crimson light. Dark blood ran down Valis' wrist, staining the sleeve of her dress. Her gray eyes blazed and her hair streamed behind her in a windswept flurry of white.

"Guards," Valis said in a voice as sharp as Aefbain's blade, "confiscate their weapons and restrain them."

The guards stirred themselves and made quick work of the floating, frozen attackers. A few guards broke off to keep the frightened crowd away from the street. Kraal ignored them all, rushing toward Valis and placing both hands upon her shoulders.

Brynn ran to join them, arriving in time to hear Kraal's rumbling voice. "You shouldn't have done that. What if they'd hurt you?"

Valis snorted. "I think not."

"What just happened?" Brynn asked from behind Kraal.

Both of them stared at her. Valis opened her mouth as though to answer, but a fierce grunt came from a few yards away.

"Traitor! Stoneskin scum!"

One of the captive frost giants thrashed between the two guards holding his arms, attempting to lunge free. He glared daggers not at Valis, but at Kraal, who swiftly positioned herself between them.

Brynn peeked around Kraal's large frame and saw the frost giant spit at her feet, leaving a hole in the snow. The guards dragged him away, shoving him into a group with the other captives.

A hundred questions raced through Brynn's mind, but there was no time to ask any of them. "Get back to the carriage," Valis said. Brynn trudged through the blood-spattered snow, trying to avoid the soupiest puddles. They climbed back into the carriage while Kraal hopped upon the driver's box. She drove down the street at a full gallop.

"Guess we're going home." Brynn's body tingled with unspent energy. She was rather annoyed with herself for being so useless in the face of an attack. If only she'd brought her bow...

Valis cupped her cheek. She'd shifted Aefbain to her other hand, caressing Brynn's face with her bloodied palm. Sticky warmth ran down Brynn's cheek, and she felt a strange, tingling tug in the muscle there. When Valis withdrew, she held a sizable glass shard between her red fingers.

Brynn touched her cheek, but there was neither blood nor a wound where the shard had been lodged. Her face was perfectly clear, and it didn't hurt at all. "Thanks. Did the window get me?"

Valis nodded. She rested Aefbain's blade flat against her palm and the flow of blood stopped. The dagger leeched what remained, still glowing a dim and unsettling red, until there wasn't a trace left. Valis sheathed Aefbain and slumped forward, resting her elbow upon her knee and massaging her taut forehead between her fingers.

"Okay," Brynn said, her mind still spinning. "Now can I ask what just happened? Because literally, a few minutes ago, you told me I didn't have to worry about assassination attempts."

Slowly, Valis lifted her head. The fires of anger had not left her eyes. Their whirling gray depths reminded Brynn of a thunderstorm. "I distinctly remember saying you needn't fear an assassination attempt while in the company of Kraal or myself. If anything, I have proven that statement true."

"Yeah, but—"

Valis silenced her with a look. "Many frost giant clans dwell within my kingdom. The ones who attacked our carriage are likely Hoarfrost.

My sources tell me they have been up in arms recently."

Brynn made the connection. "So, Kraal is Stoneskin, huh? Like that one asshole said."

"Language, please," Valis chided. "Yes, Kraal's parents were from different clans: one Hoarfrost, the other Stoneskin. The Stoneskin clan allied itself with the Aefbain dynasty when we arrived in the north. Thus, many other clans resent them. Kraal is a child of two worlds, but she has always been loyal to me as an individual."

Brynn nodded. She had plenty more questions, but sensed this wasn't the time to ask them. She leaned back in her seat, scooting toward the middle to avoid the remaining bits of broken glass, and scraping more aside with her boot so she would have a safe place to rest her feet. Next time she went anywhere outside the palace—or even inside the grounds—she would be sure to bring a dagger, at the very least.

Chapter Ten

VALIS LOWERED HERSELF GINGERLY into the warm luxury of her private hot spring. She tensed as the aching burn hit her bare skin, then relaxed as it seeped into her taut muscles, loosening the knots of tension. She sank down until only her face remained above the water and stared up at the crystalline ceiling of the cavern.

The sensation was decadent, but it would take more than lounging in hot water to solve her problems.

There was the upcoming ritual to contend with. Her marriage to Brynn, of course. It was only a matter of time before her new bride offended someone important with her stubborn, forthright manner. Brynn's intention to return the Sikah holdings to the frost giants would certainly require careful attention, but Valis was determined to make it happen. Honestly, she wished she'd thought of it first, but in her all-consuming grief, simply bathing and dressing, appearing in public, and keeping up with the ritual had sapped every scrap of energy she possessed.

Then there was the more pressing problem of the frost giants who had attacked her carriage. A similar ambush had stolen her mother's and sister's lives, but Valis couldn't allow herself to think about that. It helped to pretend the attack had happened to someone else. Memories of angry shouts and pools of blood in the snow pressed in on the borders of her mind. The delicate equilibrium she'd achieved over the past year threatened to shatter.

Valis took a deep breath and ducked beneath the surface. It was blessedly silent beneath the water, with only the sound of her own slow heartbeat in her ears. The tension headache she'd fought for the past two days finally began to dissipate. She stayed safe under the water until her lungs protested, forcing her to breach the surface.

As she pushed her wet hair off her face and opened her eyes, she noted a large, looming figure standing on the other side of the hot spring. Kraal was naked except for a towel wrapped around her waist. She inclined her head but didn't bother with a greeting.

Valis forced a smile. She was happy to see Kraal, but smiling at anything was difficult these days. "Get in," she said, leaning back against the spring's smooth rim. "I could use the company."

Kraal discarded the towel and dipped her toe in the water. Valis felt a flicker of amusement as Kraal's nose wrinkled at the temperature. "Best get it over with," she said. "It's not getting any colder."

"Easy for you to say," Kraal grumbled. "You're already in." Even so, she followed the advice and climbed in all at once, going through the same tensing-then-sighing ritual as she relaxed against the edge of the spring. A happy grin spread across her face. She rolled her head, cracking the vertebrae in her neck loud enough to make Valis' eyes widen.

"So, is it coincidence you decided to go for a dip now, or are you checking up on me?"

Kraal closed her eyes, spreading her muscular arms along the spring's curved lip. "I'm your attendant. Hard to do my job if you're hiding away."

Valis knew better. Kraal was obviously worried about her. Her demeanor didn't show it, but after so many years together, Valis knew that worry was a constant state of being for Kraal.

"I'm fine, really," she protested.

Kraal cracked one eye open. Her easy smile sank into a mild frown. "You were almost killed the other day. No one in their right mind would call that fine."

"But I wasn't killed," Valis said. "In no small part thanks to you."

Kraal closed her eye again. Her large feet kicked lazily beneath the water, stirring it slightly in Valis' direction. "As a hypothetical, let's assume you aren't fine. How can I help?"

Valis sighed. "I appreciate it, but I don't think you can help with this. Unless..." A thought stirred at the back of her brain. Perhaps there was a matter Kraal could advise her on. "The frost giants we apprehended are the first political prisoners taken during my reign, aside from..." Her voice trailed off. "Well. You know. Under our laws, treason means automatic execution."

"But you don't want to do that," Kraal said.

"Part of me does," Valis murmured. She was grateful Kraal's eyes were closed, because admitting it made her feel even more exposed than her nakedness. "Part of me wants vengeance, but another part of me is so tired of this. What good would it do? Murta's execution has only heightened tensions between snow elves and frost giants."

"Hmmm." Kraal rubbed one of her bejeweled tusks between thumb and forefinger, then sat up straighter, looking across the hot spring at Valis. "Why not banish them?"

Valis blinked. "Banish them where? Into the wilderness to die? How is that better than execution?"

A sly smile curled across Kraal's full lips. "It's an ancient frost giant punishment for the young, rowdy, and misguided. You 'banish' the troublemakers to the wilderness but send a Huntmaster after them."

Huntmaster. If memory served, it was one of the most important roles in traditional frost giant society. Huntmasters led the groups who brought life-giving game back home to feed the rest of their community. "So is it a punishment or a learning experience?"

"It's an opportunity for those who have wronged their community to serve and grow," Kraal said. "Both themselves and their community. Send them into the northern wastelands to hunt with an experienced eye to keep them honest. I'll help you write the speech for their judgment. There are certain traditional phrases you can use to let the frost giant community know what you're doing."

"Is that something snow elves would understand?"

"Very few, I'd imagine." With half-lidded eyes and a satisfied smirk, Kraal looked quite pleased with her own cleverness. "As far as most of them are concerned, you're following through on the expected execution. I'm sure there's a small community up north that can use the extra food and labor."

Valis allowed herself a genuine smile. "Thank you, Kraal. You are so much wiser than me. I have no idea what I'd do without you."

"I'm only wise about some things," Kraal said. "Other things are completely beyond me."

"Still, you've lifted a heavy burden from my heart."

Kraal sat up, wading across the hot spring to stand before Valis. She crouched down and placed a heavy palm on Valis' narrow shoulder. "A burden shared is a burden halved, my friend. We come from different worlds, but you've always done right by me, and it was an honor to stand with you at your wedding. I hope it didn't cause too much of a scandal."

Valis placed her hand atop Kraal's and squeezed. "Consort Woodwarden was scandal enough on her own to dominate the inevitable post-wedding gossip."

"Good." Kraal squeezed Valis' shoulder, then withdrew. "I know you carry the weight of an empire on your shoulders, but you don't have to carry it alone. In fact, it's better if you don't."

Valis began to reply, but the sound of a startled gasp drew her attention to the crystal arch at the cavern's entrance. Brynn and Delia stood in the archway. Delia smiled and waved in her usual friendly manner, but Brynn looked positively stunned. Her mouth hung open, and her green eyes were wide with shock.

"Good morning, Your Majesty," Delia said. "My apologies for the interruption. I was just showing Consort Woodwarden the amenities available to her, as requested. Do you need me to fetch anything for your soak?"

"No, thank you, but you're free to join us, if you like." She addressed the comment to Delia, but her eyes lingered on Brynn. She looked quite handsome in her fur-trimmed shirt and jaunty matching cap. Her leggings hugged her lean hips and muscular thighs.

Brynn's mouth snapped shut as though she'd suddenly become aware of Valis' scrutiny. She cleared her throat, but her upright ears belied any calm. "Um..." was all she managed to say.

"I wish," Delia said. "Unfortunately, my to-do list is a mile long today."

Kraal turned toward Delia. "Need help with anything?"

Valis didn't miss the gentle smile that softened Kraal's face in profile. Her attendant had always been quite fond of the bubbly human.

Delia's long lashes fluttered. "I can always find a use for you, Kraal."

"Go on, Kraal," Valis said. "I give you my word, I'll remain here or I'll read in my chambers. I could use the break."

Kraal nodded. "Of course, Your Majesty." She climbed out of the hot spring, retrieved her towel, and followed Delia to the adjoining steam room.

Once they left the cavern, Valis considered Brynn. She'd removed her cap, holding it awkwardly in front of her. She looked far more uncertain than her usual brash, confident self. "Join me if you wish." Valis settled back against the edge of the spring. "Unless you prefer standing there and staring at me?"

* * * *

Brynn swallowed, clenching her jaw so she wouldn't continue gaping at Valis' naked form. Casual nudity was common among wood elves, and given Valis' lack of reaction, snow elves held similar views. That, or Valis wasn't fazed by nudity. Recalling their wedding night, Brynn suspected the former. Perhaps hot springs were an appropriate place to shed such inhibitions.

To avoid staring, she gazed up at the ceiling. The crystalline mosaic formed a dome above them, a gorgeous and detailed relief of the Aefain dynasty's snow-and-dagger crest. "This place is beautiful," she said without looking at Valis. "Sometimes it's good to be queen, huh?"

The silvery sound of Valis' laughter made Brynn's heart thump faster. "Indeed. It seems Delia and Kraal have abandoned us, but you are welcome to try my hot spring for yourself."

"Your hot spring?" Brynn lowered her gaze, which proved a grave mistake. Though Valis was partially concealed by white, frothy bubbles and tendrils of steam wafting off the surface, the view was still decent. Or not. She resisted the impulse to lick her lips as her eyes darted to Valis' dark, purple nipples. She tried not to remember how her mouth had felt wrapped around the stiff points.

Stop it! That was just a ritual, one you won't be repeating.

If Valis noticed Brynn's impolite gawking, she gave no outward indication. She merely shrugged. "As you so aptly stated, sometimes it's good to be queen. You, however, are welcome to make use of it whenever you like. Kraal and Delia have similar access, so you wouldn't be the only one."

Brynn gnawed her lip. She could continue standing in the archway, making awkward conversation, or she could strip and join Valis in the luxurious warmth of the hot spring. It looked like pure paradise from where she was standing, and she'd been in a constant state of cold ever since arriving in Winterwail.

The opportunity to soak in some real heat got the better of her. She stripped quickly and efficiently, although she took the time to fold her fancy new clothes and set them on a nearby stone bench.

As Brynn removed her underwear, she felt more than saw Valis' icy gaze studying her. Her face flushed, but she tried to remain calm. She forced what she hoped was a casual smile and met Valis' stare with her own. She wasn't about to let the obvious weirdness hanging between them ruin this treat.

"It's nice of you to share with Kraal and Delia," she said in an effort to fill the awkward silence. "And me, of course."

Valis' ears perked. She tilted her head as though surprised. "Yes. Well, Kraal and Delia have earned my trust. They are perhaps my only true friends in this kingdom."

"That's a bit sad." Brynn gathered her courage and strode over to the hot spring. She tested the water with her foot. It was too hot for comfort, which meant it would be perfect in about twenty seconds. She slid in, groaning in pleasure as she sat on the shelf of rock beneath the water. She grinned in spite of herself. "Spirits, this is amazing. I didn't know how bad I needed this. Lately, my knots have knots."

"I can relate," Valis said coolly. She shot Brynn another scrutinizing look, brows knitted and lips slightly pursed. "What did you mean, sad? I'm simply grateful to have friends in my position."

Brynn bit her inner cheek. As usual, she'd phrased things poorly. "No, I didn't--ugh. I'm so bad at small talk. I meant, it's sad that out of all the people who'd want to be a queen's friend, you can only trust two."

Valis' brow softened. The edges of a smile returned. "Ah. Unfortunately, you're right. It can be hard to tell the difference between genuine overtures and..."

Brynn gave Valis a toothy grin. "Ass kissing?"

Valis gently cleared her throat. "Precisely, although I would have substituted a polite euphemism." She pushed a wet lock of long, white hair behind her ear. "Somehow, I doubt I will have that problem with you. I must admit, I find it rather refreshing."

Brynn rested one elbow on the edge of the hot spring to stretch out her shoulder. As an archer, her right side was always a bit stiffer than her left. "You aren't what I expected, either. I find you refreshing as well, for royalty I mean. I thought you'd be way more stuck up, to be honest."

"Thank you," Valis said. "I will take that as a compliment. We married for political reasons, but that doesn't mean we can't be friendly with each other."

"I'm glad you feel that way." Brynn allowed herself to relax a little more. Initial awkwardness aside, this conversation was going surprisingly well. So what if she was fighting a constant battle not to stare at Valis' long, toned legs under the water? It wasn't like all that smooth periwinkle skin had been supremely soft and pliant under her hands.

Come on, Brynn. Stop being a pervert. That was then, this is now. Still, she couldn't deny that the memory made the gently churning waters of the hot spring feel even warmer. A trickle of sweat rolled down her spine, dissolving into the heavy steam.

"So," she said, afraid of lapsing into another silence, "how did you make friends with Kraal and Delia, anyway? They seem lovely and forthright, but they aren't the sort of friends I'd expect the queen of the snow elves to have."

"True enough," Valis said. "I grew up with Delia. Her mother held the same position before her. One of Queen Ruith's better choices. Sadly, playmates were scarce while I was growing up, busy as I was kept. Spending time with Delia was a welcome reprieve. I remember long afternoons playing hide-and-seek in the library when I was supposed to be reading...although I did a lot of that as well."

Brynn smirked. Somehow, that didn't surprise her. Valis looked and acted the part of a bookworm. It was also strangely nice to think of her having at least a little fun as a child in such a fancy, adult-centered space as the royal palace. "That sounds fun. I guess you couldn't play outside as often as I did."

Valis reclined against the stone lip with a knowing smile. "I'll just bet you lived outdoors growing up, didn't you?"

"Me and Darrow," Brynn said. As always, merely saying her brother's name hurt, but in the years since his death, she'd learned the least painful way to revisit the golden memories of their youth. "I loved having a twin. It was like having a built-in playmate who always wanted to do the same things I did."

"That does sound nice," Valis said. "Because of the age difference, Shalana behaved almost like a second mother to me. She was perhaps my most intensive blood-magic instructor." A shadow flickered across her face, one that Brynn recognized all too easily as grief welling up inside. "I remember her lessons fondly."

Brynn tried not to analyze the sympathetic ache in her heart too closely. She had experience with losing a sibling, after all. It wasn't so strange that it hurt to look at the sadness shining in Valis' eyes. "What about Kraal?" she asked in an effort to divert the conversation. "How did you befriend her?"

Valis tilted her head. A secretive, almost smug expression settled on her beautiful face. Her eyes narrowed and a smirk played at the corners of her full, plum-colored lips. Brynn tried desperately not to ponder the rich purple color, or where else on Valis' body it appeared.

"Ah. Kraal's parents worked in the palace kitchens. One day, some other frost giant children were teasing her in the palace courtyard while I was nearby in the gardens. When it escalated to throwing rocks, I stepped in. Not that I needed to. Kraal had already doled out quite a few black eyes, if I recall."

Brynn sat up straighter. "Is it because of her heritage?"

Valis pursed her lips. "The rest of the details are hers to tell. Suffice to say, we often met in secret and played in the gardens after that. After months of pleading, I finally convinced my mother to have her trained as a bodyguard and personal attendant. I think she gave in because I wanted it so badly, but it was also a convenient way to keep an eye on the two of us. Otherwise, all the time I was spending with a frost giant child might have raised eyebrows."

"And we couldn't have that," Brynn said with a light laugh.

"Precisely." Valis sighed deeply. "My mother was a kind woman bred for a role that, in some ways, limited her perspective. Being born into such privilege is difficult to explain to others...having the weight of a royal dynasty on your shoulders, as well as sense of pride and responsibility for the family name instilled from birth, yet also learning the extent of your ancestors' sins as an adult."

Brynn nodded. "I can see that."

Valis gazed up toward the crystalline image of her family's crest. "I appreciate the positive reforms my mother signed into law, but she didn't go far enough, or fast enough. I loved her more than words can say. She was not perfect, but I cannot help hating the person who slew her."

"She was your mom," Brynn said softly. "We're made to love our parents, so long as they do right by us as their children." When Valis' forlorn stare remained fixed on the domed ceiling, Brynn stood and crossed the hot spring to sit beside her. She left enough space between their thighs to be polite but rested her elbow beside Valis' on the smooth rock. "I'm sure she'd be proud of you."

At last, Valis lowered her gaze and turned toward Brynn. Yet again, Brynn found herself drawn into those stormy, gray eyes, unable to look away. Her breath caught in her chest and her face burned as she realized how close their faces were. "Thank you," Valis murmured. "You may be unnecessarily blunt at times, Brynn Woodwarden, but you are also kind."

Brynn managed an awkward, croaking sort of laugh. She reached back to rub her shoulder. "I suspect the first half of that statement is another polite euphemism for asshole."

Valis closed her eyes and shook her head, but her smile lingered. Her high cheekbones flushed a lovely shade of lavender. "Perhaps."

Brynn exhaled, scooting a few inches away. She was grateful for the hot water and steam, because she suspected she'd have been visibly sweaty regardless of their surroundings. "Anyway...you mentioned the palace gardens. Want to tell me more about those? Because I'm getting really fucking tired of snow, snow, and more snow."

Valis looked up. Her gray eyes sparkled with renewed enthusiasm, threatening to steal Brynn's breath all over again. "Of course. It would be my pleasure."

Chapter Eleven

THE FOUR BODILY ICHORS, in confluence with magical energy streams and their varying forces, possess predisposed affiliations with specific methods and types of spellwork. However, these affiliations are merely guidelines that can be altered with specific levels of ichor and differing sources of energy, also depending on the caster's surrounding environment and inner state of being...

Brynn rolled her eyes and shut the leather-bound *Ansow's Treatise On Basic Magical Theory For Beginners* with a bit too much force. "Pretentious nonsense," she grumbled, leaning back to sulk in her squishy armchair.

The royal library was undeniably impressive, but the rows of beautiful books upon the shelves and the smell of ink and paper wore thin as Brynn struggled to interpret the dense tome. She heaved a sigh, gazing out a nearby window.

Glittering white snow covered the courtyard below. Dark purple mountains rolled in the background beyond the city walls. It was nothing like the forests of home, but Brynn had to acknowledge the majesty of the northern landscape. She longed to be outdoors despite the cold, bow strapped upon her back, discovering what native creatures she could observe or perhaps hunt.

But there was no need to hunt anymore. The palace had more food than she could eat in a lifetime. There were few animals to be found in the city, other than vermin. She'd have to travel well outside Winterwail to find what she wanted. After the attack on the royal carriage, she doubted such an excursion would be allowed.

Focus, Brynn. Do it for Darrow. Magic might be the only way to kill the Rot.

Reluctantly, she opened the book. After reading the same wordy paragraph five separate times while failing to retain its meaning, she groaned and threw it aside. The book flew from her hand with more force than intended, toppling another stack of books onto the floor.

"Bear's balls!"

Brynn left the armchair to restack the fallen books. Most were as thick and dusty as the boring treatise she'd chucked, but a thin, colorful picture book caught her eye. The pages were thicker than usual, as though made for a child's small hands. Curious, she examined the cover. The title read *That Which Dwells Beneath* above a picture of a glittering cavern. Brynn opened the book.

Long, long ago, the People were driven from their homes by human invaders from the Golden Sea.

The accompanying picture showed a line of elven families trudging away from golden sand dunes, carrying packs upon their backs.

The People went north to settle anew, but there they found the frost giants.

Brynn scowled at the exaggerated depiction of frost giants with evil, red eyes and hulking bodies, brandishing crude weapons.

"Let us live together in peace," said the People. The frost giants refused. So the People had no choice.

A large illustration spanned two pages and displayed a raging battle between frost giants and snow elves.

When it seemed all hope was lost, Vladric the Clever came up with a plan.

"I would skip that particular book if I were you," said Valis, her voice floating across the quiet library.

Brynn dropped the book in surprise. She shot up, feeling as though she'd been caught snooping. Her face burned as she tried not to notice the particularly high slits on either side of Valis' clinging crimson dress. "Not the best book I've ever read." She brushed the dust from her breeches. "I'm no expert on northern history, but it seems to me the frost giants were here first."

Valis tilted her head. Her pale, gray eyes filled with an emotion Brynn could not quite name. "It was one of my favorites as a child. I did not learn the truth until I was an adult. It was deliberately concealed from me for a long time."

"What truth did you learn?" Brynn asked.

"That the People were driven out by invaders, only to become invaders ourselves."

"Not all of the People," Brynn said.

Valis placed a hand upon her hip. "Only because you wood elves managed to avoid most of the second war."

Brynn snorted. "I wouldn't call winning the second war avoidance."

"You won nothing. You held off the Golden Horde until it collapsed under its own weight."

"Which is more than the snow elves did."

Only then did Brynn realize she was arguing not only with Valis, her wife, but the queen of the snow elves. Insulting her empire, even.

Great job, Brynn. Fantastic way to start off your new marriage.

Brynn studied Valis' face for any signs of anger but saw none. The upward tilt of Valis' dark purple lips seemed almost amused.

Maybe she finds it refreshing to discuss history with someone who tells it like it is instead of kissing her ass?

"You see the tightrope I walk, then," Valis said. "I must come to grips with the fact that my people are invaders, while also acknowledging that our ancestral home is gone. Rightfully or not, we are established in the north now. Snow elves and frost giants have no choice but to forget old grudges and live together."

"Good luck convincing the frost giants of that," Brynn said.

"Many frost giants wish for greater representation in government, rather than vengeance. I find that more than reasonable."

"While others try to assassinate you on carriage rides."

"Sadly, I understand that viewpoint, too." Valis studied Brynn with such intensity that a shiver raced along her spine. "Since we're on the subject, were you serious about returning the Sikah holdings to the frost giants? Because that might be an excellent first step toward further reparations."

"Of course," Brynn said, ignoring the heat spreading across her face. Something about Valis' stare made her uneasy. "People shouldn't own land anyway."

"That perspective would definitely be a step too far for my advisers. However, if the return were to come from you instead of me...well, most nobles would be scandalized, but some might chalk it up to my progressive, perhaps even unruly, new bride instead of pinning all the blame on me."

"So you want me to be your scapegoat." Brynn struggled to hide her smile.

"From what I know of you, I suspect you would relish the opportunity."

Brynn allowed the grin to spread across her face. "Put the paperwork in front of me and I'll sign it, meaningless as it is."

"Good. In the meantime, how have your studies progressed?"

Brynn's ears drooped. She raised a hand to scratch one of them. "Uh..."

"Not well, I presume?"

"No. Not exactly."

Valis' brows furrowed. "At the risk of causing damage to my palace and possibly my own person, I shall hesitantly suggest that a more hands-on method of training would serve you better."

Brynn sighed with relief. Anything to get out of the stuffy library and do something physical. "Please. I've always learned better by doing."

With a tight-lipped smile, Valis turned to leave. She paused and looked back expectantly. Brynn followed, still grinning at the thought of leaving Ansow's treatise behind. *The only thing that dry volume is good for is straightening an uneven table.*

Valis led Brynn out of the library, down to the first level of the palace and into an interior garden ringed by stone walls. A decorative pond dominated the middle, surrounded by stone benches and swaying willow trees. Despite the cold, the garden was in full bloom. A rainbow of flowers, most of which Brynn doubted grew naturally in the north, opened their petals to the sun as though it were spring.

"By the Great Root," she murmured, gazing around in wonder. "I'm glad to know this place exists. No offense, but your palace doesn't have much natural beauty. This is like a tiny slice of the Vale of Sunbeams."

"Hmm. We call it the Valley of Eternal Summer. Pretty euphemisms for the chill of death, aren't they?" Though Valis' voice was smooth and detached, Brynn recognized a flash of something in her soft eyes. Grief. The brief glimpse was enough for recognition. Brynn was intimately acquainted.

Makes sense, I suppose, since Valis lost her mother and sister.

"Mm," Brynn mused. "Those 'pretty euphemisms' helped my mother make sense of a senseless tragedy, but I've always found them rather hollow."

Valis quirked a brow. "Do you?"

Brynn shrugged. "All well and good for Darrow, I suppose, if the Veil of Sunbeams even exists, but he's still gone. His voice, his laughter, even the awful smell of his herbal tea in the mornings. Just gone. As though they never existed at all."

Valis opened her mouth, then pursed her lips in that distant way of hers. She cleared her throat. "Well then. Magic. How far did you get in Ansow's treatise?"

"Something about the four ichors," Brynn said, relieved at the change of topic. Perhaps she'd shared too much with Valis, who was little more than an acquaintance for all the fancy papers that said they were married.

"Blood, saliva, tears, and seed." Valis sounded every bit the boring, clinical teacher, despite the embarrassing nature of the final ichor. "Saliva is the weakest, of course. It only works because of the minute traces of blood it possesses."

"Gross," Brynn said.

"Its weak nature makes it useful for specific spells, but those are few in number. Tears feed some of the most primal and powerful magics in existence. Their effectiveness varies greatly and depends on the sincerity of emotion behind them. As you may imagine, they are somewhat unpredictable. Therefore, we will focus on blood."

"Great." Brynn felt far less enthusiastic than she had been minutes before. She'd wanted to do something physical, but blood magic was very low on her list of options. Damn well near the bottom, in fact.

Valis adjusted the slit of her dress to draw Aefbain, offering a tantalizing glimpse of pale blue thigh. Brynn fixed her eyes upon the ground, refusing to look up again until Valis offered Aefbain in an outstretched hand. "Take it."

Brynn took the dagger gingerly, as though it might nip her fingers.

"The ichors are merely a bridge between magic and the physical realm," Valis said. "Magic exists in a plane beyond our own. Your blood is a thread capable of connecting these two planes. Druids use the natural energies in various forms of wildlife to create similar bridges. Obviously, I have no Druidic training, so blood magic it is."

"Great." Brynn tried to hide her distaste.

If Valis realized, she gave no sign. "We will start with an easy exercise. Cut the pad of your thumb. A tiny prick will do."

Fighting a grimace, Brynn tightened her hold on Aefbain's oddly warm hilt... trying not to remember where else that hilt had been. She pricked her right thumb, watching a droplet of blood well there. The cut was shallow, the pain no worse than if she'd stuck herself with a needle while fumbling to repair a hole in her breeches (before giving up and asking Darrow or her mother to finish it for her).

"Close your eyes," Valis instructed. "Pay attention to the heat of your blood where it springs from your body. To the rhythm of your pulse. Feel the area growing warmer."

Brynn tried her best but felt nothing aside from the smallest of aches. "All right?"

"Sink into that place of warmth and energy. Allow it to spread down your thumb and into your palm."

Brynn's attempts bore no fruit. She felt nothing but slight dampness as another drop of blood welled from the cut.

"Should something else be happening, or..."

"Hmm."

Eyes still closed, Brynn felt Valis take Aefbain. Moments later, slender fingers entwined with hers. Another thumb brushed against her own and she realized Valis had pricked herself as well.

"Oh."

Brynn opened her eyes. Valis, meanwhile, had closed hers, lashes fluttering against her flushed purple cheeks. Her lower lip quivered, a hitch of breath skating through her sharp, white teeth.

She's so pretty it's unfair. Brynn chewed the inside of her cheek. She'd only seen such an expression once before, but it was one she couldn't forget if she tried.

All of a sudden, fiery heat flashed between their joined hands. Brynn jerked hers away, but not before a shower of sparks sprayed directly from her thumb like a hammer had struck an anvil. She gripped her wrist with her other hand, trying to aim the sparks into the air. They sped up, spurting like a flaming geyser.

"Valis, what's happening?!"

Valis recoiled, but her surprise lasted only an instant. Her face hardened as she swept her own bleeding thumb across her palm and made a sharp gesture with her hand. A transparent, purple bubble appeared around Brynn's hand, containing the sparks. "Hold still," Valis said, her voice all tight control.

Brynn didn't dare relax until the sparks had died away, as though the bubble had starved them of air. Her heart thumped against her ribs.

Her breaths came short and shallow.

Her fear receded with the danger. She let her shoulders sag, exhaling as the bubble disappeared. "What happened there? I definitely didn't do that on purpose." Her voice trailed off as Valis studied her with cold, calculating eyes. "Did I—did I mess up? Do something wrong?"

The steely look in Valis' eyes cleared. "Not at all. In fact, I believe I am beginning to understand Aefbain's decision. You are no blood mage, Brynn. Nor are you a Druid. Tell me...your father. I met him at our wedding. An unusually tall and large man, for a human. Do you know his lineage?"

"Well, he isn't entirely human," Brynn said, still confused. "He's got some wood elf in him as well, way back. At least, I think so? I don't know my family tree on that side. We don't care much about bloodlines back home."

"Hmm." Valis prowled around Brynn, examining her from all angles. She felt like a rabbit caught in a fox's hypnotizing gaze. "What about your mother? Does she come from magical stock?"

"Definitely," Brynn said. "Grandmother—that is, my great-something grandmother's aunt—is the most powerful Druid in our village. Mom's not half bad herself. And Darrow was...well, he was extraordinary."

"Not as extraordinary as you, I'll wager," Valis said.

Brynn placed her hands on her hips, ignoring her bleeding thumb. "What's that supposed to mean?"

"This is only a theory, but I strongly suspect your father has some frost giant in him, which means you do also. Frost giants have a strong natural resistance to magic. Elves cannot produce offspring with frost giants, of course, but frost giants can reproduce with humans on rare occasions."

Understanding dawned. "And humans can reproduce with elves," Brynn said, breathless. "So you think I'm part frost giant, part human, and part wood elf?"

"Indeed," Valis said. "You have an exceptionally strong link to the magical plane, yet also substantial resistance to its energies. This dichotomy produces highly unusual effects—for example, uncontrolled explosions. It also explains why you act as a near-bottomless energy source whenever I come into contact with your blood."

"Bottomless source?"

"You act as a conduit: highly attuned to arcane energies, yet naturally resistant to them. The channeling of such power would eventually tire and weaken the most exceptional arcanists, but your natural resistance means you don't feel the magic flowing through you at all until it explodes. Or until a skilled blood mage harnesses it."

With some trepidation, Brynn realized Valis was grinning. Not merely a polite smile for propriety's sake, but grinning, showing almost every one of her sharp teeth. Her gray eyes shone with excitement.

"What does this mean for me?" Brynn removed her hand from her hip, cradling it protectively against her chest. She instinctively doubted she would like whatever Valis had in mind.

"It means you are absolutely perfect for the ritual."

Brynn swallowed around a cold lump in her throat. The stone sank down into her stomach. "No, what does it mean for *me*? Is it...?" She felt like a fumbling child, without the proper vocabulary to express her fears. "Is it safe?"

Valis offered a shy, almost contrite smile. "My apologies. Eagerness got the best of me. It means the ritual should be painless and not nearly so taxing for you as I had anticipated. If my theory is correct, this is extremely good news for both of us."

Brynn chewed her cheek. "Are you sure?"

"As I said, it is only a theory, but I know how we can find out. Tonight, at midnight, I shall come to your rooms and collect you for the ritual."

"Tonight?!" Brynn barely smothered her rising alarm. She'd hoped for more time to acclimate, but part of her agreed that it was better to see what she was in for. She'd never been the type to run away before. "Fine. Tonight."

"Excellent," Valis said. "I must introduce you to my Artificers as well. They may well find special uses for your blood—"

Brynn's smile fell away. "Absolutely not. I'll do the ritual, but I never agreed to be experimented on or...or...drained by a bunch of crazy magic scientists! I'm currently using my blood, you know."

Valis quirked a brow. "Would your opinion change if I told you said experiments might provide a solution to the problem of the Rotted infestation? You have previously expressed a strong desire to see them eradicated from your forest, and since you cannot harness arcane energies yourself, it may be the best way for you to help."

Brynn's brain slammed to a halt. Empty. She blinked in confusion, then sighed and squared her shoulders. "I'd do anything for a solution. Anything, Valis."

"Very well." Valis closed the distance between them, taking Brynn's injured hand and placing Aefbain's blade against her thumb. The cut sealed itself, leaving behind no trace of blood or injury.

"Thanks," Brynn said.

"You are welcome, though I should probably be the one thanking you. This experiment was most enlightening."

Brynn rubbed her neck, struggling to sort through a confusing swell of emotions. "You can say that again."

Chapter Twelve

VALIS APPROACHED BRYNN'S BEDROOM door at two minutes to midnight. Snow elf etiquette dictated she should arrive late, but she'd been on edge since their magic lesson that afternoon. *More of a disaster, really...though a disaster that may yield an advantage.*

She'd barely been able to focus that evening, her mind full of questions. *Is Brynn really part frost giant? How will her blood react to different kinds of spells? Will it be suitable for the ritual?* Valis sincerely hoped so. Otherwise, their entire marriage was for nothing.

No need to worry, Your Majesty, Aefbain purred inside Valis' head. *Your wife's body may resist the magic that flows within, but her blood is positively ripe for spell work.*

I will keep your opinion in mind. Valis was somewhat reassured. Aefbain was bothersome, nosey, and smug, but it had never lied to her. She rapped on the door.

Brynn peeked out, blinking sleepily, but awake and fully dressed. "Er, good night." She opened the door wider, rubbing the back of her neck. "Sorry, that sounds strange as a greeting. It's just, I usually see you in the mornings—"

Valis said nothing. Brynn looked surprisingly adorable in her groggy state, her amber eyes narrowed and the bridge of her nose slightly wrinkled. Valis concealed her embarrassing thoughts with her blankest expression.

Brynn cleared her throat. "Did you want to come in?"

"We should proceed to the ritual site." Valis flicked her eyes up and down, giving Brynn a brief once-over. She had to admit, Brynn's hips filled out her wolfskin leggings in a rather pleasing way. Her flowing white shirt cut off at quarter-sleeve, showing off muscular forearms. A result of considerable archery practice, no doubt. "Bring a cloak. It's quite cold beneath the palace."

Brynn ducked back into the bedroom, reemerging with a fur-lined cape. She threw it over her shoulders and fastened the clasp at her neck. "Lead the way." She smiled, the haze of sleep mostly gone from her eyes.

She seems almost eager, Aefbain commented as Valis turned and started down the hall. *For your company, perhaps? I doubt your new bride is excited about an ancient and dangerous blood-magic ritual.*

Enough. Valis pulled her own cloak over Aefbain's scabbard, hoping the dagger would take the hint. Brynn was likely anything but eager to fulfill this part of their marriage contract, with her loudly professed distrust of blood magic. Valis slowed her steps, falling back so Brynn could walk by her side instead of trailing behind.

"The ritual should not cause you any pain or discomfort," Valis said, stealing a glance at Brynn's face. Her smile remained in place, though it seemed a bit forced. "You are merely lending me extra power. Should there be any complications, which I highly doubt, they will be mine to deal with."

Brynn gave a raspy chuckle. "Was I that obvious?"

"Your nervousness, you mean?" Valis turned toward Brynn, arching a brow. "We have only known each other a few weeks, but you hardly strike me as the type of person who swallows their opinions."

"I suppose no one could accuse me of being subtle," Brynn said. "Well, Your Majesty, I'm also a woman of my word. I agreed to this before we got married. As long as you keep your end of the bargain, you can use my blood for whatever weird spells you want. Just try not to kill me, please. My magic is… well, you remember what happened earlier."

"I assure you, these are entirely different circumstances." Valis was actually starting to appreciate Brynn's straightforwardness. It was a refreshing change from the nobles she normally dealt with, particularly a certain Lord-Adviser. "Come with me, but please, Valis. Not Your Majesty."

"Okay…Valis."

* * * * *

"This isn't creepy," Brynn muttered as she descended the steep staircase of ice, following Valis down into darkness. Valis held Aefbain aloft, lighting the way with a red glow that reminded Brynn of dying embers… or perhaps blood. "Nope. Not creepy at all."

The fur-lined hem of Valis' gown trailed through the snow. She showed no fear of the treacherous drop to their left, completely ignoring the frozen railing on the wall, as she glided down the steps.

Brynn gulped, fighting the impulse to peek over the edge. *Of course we have to do this weird blood magic in a dark pit underneath the castle. Why am I even surprised?* Nevertheless, she followed Valis' lead.

Valis had assured her the ritual wouldn't be painful. *Not for me, anyway.*

Silence pressed in on Brynn from all sides. She stifled the impulse to whistle a tune in hopes of staving off the chill that crept along her spine—a chill that wasn't a result of the cold temperature.

They climbed down, down, down until Brynn caught a glimpse of pale, gray light somewhere far below. Valis sped up, so Brynn did the same. Cold, stale air burned in her lungs. She sighed, as she realized that climbing back up would be even more arduous.

The dark shaft opened into a giant glittering cavern, and Brynn forgot her discomfort. The floor glowed with pale light, and rainbow refractions bounced from the long, blue stalactites above. The rainbows danced around the room, casting colorful patterns onto Brynn's hands and Valis' snow-white hair.

Brynn craned her neck to drink in the sight. "Incredible." A grin spread across her face. "Why is this place hidden beneath the palace? Long staircase aside, this would have been an amazing throne room."

Valis lowered Aefbain. The rainbows from the ceiling hit the dagger's onyx surface, swirling like oil in sunlight. "This is Winterwail's best-kept secret." She looked up from the dagger, staring directly into Brynn's eyes as her own narrowed in warning. "If you reveal its existence to anyone, the consequences could be disastrous. I would be forced to begin divorce proceedings and arrest you for treason."

Brynn stepped back, holding up her hands. "Okay, okay. My lips are sealed." She waited a beat before curiosity got the best of her. "Will you at least tell me why it's secret?"

"I am not entirely sure of the details myself." Valis turned toward a short podium in the center of the room, perhaps three feet tall. An orb of shockingly clear ice sat atop the pillar. Dark crimson tendrils floated within its center, swirling like traces of blood in water. Brynn watched, hypnotized.

Valis gestured at the orb. "This is a focus object. Have you reached that point in Ansow's treatise yet?" A smirk twitched at the edges of Valis' purple lips, before her face became a blank, emotionless slate once more. "Never mind. I suspect not."

"That's a safe assumption." Brynn was still staring at the orb. She should have been offended, but she couldn't seem to tear her eyes away from the whorls of blood.

"As I was saying, focus objects allow blood mages and Artificers to channel various magical energies into sharper focus, thus amplifying their power. Aefbain is a focus object as well."

"Ah," Brynn said. "Like starting a fire with curved glass."

Valis blinked. "Wood elves start fires with glass? Why not use magic, or at least flint?"

Brynn arched a brow. "You've seen my magic. Any fires I start either fizzle or explode. Glass is my backup plan. I always carry flint on me when I'm hunting."

"I see." Valis cleared her throat. "As far as I am aware, there is an ancient source of power sealed away beneath the ice. My ancestors called it That Which Dwells Beneath. I have never found any references to what it might be in the palace library, despite our extensive collection. A cursed object, a creature, a split in the dimensional fabrics that separate our universe from others... it could be any of these, or something else entirely."

Brynn folded her arms, blowing a strand of hair away from her forehead. "Seriously? In all the centuries your family's lived here, no one's bothered to find out? You aren't the least bit curious?"

Valis' eyes sharpened, becoming almost as frosty as her demeanor. Brynn shuddered. For someone of such slender build, Valis positively radiated authority.

"That Which Dwells Beneath is immensely powerful, and therefore immensely dangerous. Imagine if Winterwail's enemies seized control of it? A violent extremist from the Hoarfrost clan or even some of my own nobility? What do you think would happen?"

Brynn licked her dry lips. "I get the point." Still, she tucked the information away in the back of her mind. *If it's that powerful, maybe it's strong enough to fight the Rot? If I can figure out what it is...*

"Good. We shall begin."

Valis sheathed Aefbain. She peeled off her long, white gloves one at a time, a graceful action Brynn spent a few seconds too long observing. Valis tucked the gloves in her cloak's inside pocket, then drew Aefbain again, offering a teasing glimpse of thigh as she adjusted the slit on the side of her dress.

"Brynn?"

Brynn's eyes snapped up. She hesitated, then took the hand Valis extended. Her fingers were surprisingly soft and warm. Brynn gripped tighter, telling herself it was to warm up her own hand.

Valis led Brynn toward the pillar. "This shouldn't hurt." She turned Brynn's hand in hers, then raised Aefbain, slicing the middle of Brynn's palm before she could even flinch. As promised, there was no pain— only a warm, wet sensation. Blood welled from the cut, following the creases of Brynn's hand like tiny red rivers.

Next, Valis sliced her own palms: first the left, then the right. She grasped Brynn's hand again, lacing their fingers tight. Brynn held her breath, as hot blood ran between their palms. She fought the instinct to pull away.

Valis placed her other bleeding hand atop the orb, still holding Aefbain. The crimson ribbons floating within stirred like tiny serpents, rising to meet her touch. The white glow beneath the floor pulsed as though in answer. Valis closed her eyes and began to sing. Her voice was high and clear, with a haunting echo that spread to all corners of the cavern.

"I am Aefbain, daughter of Aefbain.
Look upon my mother's blade.
That which dwells beneath the ice,
Tis I shall see your blood price paid.
Magic blood into the deep.
Magic blood to soothe your sleep.
I am Aefbain, daughter of Aefbain.
Through my blood, the compact keep."

Aefbain flashed red, and the orb exploded with white-hot light. Brynn shut her eyes against the burning brightness. It bored through her closed lids, piercing into her brain through her eye sockets. A low hum filled the room, starting softly, then swelling like a roaring swarm of midsummer cicadas.

Brynn flinched, only able to cover one ear. Valis' hold had become an iron death grip.

Everything stopped all at once. The light disappeared. The hum died. Silence filled the cavern.

Black spots floated behind Brynn's half-opened eyes. She saw Valis remove her hand from the orb and sway precariously.

Brynn leaped forward and caught Valis against her chest. Her slender body hardly weighed anything at all. "Valis?" Brynn peered down at the crumpled form in her arms. "Are you all right?"

A soft giggle came from beneath Brynn's chin.

"Brynn?" Valis' long lashes fluttered above glassy, gray eyes, and that giggle spread to a wide grin that showed most of her sharp teeth. "You're handsome, Brynn."

Brynn barked a short laugh. "What?"

"You." Valis gripped Brynn's forearms but didn't use them to find her footing. Instead, she squeezed as though to test the muscles there. "You have nice arms. Lovely jawline. Why is everything glowing? Turn off the light, please."

Brynn shook her head in disbelief. She'd expected a strange and bewildering night, but certainly not this. "At least you're polite when you've gone temporarily insane. Come on, let's sit down." She lowered Valis onto the floor, then sat beside her, unsure what to do. "Did my blood do this? Was it the ritual? How can I help? Valis, are you listening to me?"

Valis rolled onto her back, limbs sprawled in every direction. She stared up at the ceiling with wide eyes. "Pretty colors..."

Brynn pinched the bridge of her nose. "Okay. You're magic drunk. Is that a thing?"

Valis flopped her head to one side, sticking out her lower lip in a pout. "I'm not. I'm perflect...plerfecty...fine..." She attempted to sit up but wobbled and flopped back down onto the ice. "Maybe a little. Your blood is... there's *so much* magic, Brynn. Like I cut open an artery of the universe." She laughed. "I'm fine. I'm not tired at all! The ritual was easy this time. I might have... might have..." A soft look crept over her sharp features. Her lashes fluttered as though she were fighting sleep.

Brynn smirked. "Not tired, huh? Will you be okay here for a few minutes? I doubt I can carry you all the way up those steps by myself."

Valis' eyes snapped open. "No, no! I can fly up the stairs myself. Black Wolf take me, why haven't I done that before? It's brilliant." She scrambled onto hands and knees, leaving blood-streaked palm prints in the snow. "Watch, Brynn!" Faint red mist surrounded her as she floated into the air, waving her arms as though treading water. "See? Fly!"

Brynn stared in shock, then burst out laughing. She couldn't help it. The sight of the poised and stoic Queen of Winterwail flailing through the air was simply too much. However, when Valis began rising toward the stalactite-strewn ceiling, the situation didn't seem quite so funny. Brynn grabbed the hem of her dress and pulled her back down. "No, you don't."

"It's fine." Valis tried to pry Brynn's hand off, but only succeeded in batting at it. "I'm fine." Gravity abruptly reasserted itself. Valis fell. Brynn lunged. Her knees wobbled as Valis plopped into her arms, still giggling.

"Good thing you're a stick," Brynn sighed, lowering Valis back onto the ground. A glint of light caught her eye, and she noticed Aefbain lying close by. She picked it up, handing it to Valis. "I have a feeling I'm going to regret returning your dagger while you're... like this... but can you at least make our hands stop bleeding?" The cut on her palm stung, and Valis had stained her shirt with bloody handprints.

"Oh, sorry!" Valis said, her voice a level too loud. She grabbed Brynn's hand, resting the flat of the dagger over the cut. The bleeding slowed, then stopped. Fresh pink skin closed over the wound. Valis did the same to her own hands, humming as she did.

"Thanks." That was one problem resolved, but Brynn had no idea how to get Valis up the stairs. *Kind of funny though, seeing the stuck-up queen act like she's downed an entire bottle of wine. Guess this proves it. The snob thing is more of an act than I thought. She's been honest with me from the start and got me that lovely snow hawk...*

Wait.

Have I been the asshole for judging her? Ah, great seasons. It's me. I'm the asshole.

Brynn glanced at Valis, who had resumed watching the dancing rainbows on the ceiling. She spoke in a soft, sympathetic voice. "Why don't you lie down for a bit? Once you feel better, I'll help you up the stairs. Okay?"

"I don't need to lie down..." Valis' drooping eyelids betrayed her. She covered a yawn with the back of her hand. "I feel fine. Wonderful, actually. I just need..." She rolled her head to one side and began snoring.

Brynn unfastened her fur cloak, folding it over and sliding it beneath Valis' cheek. Valis gave a muffled groan but didn't wake. The ritual must have sapped all her energy—or her current state was a reaction to Brynn's blood.

Brynn studied her own palm where the faint scar had already disappeared. There wasn't much else to do until Valis woke up. She certainly wasn't about to inspect the orb or the white glow beneath the ice after what she'd witnessed. Later, she'd see what she could discover through safer means.

She glanced once more at Valis. Her face remained soft in sleep, mouth hanging open slightly. Brynn couldn't resist a smile. This certainly wasn't how she'd expected the ritual to end, but as long as Valis ended up all right, she couldn't say she was too upset.

Chapter Thirteen

SHORTLY AFTER DAWN, BRYNN woke to loud, persistent thumping on her bedroom door. She gave an ear-popping yawn and glanced out the nearest window. The sky was pale gray with little sunlight, one of the dull, snowy dawns she'd grown accustomed to in Winterwail.

The thumping grew more urgent. "Consort Woodwarden? I must speak with you."

Brynn recognized Kraal's gruff voice. She threw off the fur blankets and dragged herself out of bed, grateful she'd fallen asleep in her nightgown. Slowly, she shuffled into her slippers and trudged toward the door on leaden legs.

She opened the door to see Kraal waiting in the hallway. The frost giant was dressed in tailored blue slacks and a neatly buttoned white and gold vest. Her posture was rigid and her face politely blank. She carried no weapon, but after watching her fight to defend Valis' carriage, Brynn knew she didn't need one.

"Morning, Kraal," Brynn said. "Is Val—er, is Her Majesty all right?" The night before, she'd assisted Valis up the ridiculously long spiral staircase and deposited her safely in her suite. Valis had collapsed onto the bed fully clothed and fallen asleep straight away.

Kraal frowned, which made her stony face look even more severe. "Queen Aefbain is ill today, but she asked that I deliver this." She held out a piece of parchment, folded in thirds and sealed with red wax.

Brynn recognized the same snowflake-and-dagger seal she'd seen on her initial invitation to Winterwail. It seemed like an eternity had passed since then, even though it had only happened six weeks ago.

She took the letter from Kraal and broke the seal. Valis' handwriting was unexpectedly easy to read despite its exaggerated flourish. Definitely a royal's handwriting, in Brynn's opinion.

* * * * *

Consort Woodwarden,

I must apologize for my highly inappropriate behavior last night. Partaking of your blood in such large quantities caused me to enter a state of temporary hysteria. I promise it will not happen again and earnestly ask your forgiveness.

Although I have imposed upon you a great deal already, I must ask one more favor. I am currently indisposed, due to exhaustion. However, I am scheduled to take tea with my advisers between breakfast and lunch. Please attend this meeting in my stead.

I recall my promise that I would not force you to participate in political functions unless absolutely necessary, but it would be an excellent opportunity to discuss your decision to return your landholdings to the frost giants. Sending you in my stead will both placate my advisers and allow you to proceed with your plan.

For your kindness and understanding, you have my greatest thanks. Queen Valis Aefbain of Winterwail

* * * * *

Brynn refolded the parchment while she considered Valis' request. The last thing she wanted to do was waste her morning with the smarmy Lord-Adviser Naddox. Lady-Advisers Fayeth and Galesha weren't stellar company either. Despite their initial warmth toward her, they were still politicians.

Ugh. Why me? But I want to return those landholdings. Might as well get the ball rolling and do Valis a favor at the same time.

Kraal cleared her throat softly.

Brynn smiled at her. "Thank you, Kraal. Will you please tell Queen Aefbain I'll have tea with her advisers in her place?"

Kraal's responsive smile made her sharp features look warmer. Brynn noticed, with private amusement, that the intimidating frost giant had dimples. "Of course, Lady Woodwarden. Tea will be served at half past ten."

Another door opened, causing Brynn and Kraal to turn. Isuna stood in the doorway across the hall, fully dressed and well-groomed, but with slightly drooping eyelids that gave away her exhaustion. "Sorry," she said when she noticed Brynn and Kraal staring at her. "I heard voices..."

"Everything's fine, Mom." Brynn scooted over to wrap an arm around her mother's waist and rest a cheek on her shoulder. Isuna folded her arm about Brynn's shoulders in return and kissed the top of her head. "Kraal just came by to tell me about an appointment. I'm having tea with the queen's advisers this morning."

Isuna's green eyes brightened. "Oh? You'll need something formal to wear then, won't you?" She pulled away from Brynn and clasped her hands. "Wonderful! This will give us a chance to look through some of the lovely outfits Shalure designed."

Brynn's ears drooped. Unfortunately, her mother had a point. She probably needed to wear something nicer than usual.

Kraal smirked, obviously having noticed Brynn's despondence. "Shalure is an artist without compare. To wear their designs is an honor."

"Yes, of course." Brynn willed her ears to perk up. She summoned her courage and asked, "Do you want to help me pick something out, Mom?"

"Of course!" Isuna grabbed Brynn's hand, dragging her into her chambers.

"Thanks, Kraal," Brynn called over her shoulder, nudging the door shut with her foot before Isuna pulled her too far.

She braced herself for an unpleasant morning of trying on outfits for her mother's benefit. Isuna had a good eye for fashion, but Brynn had never enjoyed being a dress-up doll. She would grin and bear it; a sharp appearance might prove beneficial for this particular meeting.

* * * * *

Brynn clenched her teeth to maintain her tight smile. She'd only spent fifteen minutes with Lord-Adviser Naddox and Lady-Advisers Fayeth and Galesha, but her nerves were already frayed. No doubt this 'friendly' tea would continue to be an exercise in restraint.

"You see"—Fayeth set her teacup on the white, lace table cover— "signing away your landholdings has the potential to considerably lower your standing at court." She aimed a thin, painfully polite smile at Brynn from across the table.

"Quite right," Galesha said. "I mean no offense, Lady Woodwarden, but your background is not what one would normally expect from a royal consort." She sipped her tea slowly and gracefully, in tiny mouthfuls with a minimum of noise.

"I see." Brynn found an outlet for her rising frustration by imagining herself climbing onto the table and emptying the steaming kettle straight into Galesha's lap.

"Not to mention the whispers that will spread at your refusing Queen Aefbain's generous wedding gift," Fayeth said. "Some might even interpret such a disrespectful act as an ill omen."

Another thread of Brynn's dwindling restraint snapped. Fortunately, Lord-Adviser Naddox spoke before her temper got the best of her. "Now, now, ladies. Appearances are important, but the decision is Lady Woodwarden's. The holdings are hers, after all."

Naddox's smile made Brynn's skin feel slimy and her scarf suddenly restrictive. She resisted the temptation to loosen it. "Thank you, Lord-Adviser. The truth is, I don't know anything about managing landholdings. And the frost giants lived there first, before the snow elves. It's their home."

"Why, that was over a thousand years ago." Fayeth gestured airily, causing the sheer gauze flowing beneath the sleeve of her dress to flutter as though in a nonexistent breeze. "The frost giants of that time were understandably upset, but this is the present. We are all equal citizens of Winterwail now."

Upset? I wonder if she knows what understatement means. Brynn resisted the temptation to roll her eyes. She lifted her hand to brush away an uncomfortable stripe of sweat beading along her hairline but stopped herself in time. *Ugh, why am I so hot? The room is literally ice cold.*

Galesha either failed to notice Brynn's rising frustration or pretended otherwise. "Besides, no one says the current residents have to move, simply because you own the land." She began to fill her teacup from the kettle, only to find it empty.

Naddox raised his hand, summoning one of two attendants who waited by the wall. The first was a tall snow elf and the second a bald, fair-skinned human. "Fetch another kettle," Naddox said.

The snow elf took the empty kettle with a bow and hurried off. The human took the empty platter of frostberry pastries, presumably to bring more.

Brynn experienced conflicting emotions. She'd eaten half the pastries herself, both because they were delicious and because she considered it a small act of rebellion. Her overindulgence had certainly annoyed Valis' advisers, but they were too polite to mention it. However, Brynn's stomach was uncomfortably full. It churned, forcing her to swallow down a wave of nausea.

"Now," Naddox said, "where were we?"

"The landholdings," Fayeth said.

"Ah yes. As I was saying, we may offer our counsel, but it is ultimately Lady Woodwarden's decision."

The hairs on Brynn's neck prickled. Naddox was working an angle of some sort, but she had no idea what it might be. She decided the best course of action was to continue behaving in a firm, straightforward manner. She wasn't about to join the advisers in their stupid game of politics.

"Thank you, Lord-Adviser." Brynn shifted in her seat, hoping a new position might calm the aching cramps in her belly. They seemed to be getting worse. "Do you know the frost giant clan leaders in that area? Someone I could talk to?"

Fayeth and Galesha exchanged glances.

"Of course," Galesha said in an overly bubbly voice.

"We would be happy to provide you with a list of names..." Fayeth's voice suddenly trailed off. Her smile fell away. She sat back in her seat, groaning as she rested a hand on her stomach. "Oh my, I do apologize. I'm afraid something isn't agreeing with me."

The comment made Brynn's stomach churn again. It gurgled painfully, and her face burned with intense heat. An icy chill raced down her spine, sending an involuntary shudder through her body. "I don't feel well myself. What was in those pastries...?"

A furrow creased Naddox's brow. "Only a pastry crust with frostberry preserves in the middle, as far as I'm aware. I had a filling breakfast, so I didn't partake myself."

"Neither did I," Galesha said. Her eyes darted nervously between Fayeth and Brynn. "I found the tea more than sufficient. Are you quite all right, Lady Woodwarden? Fayeth?"

Brynn opened her mouth to answer, then clamped it shut again, gritting her teeth to keep from crying out. The churning in her stomach became a sudden, stabbing pain. She tensed and shivered as cold sweat soaked through her clothes.

"I—I believe I should lie down." Fayeth released a low moan. "I sincerely apologize—" Eyes narrowed and lips pursed, pain flickered across her face.

Brynn winced with empathy. Her vision blurred as tears welled in her eyes. *Oh. Oh shit... was I...?*

Merely thinking around the word poison made Brynn's entire body seize. Black spots floated in front of her face. She gripped the table in a desperate attempt to steady herself.

It wasn't enough.

Her muscles went slack, her limbs dissolving into putty. She kept her grip on the lace tablecloth, but slumped sideways out of her chair, collapsing into a heap on the floor and pulling several dishes down with her. The loud crash sounded distant to her ears, which throbbed with her own heavy heartbeat.

Fuck, was Brynn's final thought before darkness crept in. The last things she saw were the worried faces of Naddox and Galesha hovering above her.

* * * * *

Valis threw open the door to Brynn's suite without bothering to knock. She rushed into the bedroom in a flurry of skirts, startling Bloodtender Horys. The old healer looked up in surprise from his post by the bed, his bushy eyebrows rising toward his receding hairline.

Horys bowed, offering his palms. "Your Majesty? I didn't expect you so soon—"

Valis hurried to the bed, peering past Horys at the figure lying there. It was Brynn, but not as Valis remembered. Her golden-brown skin had gone sallow. A layer of sweat gave her forehead a sickly sheen. Her eyes were closed, but her dry, cracked lips remained parted as she sipped shallow breaths.

Valis questioned Horys without taking her eyes off Brynn, paralyzed by the irrational fear that if she stopped watching for even a moment, Brynn might somehow slip away. "How is she? Will she recover?"

"A full recovery seems likely, though I fear Lady Woodwarden was touch and go for a while," Horys said. "We—forgive my crudeness, Your Majesty—encouraged her to regurgitate before performing the usual rituals to purify her bloodstream. Based on her symptoms, we suspect blackspine poisoning."

Valis covered her mouth to stifle a gasp. Blackspine was a native tundra shrub that grew mainly in the northern area of the kingdom. When consumed in large quantities, it often proved fatal. She bit her lip behind her hand. Her vision narrowed to a dark tunnel with Brynn's face at the center. She could draw only one conclusion.

Someone tried to kill Brynn! Or me, if they didn't realize I'd sent

Brynn in my place. Either way, it's my fault.

Valis dropped her hand, reaching down to smooth Brynn's curly hair away from her forehead. Her fingers trembled, but Brynn remained still as stone. Why had this happened? Brynn was kind. She was funny. She was brave and self-sacrificing, having married Valis in hopes of saving her home. What she lacked in polish, she more than made up for in compassion.

And she almost died because of me.

Tears stung Valis' eyes. It took all the restraint she possessed to hold them back. She pretended she was an ice sculpture before she finally looked at Horys. "You are to make sure the infirmary is well stocked with every possible antidote. Believe me, this incident will be thoroughly investigated. In the meantime, I won't allow anyone else to be poisoned in my castle. Do you understand?"

Horys nodded frantically. His round spectacles slipped down his nose in the process. He shoved them back up with a nervous gesture. "Of course, Your Majesty. Is there anything else—"

Valis waved him away. "Unless my wife requires further medical supervision, I would prefer to be left alone with her."

Horys said nothing more. He offered a deep bow with outstretched palms and scuttled toward the door, closing it softly behind him. Valis didn't watch him leave. She continued staring at Brynn, who remained motionless aside from her slow breaths.

Valis sat on the bed and took Brynn's hand in hers. It was cold, much colder than usual. Though Horys had said Brynn was likely to recover, Valis' heart remained lodged in her throat, a burning lump that made it difficult to breathe. The fear of watching Brynn die was a sickeningly familiar feeling, one she'd hoped never to experience again.

The images came to her unbidden, as fresh and raw as they'd been that horrible day.

Clan leader Murta's followers had ambushed their royal convoy, pushing boulders over a cliff and onto the road below. Shalana reacted swiftly, throwing a forcefield over Valis, their mother, and the closest guards. It wasn't enough. While Shalana maintained the magic barrier, another boulder fell on top of her, crushing her completely.

Valis recalled every second of what transpired after. The horror replayed in her memory with agonizing slowness. The bloom of crimson blood on snow. Shrill screams of terror. The charred smell of magic, like the scent of fresh lightning. She remembered her mother, both arms raised, clutching Aefbain in one hand and holding out her bleeding palm as her long, white hair whipped behind her.

While Valis stood frozen with fear, unable to draw her own bloodletting dagger, her mother had blown away half the cliffside with a bolt of pure force. The frost giants tumbled in an avalanche of snow and rock. Ruith failed to notice Murta and a few chosen warriors emerging from a ditch on the other side of the road. Valis watched, too terrified to scream, as Murta's spear drove straight between her mother's shoulder blades and sprouted out the other side.

In the present, Valis closed her eyes for several moments. She wiped away the tear tracks on her cheeks and swallowed the lump in her throat, though a dull ache lingered in her chest. She'd seen her older sister fall. She'd watched the spark of life leave her mother's eyes. She would not let Brynn die, too. She would not lose another family member, even if that someone was only part of her family through a political marriage of convenience. She would not.

"I will find whoever did this to you." Valis squeezed Brynn's hand tight, relieved to find it warm. Her fear began to fade, replaced by rising anger. Her jaw hardened and her eyes narrowed. "And when I do, they will pay most dearly. You have my word as sovereign of Winterwail."

Chapter Fourteen

"PLEASE, THERE IS NO need to get up on my account. I only stopped by to leave some books…"

"Nonsense. You're the queen, not to mention her wife. You have as much right to be here as I do."

"You're her mother. I would hate to interfere…"

"It's all right. I know you're worried about her, too."

Brynn's head throbbed with a dull, persistent ache. Gray mist enveloped her as though she were wrapped in a raincloud. Faint, ghostly shapes flickered above her face, shifting out of focus before she could make sense of them. Something soft was draped over her.

Ugh. Where am I? Brynn tried to open her eyelids, but they weighed a hundred pounds, at least. She attempted to wiggle her fingers, then her toes. She wasn't sure whether she succeeded.

Beyond the mist, the distant voices continued their conversation.

"Brynn's never been much of a reader, if I'm being honest." Isuna's low, familiar voice eased some of the pounding in Brynn's head. "She was more of an outdoors child. Still is."

Silver laughter drifted into Brynn's ears. Valis. She'd only heard it a few times, but she recognized the sound. It made her chest feel strangely light and buoyant. "No surprises there, but I know what being stuck in a sickbed is like. Books are better than nothing."

"She'll try and sneak out of bed as soon as our backs are turned, Your Majesty. I guarantee it."

"Then we must not turn our backs. Blackspine extract is fatal if not treated immediately. Brynn is lucky to be alive."

Brynn frowned, or at least tried to. She couldn't see anything through the monotonous gray mist. Though she sensed parts of her body, most of which were uncomfortably sore and tender, they didn't seem to react to her brain's commands.

Blackspine… Wait, I was poisoned?!

She tried once more to open her eyes. This time, she raised her lashes slightly, allowing a sliver of warm, orange light to creep in. Candles. She lay in her own bed, covered in blankets that smelled like her own sweat. Shadows flitted above her, though she couldn't make out the details of their silhouettes.

Isuna gasped. "Brynn?"

"Are you awake?" Valis asked.

Brynn could only groan, but considered it a sign of improvement. At least she could make noise. She wrenched her eyes open. Sharp pain pierced her skull, protesting the sudden flood of light. She hissed, flopping one arm around as she tried to cover her eyes.

"Brynn..." Soft, trembling fingers caressed Brynn's cheek. Above her, Isuna's face came into focus. Her mother looked exhausted, with dark circles under her eyes and several new wrinkles on her brow.

Probably some gray hairs, too. Sorry, Mom.

Brynn tried to speak. Her mouth was cotton dry. All she managed was a raspy sort of, "Mmm..."

"Here." Different hands came into view, pale blue with slender fingers adorned with rubies on shiny, silver bands. "Drink this."

The delicate, bejeweled hands lifted a cup to Brynn's mouth. She parted her cracked lips, shivering as cool water trickled down her throat. She swallowed greedily. It was only plain water, but it was the most delicious thing she'd ever tasted.

The cup pulled away. Brynn licked her lips, already thirsty for more. "Not yet," Valis said, her pale face swimming beside Isuna's. "You will make yourself sick."

Brynn managed a short laugh. She instantly regretted it when her ribs rattled painfully in her chest. "Already sick." The croak of her own voice reminded her of an evening tree frog.

"Precisely." Isuna swept Brynn's curls away from her forehead, tucking them behind her ear. "You won't get better unless you take it slow."

Brynn's headache subsided under Isuna's palm. Her eyes finished adjusting to the flickering candlelight. "How long was I out?"

"Two days," Valis said. Something soft brushed the back of Brynn's hand, then cool fingers laced with her own. For some reason, Valis was holding her hand. "You are still very weak, but you should make a full recovery."

Brynn started to speak but ended up coughing. Jagged spikes of pain drove through her chest. Valis lifted the cup to Brynn's lips. She took a long, grateful sip, then licked her lips and tried again. "Was it meant for me, or...?"

"I wish I knew," Valis said. "Rumors that you wish to return the northern territories to the frost giants have made you unpopular among some of my courtiers, but..." Her eyes darted away briefly. She took a deep breath. "I am a far more likely target. I have many enemies, even within my own kingdom. Especially within my own kingdom."

Isuna laid her other hand on Valis' forearm, to Brynn's mild surprise. "It isn't your fault, Your Majesty. You didn't poison my daughter." Her eyes narrowed, lips pressing into a thin line. "But when we find out who did..."

Brynn stifled another laugh, knowing it would hurt. *That's Mom, all right. But since when is she comfortable touching a queen?*

Valis arched a brow but said nothing. She ignored Isuna's touch, stroking her thumb back and forth over Brynn's knuckles almost absentmindedly. "The apothecaries and bloodletters were able to extract the worst of the poison." Her gaze settled on Brynn's wrists. "I promise you, we will find its origin."

Brynn looked down as well. Her forearms were bandaged with clean, white dressings. Her stomach churned as she realized what Valis meant. She didn't know much about snow elf medicine, but bloodletting didn't leave much room for interpretation.

"I heard something about books?" Brynn needed to change the subject. Isuna kept staring at her like she might fade away at any moment, while sorrow shone in Valis' wide, gray eyes. Slowly, like the creeping of early dawn, Brynn realized that Valis' look of sadness made her chest feel heavy. "Thanks for those. What did you bring me?"

As Brynn had hoped, Valis brightened. She placed her free hand upon a short stack of books on the nightstand. "I took the liberty of choosing works of fiction and a few of the more action-oriented biographies."

Brynn smiled, a gesture that became easier as she regained more strength. "Thanks. I'm not much of a reader—"

"So I told Queen Aefbain," Isuna said.

"—but I guess there won't be much else to do while I'm stuck in bed. You said I might be here a while." Her heart sank at the prospect. The thought of tracking down the poisoner was already at the back of her mind.

Isuna frowned. "I know that tone of voice, Brynnflor Woodwarden.

You're already planning your escape, aren't you?"

"I'm not," Brynn whined, but her voice sounded unconvincing to her own ears. She'd always been a terrible patient, as her mother well knew.

Valis' soft look of concern hardened into something sterner. Her sharp jaw hardened and her icy mask fell in place once more, erasing all emotion from her eyes. "You need rest. Even with immediate treatment, blackspine can severely damage one's internal organs."

Brynn scoffed, rolling her eyes. "Why are you both acting like I'm about to run out of the room in my underwear and fight a grizzly bear?"

"Because you're my daughter," Isuna said. "I know the sorts of foolish stunts you're capable of."

Valis tilted her head. "Oh? That sounds like an interesting story."

"Several interesting stories," Isuna said.

"I'll stay in bed like a good girl," Brynn grumbled. The last thing she needed was for Isuna to recount her embarrassing childhood antics in front of Valis.

"Thank you." Valis hesitated. "I know you are a relatively new member of the royal family, but I have already lost my parents and older sister. I would rather not lose my wife as well." She tugged her lower lip briefly between her teeth before catching herself and emptying her expression. Too late. Brynn couldn't unsee the gesture.

My wife. Is that a note of wistfulness in her voice? Brynn allowed herself a smile. She wasn't so cocky as to believe that Valis was in love with her or something ridiculous like that, but she could tell Valis was warming up to her. They might even end up as friends.

"I promise," Brynn said.

"That's my girl." Isuna squeezed Brynn's shoulder. "Now, I'll see about some soup for you. Tested first, of course."

"By a poison taster, right?"

Isuna rose from her chair and did not answer.

"Mom! *By a poison taster, right?*"

"There are other means of testing Brynn's food," Valis said to Isuna as she approached the door.

Isuna turned, hand on the knob. "I know. But this is my baby girl's life. I'm tasting everything that passes her lips until the poisoner is caught. I insist."

"Mom, no!" Brynn tried to push herself up, but her ribs protested and the muscles in her arms shook with exhaustion.

Valis stood as well. "I'll take care of this," she whispered to Brynn before joining Isuna. "Come. Let me familiarize you with the safety procedures I have recently put into place."

"Of course, Queen Aefbain. Brynn." Isuna fixed her with a stern glare. "Go back to sleep, all right? Get some rest."

"Yes, Mom," Brynn drawled. She softened her insolent tone with a sincere smile, pleased when Isuna and Valis both smiled back. They exited the room, leaving Brynn alone.

"Fuck." She pulled the blanket beneath her chin and stared at the ceiling. She closed her eyes, hoping a quick nap might delay her next meal. Her stomach grumbled, but weariness outweighed hunger. She had a feeling the battle to prevent her mother from acting as her personal poison taster had just begun.

* * * * *

First Apothecary Ivoss was a thin, balding gentleman of short stature. His round, thick-lensed spectacles hung off the edge of his long nose. He was constantly pushing them back up as he squinted at Valis. Though of no great height herself, she had a few inches on him.

"I'm afraid, Your Majesty," Ivoss said in a warbling tenor, "that I have little more to report on the blackspine extract used to poison the royal consort. Though it is a rare plant except in the northernmost reaches, blackspine is mostly homogeneous. I have no way of narrowing down the source."

Valis ignored the sinking feeling in her chest. "What about the royal consort's treatment plan? Do your findings, or lack thereof, further inform it in any way?"

Ivoss smiled, his sharp, white teeth in excellent condition for a man of his advanced age. "Royal Consort Woodwarden's prognosis is still good. Bloodtender Horys and I were able to filter out the majority of the poison in time. It will take a few more days, perhaps a week, for her to regain her full strength, but she should make a full recovery. Unless..." His voice trailed off awkwardly, as though he were rethinking what he was about to say.

Valis narrowed her eyes. "Unless, what?"

"It is outside my purview—"

"Speak freely, First Apothecary." Valis folded her arms, causing the long sleeves of her robe to swish by her sides. "Unless what?"

Ivoss sighed. "Blackspine extract is not the sort of thing one builds up a tolerance for. Quite the opposite. If Consort Woodwarden is exposed a second time, the reaction will be even more severe."

Valis bit down on her cheek before catching herself and relaxing her jaw. She doubted Ivoss noticed. He wasn't constantly staring at her face with the deep, searching looks Brynn often used. In fact, Ivoss deliberately avoided eye contact. "I understand. The poisoner has not yet been apprehended."

"No doubt they will be caught soon." Ivoss' bushy eyebrows drew together sympathetically, making him look less like a sycophantic member of her staff and more like a concerned, elderly relative.

Valis felt a small flicker of amusement. It looked as though the hair he'd lost on top of his head had regrown above his eyes. Hmm. *That observation sounds like something Brynn would say...*

A brisk knock sounded upon the door to Ivoss' workroom.

"Enter." Valis commanded.

First Arcanist Listra, a plump, older woman wearing crimson robes, walked in. Her long, silver hair was pulled into a braid that fell all the way down her back, but both sides were shaved short and carved with intricate designs that ran horizontally along her scalp. Though not as long as her queen's, her sleeves trailed low as a symbol of her station.

"Oh, Your Majesty." She strode forward, dipping her head and offering both palms. "My apologies. I didn't expect you here..."

Valis took Listra's hands, joining their palms for a brief moment before withdrawing. "No trouble, First Arcanist. First Apothecary Ivoss is updating me on the royal consort's prognosis."

Listra straightened. "Ah. I hope she's doing well?"

"As well as can be expected after the attempt on her life," Valis said.

Listra's blue eyes widened. "Oh." She seemed to struggle for an appropriate response, only to decide that one didn't exist. "I also have news, Your Majesty, though not about the poisoning. My intention was to consult with the First Apothecary before requesting an official meeting with you, but since you're here..."

The pleasant arcanist usually had full cheeks and a warm smile, but

Valis noticed her heavy-lidded eyes and the deepened wrinkles in her forehead. "Ill news, I take it?"

Listra inclined her head once more. "My fellow arcanists and I have searched diligently for the source of the Rot. Despite extensive testing, we've only been able to determine that our samples aren't magical or arcane in nature. We discussed it amongst ourselves and determined that this is a more suitable task for the First Apothecary and his colleagues... so long as you agree, Your Majesty."

Valis failed to summon her usual polite, distant smile. She cared because Brynn cared, and Brynn had already endured enough awfulness over the past few days. *How will I tell her? Perhaps I should wait until she's feeling better...*

Listra and Ivoss looked to her, awaiting a response.

"I understand, First Arcanist," Valis said. "If the Rot is natural rather than arcane in origin, First Apothecary Ivoss should continue the research." Valis turned to address Ivoss. "You and your alchemists will make sense of this. You shall have as many samples and as much funding as needed."

Ivoss cleared his throat. His eyes shifted in a noticeably nervous manner. "It would be my honor to study the samples, Your Majesty. Assisting our southern cousins and new allies is a worthy endeavor." He bowed again, offering his upturned palms.

Valis nodded but didn't take them. "Consider it done. First Arcanist, you and your arcanists shall remain available for anything Ivoss may require. They may need your assistance. Continue to consider this an urgent priority."

Listra bowed in the same manner as Ivoss. "Of course, Your Majesty."

"Thank you for your reports. I shall leave you to collaborate while I visit the royal consort. She should be informed of this development." *Or lack of development... if I can find the courage to tell her.*

Tired of the constant bad news, the endless bowing, and being addressed as Your Majesty, Valis made a hasty exit. She left the First Apothecary and First Arcanist to deal with logistics, exiting the room and releasing a heavy sigh as soon as the door closed.

Kraal stood in the hallway, back braced against the wall. She straightened as Valis approached. "I heard the bad news. Sorry about eavesdropping, but none of you were quiet."

Valis managed a weak smile. "No need to worry, Kraal. I know you never listen at keyholes unless I ask. Besides, learning what the Rot is not may be another step toward learning what it actually is."

Kraal looked both ways down the hall to make sure they were alone, then placed a hand on Valis' shoulder. Though the touch was careful and light, its weight was considerable. Valis found it comforting. She appreciated that Kraal touched her when they were alone, since so few others could.

"If it helps, I have slightly better news," Kraal said. "I went through the apothecary logbooks and compared them with the palace's stock of herbs. The First Apothecary likely hasn't been informed yet, since the audit was completed only a few minutes ago. What little blackspine extract we have is accounted for... but some silverleaf was missing."

Valis' brow furrowed. "Silverleaf." Her eyes widened. "You mean to disguise the taste of the poison?"

Kraal smirked. "Exactly. I believe the poisoner is someone in the palace with access to our stores. They purchased the blackspine secretly, assuming we would check for that right away, but assumed some missing silverleaf would go unnoticed. I was very thorough in my investigation. None of the apprentices remember distributing the missing vials to anyone. I questioned them all, and I seriously doubt they were lying."

Valis managed a smile. Kraal's enormous stature and well-developed muscles, not to mention her position as Valis' attendant, almost guaranteed that the young apprentices wouldn't dare lie. "Question them again anyway, perhaps under the influence of a truth serum. Should any refuse, we have our primary suspects."

"As you wish, Valis. Where are you going next? I should escort you."

"To check on Brynn. I should tell her about... well, you heard."

Kraal removed her hand. "You haven't given up on your promise. You're just consulting a different field of experts."

"Consulting a new field of experts." Valis managed a soft laugh. "That does sound better."

Kraal winked. "I learned from the best."

"Very well. You may escort me to Brynn's room. If she is asleep, I plan to sit and read until she wakes up. Feel free to continue your investigation."

"Excellent." Kraal flashed a toothy grin. "The official investigators have their knickers in a twist about me pursuing leads. It isn't often I have royal permission to step on snow elf toes."

"And you will surely enjoy watching them squirm," Valis said.

"Very much."

"Please keep them apprised of anything you discover... after telling me, of course."

"Of course."

They left for the infirmary in companionable silence, with Valis taking comfort in Kraal's reassuring presence. Consulting another field of experts. *Very smart, Kraal. Maybe I will manage to tell Brynn the truth after all.*

* * * * *

A knock sounded on Brynn's bedroom door. She stirred, blinking away the haze of sleep. With a yawn, she rolled onto her back and propped herself up against the pillows. "Mom? That you? We seriously need to discuss the whole poison taster thing..."

Brynn fell silent as the door opened. Her eyes widened, riveted to the slender figure in the doorway. Valis was an unexpected but certainly not unpleasant sight, especially in a clinging, purple silk dress with gold trim.

Valis took a step toward the bed. "Brynn? Are you all right?"

Brynn realized she was staring and cleared her throat. "Hey, you," she said with a sheepish smile. Hopefully, Valis would attribute her delayed response to exhaustion.

Valis exhaled a long sigh but returned the smile. "Black Wolf's teeth, I appreciate you so much right now. You and Kraal are the only two people in the kingdom who don't insist on calling me Your Majesty at every opportunity."

Brynn's smile became a grin. "It's my pleasure to disrespect you at every opportunity."

Valis laughed. The soft, sweet sound sent a tingle down the back of Brynn's neck. Valis entered with her usual graceful glide, shutting the door behind her. She approached the chair beside Brynn's bed and sat down. "How are you feeling today?"

"Better," Brynn said. "Tired. Frustrated."

"Because you are confined to bed?"

"Yeah." Brynn scrunched her nose. "Also, my head feels like it's full of rocks, my muscles are noodles, we don't know who attempted to poison one of us, and my mom insists on tasting all my food before I eat."

"When you put it that way, your frustration is more than understandable." Valis leaned closer and lowered her voice into a conspiratorial whisper. "Let me handle your mother. I can be quite persuasive." She rested her hand on Brynn's.

"No doubt, but my mom can be very stubborn." Brynn's headache began to fade. It felt good to vent about her situation. She suspected she'd been right about Isuna and Valis forming a friendship.

"Let me handle this. You have enough to worry about." Valis withdrew her soft hand sooner than Brynn would have liked, then sat up and straightened her shoulders. "I also have some news about our research into the Rot."

Brynn's ears perked up. "Good news?"

The tips of Valis' ears drooped. "Not good, no... but not exactly bad. My most accomplished arcanists have determined that the Rot isn't magical. I have ordered them to collaborate with my First Apothecary and his staff. If the Rot is natural in origin, we will learn how to destroy it."

For a moment, Brynn forgot to breathe. A shard of ice lodged itself in her heart, sending frost through her body. Cold dread crawled down her spine and numbed the pit of her stomach.

"Not magical? That... that can't be right. The Druids are nature experts. If the Rot is part of nature, they'd have figured out how to fix it years ago!"

Valis touched the back of Brynn's hand again. Brynn realized she'd twisted the fur covers in her clenched fists but couldn't figure out how to uncurl them.

"I'm sorry." Valis' thin, white brows drew into a wrinkled line over her sorrowful gray eyes. "I realize this is not the news you hoped for..."

"Not what I hoped for? My people are doomed!" Brynn yanked away from Valis, pulling into a curled position with both arms around her knees. "If your arcanists and my Druids can't stop this curse, no one can. We'll be gone in less than a generation, turned into those...things."

Her heart thundered, as her mind conjured the infected panther, its monstrous jaws dripping, Rotted purple boils erupting through bare patches in its ragged black fur. Her throat squeezed shut as the cloying smell of decomposition rushed back, its memory strong enough to fill her nose.

Valis shifted forward in the chair, placing her hand on the edge of the bed, but not attempting to touch Brynn again. "We will find the answer. I made a promise."

Brynn ground her teeth, pulled between two different times and places. She dragged herself forcefully into the present. When she spoke, her voice was strained. "It isn't about promises or what you want to do. It's about what you and your people are actually capable of."

Valis' sharp eyes narrowed, flashing like the polished edge of a blade. "I never took you for the type to give up so easily, Brynn Woodwarden. I thought you were stubborn, like your mother. Like I'm sure the rest of your people are."

The heat of anger flared in Brynn's belly, burning away some of the constricting cold. "You don't understand. You haven't seen it—"

"You're right. I haven't. Even so, I won't give up, and I refuse to let you give up either."

Valis rose from the chair. At first, Brynn thought she was about to leave and felt a twinge of regret in her heart. Instead, Valis sat on the edge of the bed, close enough for Brynn to catch the scent of her perfume. Brynn relaxed in spite of herself. Her memory of the Rot's smell faded, replaced by something crisp and floral.

"We will find a solution, Brynn. Not only because I promised, but because I refuse to see an entire civilization wiped out. It will restore some of the snow elves' lost honor to help people for a change instead of plundering their ancestral homeland."

Brynn gazed into the depths of Valis' liquid-silver eyes. No longer burning with anger, they shone with earnest emotion. In spite of her frustrations, something inside Brynn melted. "Sorry," she rasped. "None of this is your fault. I'm just scared. My people could lose everything."

Valis touched Brynn's cheek with the tips of her fingers. "No need to apologize. I understand."

Brynn waited, expecting Valis to say something else. She silently stared directly into Brynn's eyes, her face leaning closer. Moments later, Brynn realized she was leaning in as well.

Her gaze dropped to Valis' lips. Dark plums. Full and slightly parted. Irresistible. Brynn couldn't help but wonder how soft they would feel against her own. *What am I doing?! Am I going to kiss her?* She hesitated, unsure. Valis remained exactly where she was. Close enough to share the same breath.

Brynn wasn't sure which of them closed the gap. Suddenly, Valis' lips were pressed against hers, soft as a butterfly's wings and trembling slightly. This time, Brynn knew exactly what she needed to do. She parted her own lips, applying gentle pressure.

A low sigh escaped Valis' mouth. Brynn covered it with her own, resting a hand on Valis' hip. She scooted closer, her eyes fluttering as Valis grasped one of her shoulders. Fingers curled tight into the fabric of Brynn's nightgown, the grip shaking, yet firm.

I have no idea what I'm doing... but I don't want to stop.

Chapter Fifteen

VALIS FROZE AS HER mouth touched Brynn's. Her mind went white like the silence after a snowstorm. She knew she should move to deepen the kiss, or at least pull away, but leaning in had taken all her courage.

She tensed when Brynn's hand touched her side, then relaxed as it curled around her waist. The thump of her own heartbeat filled her ears. Her blood burned, thawing her uncertainty. Brynn's lips were so soft beneath hers. The gentle pressure of her palm was a welcome reassurance.

No! I need to stop! She began to pull back, then Brynn's tongue brushed her lower lip. All the heat in Valis' body rushed straight between her legs. A quiet whimper escaped her throat, barely muffled by Brynn's mouth. She parted her lips only for Brynn to break away first.

"Valis?"

"Hmm?" Valis blinked, lost in Brynn's forest-green eyes. Then she noticed Brynn's furrowed brows and the concerned tilt of her head.

The tips of Brynn's ears wilted. "Did I guess wrong?"

"I—" The memory of Brynn's mouth was like a brand upon her own, but Valis knew she shouldn't be kissing Brynn or anyone else. She'd lost far too many pieces of her heart to give away another.

Brynn withdrew her hand. "I'm sorry—"

Valis stared at her own hand, curled over Brynn's shoulder. She couldn't seem to remove it. "Don't be. I kissed you first."

Brynn's ears perked. "I thought I kissed you."

Valis averted her gaze, staring down at her lap. "I suppose we kissed each other."

Brynn sighed heavily. "I'm a fool, aren't I? Stealing a kiss during...well, everything."

Against her better judgment, Valis looked up. "We aren't fools," she said, although she very much felt like one. Her gaze fixed on Brynn's mouth, remembering the tenderness of the kiss. "I kissed you because I wanted to, but I've lost too much already. I'm not sure how to..." She trailed off, hoping Brynn would understand.

"Hey." Brynn laced their fingers together. Valis couldn't help but notice the warmth, the slight roughness of archer's calluses. "I know it's scary, but you can't just choose to stop feeling things. Sure, caring about someone can hurt, but it's part of life. It's part of who you are." She squeezed Valis' hand. "You aren't the ice queen I thought you were. You have a really big heart that isn't frozen at all."

A lump caught in Valis' throat. She tried to summon her usual emotionless mask, but hot tears spilled free instead. "Is it really that simple? Stop fighting? Accept that caring is worth the inevitable pain?"

"I never said it was simple." Brynn wiped away the wet tracks of Valis' tears. "But we're all just people. We're built to care about each other."

Valis leaned into Brynn's hand. She felt raw inside, like an open wound, but an agonizing pressure released somewhere deep within her heart. She sobbed, burying her face in Brynn's shoulder. Beneath the scent of her freshly laundered nightshirt and a hint of sweat, Brynn smelled like fresh pine. A comforting scent.

I was always fighting a losing battle, wasn't I? I care for Kraal and Delia... and now Brynn, too.

When Valis lifted her head, blinking through what she hoped were the last of her tears, she got lost in Brynn's eyes all over again. She'd always thought them beautiful, but now they shone with the warmth of dappled sunlight through a canopy of trees.

Answering warmth tingled in Valis' chest, spreading down her spine and lower still. She tightened her hold on Brynn's shoulder, tilted her head, and leaned in.

Their second kiss was deeper. Intentional. Perhaps even inevitable. Valis shivered as Brynn's tongue brushed her bottom lip again. With a nervous hitch of breath, she parted her lips, hoping Brynn would take her offer this time. Brynn's tongue pressed forward, gently at first, and Valis met it with her own.

Brynn wrapped an arm around Valis' waist, coaxing her to swing a knee over her lap. Valis' cheeks burned at the brazen position, but the urge to flee never came. She wanted to remain right where she was, straddling Brynn's thighs with her arms draped around Brynn's neck.

When Valis broke their kiss, it was only to draw in a quick breath before seeking Brynn's mouth again. It tasted of heat and salt and her own tears. She moaned in disappointment when Brynn brushed her forearms aside, then fell into stunned silence.

Brynn pulled her nightshirt off, revealing the landscape of her rich, bronze skin. Last time, Valis hadn't gotten much of a chance to admire Brynn's body. She'd glimpsed it of course, but the bedroom had been dark, and Brynn had spent most of the time between her legs. Now, she drank in the sight, in awe of every detail.

Though Brynn's form was lean, her shoulders were exceptionally well-defined, with the sculpted lines of an archer. Her breasts sat high on her chest, thick brown nipples stiff against the air. And her stomach... Valis barely swallowed a whine. Brynn's muscles were taut and prominently outlined, leading down toward the dark curls between her legs.

"You can do more than just stare." Judging from Brynn's lopsided grin and the sly narrowing of her eyes, she'd noticed Valis' reaction. Brynn leaned back, folding her hands behind her head. "I'm on bed rest, remember? You take the lead this time."

Valis tried to summon her noble bearing, her carefully cultivated aura that commanded attention and obedience, but they were nowhere to be found. Before...everything, she'd been a shy, introverted arcanist, far more interested in researching advanced blood-magic theorems than running a kingdom.

Maybe—while she and Brynn were alone, at least—she could behave more like her old self. As though the two of them were equals.

Valis gathered her courage and ran two fingers across the tear tracks on her cheeks. With wet fingertips, she traced a sigil in the air. Her fur-lined gown vanished, leaving her as naked as Brynn was beneath her.

She recalled the first night they'd spent together, a night that had offered some unexpected pleasures amidst all the awkwardness. "I want your fingers again," she whispered, barely stifling a please.

Brynn didn't seem the least bit fazed. She removed her hands from behind her head and motioned for Valis to scoot closer.

If I'm set on doing this, I may as well commit.

Despite the shiver that raced down her spine, Valis shifted to kneel over Brynn's cut abdomen. She sighed as Brynn's hands grasped her hips and squeezed briefly, just enough to make Valis dizzy, before running down along her outer thighs.

"Gods below, I wish I had the stamina to flip you over right now." Brynn slid her hands up, reaching behind to grasp Valis' backside. "But whatever you want, I'll make sure you get." With a possessive squeeze, Brynn brought her left hand back around, cupping between Valis' legs.

Once more, Valis froze. Not because she was afraid, but because she had no idea how to respond. She wanted Brynn's hand there—by the Black Wolf, she did—but what was she supposed to do? Just keep kneeling in place? Begin rocking? Where was she supposed to brace herself? Sex, it seemed, never stopped being awkward, even when you chose to have it for pleasurable rather than political reasons.

Fortunately, Brynn was keen to offer suggestions. "Lean forward," she whispered, tracing the sensitive crease at the top of Valis' inner thigh.

Trembling, Valis did so, realizing Brynn's intent when she leaned up for another kiss. As their mouths met, Valis relaxed again. Kissing Brynn felt extraordinarily right. She would have been content to drink from that particular well forever, but Brynn's fingers found her, stroking in a soft line.

She spilled a moan into Brynn's mouth. She'd expected the touch but underestimated its intensity. Even though Brynn was being exquisitely gentle, heat flashed through Valis' core, followed by slippery warmth between her legs.

Valis gasped as Brynn's fingers toyed with her. Brynn broke away from her mouth to string kisses along her collarbone. Valis tried to protest, but her mouth went slack and her lashes fluttered as Brynn's teeth grazed the base of her throat.

Rather than bite down, Brynn withdrew almost immediately. "Is biting okay?" She stared up at Valis with a worried furrow between her brows. "Sorry. It's kind of a thing for wood elves, but I should have asked first…"

Valis stretched her body over Brynn's, resting fully on top of her. She buried her face in the crook of Brynn's throat, fitting her own teeth there and digging in as hard as she dared. A low rumble vibrated in Brynn's chest and the hand on Valis' backside squeezed harder.

The hand between her legs took greater liberties. Valis whimpered through her teeth as Brynn's thumb found her clit, massaging in slow circles. Hot sparks shot along her spine, but it wasn't enough. She rocked her hips, no longer the least bit uncertain.

One of Brynn's fingers slipped inside. There was no pain, no resistance. Valis was more than slick enough, more than ready. Then Brynn's finger curled forward and up. Valis' entire body jerked. She bucked, forcing Brynn's thumb out of place.

Brynn adjusted quickly, adding a second finger and offering Valis the rough heel of her hand to grind against.

For once, Valis knew exactly what to do. She rocked greedily against Brynn's hand, shifting until she found an angle that made white spots float behind her closed eyes. She relaxed her bite on Brynn's neck and nuzzled there, struggling to breathe through the sharp spikes of pleasure.

"That's it," Brynn whispered, her breath warm and reassuring. "Fuck, you're so hot. So tight."

Valis arched, clenching around Brynn's fingers as they gave another purposeful curl. She chased Brynn's lips, eager for another kiss, but her mouth fell open as warmth wrapped around her nipple. Brynn had scooted underneath her to lavish attention upon her breasts.

She tightened around Brynn's fingers, trying to make sense of the stretch, the wonderful pressure. Somehow, everything felt more intense while Brynn sucked, sweeping her tongue in flat circles. The strokes became faster and firmer as Brynn's fingers moved, pumping deeper.

Valis arched, bracing herself on trembling forearms to give Brynn more access. She rocked frantically, tensing each time her clit dragged against the heel of Brynn's hand. Her peak was close. It built and built, a ball of fire burning low in her belly.

Somewhere within her fuzzy mind, she realized this release would be different. She wasn't resisting. Wasn't fighting it, struggling to maintain some semblance of composure. Wasn't closing off her body or her heart to shield herself. She wanted to come. For Brynn.

Brynn sensed it too. She tugged Valis' nipple lightly between her teeth, then drew back and gazed up at her. "Let go. I've got you."

It wasn't only Brynn's words, but the adoration that shone in her green eyes and her tender smile that pushed Valis over the edge. Her peak hit suddenly, every bit the roaring flame she'd braced for. There was no controlling it, even if she'd wanted to. She threw her head back and cried out, pulsing around Brynn's fingers, spilling into her waiting hand.

Brynn latched onto Valis' other nipple, sucking hard as her fingers curled. They neither stopped nor slowed, showing no mercy.

Valis was grateful. Although her hips had frozen above Brynn's stomach, she desperately needed the extra pressure. She throbbed whenever Brynn hooked into her front wall, sending streams of heat down Brynn's wrist.

Eventually, the waves of pleasure passed. Valis collapsed on top of Brynn, sighing into the sweet-smelling curve of her wife's neck. *My wife... Does this mean we are? By our own choice?* She wasn't sure, but she was too happy to care, wrapped up in bliss as she was.

"You're okay," Brynn murmured, kissing the top of her head. "You're okay... I've got you. You did so well."

Valis whimpered, fluttering weakly around Brynn's fingers. They'd finally stilled but made no move to withdraw. She closed her eyes, allowing herself to enjoy the way Brynn's heartbeat thumped beneath her. "Thank you," she whispered, the only words she could manage.

Brynn laughed and kissed her hair again. "Thank you. Watching you come just now was the hottest thing I've ever seen."

Valis' lashes fluttered. She began to stir. The line of Brynn's lithe body radiated tension beneath her, and she realized she had yet to repay the favor. Although Brynn hadn't asked, Valis began kissing her way down, starting at the sharp line of Brynn's jaw and continuing on.

Brynn stiffened beneath her. "Hey, it's okay. Take a minute to— unhhh..." She tilted sideways as Valis kissed her neck, hips rocking upward. The movement caused Brynn's fingers to shift. Valis clenched around them, rising only reluctantly.

Determination lent fresh energy to Valis' exhausted body. She dragged her tongue along Brynn's collarbone, enjoying the way Brynn's stomach tensed between her thighs. She gave a gentle nip to see if it would happen again, delighted by the way Brynn's hips jumped.

She kissed down toward Brynn's breasts, pausing to drag her tongue across a stiff, brown nipple. Brynn shoved rough fingers through her hair, not quite pulling, but holding her in place.

Valis was more than happy to settle for a while, only withdrawing to switch between Brynn's breasts. Brynn began a steady grind beneath her, rubbing against her stomach and leaving a slick stripe of need.

That sensation tugged at Valis' memory. She released Brynn's nipple with a wet pop and peered down, her eyes widening as she took in the glorious sight of Brynn's beautifully formed abdomen. Her muscles flexed, shimmering with slick lines of what Valis realized was her own release. Too eager to be embarrassed, she pulled away and ducked beneath Brynn's knees, following one of the lines with her tongue.

Brynn grunted, hips moving restlessly. "Fuck, you're wonderful." A wide grin spread across her face, dimpling her cheeks. "Insatiable..."

Valis took her time cleaning the mess she'd made, enjoying each low moan that rumbled in Brynn's chest, every subtle shiver that raced through her body. Those reactions were proof that despite her inexperience, she was doing something right.

When Brynn's hand tightened in her hair, pushing gently downward, Valis allowed herself to be guided between Brynn's shaking thighs. She scooted down on the mattress and pulled Brynn's legs over her shoulders, hesitating only long enough to admire the view.

Brynn's clit was stiff and shiny, straining beneath its hood. Her puffy outer lips had blossomed open to reveal the soft pink inner folds. Everything glistened. Valis' mouth watered. Though she'd never done this before, she wasted no more time. She lowered her face between Brynn's legs.

Valis swiped her tongue. The taste was strong and salty, but by no means unpleasant. She started with flat strokes, acclimating to the sharp flavor and the heavy scent that filled her nose. She soon craved more. She pushed her tongue deeper, swirling it against Brynn's entrance.

Brynn's other hand tangled into Valis' hair alongside the first. She lifted her hips, pulling Valis' face closer. "Just... just give me a tap if— *fuck,* if I'm pushing your head around too much... yes, right there!"

If Valis' mouth hadn't been thoroughly occupied, she would have smirked. It seemed Brynn's entrance was especially sensitive. Valis circled her tongue a few more times before pushing inside, ignoring the strain at the corners of her jaw in her efforts to get deeper.

Brynn threw her head back and cried out, her fingers trembling in Valis' hair. Her thighs tensed, heels digging in behind Valis' shoulders. Valis' heart swelled. Definitely doing something right. She tried to tease Brynn with slow thrusts, moaning as warm salt spread across her tongue and throughout her mouth.

The sounds Brynn made were divine, low groans interspersed with an occasional breathy whine. When Valis decided to try something different and suck the swollen bud of her clit, Brynn gave a full-throated shout that echoed throughout the room. "Valis!"

Her name. Brynn had cried *her* name.

Valis glowed with pride as she sucked Brynn's clit, lavishing it with all the attention she could. She swirled her tongue over and around, maintaining firm pressure, relishing the way it pulsed within the seal of her lips.

Brynn untangled one hand from Valis' hair and grabbed one of hers. "Fuck me," she muttered, guiding Valis' fingers between her legs.

Valis obeyed happily. She tested Brynn's entrance with one finger first, sighing around Brynn's clit as the finger slipped effortlessly inside. She added a second soon after, curling forward as Brynn had done for her. Brynn rocked faster onto her fingers and into her mouth. Valis felt Brynn's inner walls squeeze while Brynn's clit throbbed beneath her tongue.

"So close... Just keep—keep sucking me..."

Valis disliked foul language, but hearing the muffled curses that spilled freely from Brynn's mouth sent warmth tingling through her body. The thought that she was the cause of this loss of control made her roll her hips down hard into the mattress.

She found more than she bargained for. To Valis' surprise, she came first. Her core clenched and slippery heat ran down her thighs. It wasn't as intense as before, but a great relief nonetheless. She forgot to move her fingers as the waves took her, but it seemed she'd already done enough. Brynn tugged the roots of her hair and arched off the bed, flooding Valis' mouth and chin.

Once the initial shockwave passed, Valis did her best to keep sucking Brynn's clit. Her inner walls rippled right along with Brynn's as more slickness spilled onto the sheets below. Brynn tugged the roots of her hair, but Valis relished the sensation. For once in her life, she was happy to let someone else make a mess of her.

At last, Brynn slumped back onto the mattress. She sprawled her limbs out with a long sigh, panting heavily. When Valis looked up to admire Brynn's toned and glistening body, she noticed Brynn grinning down at her. "Shit," Brynn rasped, her voice low and rough. "I'm not sure I'll survive you once you've had more practice."

Valis kissed Brynn's inner thigh, then rested her cheek there, not minding the trails of slickness that touched the side of her face. "I've been told I'm a fast learner. With a good teacher, that is."

Brynn winked. "Come here. Let me kiss you."

Valis crawled on top of Brynn and braced herself on her elbows, bending down for a soft brush of mouths. Brynn surprised her by opening, inviting her in. Valis slid past Brynn's lips, shuddering as Brynn's tongue brushed hers.

They kissed slowly and deeply until the need for air broke them apart. Brynn stared up at Valis with glassy eyes, grinning ear to ear. "Not sure you need much instruction, but practice? That, I'm more than happy to provide."

"In a little while," Valis said. "Rest first. You're still recovering your strength."

Brynn waggled her eyebrows. "When I get it back, you'll really be in for it."

"We will see about that." Valis rolled over and opened her arms. Brynn cuddled into them straight away, resting her head on Valis' shoulder. She soon dozed off, snoring while Valis stroked her hair.

Valis closed her eyes as well, not sleeping, but entering a state of languid satisfaction as she listened to the steady thump of Brynn's heartbeat. They hadn't talked any more of feelings, hadn't clarified what they were to each other, but Valis knew. She knew, and at least for the moment, she wasn't afraid.

* * * * *

Cold. Fierce, numbing cold flashed through Valis' limbs, rooting them to the ice below. The cold burrowed into her bones, eating its way through her body from the inside.

Valis cried out, but her voice vanished into the vast, endless white of a violent blizzard. Cruel lashes of wind whipped her face, pulling hot tears from her eyes—tears that froze partway down her cheeks. She bowed her head and threw an arm across her face.

The snow beneath her feet wasn't white. It was red. Redder than roses or rubies. Redder than Aefbain's crimson glow in her hand. Steaming puddles of blood blossomed beneath Shalana's limp body, her chest and part of one shoulder crushed beneath the weight of a heavy boulder.

"*Shalana!*"

The howling wind stole Valis' scream. She fought for control of her frozen limbs. Fell to her knees beside Shalana. Reached for her. Blood stained Valis' palms. She wrenched her stiff lips into movement, muttering soundless spells or perhaps prayers.

Nothing happened. Shalana's glassy, blue eyes stared up into the blurred, white sky above.

More blood soaked the fur-lined hem of Valis' dress, trapped beneath her knees. She turned. There lay Queen Ruith, curled on her side. The stone point of a spear sprouted through the center of her chest. Snow came down in torrents, threatening to overtake her face.

Valis crawled toward Ruith, discarding Aefbain without a second thought. She scooped the snow off her mother's body with both hands, but more took its place, forming a white mound over the still form.

"No, no, no..." Val's dug until her fingers split and bled. It was useless. Ruith was disappearing faster than she could scoop away the snow. She stole a glance at Shalana. Her sister was completely lost except for a streak of inky black hair and the tips of her ears.

Valis collapsed into a heap of silent sobs. She couldn't save them. They were gone. Swallowed whole by the endless frozen whiteness. Stolen away forever. She would never hear their voices or feel their embraces again. Her mother... Her sister...

Miraculously, Aefbain lay atop the piling snow instead of sinking beneath, pulsing with faint red light. With love comes loss.

Every one of your ancestors learned this lesson. The question is, how will you protect yourself?

* * * * *

Valis jerked upright. Her bare skin dripped with cold sweat and her lungs still burned with the biting memory of cold. She panted, whipping her head around. There was no blizzard. There were no corpses. She was in Brynn's bed, tangled amidst sheets that smelled like sex and warm bodies.

She glanced down. Brynn lay on her stomach, limbs sprawled spread-eagle, snoring and drooling slightly onto the pillow. She groaned, mumbled something unintelligible, then flipped onto her back and continued snoring.

Valis exhaled a long, shaking breath. She wiped away the sweat rolling down her face, combing her fingers through her tangled hair. She needed a scalding hot shower. More urgently, she needed to make her escape before Brynn woke up.

This was a mistake. A stupid, selfish mistake. I'm the reason Brynn nearly died. And what if she had? I would be ruined all over again. Unfit to rule. Unfit to take even the most basic care of myself.

She remembered how Kraal and Delia had slowly pulled her out of her all-consuming depression, bit by agonizing bit. They'd fed her when she wouldn't eat. Forced her to bathe and dress when she wouldn't leave bed. Only in the kindest way possible, but still. She couldn't have managed without them. She probably wouldn't have survived to take the throne.

That's it then. My feelings are irrelevant. Winterwail needs a queen. I cannot afford to slip into the darkness again. I might never find my way out a second time.

Valis slipped out of bed as stealthily as possible. She paused when Brynn stirred again, waiting until it was safe to grab her discarded clothes. She considered borrowing one of Brynn's nightgowns from the armoire, but embarrassment forced her back into her previous outfit.

A bit clumsily dressed, Valis removed Aefbain from the nightstand and tiptoed away. She waited for the swell of Brynn's next snore before opening a door and ducking into the suite beyond the bedroom. She closed the door behind her and breathed a sigh of relief.

Though guilt gnawed at her heart, Valis squared her shoulders and held her chin high. Later, after she showered and dressed in clean clothes, she would explain everything to Brynn. Despite her flares of stubbornness, Brynn could be reasonable. Surely, she would agree that they couldn't be romantic with one another, not with an assassin on the loose and two kingdoms depending on them.

Brynn will understand. She has to understand.

You made the right decision, Your Majesty, Aefbain said, with none of its usual smugness. As in the dream, its voice was calm, almost reassuring. Almost like a parent expressing pride in their child. *It is only natural for the living to form attachments, but you are destined for far greater things. Your growing affections for your consort will only weaken you.*

Valis peered into Aefbain's shiny black blade. Her own face stared back at her, looking almost like her mother. "Aefbains cannot afford to be weak."

Good girl. Your mother would be proud.

"I'll never know, will I? She's gone."

Not entirely. An echo of her wisdom lives within me, and all your ancestors before her. Follow my advice and you will be one of the greatest queens of your dynasty.

Valis swallowed around a hard lump in her throat. She knew if she spoke, her voice would crack. She stole quietly away from Brynn's suite and returned to her own. That shower sounded like a good idea, and if she cried beneath the water, no one else would know.

Chapter Sixteen

BRYNN WOKE TO BEAMS of late afternoon sunlight streaming through the partially drawn curtains. She groaned, rubbing sleep from her eyes. Her surroundings smelled different from the lingering scents of sweat and soap she'd grown accustomed to over the past few days. The tangled sheets only covered her lower half and faint floral perfume clung to the pillow beneath her cheek.

Her eyes popped all the way open. She sat up, but Valis was nowhere to be found. The other side of the bed was empty.

For a moment, she wondered whether it had all been a dream. If so, it was by far the best dream she'd ever had, but the memories were much too clear. She recalled warmth and slickness around her fingers, Valis' soft sighs of pleasure, the heat of that clever tongue between her legs.

Great Root. We really did that. Heaving a sigh, Brynn flopped back onto the bed and folded her hands behind her head. Why had Valis snuck away while she slept? Had it been an act of kindness to let her rest a while longer? Or was she ashamed of what they'd done?

The bottom of Brynn's stomach felt hollow. Summoning her energy, she climbed out of bed and staggered toward the washroom. A shower was the first order of business. Then clothes. Then maybe, she'd look for Valis. Straighten things out. Brynn had never been the sort to avoid confrontation.

As Brynn scrubbed the smell of sex from her skin under the scalding water, she found herself growing annoyed. The more she thought about it, the more certain she became: Valis had run away. Why else would Valis leave without waking her? Without leaving so much as a note?

Once she'd scoured her body clean, Brynn returned to the bedroom with a scowl on her face. She selected a linen shirt, sealskin vest, and loose trousers. Not the fanciest affair, but finely tailored. She refused to deal with laces or buttons today.

A knock on the door made Brynn turn her head. Her heart leaped. "Valis?" Brynn hurried to the door only for that hope to condense into a cold, heavy lump of disappointment.

Kraal stood outside, her broad-shouldered frame filling the

doorway. "Consort Woodwarden. Good to see you up and about. How are you feeling?"

"Better, thanks." Brynn forced a cheerful note into her voice. Kraal wasn't the reason for her bad mood, after all. "Please, call me Brynn."

A subtle smile curved Kraal's lips. "Of course, Brynn. I know titles can seem tedious when you come from the wider world beyond Winterwail's court."

Brynn forced an answering smile. "Right. Do you know where Valis is?" The question spilled out before she could swallow it back. She cursed herself for asking but desperately wanted to know the answer.

Kraal's brow furrowed. "Her Majesty is very busy, so she sent me to check on you."

The lump of disappointment in Brynn's chest sank into her stomach like a stone. If Valis had sent Kraal, that was answer enough. She struggled to keep her smile in place. "How kind."

Kraal said nothing but maintained a level stare.

Brynn scratched her neck. Something about Kraal's stare made her feel like an uncut stone beneath a jeweler's eyeglass, as though she were being scrutinized very closely.

"Anyway, I'm fine, so... I'm sure you have other things you need to do today..."

Kraal remained in the doorway. She gazed into Brynn's eyes as though searching for something hidden within.

Brynn sighed. "Is there anything else I can do for you, Kraal? Not to be rude, but I could use some more rest."

"Of course. I wouldn't want to disturb your rest. It just occurred to me that you might want to learn more about your snow eagle, should you intend to fly her."

Brynn had nearly forgotten about the snow eagle. She'd been preoccupied with her obstinate magic, the mysterious ritual, and two separate assassination attempts. She felt guilty that it had slipped her mind. Snow eagles were living creatures, after all.

"Someone's been minding her, right?"

Kraal nodded. "The palace falconer and I have been flying and feeding her. You strike me as a lover of nature and the outdoors, so I thought you might enjoy learning to handle her yourself."

Brynn managed a genuine smile. Caring for the snow eagle was an excellent excuse to get up and about, not to mention an effective distraction. She'd been cooped up in her bedroom long enough. A change of scenery would surely do her good.

"Absolutely. Would you be willing to show me?"

"Of course," Kraal said. "She needs a proper name as well."

"Hmm. I'll have to think about that…"

* * * * *

The afternoon was beautifully clear but bitterly cold. Brynn appreciated her heavy coat and the warmth enchantment stitched into it. The frigid air bit her cheeks, freezing the tips of her ears. She tucked them into her fur cap and pulled her arms in close as Kraal led her past the stables.

They stopped at a narrow, triangular building behind the palace stables. "This is the mews." Kraal opened the door and held it for Brynn. "All the royal birds live here, including your fine-feathered friend."

Brynn adjusted her cap again. She was used to holding doors for others rather than having them held for her. "Thanks," she said, entering the mews.

The interior was dark except for a single skylight. A dozen wood and wire hutches lined the walls, occupied by shadowy winged forms. The smell of droppings mixed with hay was unpleasant, but not unbearable.

"The dark keeps the birds calm," Kraal explained. "Their keepers fly them regularly, so they get plenty of sunlight and fresh air."

Brynn blinked. It was unsettling how easily Kraal could predict her thoughts. "Where's Wytestryke's hutch?"

Kraal arched a brow. "You've named her already?"

"Just testing it out. I thought of it on the way down," Brynn said. "What do you think?"

"I've been calling her Thas'dun. One of many frost giant words for blizzard."

"Thas'dun." Brynn tested how the name felt in her mouth. "That has a nice ring to it. Do you know how many languages the frost giant clans have? What's the most common?"

A subtle smile cracked Kraal's stony face. "Full of questions, aren't you? The answer is several. Most of us speak elvhen out of necessity and common out of spite. Some of the old tongues have already died."

"Yes, but I'd like to learn at least a few words of the more common languages. I've recently had a bit of a revelation..." Brynn paused. She doubted she was qualified to claim frost giant ancestry based only on Valis' suspicions and a drop of blood at most.

Kraal blinked, waiting.

"You know, since I live here now, it'd be good to understand the local culture."

"Full of surprises, too. Most elves would assimilate to the so-called dominant culture of Winterwail."

"I'm mixed," Brynn said. "Human, mostly. Many wood elves are. We don't care about bloodlines the way snow elves do."

Kraal hummed in acknowledgment, then turned to walk between the hutches. Brynn followed. Now that she wasn't the sole, unwavering focus of Kraal's attention, she didn't mind the frost giant's silence. She seemed like a woman of few words anyway.

They stopped at a large enclosure near the back of the mews. The skylight didn't offer much illumination, but Brynn made out a large shadow on a wooden perch. She leaned in for a closer look, then pulled back as the loud rustle of wings filled the space. Other birds in nearby hutches stirred at the disturbance.

"Easy, girl," Kraal crooned. She approached the enclosure, removing a leather pouch from her coat pocket. "I've got yummies if you behave."

Brynn barely stifled a laugh. It seemed Kraal had a hidden soft side. "Do I want to know what these yummies are?"

Kraal reached into the pouch. "Caribou jerky. She can't get enough."

On cue, the eagle leaped from her perch. She hooked her talons into the wire netting and jabbed her beak through the holes.

"Naughty!" Kraal wagged a finger at the eagle, who seemed unperturbed. She withdrew her beak, staring at them with piercing yellow eyes. "Go on, get back where you belong."

To Brynn's surprise, the eagle settled back on her perch. She studied them through the wire hutch, tilting her head ninety degrees. Brynn smiled. Watching the snow eagle's strange movements was fascinating.

"That's better." Kraal offered a strip of jerky through the wire. The eagle snapped it up in a single bite, then clacked her beak and stared intently at Kraal's coat.

Kraal offered Brynn another piece of jerky from the pouch. "Here. Mind your fingers or she'll take them clean off."

Brynn snorted. "Thanks for the encouragement." Carefully, she offered the stick of jerky through the wire. The eagle snatched it away, tossing her head back to gulp it down.

"That's enough for now," Kraal said. "Brynn, see that wall over there? Grab a glove that fits you, a longer jess, and a large anklet."

Uncertain what those things were, Brynn headed over to the wall. A pegboard had been mounted in the middle, with several items hanging on it. She soon found an elbow-length glove and a small loop, which she assumed was an anklet. After that, she frowned and studied the pegboard, unsure where to find the jess.

"It's just a strap that fastens the anklet to your glove," Kraal called out.

Brynn selected a leather strap, clipped one end to her glove, and fastened the other to the anklet. She returned to the enclosure, watching Kraal withdraw a key and unlock the door. "What do I do?"

"Stick the glove in. She'll hop on."

Hesitantly, Brynn stuck her gloved hand through the door. Just as Kraal had promised, the eagle hopped on. The pressure of her large talons squeezed tight around Brynn's forearm with more power than she'd expected. "Incredible. I had no idea she was so strong!"

"Bring her here."

Brynn withdrew her arm as slowly and carefully as possible. The eagle remained on her forearm, studying her with unblinking yellow eyes. The snow-white feathers behind her head puffed out as she rustled her wings, but she didn't launch herself into the air.

Kraal took the anklet and fastened it around the eagle's leg with a deftness born of practice. "There you go," she cooed, stroking the top of the bird's head with her finger. "Good girl." The eagle's feathers fluffed higher, but she didn't seem to mind the attention.

Brynn followed Kraal out of the mews and into the bright, cold afternoon. She shuddered at the drop in temperature, but the eagle seemed to relish the brisk wind and clear sky. She shifted from foot to foot on Brynn's forearm.

"What do you say, Thas'dun?" Brynn asked. "Want to stretch your wings?"

The eagle gave a full-body shiver from head to tail.

"She's aligning her feathers," Kraal said. "Unclip the jess and give her a short toss. Don't worry, she's well trained. She won't fly off without instructions."

Brynn dropped her arm, then jerked it upward. The eagle launched from her glove with a heavy push, flapping her powerful wings and rising into the sky. Once she was high enough, she flattened her wings and sailed in a wide circle. Her wheeling cry rose above the wind as she soared above them. Brynn's heart rose as well. She grinned, a sense of elation bubbling within her.

"Marvelous, isn't she?" Kraal said.

Brynn knew it was rude, but she didn't look over at Kraal. She couldn't stop watching the small, dark speck that spiraled overhead. "Absolutely. It's hard to believe anyone can 'own' a creature like that, especially not me. She could fly away and live her life in freedom if she wanted."

Kraal laughed. "She enjoys food far too much for that, but you're right. You can't own a creature like her. She stays because she wants to. Because she enjoys being here. The food, the work, the training. Something most elves don't understand."

Something in Kraal's voice finally made Brynn look away from the eagle. She stared up at Kraal's stony gray face and into her dark eyes. "I suppose not, in your experience."

"Hmm." Kraal scratched her chin. "Perhaps I misspoke. Perhaps it's something most snow elves don't understand."

Brynn shrugged. "I understand why you phrased it that way."

Kraal's brown eyes settled on Brynn, but a subtle smile made the stare seem curious rather than judgmental or threatening. "You come from a community of Druids, don't you? Wise elders who show you how to live in harmony with the land? That isn't so different from frost giant communities."

"It does sound similar." Brynn returned Kraal's smile with a hesitant one of her own. Maybe she was more connected to this newly discovered part of her heritage than she'd assumed. "Could I ask you for some advice?"

Kraal's brows rose. "About?"

"I intend to return those northern holdings Valis 'gave' me"—Brynn
made quotation marks with her fingers—"to the frost giants who live
there. Simple in theory... complicated in practice. I'd hate to leave a
power vacuum that makes things worse, or shut down any systems in
place that the residents use..."

Kraal's smile fell away, her stare becoming brighter and more
intense.

Brynn's voice trailed off. Silence stretched between them for
several long moments.

"You were serious about that?" Kraal said after what felt like years.

"Of course," Brynn said. "Anyway, I know what I have to do. What's
right. But I don't know how other than signing some meaningless
papers. Do you know anyone who could advise me? Even better, some
frost giants I could put in charge of the process?"

Kraal gave a slow blink, her expression thoughtful. "Some frost
giants would be furious at the thought of a Stoneskin giant advising you
in this. Many of my kind see my mother's people as traitors." She
sighed. "But I do know someone. A priestess, Gruush. She is the
custodian of the largest frost giant temple in Winterwail, with many
connections in the north."

Brynn's ears perked. "Would you introduce me? Please. I need to
do this."

Before Kraal could answer, the eagle swooped back down. She
landed on Kraal's shoulder, nipping lightly at the frost giant's ear.
"Away, nasty bird," Kraal huffed, swatting at the eagle until she
dismounted. "And I was just bragging about how well trained you are.
Try that on an elf ear and it'll be bitten in half, you scoundrel. Brynn,
hold out your glove."

Brynn extended her arm. The eagle landed on her glove, staring at
her expectantly. Kraal laughed and withdrew another piece of jerky.
Brynn gave the jerky to the eagle, who threw back her head and
swallowed the meat in a single gulp.

"Give her enough of that," Kraal said, "and you'll never find a more
loyal friend."

Brynn grinned. "Glad you know the secret to her heart." She licked
her dry lips, then added, "I like Thas'dun for her name. It's grown on

me."

"Wouldn't you prefer to name her yourself?" Kraal asked.

"It feels right." Brynn studied the eagle, who lowered her neck into her shoulders as though settling in for the duration. "You and I are going to be good friends. Right, Thas'dun?"

Thas'dun blinked her large yellow eyes in apparent understanding. Something like peace swelled in Brynn's heart. Her relationship with Valis was... complicated, but she had several other things to be getting on with. Things that would be easier with friends.

* * * * *

Brynn would have preferred to stay outside until nightfall, but eventually, the biting cold and her own weariness got the better of her. It was only with gentle prodding from Kraal that she surrendered to exhaustion. She returned Thas'dun to the mews and went back inside the palace, unsure whether a warm bowl of soup or a long nap should be the first order of business.

The desire for a nap won out.

"Blackspine poison is no joke," she told Kraal, holding the railing tight as they went up the rear servants' stairs. "My legs feel wobbly as a brand new fawn's in spring."

Kraal made a sympathetic noise but didn't offer Brynn her arm. Brynn appreciated that. No doubt Kraal would leap to her assistance if she asked, but the frost giant seemed to understand that Brynn's pride would be wounded.

Grandmother would call me an idiot. Asking for help doesn't make you weak, she'd say.

"Give me a hand please, Kraal?"

Kraal took Brynn's arm in her enormous hand. Despite the sheer size of her fist, her grip was gentle as she encouraged Brynn to lean against her. They made it up the stairs sooner than they would have if Brynn had continued struggling alone.

"You should get some rest," Kraal said. "I might have taken you outside too soon. Blackspine is particularly poisonous to elves. Even the smallest dose can fell the strongest of your kind. In fact, I'm surprised it didn't. Glad, but surprised."

Brynn's brow furrowed. "I don't suppose frost giants are immune?"

"Not immune, but resistant. Why?"

"Just curious." Brynn let go of Kraal and opened the door to her chambers. Everything was just as she'd left it. *I guess Valis didn't stop by to see me, although she might not leave any sign if she did.*

Swallowing her disappointment, Brynn began the arduous process of shucking her cap, gloves, scarf, and coat. Far too tired to put them away in their proper places, she left them in a haphazard pile on the couch, then sat down to pull off her sealskin boots.

"What's this?" Kraal said from somewhere beside her.

Brynn looked up. Kraal stood beside the couch, staring down at the coffee table. She followed Kraal's gaze. "Oh, those? Valis thought I'd enjoy some light reading while on bedrest." She snorted through a smile. The stack of books certainly wasn't light reading by her standards.

"No, I mean this." Kraal picked up a thin book, which seemed out of place amongst the thick, dusty tomes. She opened it, flipping through the illustrated pages.

Brynn frowned. She recognized the book's cover from several weeks ago, and doubted Kraal would appreciate its contents. "You might not want to read that one. It's trash about how the snow elves colonized the north. From their perspective, of course. I'm sure Valis didn't mean to include it..."

Her voice trailed off as Kraal held the book open, bringing it close to her face and staring intently. An awkward silence stretched between them, but Kraal's face didn't twitch. Aside from her look of unbroken concentration, it gave no hint as to her emotions.

"Kraal?"

"Look here." Kraal lowered the book to Brynn's eye level, pointing to an image that spanned two pages.

The illustration was dark and stormy, made of restless gray shadows that billowed across the paper like rain clouds. There was a mysterious but undeniable sense of movement to the ink on the paper. A smooth, silver oval glowed in the center of the picture, shining bright within the surrounding blacks and grays. The way it shimmered made Brynn wonder which materials the artist had used to produce such a striking effect.

As she unfocused her eyes, the shadowy clouds gathered into a recognizable shape: a massive dragon wreathed in smoke. Its hooked claws curled around the silver oval in a possessive grip. Above, its glowing blue eyes seemed to brighten, then dim like flickering candles.

"Hadronax," Kraal whispered.

Brynn looked up. "What was that?"

"Hadronax," Kraal repeated, her brown eyes wide and shining with emotion. "Last of the great frost wyrms. Long ago, we worshiped them as gods. Some of us still do." She pressed her lips together, her eyes darting back down to the page. "Unfortunately, the snow elves hunted them to extinction many years ago."

"That's fucked up." Brynn shook her head, feeling a sorrowful ache in her chest. "It's awful when any creature is hunted to extinction. Not to mention destroying something of such religious importance."

"Yes," Kraal said, "but look closer. What do you see in the middle of the page?"

Brynn squinted at the shining oval. At first, she saw only its unusual sheen, but then she noticed shining white lines that crawled along its surface. She gasped. Could the parchment be enchanted, like the blood-activated summons she'd received? She focused on the wavering white lines, trying to make some sense of their pattern, but any potential meaning escaped her.

"Looks like some kind of symbol, but I don't recognize it. Do you?"

Kraal leaned closer, pinching her chin between thumb and forefinger. "It's a frost giant rune. An old one, unless I miss my guess. Unfortunately, I have no idea what it might mean."

Brynn chewed her lip. "What about that priestess you mentioned earlier? Gruush, right? Would she know?"

"Possibly." Kraal straightened, smoothing the wrinkles from her shirt. "But you should finish recuperating first." Her brows drew together over narrowed eyes, with what looked to Brynn like uncertainty.

"I feel fine," Brynn said. The initial spark of curiosity had caught within her, growing into a steady and persistent flame. Even the backs of her ears itched, as they did when she couldn't put a finger on what was bothering her. There was definitely something strange, perhaps even magical, about the illustration. "I've got a strange feeling about this. I can't explain it exactly, but I know it's important somehow. Grandmother calls it spider skin. It feels like they're crawling down your spine."

Kraal folded her arms. "I agree. There's something strange here, but it will keep a few more days. The mystery is interesting, I'll admit, but not urgent."

Brynn's head snapped up. The crawling sensation spread out from her spine, sending a shudder through her body and raising the hairs along her arms. The illustration wasn't simply interesting, as Kraal had said. Something about it burrowed into her brain, a fuzzy connection that hovered just out of reach. She was no Darrow, who'd been blessed with more than a touch of the Sight, but she had a hunter's instincts. She knew which game trails were worth pursuing.

"But Kraal—"

Kraal shook her head. "The first and only time you went into the city, we were attacked. Now, someone may be trying to take your life. If they're determined to do so, they won't stop at poison. Leaving the safety of the palace could allow them to try again."

"Then I'll ask Valis," Brynn blurted out. "She can provide some sort of protection." She felt a pinch of regret as soon as she made the suggestion. Asking Valis meant talking to her, which meant they'd likely have to address what they'd done. A very embarrassing prospect.

"I am your protection," Kraal said. "I'm under orders from Her Majesty to make sure you stay safe."

"Is that why you spent the day with me?" Brynn's ears drooped and a twinge of sadness shot through her chest. "Silly me. I thought we were becoming friends."

"We can be friends," Kraal said, "but I wouldn't let a friend wander the city days after being poisoned. Be patient, Brynn. I'll see about summoning Gruush here, to the palace. She might refuse, but it's worth a try. Or I could show her the book myself."

"Come on, Kraal," Brynn huffed. "Don't cut me out. I'm bored to tears in here! Today was the first fun I've had since the incident." Her cheeks grew suddenly hot as she reflected on that statement, but she told herself it was with justifiable frustration. Definitely not the other 'fun' she'd stumbled into with Valis. That didn't count anymore, considering the sour aftertaste.

"The 'incident'? You mean the attempt on your life?" Kraal said. "This is a bad idea, Brynn. I promise to keep you updated if I learn anything more."

Brynn opened her mouth but closed it again. Kraal's infamous stony expression had returned, shutting down any attempts at argument. Brynn knew her protests would be ignored. Better to figure out some other way. Perhaps going directly to Valis was the right idea after all.

"Fine," she grumbled. "I see your point." Then, she added a grudging, "Thank you for introducing me to Thas'dun and spending the afternoon with me. We should do it again, sometime." Annoyed as Brynn was, she acknowledged Kraal had been good company and didn't want their outing to end on a bad note.

Kraal's smile returned for a fleeting moment. "You're welcome. The two of you should be fast friends in no time."

"I hope so." Brynn's mind was already elsewhere, putting together her argument for Valis. Hopefully, she'd feel guilty enough about leaving Brynn alone in the bed they'd shared to grant her request.

Chapter Seventeen

VALIS SAT BEHIND THE desk in her study, elbow braced and chin in hand, gazing at a portrait of Queen Ruith which hung above the fireplace. Her doleful gray eyes stared back in silence, realistic enough to give Valis the sensation of being watched.

Normally, Valis enjoyed the portrait. Bouts of grief flared up on occasion, like a hot spring's steam bubbling up through the ice, but the portrait also made her feel as though her mother was looking out for her, whether from within Aefbain or through the Veil.

Today, Queen Ruith's gaze seemed colder, more judgmental. Valis knew it was a reflection of her own feelings. Her mother wouldn't have begrudged her affections for her own consort. She would have seen it as an unexpected but positive benefit, but Valis couldn't keep from judging herself anyway.

It wasn't that Brynn was a wood elf. It wasn't that she came from a place most snow elves would consider the back end of nowhere. It wasn't her forthright manner of speech, nor her ignorance and disdain for courtly affairs and certain ancient traditions. No. Love was simply too much of a risk.

Valis blinked, realizing she'd dropped her gaze from the portrait to the dancing flames in the fireplace. She'd been imagining Brynn's face: the lopsided smile and its dimples, the square jaw, tight coils of brown hair, sparkling green eyes...

She tore her gaze away from the fire. "So what if I do love her?" she asked the portrait. "Feelings can be managed." She knew that all too well, though some, like grief, tended to linger. Her loss gave her hope, however. She'd always carry a scar, but she was functional now. A proper queen who attended to her duties. Surely a love wound would close faster than the death of her family.

You do realize you're speaking to a portrait? Aefbain said from the desk. Valis had placed the dagger there, sheathed in its scabbard.

Valis glared down at Aefbain. "Precisely. I was speaking to a portrait. Not you. It is extremely rude to interrupt a conversation that does not include you."

Talking to yourself does not qualify as a conversation.

Valis lifted her chin from her hand and leaned back heavily in her chair. "What more do you want from me, Aefbain? I'm following your advice, but I'm not a cold, unfeeling block of ice. I'm a living being. These things take time. Not that you would understand."

I do understand. How quickly you forget that I have absorbed all the wisdom of your ancestors.

"I haven't seen her in four days—"

Four entire days! Would you like a medal for your incredible show of restraint?

"That's enough." Valis took Aefbain and threw it into her desk drawer with a clatter.

Valis, don't—

Valis slammed the drawer shut and stood up from her chair. Being without Aefbain always left her feeling somewhat naked and vulnerable, but there was only so much ancestral oversight she could withstand.

She ignored Aefbain's muffled curses at the edges of her mind, regarding the portrait of her mother once more. "I have no idea know how you dealt with it for so long."

A tentative knock upon the door caused Valis to start. She reached instinctively for her thigh, then remembered Aefbain was in the drawer. She relaxed and turned away from the portrait. "Enter."

The door opened.

Valis expected to see Kraal or Delia. The sight of Brynn's lithe form filling out a white fur vest and silk trousers made Valis' heart thump faster. It was far too easy to remember how Brynn looked entirely naked, all those lean muscles and bronze skin...

Outwardly, Valis kept her expression as neutral as possible. "Good afternoon, Consort Woodwarden. This is an unexpected pleasure."

"Good afternoon." Brynn didn't bow or offer her palms, but she did remove her fur-lined cap and hold it in front of her, revealing a crown of neat braids atop her head.

Valis swallowed around a dry lump in her throat. She decided a compliment might ease the tension. "Your hair looks lovely. Have you found a suitable stylist, or did your mother do the braids? I hope it means that you're feeling better."

Brynn offered a small smile. "The stylist Delia hired is wonderful, but my mother did these. She... well, hovers."

"Understandable. On that topic, I believe I have convinced her to stop tasting all your food for poison. However, she insists on overseeing its preparation, much to the annoyance of my chefs. I fear that is the extent of my persuasive abilities, for now."

Brynn shrugged helplessly. "Mom's always been stubborn. I come by it honestly."

Valis managed a smile of her own. Perhaps losing Brynn wouldn't be like losing her family. Unlike her mother and sister, Brynn was still very much alive and present. Here they were, having a casual conversation. Never holding or kissing someone again wasn't the same as grieving their death, even though it might feel that way sometimes.

"In some situations, stubbornness can be a tremendous asset," she said to Brynn. "Now, is there something I might assist you with? An update on our investigation into the Rot, perhaps? Our attempts to find the poisoner?"

She immediately wished she hadn't mentioned either prospect. There wasn't any progress to speak of on either front, but now she'd probably gotten Brynn's hopes up. She'd simply been desperate to discuss an item of business instead of... other things. To justify their conversation in some way.

"Of course." Brynn took a few steps closer. "If there are any updates you can give me."

A chill crawled down Valis' spine, but her face warmed as she looked at Brynn's hands, still holding the fur cap. She tried and failed not to remember how the archer's calluses felt against her skin.

"Kraal and the First Apothecary's apprentices took stock of our herb stores. There was no blackspine missing, but someone dipped into the supply of silverleaf, likely to conceal the poison's taste. That leads me to believe the assassin may work within the palace. A frightening prospect."

Brynn's smile fell. "That's... yeah. Not good. But Kraal's looking into it? I trust her. She's been helping me with Thas'dun."

Valis arched a brow. "Thas'dun?"

A wider, more genuine smile spread across Brynn's face. Valis noted, then dismissed a slight twinge in her chest that couldn't possibly be jealousy. "The snow eagle. She's a marvelous bird. She's also a good excuse to go outside and rebuild my strength."

Valis' heart sank. "You really shouldn't overexert yourself." She justified the serpent's knot that coiled in her belly as concern for a woman who had become something like a friend to her, rather than a lover.

Brynn's expression sharpened into a glare. "With all due respect, Your Majesty, I feel comfortable assessing my own body's limits."

Valis squared her shoulders. *We're back to Your Majesty, are we?* "So long as you follow Bloodtender Horys' advice."

"I'm actually feeling much better."

Valis hid a frown. Brynn was right. She came by her stubbornness honestly. "I'm simply concerned for your welfare."

Brynn shoved her cap in her pocket and folded her arms across her chest. She shifted her weight back onto one hip, regarding Valis coolly. "Really?"

No. The unpleasant pull at her gut and the tightening of her throat definitely weren't guilt. She had nothing to feel guilty for, except perhaps delaying this conversation about the status of their relationship, such as it was. "Yes, I am. I consider you a friend."

Brynn drummed her fingertips above her left elbow. "Friends don't leave each other alone in bed after making love without so much as a kiss goodbye or a note."

Valis resisted the impulse to squirm when Brynn said *making love.* It was so much easier to define what had happened between them as simple sex, but denial would only delay her efforts to move past the incident. "I apologize for putting distance between us without speaking to you first."

Brynn uncrossed her arms and dropped her hands to her sides. She stared at Valis with wide, curious eyes. "I wasn't expecting an apology," she said in a much softer voice. "Queens don't usually admit when they're wrong... I assume. You're the only one I've ever met."

Valis sighed. "We have always been straightforward and honest with each other, haven't we? I physically enjoyed what happened between us, and I would hate for you to think otherwise, but..."

"You weren't ready," Brynn said slowly, as though tasting the shape of the words on her tongue. She paused for a beat, a thoughtful furrow forming on her brow. "You don't need to explain, Valis. I get it."

It took an effort of will to maintain eye contact with Brynn rather than dart away in shame. "I may never—" She steeled herself. She had nothing to be ashamed of. This was the correct choice. "I will never be ready, Brynn. My position is too important. I have a duty to this kingdom and the people in it that I cannot ignore in favor of a selfish interpersonal relationship."

"Selfish interpersonal relationship?" Brynn stared at her, chin drawn back as though to put more distance between them, mouth partway open in disbelief or perhaps disdain. "Is that really how you feel about what happened between us?"

"Yes." It was Valis' turn to fold her arms, long sleeves rustling in response to her irritation. "I appreciated your willingness to comfort me in a moment of weakness, but I have my position to consider."

Brynn scowled. Her hands balled into fists at her sides. "And slumming it with me would get in the way. I see."

Valis didn't hide her frown this time. "I am completely serious, Brynn. This is not about you—"

"Not to be crude, *Your Majesty,* but don't pull that shit with me. What happened to being honest with each other? You're running away. I know you felt something when we were together."

Something sharp and urgent tugged at Valis' heartstrings, but she ignored the painful sensation. She drew upon the calm demeanor she had practiced over the years, behaving in a way she hoped would make her mother proud. She would not respond to Brynn's anger, however justifiable, with more spite. "This isn't personal. My duties to my station and my people must always come first."

Brynn snarled, showing a flash of white teeth beneath her curled upper lip. "Right. It isn't personal at all. You're Queen of Winterwail and I'm just the peasant who won the magic blood lottery. How could I have forgotten?"

"I—" Valis paused, then sighed. Better to move on as quickly as possible. "Was there something you needed, or did you simply desire an apology for my actions?"

Some of Brynn's anger faded in favor of a more serious expression. She remained physically distant, but a little of the spite faded from her voice. "Actually, there is something. Remember that children's book I found in the library?"

Valis recalled the day she and Brynn had discussed magic lessons in the library. "The one with the offensive illustrations of the frost giants?

Yes, I remember it."

"Well, it somehow got mixed in with the books you lent me." Brynn rolled her eyes. "Unless you decided I would enjoy some snow elf propaganda as a little light reading before bed."

"Definitely not," Valis said. "That book is horrid."

"Regardless, Kraal found it."

Valis' frown deepened. "I hope she didn't take offense."

"No. She noticed a secret frost giant rune hidden in one of the illustrations." Brynn's voice rose in volume and her eyes burned with a sense of purpose. "She didn't know what it said, but she knows someone who might—Gruush, a frost giant priestess in the city."

"That is unusual," Valis said. "I have no idea why that might be. As for Gruush..." She knew of Gruush by reputation. Not a loyal subject of the Aefbain dynasty by any means, but she didn't advocate purposeless violence either, against elves nor frost giants. Not like Murta and her followers. "I'm still uncertain why such a small mystery matters to you, but I see no harm in allowing Kraal to show Gruush the rune."

"Actually, I'm going to ask her in person."

Valis did a double take, uncertain she had heard correctly. "Sorry, did you say you wanted to speak with Gruush yourself?" From the stubborn look Brynn gave her, that was exactly what she'd said. "Surely you understand why that isn't possible while someone is trying to kill you?"

"Or you," Brynn said.

"Either way, you are in grave danger. Are you truly that bored here?"

"Yes," Brynn said, "but it's more than that. I got spider skin when I looked at it."

Valis wrinkled her nose. "Spider skin?"

"You know. When you get this strange, urgent feeling that something is important." Brynn gestured outward with her hands, as though trying to make Valis see something invisible between them. "Part of you just knows it's connected to something larger and you have to see it through. Grandmother says spider skin is never wrong. It runs in our family."

Valis sighed. "I sympathize with your curiosity, but the fact remains that it is far too dangerous for you to venture into the city. Send Kraal.

She already knows Gruush, who may not even agree to speak with an elf."

"I'm not a snow elf."

"But you are Royal Consort Woodwarden."

"Who's about to return a bunch of stolen land to the people who lived there first. How is that going, by the way? Or is your desire to begin reparations all talk and no action?" The dash of bitterness in the question was unmistakable.

"Too slowly," Valis said, refusing to rise to the bait. "Galesha and Fayeth keep rescheduling the meeting wherein they are to approve the frost giant leaders we are consulting."

Brynn scoffed. "Why do they need to approve the people in attendance? Just make a list and stick to it."

"It isn't that simple..."

"Yes it is," Brynn insisted, throwing up her hands. The line of her shoulders went tense and rigid. "It is that simple, Valis! Look. I know your ancestors did this, not you, but you know it's the right thing to do. You need to fix their mistakes. You agreed when I said I wanted to do this. Also, you aren't the boss of me! I can go into the city and speak to whoever I want."

Valis raised her chin high. "I am Queen of Winterwail, so in all respects, I *am* the boss of you. Right now, you sound like a petulant child who won't eat your snow leeks. I will summon my advisers first thing tomorrow, because you do make a valid point about this process being too slow, but you absolutely will *not* disregard your safety and the stability of my kingdom."

"Why do you even care about my safety?!" Brynn closed the gap between them so rapidly that Valis almost started. Suddenly, Brynn was in her face, nearly nose to nose, close enough for Valis to feel the warmth of her breath. She couldn't help but stare into Brynn's burning green eyes and face the fury within them. "You said our night together meant nothing, so what does my safety matter? Or are you just afraid of losing your *precious* blood bag?"

"Your safety does matter to me, but so does your blood." She refused to draw back. "I wouldn't have gone through all the trouble of finding you if I didn't need it."

Brynn's glare never wavered. "But I bet you wish my blood was in someone else's veins. Face it. You're ashamed of me. You let yourself slip up once, but then you remembered who I am. Unfortunately for you, I also know who I am, and I'm not the kind of person who takes orders from someone who doesn't even respect me."

Valis remained perfectly still, a cold and unfeeling block of ice before the emerald fire of Brynn's stare. "If you are determined to throw yourself at your assassins, it's obvious you don't even respect yourself. How would your mother feel if she knew you were doing this?"

Brynn recoiled—only a few inches, but Valis claimed the victory. "Don't bring my mother into this!"

"This is your foolish idea," Valis said. "I'm merely warning you of the consequences. If the possibility of your own death and the potential destruction of a kingdom isn't enough to dissuade you, perhaps the thought of your mother losing her only remaining child will put some sense back into you."

"How *dare*—" Brynn spluttered, too furious for words.

Normally, Valis enjoyed winning arguments. This one was different. She felt terrible and awful and cruel. *No. It had to be done.* "You will see sense and thank me once you calm down. I think this conversation is over."

"It isn't over." Brynn whirled and stormed toward the door, pausing only to toss one final caustic remark over her shoulder. "And you still aren't the boss of me!" She threw the door open, stomped through, then slammed it shut behind her.

Valis waited to make sure Brynn wouldn't bluster back into the study, then sighed heavily, pinching the bridge of her nose. "Well. That went even worse than expected."

What did you expect? Aefbain drawled, its voice somewhat muffled even in her mind. *She's only a wood elf.*

"Keep your silence for once in your miserable existence, you vile thumbtack," Valis hissed, scowling at the desk. "My problem with Brynn isn't her heritage. It's that she's a stubborn mule with a head harder than a boulder! Besides, you picked her."

A choice that may have been a mistake, in retrospect.

"I thought the high and mighty Aefbain didn't make mistakes? Oh, I remember now. You carry the 'wisdom' of my ancestors... the same ancestors who stole from and nearly decimated an entire civilization.

Brynn may be an idiot, but she's right about one thing. Why do I even listen to your nonsense? I'm honestly ashamed it took her nudging me to take some kind of action."

She stormed out of her study before Aefbain could have the satisfaction of responding, unsure where she was going, but knowing she couldn't stay in its presence any longer. She hurried from the room, without slamming the door. She wouldn't stoop to that level of childishness, at least.

I should warn Kraal. If Brynn sneaks off to visit Gruush—which she definitely will—someone should make sure she doesn't get herself killed, or all of this will be for nothing.

* * * * *

Brynn pulled up her fur-lined hood and strode through the northwest rear gate with confidence. Sneaking out of the palace was simpler than she'd anticipated. She held her breath as she passed the frost giant guards, then exhaled when they didn't stop her. Without a clear view of her face, they probably assumed she was a servant going about her duties.

Beyond the palace walls, it was easy to lose herself in the city. The crowd was thick, winding through the narrow streets like a slow-moving river, swollen after a rainstorm. Snow elves, frost giants, humans, and more mingled in ways they didn't within the palace. Her short height was little help as she struggled to navigate the sea of busy people. She had to twist her shoulders and sidestep several times to avoid collisions.

Once Brynn decided she'd gone far enough to relax her guard, she realized she had no idea where Gruush's temple was. All she had was Kraal's description of a large temple in the city center. Since the palace was already near the middle, she edged toward a clearer patch of street between two shops and scanned her surroundings.

Her eyes locked onto a tall iron spire some short distance away. Higher than the surrounding buildings, a jutting black spike pierced the muted gray sky. The use of iron caught her attention. The royal palace was made of magically preserved ice. Without such magic at their disposal, frost giants had to use different building materials. She steeled herself and braved the crowded street again, heading for the spire.

Up close, the building was even more impressive. Three triangular roofs were stacked on top of each other, with the largest at the bottom.

They had some of the steepest slopes Brynn had ever seen, likely to prevent snow buildup. Tall, stone columns lined the lowest level, surrounding the temple on all sides.

As Brynn approached, she saw that the columns were carved in the likeness of frost giants. She paused, craning her neck to admire the workmanship. Their faces were molded into peaceful expressions, but their raised arms bulged with muscle, seeming to hold the upper floors aloft.

Something about their poses stirred a warm feeling of reverence within Brynn's chest. The statue columns reminded her of Grandmother's teachings. All wood elf knowledge, both Druidic and practical, grew from the roots their ancestors had planted eons ago. Based on this design, modern frost giant culture and traditions quite literally rested on the backs of their ancestors.

"No tours today."

A low, gruff voice interrupted Brynn's solemn admiration. She turned toward the source and saw an old frost giant woman stooped beneath a heavy, fur-lined cape. Even with a bent back and leaning on a carved walking stick, she stood quite a bit taller than Brynn. The woman peered at Brynn with dark, narrow eyes.

"That's a beautiful piece of work, madam," Brynn replied in common. She nodded toward the woman's staff. Flowing runes wound around the length of the staff like a serpent, spiraling up toward the knobby tip. "Grandmother carries something similar. Bet it's positively ancient."

The woman's lips remained in a stiff line, barely moving as she spoke. "Two centuries old. You aren't a snow elf, are you, love?"

Brynn lowered her hood, tucking a stray lock of hair behind her ear. "Wood elf. And possibly part frost giant, as I've recently discovered...in the very distant branches of my family tree."

The woman pulled her bony shoulders back, straightening slightly. She studied Brynn even more intently, causing Brynn's face to flush at such close scrutiny. "Must be part human as well, then. That why you've come all this way? If you're looking for answers, I'm afraid you'll be disappointed." A shadow flickered over the woman's face, like a brief flinch of pain. "Most of the oldest written records were destroyed. Had to be reconstructed from oral recitations."

"I'm sorry to hear that, but I'm not here for genealogy research." Brynn licked her lips. "I know this sounds strange, but I found a frost giant rune hidden in a picture book. When I saw it, I got the feeling it was important. My friend Kraal—she works at the palace—told me to inquire with a priestess named Gruush."

"Kraal, eh? Yes, I know her." The woman gestured toward the stone steps leading up to the large front doors. "Come with me and we'll bother Gruush."

Brynn chuckled. "Well, I don't want to bother her, but if you say so..."

"Trust me, she'll appreciate the interruption. She despises cleaning. Name's Madge, by the way." Madge's dark eyes twinkled as she hobbled toward the steps, leaning on her stick. "Gruush happens to be my daughter."

"I'm Brynn, and I'm lucky to have run into you. Lead the way, my good Madge."

Brynn offered Madge her elbow, but due to the height difference, ended up with a knobby hand on her shoulder instead. She allowed Madge to lean on her as they went up the steps and through the large iron doors, which stood open to reveal the temple's interior.

It was much brighter inside than Brynn expected. Warm torches lined every wall, and candles flickered everywhere. The pleasant smell of incense and burnt offerings drifted into Brynn's nose. All three floors were connected through open ceilings, with wide balconies following every wall. A large skylight dominated the middle of the roof, allowing sunbeams to brighten the stone floor.

Brynn lowered her gaze to admire the first floor. A giant hearth dominated the rear wall, surrounded by shag rugs and stone furniture covered in fur blankets. Long tables took up the rest of the space. It looked more like a dining hall than any sort of religious space Brynn had ever seen, although she had little to compare it with. Druids worshiped in the wilds, with the earth itself as their temple.

"It feels like a cozy house, but huge," she murmured.

"That's exactly what it is," said Madge. "The temple is everyone's home. Eating, sleeping, and socializing together is part of our worship as well as our culture."

Brynn nodded. "And the skylight?"

Madge gazed up at the patch of light-gray sky above them. "It's difficult to connect with nature in the city, especially a city like Winterwail. The least we can do is remember to look at the sky above us and pay our respects."

"Who have you got there, Mother?" A low, feminine voice came from a stairwell leading to the second floor. "Not harassing some poor tourist again, I hope?"

Brynn turned to see a tall, wiry frost giant with stark, white hair and intricate patterns shaved into the close-cropped sides of her head. The rest fell in a long braid that reached the base of her spine. Her size might have been intimidating on its own, but her face was soft and friendly. She smiled warmly at Brynn, and Brynn made sure to smile back.

"Not harassing," she said. "You must be Gruush. Your mother's been quite helpful, actually."

Gruush looked Brynn up and down. "That's because you're a wood elf. She likes Druids. Not that we see many around here."

"Oh, I'm no Druid," Brynn said. "Just a humble archer." *And Winterwail's Royal Consort.* She swallowed hard. The skin on the back of her neck prickled. She felt as though she were lying by omission, but it definitely wouldn't help her cause and might very well harm it.

Gruush descended the steps and stuck out her hand. Brynn clasped her forearm and squeezed. Gruush's hand completely swallowed her narrow wrist. "And what brings you here, humble archer?"

"Her name's Brynn," Madge said. "She's come to show you a picture book."

Gruush's brows rose. "A what?"

"A picture book," Madge repeated, smirking. "Thought you'd find it more interesting than sweeping."

"Anything's more interesting than that," Gruush said. "But why?"

Brynn shrugged off her pack and withdrew the picture book. "It's pretty vile, as a warning—but I found a frost giant rune hidden in one of the pictures. My friend Kraal couldn't translate it. She suggested you might be able to help." She flipped through the pages, searching for the illustration of the dragon and the shining orb within its claws.

Gruush circled to stand behind Brynn's shoulder, peering down at the book.

Brynn lifted the book so Gruush could examine it more comfortably. She tilted the pages, catching the sun streaming down through the skylight. At a certain angle, the spiderweb design in the middle of the orb sparkled and glittered.

Gruush snatched the book from Brynn, bringing it closer to her face and burying her nose between the pages. "Where did you say you got this?"

"The royal library," Brynn said.

Gruush hardly seemed to hear her response. Madge shuffled over, straightening as best she could to examine the illustration. She frowned and shook her head. "This should not exist. Those of us in the priesthood no longer write or record Hadronax's name. There are only images and carvings."

Brynn's ears perked. "Hadronax? That's the name Kraal told me when she saw the picture."

Gruush sighed and closed the book but didn't return it to Brynn. "Hadronax is… was… the great mother of all frost wyrms."

Madge nodded. "Aye. Dangerous, wild, and beautiful. They're all gone now, of course. Snow elves hunted them to extinction. Our people hunted them too, of course—but only for meat, bones, and hide. A single frost wyrm could feed an entire village. They often meant the difference between sustenance and starvation in the leanest times."

"We always showed them the proper respect," Gruush continued. "We only hunted males, never females. Wouldn't want to orphan a clutch of eggs. I can only assume that's what the silver orb represents."

"What about the rune?" Brynn asked.

Gruush hesitated, pursing her lips, but seemed to come to a decision. "Rebirth. The legends say that if Hadronax fell, she would be reborn as an egg. A new life. There are stories of Hadronax offering herself to starving villages in the dead of winter. When they butchered her body, they found an egg within. They kept it safe and warm until a new wyrmling hatched, then released it back into the wild."

Brynn frowned, scratching her neck. Something wriggled in the back of her brain, an insistent thought she couldn't quite grasp. Whenever she tried to get hold of it, the thought slipped further away. "Can I see that book again?"

Gruush averted her eyes. Her hands tightened around the book.

"This must be destroyed. We do not keep written records of Hadronax any longer, only artistic images. It is insulting and blasphemous to hear the great mother's name on snow elf tongues, from the mouths of those who murdered her and her kin."

Before Gruush could protest further, Madge plucked the book from her grasp and handed it to Brynn. "Come now. I'm sure Brynn here will let you have it back. Let her see the picture."

"You can destroy it once we're done." Brynn flipped through the pages. She studied the image again, focusing on the orb—the egg. It glowed faint silver like a waning moon, reminding her of something she'd seen before. Something the Aefbain dynasty had kept buried beneath the ice for centuries.

"Great seasons, it's real!"

Gruush stared at Brynn with wide eyes. "What?" she stammered.

"Hadronax's egg?" Madge asked.

Brynn shoved the book into Gruush's hands. "Do whatever you like with this. Can't explain now." She swung her pack onto her back and turned for the door. "Thanks for all your help. I'll be back with amazing news very, very soon!" She jogged out of the temple, ignoring Gruush and Madge's calls. She needed to speak with Kraal and Valis right away.

There was no doubt in Brynn's mind that Valis, despite her cold and aloof persona, would listen. She'd always seemed sympathetic to the frost giants but hadn't yet found concrete ways to help them—no thanks to her useless advisers. *This could be her chance. Once she knows what she has locked away, I'm sure she'll do the right thing.*

Brynn ran into the street, darting and weaving through the milling crowd outside the shops. She ignored their gasps and dirty looks, heading for the glittering spires of the palace. A sudden, sharp cry sounded behind her. She whirled in time to see Kraal erupt from the tightly packed crowd, then the flash of sunlight on steel.

Something cold and sharp plunged behind Brynn's shoulder blade. She stumbled, hitting the ground palms first. Her vision narrowed to a dark tunnel. She saw only her own hands splayed on the cobblestone street. She reached instinctively for her bow but felt only the hilt of the dagger.

"Don't," Kraal barked. "Leave it in."

Brynn gritted her teeth against the pain and rose to her knees.

Kraal stood nearby, holding a skinny cloaked figure by the throat. Only when she dropped the figure into a heap on the ground did Brynn notice the unnatural angle of their head. Dead, then.

Hot, sticky blood bloomed across Brynn's back, soaking through her shirt. "Did they..."

"I told you not to go anywhere alone," Kraal said. "Luckily, Valis sent me after you."

Brynn coughed. "Hurts. Dizzy..."

Kraal crouched beside Brynn, removing her cloak and widening the tear in her shirt. "You're lucky. This assassin had poor aim—probably because I crushed his windpipe. I think I can remove this without your bleeding out. It's lodged in the muscle."

"You... think...?" Brynn forced a hoarse laugh.

Kraal pulled the dagger out.

Deep, white-hot pain—then a surge of relief. Brynn grunted, exhaling a shaky breath. "No warning?"

"You would have tensed. Hold still. This needs pressure."

Kraal ripped Brynn's caveworm silk cloak into strips, then wound them tight around Brynn's torso as makeshift bandages. The searing pain in Brynn's shoulder became more of an itchy ache. She barely resisted the urge to reach back and feel the injury.

Frightened shouts and frantic murmurs reminded Brynn of where she was—on her knees in the middle of a public street. A sizable crowd gathered around them, forming a circle as Kraal tied off the bandages.

"Quick! Someone call the marshals!"

"—Black Wolf's breath—right here in the street..."

"... saw the whole thing. That fellow on the ground did it."

"Stop that. Get back and give them some room."

"Everyone, back off and go about your business," Kraal barked, straightening to her full height. "The marshals will be here soon. In the meantime, this woman is my charge. I've got the situation under control." She withdrew a golden, ruby-studded dagger from her belt. It was useless as a weapon, but the design reminded Brynn of the dagger in the royal seal, minus the snowflake design.

Another wave of dizziness overcame her. She curled forward, sipping shallow breaths. Each one sent a sharp pang through the stab wound, but the bandages seemed to be helping. She didn't protest when Kraal scooped her up and held her, grateful for the warmth of her body heat and the fur cloak she wore. "Think I might pass out…"

"Stay awake." Kraal shook Brynn lightly, then wrapped her further in the depths of the cloak. "You won't get out of explaining yourself to Valis so easily."

Brynn's stomach twisted. That was a conversation she desperately didn't want to have. She remained still and silent until the marshals arrived and forced the crowd to disperse. Despite the raised voices, stomping of boots, and chaos all around, Brynn remained numb to it all.

The numbness persisted as the marshals cordoned off the street. Thankfully, Kraal refused to entertain their questions. "The palace will handle this," was all she said. "I'm taking Consort Woodwarden there immediately."

Brynn was both grateful and terrified. Grateful to get away, terrified as she imagined the devastated look on Valis' face upon her return. The icy mask Valis wore was just that—a mask. A facade. In a few minutes, she'd have to admit she'd put herself in danger, and had almost made Valis suffer another loss. Strangely, that upset Brynn more than her third recent brush with death. *I hope she doesn't cry because of me.*

Kraal bore her back to the palace, escorted by several armed marshals. Maybe it was the dizzying drop that followed the dramatic spike of fear and pain, but the thought of Valis crying felt worse than being stabbed. Much worse.

Chapter Eighteen

BY THE TIME KRAAL and a growing number of palace guards escorted Brynn to her rooms, she was mostly numb to her pain and well on her way to annoyance. "I'm fine," she told Bloodtender Horys, who arrived so fast that she suspected someone had tipped him off. "I've had worse injuries from the Rotted back home."

Horys opened and closed his mouth several times in what looked to Brynn like a silent stammer. "Forgive me, Consort Woodwarden, but you are most certainly not fine!" he declared in a strangled wheeze. "You left the palace unattended! You were almost killed—"

"Almost is an important word," Brynn grumbled. She turned around so Horys could examine her back. She wanted to cross her arms, but feared the motion would pull the torn muscle behind her shoulder. She hissed as Horys pressed his fingers on either side of the wound.

"For future reference," Horys said, "you should never remove sharp, piercing implements from an injured person without medical supervision."

"Wasn't me," Brynn said. She'd made enough stupid decisions for one day and refused to add to the list.

"I determined it was safe," Kraal said.

Horys huffed. "Well then. Congratulations on your recently completed medical training, Bloodtender Kraal."

Brynn snorted.

Kraal fixed her with a steely stare.

Brynn stifled another pained cough.

"You deserved that for laughing," Kraal said.

"Stop enjoying my pain."

"Trust me. I'm not."

Horys ignored their squabble, mumbling to himself as he probed the edges of Brynn's wound. Uncomfortable, itchy warmth spread behind Brynn's shoulder, flashing hot before subsiding. The lingering discomfort felt like a tender bruise.

"There," Horys said. "Limit the movement of your right arm and drink two of the tea packets on your nightstand at mealtimes. I cleansed the wound, but the last thing we want is an infection. And please, for the love of all those who have passed beyond the Veil, rest! Or I'll have to treat Queen Valis for shock."

"Why?" Brynn narrowed her eyes.

Horys sputtered. "Why? You could have died, that's why! Can you imagine the chaos and disarray your demise would have caused? I beg of you, be more careful."

Brynn glowered but said nothing. She couldn't argue with Horys' logic. Going out had been selfish, spider skin or not.

Her lack of response left Horys less than enthused. "Make sure she follows instructions, Kraal." He softened his nasally voice and said, "You did your queen and kingdom proud today by saving the consort."

The barest hint of a smile twitched across Kraal's lips. "I could do no less, Bloodtender."

"Of course. Now, if you will excuse me, I must inform Her Majesty of Consort Woodwarden's state—"

"Brynn? Brynn!"

Brynn's pointed ears flattened as Isuna burst through the door, holding her skirts with trembling hands. She rushed to Brynn's bedside, throwing herself on the mattress and wrapping Brynn in a tight, choking hug.

"Ow, stop. Take it easy, Mom."

Isuna released Brynn from the hug but seized the tops of her shoulders in a desperate grip. "Brynnflor Woodwarden, you foolish, stubborn—" Tears welled in her wide, green eyes, threatening to spill down her cheeks.

Brynn's stomach snake-squirmed with guilt. "I'm fine. Horys fixed me up, and Kraal stopped the assassin. Didn't you?" She looked from Horys to Kraal, hoping for allies.

"Consort Woodwarden's wound has been dealt with, Madam," Horys said frostily. With a swirl of his long, flowing sleeves and fanciful cape, he left through the door, allowing it to thud behind him.

Kraal folded her arms. She shook her head at Isuna, stone-faced and silent.

Brynn's ears drooped. "I'm sorry, Mom. I shouldn't have gone out alone when I knew someone out there wanted to hurt me..."

"Damn right you shouldn't have." Isuna swiped her sleeve across her leaking eyes. "Please, Brynn. Stay here from now on, where you're safe. I... I simply can't deal with this again. I couldn't go on if—"

Brynn's heart sank. She felt lower than the frozen mud beneath Winterwail's pervasive frost. She dropped her chin, resting her forehead on Isuna's shoulder. "I'm sorry. I didn't think."

Isuna wrapped Brynn in a far gentler hug. "A recurring problem with you, I fear."

Kraal cleared her throat. "Unfortunately, I had to dispatch the person who did this. I would have preferred to question him, but searching his body may reveal some clues. Perhaps even the identity of his employer."

Isuna kissed the top of Brynn's head. "Do you think so, Kraal?"

"It's possible."

"Then do what you need to do. I'll look after Brynn. I won't leave her side."

Brynn sighed, inhaling the familiar, comforting scent of flowers that clung to her mother's neck. She sensed there was no point in arguing. "I won't go anywhere this time," she mumbled, only a bit sulky. "No more sneaking off."

"Good," Kraal said. "You'd best prepare yourself for the incoming blizzard. Valis won't be pleased."

Brynn raised her head. Kraal's frown was deeper than she could ever remember seeing it. "From the look on your face, I suspect that's a massive understatement."

"I'll ignore your rudeness because you got stabbed, but don't expect Valis to feel as sorry for you as I do. The poor woman's been through enough. I wouldn't blame her for being furious." Kraal turned and left the room, though she didn't slam the door as Horys had.

"I'm such an ass," Brynn mumbled.

Isuna rubbed circles on Brynn's lower back. "We only worry about you because we love you."

Brynn choked on her own spit. "What? We?"

Isuna rolled her eyes, their irises still red-ringed with tears. "Please, I'm not blind. Anyway, the best you can do is apologize. The poor girl only lost her mother and sister a short while ago. Miraculously, she found a friend and confidant in you, an arranged marriage partner. Meanwhile, you're off strutting around the city like a fat hen who doesn't know she's due for slaughter."

Brynn scoffed. "Did you seriously call the Queen of Winterwail a poor girl?"

"What an interesting choice of objection, considering all the other things I just said."

"I understand how stupid I was. Really, I do." Brynn's voice rose with excitement. "But I learned something incredible at the temple. There's a frost wyrm egg hidden under the palace!"

Isuna's eyes widened. She sucked in a short gasp. "Aren't frost wyrms extinct?"

"Apparently, not all of them." Brynn hesitated, debating whether to tell her mother the rest of Valis' secret. She'd promised not to breathe a word about the cavern, but in her judgment, the weight of her new discovery overruled that oath. "There's a secret cave underneath the palace, home to a mysterious glowing orb that Valis calls That Which Dwells Beneath The Ice. It's been in a magically induced hibernation for centuries, according to her. I don't think she actually knows what it is. At least, I hope she doesn't."

"Slow down, Brynn. Give me a moment to go through all that." Isuna shook her head slowly, pausing to process the flood of information. Eventually, a wrinkle formed on her brow. "So, she's keeping a sacred beast locked away, possibly without knowing why. Will you tell her?"

"I have to," Brynn said. "She needs to release it. Frost wyrms are sacred to the frost giants. This could be the first step in returning what was stolen from them."

Isuna placed a comforting hand on Brynn's shoulder, squeezing softly. "I'm certain Valis will do the right thing. My opinion is that she's a kind, empathetic person who struggles to navigate the bloody dynasty her ancestors left behind. I think you should trust her."

"I do." Brynn squared her shoulders, staring directly into Isuna's eyes. "But if she won't return the egg to the frost giants, I will, whether she wants me to or not."

* * * *

"I understand your concerns," Valis said to her advisers. As she spoke, she walked the perilous tightrope of calmness and condescension. "This is a large and complicated endeavor. The transition will take some time, but draining *more* wealth and resources from the northern territories in order to improve their local infrastructures will only cause resentment. How are we, living in Winterwail, qualified to decide where those resources are best allocated?"

"Through our ample experience, Your Majesty." Fayeth paused to sip her tea, a choice Valis interpreted as a deliberate show of power. "Some Northern frost giant leaders must be involved in the process, of course, but this is a large financial investment on our part. If the funds *are* to come entirely from the palace treasury, as you have made clear you prefer, we need to make sure it's spent properly. You can't simply throw money at complicated problems like this."

Valis pursed her lips. You can't throw money at problems was a tired adage that only wealthy people believed. Thanks to various relationships she'd built with people from other walks of life, she knew better. Money could, in fact, solve all kinds of problems, and money was one thing she had in ample supply.

"With all due respect, Fayeth, I question your use of the word investment," Galesha said. "I fail to see how this will return any money to the palace coffers. Not that we shouldn't proceed. All Winterwail's people deserve decent living conditions and standards of care, but this is clearly an expense and should be treated as such."

"It may, however, be an investment in our own safety," Naddox drawled. His forearms and long, elaborate sleeves rested on the table with his hands clasped and steepled before him. His steely blue eyes roamed from Fayeth and Galesha to Valis, where they drew her into an intense stare. "Though I hate to bring up such a tragic occurrence, Her Majesty's mother and sister were slaughtered by frost giants who were unsatisfied with the current state of affairs. In their minds, this act of terrorism was entirely justified."

Valis ground her teeth. As usual, Naddox's tone dripped with poisoned condescension. "Murta's followers were lost individuals whose righteous anger had been twisted by Murta into something violent. Of course, I despise them for taking my family from me, but I blame Murta entirely. It only takes one charismatic leader to form a loyal band willing to commit atrocities."

"Quite right, Your Majesty." Without breaking eye contact, Naddox adjusted his sleeves, folding his hands the opposite way. "Yet surely, other Murtas exist. Someone organized the attack on your convoy following your marriage, and someone recently tried to poison either you or Consort Woodwarden. Making an effort to pacify the frost giants might cool certain tempers."

"Naddox makes a good point, Your Majesty," Fayeth said. "How is the investigation proceeding thus far?"

"Thoroughly." No doubt, her advisers would read between the lines and make negative assumptions, but it was the best response she could give without outright lying or showing her annoyance that they'd asked the question to begin with. She let the silence grow, but all three advisers continued watching her expectantly. "Rest assured, I will do whatever it takes to find the person who made these attempts on mine and Consort Woodwarden's lives, and they will be suitably punished."

"But how—" Galesha began, only to stop as the heavy wooden doors creaked open. Valis turned to see Kraal standing in the doorway, accompanied by Bloodtender Horys. In an instant, her blood ran cold. Though they hadn't said a word, she read the dark and stormy looks on their faces. The ice of true fear seeped all the way into the marrow of her bones.

Brynn. Please, please be on this side of the Veil! I don't know what I'll do if you—

"This is outrageous!" Naddox pushed back his chair and stood. He brandished a finger at Kraal and Horys. "How dare you interrupt our meeting without so much as a knock—?"

"This meeting is adjourned." It wasn't really Valis speaking. It didn't feel like her. It was as though the spirit of her mother and ancestors past were guiding her through the motions. Her heart was already out the door, searching for Brynn. "My apologies. We shall reschedule at the earliest opportunity. Do not follow me."

She rose from her chair and strode from the room without a backward glance at her loudly protesting advisers, meeting Kraal and Horys in the doorway. "Walk while you explain." She pushed through, motioning for them to follow. Valis set the briskest possible pace without falling into a run. "Please, tell me she's alive."

"She's alive," Kraal said.

Valis nearly melted with relief.

Horys trotted alongside them, struggling to keep up. "Yes, Your

Majesty, but her condition is—"

"Alive, conscious, and very sorry for sneaking out," Kraal continued for him.

Some of Valis' fear melted into molten anger. "She left the palace unattended?! That hardheaded fool. What was she—"

"Valis, stop," Kraal said.

Valis stopped dead in her tracks. Tears welled in her eyes, threatening to spill down her cheeks, but she couldn't bring herself to care. She looked up at Kraal, waiting.

Kraal flipped her cape back over her shoulder and withdrew something from an inner pocket of her vest. "Someone stabbed her in the street. I dispatched him. When I searched his person, I found this." She handed Valis a folded scrap of parchment.

Valis opened it. The parchment contained a charcoal portrait of Brynn, rendered in considerable detail. "So, they are after her." A lump grew in her throat. Her hand shook as she held the parchment.

"That isn't everything," Kraal said. "Look at the bottom."

Valis looked at the bottom of the parchment and the remnants of a red wax seal. A very familiar type of red ink, with faint but visible traces of a very familiar seal. She would have recognized the edges of the royal snowflake-and-dagger crest anywhere.

"This came from within the palace." She looked from the parchment to Kraal.

"I came as soon as I recognized it," Kraal said. "Do you think it's genuine?"

"There isn't much left, but I recognize the wax too," Valis said.

"That's impossible," Horys squawked. "Who within the palace would want to..." He sputtered. "...I mean... who would dare... regardless of any personal opinions a palace official might hold toward Consort Woodwarden, her assassination would destabilize the entire kingdom!"

Valis ignored him. "Horys, I must speak with Kraal alone. Surely you have other important matters to attend to, such as a treatment plan for Brynn?" Though she phrased it as a question, she pinned Horys with a hard stare to communicate an order.

Horys gaped for a moment but seemed to collect himself. He shoved his round spectacles further up the bridge of his nose and made a deep but perfunctory bow, offering his palms outstretched. "As you wish, Your Highness." He rose and made a swift and awkward departure down the hall.

Valis turned her stare upon Kraal. "Only three people, other than myself, have the use of this particular seal. Even from the remnants, I recognize it."

She took a breath, struggling to swallow around the idea before it left her mouth. It was almost inconceivable, and yet so much had been thrown into chaos since her mother's death. At this point, she trusted no one except Kraal and Brynn.

"It's one of the signet rings my advisers and I wear. Only they may stamp decrees and seals with the Aefbain crest."

Kraal's eyes widened, but she took the news in stride. Or seemed to. It was difficult to tell, since her stony face so rarely relaxed into readable expressions. Valis thought she saw worry in the wrinkling of Kraal's brow. "Do you believe one of your advisers is capable of such treachery?"

Valis shook her head. "I don't know what to believe anymore."

Kraal reached down, placing a heavy, reassuring hand upon Valis' shoulder. "If you believe it's one of them, I believe it too. That would certainly explain the missing silverleaf from our stores. They purchased blackspine outside the palace, but thought nothing of using our herbs to disguise its taste." She paused. "What are you going to do?"

Valis placed her own hand on top of Kraal's larger one, gently brushing it away. She stood taller, sticking out her chin. "There is a reason I am widely acknowledged as the foremost blood mage of my era. If they refuse to confess, I will force a confession out of them. And I know exactly whom to begin with."

Do you, now? Aefbain said from within its hilt against Valis' thigh. She felt its consciousness brush the back of her mind as it stirred from slumber. *Treason is far more interesting than your boring meeting, isn't it? I believe that's what you wanted.*

Believe me, this is the opposite of what I want, but I will do whatever it takes to end this.

Valis drew Aefbain from its scabbard, holding the flat of the blade against her opposite palm. The cold, sharp steel directly opposed her burning rage and bitter hatred toward the one who had tried to kill her wife. The one who had betrayed her, her family, and the entire kingdom of Winterwail. *Fine.* Hot blood made for better spell work.

"Come with me," she said to Kraal, heading back toward the conference room where she'd last spoken with her advisers. "We must pay Lord-Adviser Naddox a visit. Now."

* * * * *

When Valis threw open the conference room doors, she caught all three of her advisers huddled in whispered conversation. As one, they turned to stare at her with startled expressions. Their gazes dropped from Valis' face to her hand, which gripped Aefbain's hilt in a tense, bloodless fist.

Valis scanned their faces, searching for obvious signs of guilt, but saw none. She supposed it was too much to hope for. "Fayeth, Galesha, please leave." Her firm voice left no room for argument. "I must speak with Lord-Adviser Naddox alone."

Naddox blinked but showed only the expected amount of surprise and confusion. "Of course, Your Majesty. May I ask what this is about?"

Valis frowned. If he was indeed guilty, she would relish never again hearing that title drip from his poisoned lips. "No, you may not." She glared at Fayeth and Galesha, daring them to argue. The pair slipped silently from the room without the usual bows and palm proffering.

Once they departed, Kraal closed the heavy wooden doors. She lowered the deadbolt with a soft thud and stood guard, blocking the only exit. She made a show of tapping the base of her staff against the floor stones.

A nervous shadow flickered across Naddox's face. His pointed ears perked, and he pushed his long, white braid nervously over his shoulder. "As always, Your Majesty, I am at your disposal."

Valis withdrew the rolled-up portrait of Brynn from Aefbain's empty scabbard. "Would you care to explain this?"

Naddox leaned forward to study the parchment. "A drawing of Consort Woodwarden? What am I supposed to make of this?"

Valis stared into Naddox's eyes until they darted away. His shoulders tensed with visible discomfort. "This was found on the body of a hired assassin. An assassin who stabbed Consort Woodwarden in the back less than an hour ago."

Naddox gasped and recoiled. "What? Is she—"

"Alive? Yes. Fortunately for you." Without breaking eye contact, Valis tossed the portrait aside and sliced Aefbain across her palm. The dagger glowed red as her blood sank into its blade.

"Your Majesty—"

Valis made a sharp gesture and yanked Naddox into the air. He thrashed and kicked, gagging as though an invisible hand had grasped him by the throat. "Your own life depends on the answer to this question." Valis squeezed Aefbain's hilt. "Did you pay someone to murder my wife?"

Naddox groped for the gilded scabbard at his waist. Valis yanked his arms behind his back with another gesture. Keeping Aefbain extended, she circled calmly around Naddox to remove his scabbard and dagger. "What's that?" she said, tossing them onto the table. "Speak up, Naddox. I can't hear you."

Naddox's eyes rolled wildly, but that was all he managed. If she hadn't taken him by surprise, he might have given her a good fight. Her advisers were dangerous blood mages in their own right, but from the looks of Naddox, he hadn't seen this coming.

The thought gave Valis pause. *If Naddox is guilty, why wasn't he prepared for the possibility that I would find out?* She loosened her grip on Aefbain—and Naddox's throat—ever so slightly. He coughed and wheezed, but continued hovering helplessly in midair, surrounded by the crimson glow.

"I—I didn't... I would never—"

Valis squeezed Aefbain tighter.

Naddox's eyes bulged. His pale-blue face flushed a sickly shade of lavender.

"Brynn is a wood elf and a commoner," Valis snarled. "She sees the twisted tree of our culture down to its blood-soaked roots. Which of these things frightened you more, Naddox? Which angered you enough to commit treason against your queen, to whom you swore an oath of loyalty with your blood?"

"Was...n't...me..." Naddox coughed, more breath and sputter than voice.

Valis rolled her eyes. "Then why is my signet ring stamped into the wax here? There are only four in existence and you've made no secret of your disdain for Brynn."

"Giants…"

"Are you suggesting a coalition of frost giants planned to assassinate Brynn?"

"No, I…h-helping…giants…"

Of all the things Naddox could have said, that was perhaps what Valis least expected to hear. Slowly, she loosened her grip on his throat and lowered him to the floor. "Explain yourself."

Naddox slumped to his knees, catching himself with one hand and rubbing his throat with the other. After several gasping breaths, he croaked out a reply. "I've been in communication with a coalition of frost giants in the north for several years. We all have the same goal, to return their stolen land."

Valis lowered Aefbain. She resisted the temptation to prick herself again and check if she was dreaming. "You want to return the northern holdings to the frost giants?" she repeated, utterly flabbergasted.

Naddox clambered to his feet, nearly tripping over his long silk sleeves. It was the most undignified Valis had ever seen him. "Yes." He attempted to straighten his disheveled robes. "It may be difficult for you to believe—"

"Incredibly difficult," Valis said.

"Understandable," Naddox said. "It was Shalana who audited our meetings with Queen Ruith in preparation for her ascension. You would have no way of knowing which agendas I've pushed for in the past. And when you were crowned instead—"

Valis' eyes went wide. "You… you were playing mind games with me!" she stammered.

Naddox looked Valis up and down with an expression she couldn't quite place. Was that wariness or respect she saw in his blue eyes? "With all due respect, Your Majesty, you are very young. Stubborn, too."

"Go on." Valis tersely attempted to scrounge up what little remained of her dignity.

"Your opinion on current relations between the snow elves and frost giants has never been secret. Neither has your friendship with Kraal, nor your disdain for the royal mantle. From the moment you accepted Aefbain, you made it abundantly clear you were going to do what you wanted, regardless of what your mother's crusty old advisers said."

Valis ground her teeth. The tips of her ears burned with embarrassment. "Why not say so publicly? Why not ally yourself with Brynn? Or me, at the very least?"

Naddox scoffed. "Don't be absurd. Fayeth and Galesha hate Consort Woodwarden. She runs roughshod over everything they hold dear. As for you, Your Majesty, I supported your initiative mere minutes ago, if you may recall. I told Fayeth and Galesha it would be wise to make friendly overtures toward the northern frost giants."

"By using Murta's specter as a thinly veiled threat," Valis said.

"It worked, no? I prefer to serve the end result rather than noble principles."

Valis shoved Aefbain back in its sheath and retrieved Naddox's dagger and belt from the table.

Don't you dare put me away, Aefbain hissed. *Things are really getting interesting. This slimy toad has more brains than I gave him credit for.*

Valis ignored Aefbain's commentary and kept it sheathed. She returned Naddox's dagger with narrowed eyes, curling her fingers into her bleeding palm. Her blood was still there if she needed it. "If you didn't order Brynn's death, who did?"

Cautiously, Naddox took his belt and dagger and affixed them to his person. "With this new evidence you've shown me, I can only assume my colleagues are to blame. As you yourself pointed out, there are only four such signet rings in existence. What fools. They may as well have written *I committed treason* and signed their names."

Kraal stepped forward from her silent post by the door. She tapped one end of her staff against her open palm. "Just so we're clear, you're accusing your fellow advisers of attempted murder and treason? Speak truthfully, elf, or you'll answer to me."

Naddox seemed unperturbed by Kraal's threat. "Their guilt would not surprise me in the least," he said. "Fayeth and Galesha are capable of much worse than you know. I suspect Consort Woodwarden is not the first supposedly problematic person they've attempted to remove from the equation."

"You should have warned me!" Valis snapped.

"How would that look, Valis? Me, informing you—someone who has always loathed me—that your other two advisers are treacherous and untrustworthy? Leaving me as your only adviser in the interim?" Naddox snorted, shaking his head. "I think not."

Valis could only stare, dumbfounded, for several moments. Aefbain was right. Naddox had far more brains than she'd given him credit for. He'd thought this through from every angle, taking her own biases and preconceptions into account. "You called me Valis," she said at last, in a softer and calmer tone.

Naddox frowned. "So I did."

"Do so from now on." Valis straightened and strode purposefully toward the doors. She paused alongside Kraal and glanced back over her shoulder. "Well? Hurry up, Naddox. I ordered those two snakes to leave us while Brynn's alone and injured!"

Naddox's eyes widened. He hurried after Valis as Kraal unbolted the doors. Abandoning all pretense, the three of them ran down the corridor, heading for Brynn's suite.

Chapter Nineteen

AFTER TWENTY MINUTES OF nonstop coaxing, then pleading, then scolding from Isuna, Brynn finally made a fruitless attempt to rest. The fact that Isuna kept reaching over to stroke her hair and hold her hand didn't help, but Brynn hadn't the heart to tell her no. She sensed her mother's pain even with her eyes closed. The squirming serpent of guilt in her gut tied itself in knots, but there was little to be done. All she could do was try and sleep as Isuna had asked.

She actually managed a light doze until the sound of the bedroom door opening roused her. She sat up, wincing as the bandage tugged at her wound, and rubbed her eyes. Three smudged figures entered the room. After a few blurry blinks, Brynn recognized them as Delia and, more surprising, Lady-Advisers Fayeth and Galesha.

Delia looked even more flighty and anxious than usual, rocking forward onto her toes and back again while wringing her hands. Lady-Advisers Fayeth and Galesha wore matching expressions of concern, with deep frowns and furrowed brows.

Brynn forced a smile, ignoring the brief stab of disappointment in her heart. Guess *it was too much to hope that Valis would come see me right away. She's probably too furious to even look at me.*

"Hello, Delia. Lady-Advisers."

Fayeth and Galesha did a brief double take in perfect tandem, blinking faster than usual before adopting terse smiles. Only then did Brynn realize she'd greeted Delia before them. She decided she didn't have the energy to care. Delia was her friend. Valis' advisers weren't.

"Consort Woodwarden." Fayeth clasped her hands before her chest. "What a relief it is to see you awake and responsive. When I heard about the stabbing, I could scarcely believe it!"

"Agreed," Galesha said. "The thought of you being…" She deliberately averted her eyes and heaved a sigh in what Brynn considered an overdramatic show of emotion. "Suffice to say, we are indescribably glad that you're still with us."

Brynn had to work harder at keeping her smile in place. Something was definitely off. She'd expected the advisers to scold her as Horys and Kraal had done, not fawn over her.

"Oh, Brynn!" Delia stopped rocking and rushed over to the bed, pausing only long enough to make sure she threw her arms around Brynn in a way that wouldn't touch her back. "My heart nearly stopped when I heard. Are you all right? What did Horys say?"

Brynn patted Delia's back awkwardly. Her reaction was unquestionably genuine, although she squeezed too tight for comfort. "I'm fine, Delia. No worries. The guy who did it is dead."

"But what if someone else tries?" Delia drew back, peering worriedly into Brynn's face. Her brown eyes shone with emotion. "This is the third time you've almost..."

"I'll take the danger seriously from now on," Brynn told her. "No more sneaking out. No more ignoring the rules. I'll let the poison tasters do their job. I trust Valis and whoever she enlists to get to the bottom of this."

Delia's bottom lip trembled. "Do you promise?"

"Promise," Brynn said.

"I'm so glad to hear that," Fayeth said. She and Galesha approached Brynn's bedside as well, stepping past Isuna, who was forced to vacate her chair and retreat a few feet. From the way Isuna crossed her arms over her chest, Brynn could tell she wasn't pleased.

"We've spoken with Bloodtender Horys about your condition and treatment," Galesha said. "Oh, I've just remembered. He asked me to give you this." She withdrew a paper packet from within her robes and handed it to Brynn. "He forgot this supplement for your tea. I'm afraid the poor man was quite flustered by this awful situation."

Brynn looked at the packet in her hand, then back at Galesha. The back of her neck prickled and the hairs on her arms stood straight up. Grandmother's spider skin was back in full force. "Horys forgot this?" Her gaze shifted between Galesha and Fayeth.

"It speaks to how upsetting this horrible attack was for all of us," Fayeth said. "It wasn't merely an assault on you personally, but all of Winterwail."

Brynn tried not to snort when she caught Isuna glaring daggers at Fayeth. Even Delia gasped and placed her palm upon her chest. It had clearly been the wrong thing to say to a person who had nearly died, but Fayeth ignored their reactions, pinning Brynn with an uncomfortable, searching stare.

"Bloodtender Horys insisted you take them directly," Galesha said.

She noted the cup of half-finished tea on the nightstand and took the packet from Brynn's hands. "Hand me that cup of tea, would you, Delia? I'll heat it up." She licked the tip of her finger and twirled it twice, producing a small orange flame.

Brynn's shoulders stiffened. Her gaze darted nervously from Galesha to Delia. Something was definitely wro7ng with their behavior. The fact that they wanted to force tea and some mysterious substance down her throat thundered in her head like the warning drums back home. "I'm feeling a bit nauseous." Brynn cupped her hand protectively over her stomach. "Can it wait a few minutes? I'd hate to throw Horys' medicine back up."

"Nonsense," Fayeth said. "You must take the medicine Bloodtender Horys prescribed as soon as possible. He knows best. Delia? The tea."

"Um..." Delia's eyes flicked restlessly between Fayeth and Brynn, waiting for further instruction.

Brynn's spider skin turned cold and clammy. It had nothing to do with her weakness or her wound. With growing horror, she realized Valis' advisers were to blame. Fayeth's consumption of the poisoned pastries must have been a ruse to divert suspicion. And it had worked. Valis' advisers hadn't once crossed Brynn's mind as possible suspects.

Quickly, Brynn considered her options. She couldn't drink the tea, but she was also injured and unarmed. Galesha and Fayeth were blood mages. If she refused, they might grow desperate—with Delia and her mother as potential casualties.

If they're pushing this hard and without any subtlety, they must be in a hurry. I bet Valis knows, or will know soon. Stalling's my best hope.

"Okay, you're right. I'll take the medicine. Delia, will you hand her the tea?" She leaned toward Delia and stared at her without blinking, brows raised and ears standing straight up. She gave the subtlest nod she could manage, hoping Delia would take her meaning.

A soft gasp skated past Delia's parted lips. She went to the nightstand. Brynn noticed her hand trembling. Delia grasped the handle, then bumped her elbow against the bedframe, sending the cup and its contents onto the floor. The rug beneath the bed saved the cup, but the tea spilled everywhere.

"Oh, I'm so sorry," Delia squeaked, drawing both hands sharply to her chest. "I—it was an accident..."

Galesha's plum-colored lips peeled back over her sharp teeth, but she regained control of herself in an instant. "No need to worry, dear. We all make mistakes. Consort Woodwarden will just need to take her medicine with water."

Brynn's stomach lurched as Galesha licked her finger and curled it upward. The unbroken cup rose from the rug, floating into Galesha's hand. Meanwhile, Fayeth held her palm upward, fingers outstretched. Shimmering droplets condensed in the air above her hand, swirling into an orb of water.7

"Actually, nature happens to be calling right now. Urgently." Brynn swung her legs over the bed's edge and prepared to stand, glancing toward the bathroom door. "I'll be right back."

"No." Fayeth's voice was cold and hard. "Not before you've taken Bloodtender Horys' medicine."

Isuna placed her hands on her hips. "This is ridiculous, Lady-Advisers. Brynn doesn't have to take anything she doesn't want to. As my daughter often says to me, you aren't the boss of her."

Galesha rolled her eyes. "Charming. Very well. I was hoping to do this the easy way, but if you insist..." Quick as a cat, she cast the teacup aside and drew the bejeweled dagger at her waist.

Brynn lunged across the bed to stop her, but Fayeth was faster. With a clench of her fist, the orb of water condensed into wicked shards of ice. Snarling, she flung them at Brynn's head. Brynn barely rolled away in time. The icicles pierced the fur blanket by her head, tearing holes in the hide.

"Run!" Brynn shouted at Isuna and Delia. She dropped off the bed and ducked behind the mattress, scrambling in search of something she could use as a weapon.

Delia cowered against the wall, sliding into a crouch and wrapping her arms around her knees. Isuna grabbed a silver candle holder from the nightstand and swung wildly at Fayeth's head. Fayeth threw up her forearms to protect her face, then stumbled, slipping on the ice floor.

"Enough of this nonsense!" Galesha sliced her dagger across her palm and made a flinging motion. Isuna, who'd reared back for another strike at Fayeth, went flying full speed into the far wall. She hit the ice with a sickening thud and slid into a heap on the floor.

A scream of pure rage tore from Brynn's throat. Fighting the urge to run to her mother's side, she sprinted for her bow and quiver, which were mounted on hooks by the fireplace. A blast of crimson light streaked toward her, leaving a scorch-mark on the wall behind her head.

Brynn stopped her mad dash to take cover beside her neglected vanity. Narrowly avoiding another blast, she scooped as many bottles of lotions and potions into her arms as she could carry, then began chucking them at Galesha and Fayeth.

"You foul, impudent little brat!" Galesha waved her hand, but Brynn tucked and rolled. When she hopped to her feet, the vanity was in splintered pieces. She threw another bottle, ducked to avoid a barrage of icicles from Fayeth, and ran for the mounted wall hooks where her bow hung.

"No you don't," Fayeth spat, drawing her dagger. She cut the back of her arm, her blue eyes glowing white with fury. Spikes erupted from the ice at Brynn's feet. Brynn gasped and windmilled her arms, hopping clumsily to avoid them. The freshly healed wound behind her shoulder tore open, screaming with pain.

Hot blood soaked through Brynn's bandages, running down her back. She hopped her way to her bow, barely avoiding the icy spears. One of them sent her skidding into a nearby armchair—but not before she snatched her bow and quiver from the wall. She grabbed an arrow, dropped to one knee, and aimed for Galesha's throat.

Galesha flung up her hand. A shimmering red dome formed around her, deflecting the arrow like a shield. It fell to the floor. Brynn fired another arrow, then another. They splintered against the dome, bouncing off uselessly.

Fayeth retaliated with another blast of icicles. Brynn dove behind the armchair. Her muscles seized as her open wound protested, but she pushed past the pain.

"Come out, come out, Brynn Woodwarden," Fayeth called, striding toward the armchair. "We're finished playing games with you."

"No!" Delia shouted.

Brynn peeked around the edge of the chair to see Delia grab the abandoned candle holder, leap up from her crouch, and bash it against the back of Fayeth's head. Fayeth swayed, clutching her head with one hand and groping for the nightstand with the other.

Galesha whirled on Delia. She abandoned the shield, summoning an ominous crimson glow in her bloody hand. As she prepared to throw it, Brynn grabbed another arrow and let fly. It hit dead center between Galesha's shoulder blades. A red stain bloomed across Galesha's royal-blue robes. She swayed, then collapsed onto her hands and knees.

With a shriek, Fayeth pushed away from the wall. She grabbed Delia's hair, dragging her close and holding the dagger to her throat. "Not another move or I'll slit her throat."

Brynn's heart gave a sickening lurch in her chest. Her vision narrowed to a dark tunnel with Delia's vulnerable throat and Fayeth's gleaming dagger at the end. Fayeth would do it, no doubt. She could tell from the crazed look in Fayeth's eyes.

"Throw the bow and quiver away," Fayeth said.

Brynn hesitated. If she released her weapon, she and Delia were probably doomed, but if she didn't...

"Let her go, Fayeth," Brynn called, peeking over the armchair. "She hasn't done anything to you."

"No, but you have. And it's too late for niceties. You have three seconds to cast aside your bow. One, two..."

"Three." Valis finished the count as she burst through the door brandishing Aefbain. Clouds of crimson smoke billowed around her and her eyes flashed white. Brynn's heart skipped a beat. Valis looked like some avenging storm goddess, electrified by Aefbain's glow.

Valis pointed Aefbain at Fayeth and gave a command. Trails of smoke crawled across the floor, winding their way up Fayeth's body until they enveloped her from toes to chin. She could only stare, wide-eyed, her body immobilized. Her stiff fingers twitched and her dagger dropped to the floor.

"Thank the seasons." Brynn heaved a sigh of relief and popped up from behind the armchair.

Delia scampered away from Fayeth, pinning her back flat to the wall. "Your Majesty?!"

The smoke around Valis dispersed as she strode calmly into the room. She was followed by Kraal and, to Brynn's surprise, Lord-Adviser Naddox. "Is everyone all right?" he asked, looking around the room.

Brynn ignored Naddox. She ran to where Isuna was slumped against the wall and knelt by her side. A large goose egg had formed around a shallow cut on Isuna's head, but she seemed to be breathing normally.

"Mom." Brynn pulled Isuna into her arms, shaking her gently by the shoulders. "You hit your head. You have to wake up."

"Let me see her," Kraal said. Before Brynn could protest, Kraal scooped Isuna into her arms and carried her to the bed. She shifted Isuna to one arm as she swept aside the icicles lodged in the mattress, then laid her atop the torn blankets.

Brynn followed, wincing when she strained her injured shoulder to push herself up. When she made it to the bed, Kraal was turning Isuna's head this way and that. Brynn bit her lip. Her mother looked surprisingly small beneath Kraal's large hands.

"Is she okay?" Brynn asked.

Kraal nodded. "This bump isn't pretty, but she'll live. Delia?"

Cautiously, Delia stepped away from the wall. She made a wide circle around Galesha and Fayeth, whom Valis had relieved of their weapons while they remained magically suspended in the red smoke. "Y-yes?"

"Go and fetch Horys." Kraal offered Delia a surprisingly soft smile. "He's really earning his salary today."

"Right. Horys. Of course." Delia scuttled from the room even faster than her usual frenetic pace.

"What about these two?" Naddox asked Valis with a drawling note of disgust.

"The dungeons, of course," Valis said. "Black Wolf's hide, this will lead to a pile of paperwork higher than the Daggerback Mountains."

For the first time since Valis' whirlwind entrance, Brynn looked at her—really looked at her. Small, slender, and dripping blood down her forearm, Valis no longer seemed larger than life. She looked angry, frightened, tired. Brynn wondered at how easily she could read all those emotions on Valis' face but didn't have time to ponder. Though Brynn remained by Isuna's side, she shot Valis a concerned look. "What about you? Are you all right?"

Valis sighed. "I could ask the same of you. You're bleeding."

"I'm fine," Brynn said.

"Nevertheless, I shall have Bloodtender Horys examine you, too."

Brynn wrinkled her nose. Something about Valis' searching stare made her heart hump out of rhythm and caused her stomach to twist in knots. She knew Valis wasn't judging her, because she didn't feel like a specimen pinned to a cork board, but—

Oh. She's worried about me. Again. Fuck.

"All right," she said. Valis had saved their lives, after all. The least she could do was submit to medical treatment without complaint this time.

Valis' frown remained, but her shoulders relaxed. "Thank you."

"You're welcome."

An awkward silence followed. Brynn was keenly aware that Naddox and Kraal were listening to their conversation. Though she and Valis hadn't said anything inappropriate, it still felt unexpectedly private. Pushing past the awkwardness, she sat on the edge of the bed and took Isuna's limp hand in hers. "Horys is coming, Mom. You're going to be fine."

* * * * *

The palace guards arrived first, removing Fayeth and Galesha unceremoniously from the room. Horys came soon after, much to Brynn's relief. After tending to Isuna's head wound, he managed to rouse her with liberal use of smelling salts. Brynn hurried to comply with Isuna's request for water and spent the rest of the time holding her hand tight. Every few seconds, she squeezed just to feel Isuna squeeze back.

Once Horys finished treating Isuna, he stepped back from the bed and looked around as though for the first time. "Ancestors!" He eyed the shattered bottles, splintered furniture, and scorch marks on the wall. "What in the world happened here?"

"It's a long story," Valis said. "The short version is, two of my advisers committed treason by attempting to murder my wife."

Brynn blinked. *Wife?* Her ears perked up and her face flushed. She tried to ignore the awkward feeling—awkward because it was unexpectedly pleasant.

Horys gaped at Valis like a fish out of water, wide-eyed and slack-jawed. In the end, he simply shrugged and shook his head. "Not my circus," he muttered under his breath. "Come here, Consort Woodwarden. Let's have a look at you. Apparently, you couldn't wait even a day before disobeying my instructions to rest."

Brynn folded her arms and scoffed in offense. "I apologize for being attacked in my own room."

Horys ignored her, pulling her arms away from her chest to peel her stained shirt over her head. He undid the bloody bandages, cleaned and resealed the wound, then applied fresh bandages. Brynn tried and failed not to squirm during the process, less because Horys was hurting her and more because Valis was watching.

When Valis circled behind Brynn to observe Horys' work more closely, Brynn felt a tingle race down her spine. Her gaze roamed around the destroyed room, unable to settle anywhere for more than a moment. "Sorry about the mess."

The tingle became a shudder when Valis gave that soft, silvery laugh of hers. "It wasn't your fault." She looked around at the wreckage. "It seems you finally found a use for the… what did you call them? Lotions and potions I gave you."

Brynn laughed too. "Yeah. I liked the rose and salt scrub for my face, though. Need to get some more of that."

"There we are." Horys tapped Brynn's uninjured shoulder. "All done. Please do try and preserve my handiwork this time, Consort Woodwarden. Now, I must insist the rest of you leave. Isuna must remain awake for the next few hours, but I insist she have peace and quiet. Loud chatter may overexert her senses."

Brynn turned and glared at Horys, already opening her mouth to object.

"It's all right, dewdrop," Isuna said, her voice low and a bit unsteady. "I'm going to be fine." The barest hint of a smirk twitched at the corners of her lips. "Now you've got a taste of your own medicine."

Brynn scrunched her nose. "True. Are you sure you'll be all right?"

"Rest assured, I will remain with her," Horys said. He glanced at the toppled stack of books on Brynn's nightstand, which she hadn't even realized she'd disturbed during the fight. "You seem to have some reading material already. Lucky me."

Brynn looked from Horys to Isuna, biting her lower lip.

"Go, Brynn," Isuna said. "Besides, don't you have something important to tell Valis?"

Anxiety prickled along Brynn's neck and forearms. "Um…"

Valis tilted her head, giving Brynn a curious look.

Brynn glanced away, then down to the floor. She noticed she was twisting her hands and stopped. "Ah. Right. Should we...?" She gave an awkward nod toward the door. She didn't want to leave Isuna, but she did need to tell Valis what she was really keeping captive beneath the royal palace.

"Of course," Valis said. "Naddox?"

"Your Ma—" Naddox stopped and cleared his throat, flicking an invisible speck of something from his sleeve. "Yes, Valis?"

"See to it that Galesha and Fayeth are given potions of magic resistance, would you? Strong ones. And find proper oubliettes for their ritual daggers."

Naddox inclined his head. "Of course."

"I'll happily donate to that cause," Kraal said. Brynn noticed the light of mischief dancing in her dark brown eyes. "Fresh blood is best, isn't it?"

Valis nodded. "Thank you, darling. Go with Naddox, then. Once I speak with Brynn, I'll begin on that paperwork—including stripping my former advisers of all their titles and privileges. Oh, finding an unbiased magistrate for this trial is going to be a nightmare..."

Before she could think better of it, Brynn patted Valis' narrow shoulder. "Don't worry about that part yet. They can sit in the dungeon as long as it takes for you to get through it. Let the wheels of justice turn slowly."

Valis raised her own hand, placing it gently over Brynn's. "No less than they deserve for what they did to you. Oh... oh, I'm sorry." Her ears lowered in dismay as she looked at their joined hands. Valis withdrew hers with a swiftness that made Brynn's chest feel strangely empty.

Brynn raised a brow, then noticed the wet blood on the back of her own hand. She'd been too distracted to worry about it. "It's fine," she said. "But you should probably close that."

"Indeed." Valis unsheathed Aefbain, pressing the flat of the blade to her palm. White light flashed, highlighting faint runes etched upon the dagger, then dimmed. When Valis removed Aefbain, the cut was closed without so much as a scar. "Now, where were we?"

* * * * *

Valis followed Brynn out of the suite and into the hall.

"Let's walk and talk." Brynn slung her bow and quiver over her shoulder. She set a brisk pace, obviously expecting Valis to accompany her.

The note of urgency in Brynn's voice didn't bode well. "Where are we going?"

"The cavern under the palace."

Valis stopped dead while Brynn kept walking. "That's quite impossible, I'm afraid. The cavern is strictly off-limits except for—"

Brynn turned and walked back to Valis. Her jaw bunched, her shoulders going rigid in a visible display of determination. "You've got a frost wyrm egg sealed away down there. We have to unseal it and set it free."

Valis sighed, pinching the bridge of her nose. This unending string of shocking revelations had gone from surprising her to giving her a stress headache. She closed her eyes a moment, processing Brynn's declaration, then inhaled deeply. "How did you learn this?"

"From Gruush," Brynn said. "It's why I snuck out. The picture book—"

"The picture book I expressly told you I would consult with Gruush about so you wouldn't have to endanger yourself by leaving the palace?"

Brynn rubbed her neck, having the decency to look sheepish. "Yes, that picture book."

The ache inside Valis' skull worsened from a dull throb to more of a stabbing pain that followed the rhythm of her heart. She gritted her teeth, rubbing her temple with two fingers. "Go on."

"When I showed Gruush the illustration with the hidden rune, she told me about a frost giant deity, Hadronax, mother of all frost wyrms. Whenever Hadronax died, she was reincarnated as an egg. I think your ancestors couldn't kill her like the other frost wyrms, so they entombed her deep under the ice. That's what the ritual is for—to keep her bound."

A sharp denial rose to Valis' lips, but died there before she could utter it. As Brynn's theory burrowed into her brain, its roots began to spread. *Mother always told me That Which Dwells Beneath was a terrible and powerful force of destruction. Did she know what it was, or was that simply what her ancestors told her? How many of them knew?*

You aren't seriously listening to this nonsense, are you? The low drawl of Aefbain's voice dripped with condescension. *You can't believe the wild theories and conjectures of someone without a drop of magic in their blood.*

"Why not?" Valis said. "Brynn is stubborn and reckless, but far from stupid."

Brynn tilted her head. "Um, thanks? I think. Are you talking to your dagger again?"

Valis ignored the flash of embarrassment she felt for having answered Aefbain aloud. "Yes. Aefbain doubts your claim..." She withdrew the dagger from its scabbard at her thigh, staring down at it with narrowed eyes. "...and has denied it *with unusually forceful insistence.*"

"Maybe it has its own agenda," Brynn said. "It can lie to you, can't it?"

My agenda, Aefbain said, *is to prevent you from unleashing catastrophe upon your kingdom. I possess the wisdom of your collective ancestors, and every single one of them is screaming from beyond the Veil in protest at the idea of freeing That Which Dwells Beneath!*

"Yes." Valis eyed her own reflection in the obsidian sheen of Aefbain's blade. "It can."

Fine, Aefbain snapped. The glowing red runes along its polished surface pulsed in annoyance. *Go down to the cavern and destroy everything your ancestors spent centuries to build.*

"Offer me another explanation, then," Valis said. "What is That Which Dwells Beneath if not Hadronax? Surely you know the truth, if you do in fact possess the wisdom of all the Aefbains who have come before."

There are reasons I cannot tell you, Aefbain said. *To possess the knowledge of That Which Dwells Beneath's nature is a danger in itself.*

Valis' upper lip curled back over her sharp teeth. "Very well. If you won't enlighten me, I have no choice but to investigate for myself. Come on, Brynn." She grabbed Brynn's elbow and pulled her along, walking briskly through the hall and toward the nearest downward staircase.

"Valis...what if I'm right and it is Hadronax?" Brynn said, trotting to keep up. "What are you planning to do?"

"Release it, of course. What sort of question is that? I can't very well keep someone's god locked away under my palace, can I? If this is true, the shame of my ancestors' legacy regarding the frost giants is greater than I thought, and I didn't even know that was possible."

Brynn stopped, causing Valis to jerk back. She turned in confusion only to meet Brynn's mouth, warm and hungry against hers. She stiffened in surprise, then clutched Brynn's shoulder with her free hand, her knees wobbling beneath her. When Brynn's tongue swept gently along Valis' bottom lip, she opened, instinctively deepening the kiss. *Oh.* She'd longed for this taste ever since—

Aefbain launched into a series of strongly worded chastisements in the back of Valis' mind, but they were so distant she hardly noticed. She only heard the roar of her heartbeat in her ears and felt the warmth of Brynn's lean, sinuous body pressing against hers. She almost dropped Aefbain onto the floor when Brynn looped an arm around her waist to pull her closer.

With twin gasps, they eventually parted for air. Valis chased Brynn's lips anyway, only to find them smiling when she opened her eyes. She couldn't even remember closing them. "What?" she asked, breathless and half dazed.

"I knew you'd do the right thing," Brynn said, grinning.

Valis' heartbeat slowed to a more manageable speed. The cold reality of her situation returned, including the complications that would surely follow such an unseemly and inappropriate display of emotion. "I—" For once, she had no idea what to say.

"Come on." Brynn took Valis by the hand. "Let's go see if I'm right."

Chapter Twenty

THEIR DESCENT INTO THE cavern was dark and cold. Though Valis had taken the narrow, winding staircase numerous times, never before had it seemed this long. It was so quiet and still that the sound of her own breaths echoed in her ears. Even Aefbain kept its silence as she held it aloft to illuminate their path.

Partway down the stairs, Valis felt Brynn grope for her free hand in the shadows. She allowed it, though Brynn's fingers felt like icicles. She took reassurance in the contact as they circled toward the faint white glow below.

At last, they reached the cavern. Prisms of light bounced from the glittering stalactites overhead, flickering along with the eerie pulsations of the shining white orb sealed beneath the icy floor. Valis gazed down, staring intently at the orb, but the knowledge that it might be Hadronax's egg made it look no different.

"You're certain about this?" She turned toward Brynn. The tips of her ears burned hot in the cold air as she realized they were still holding hands. She knew she should let go, but something prevented her from doing so.

"Pretty damn certain." Brynn didn't let go of Valis' hand either. "There's always a chance I could be wrong."

Valis sighed. "I believe you. This sounds precisely like something my ancestors would have done while taking over the northern territories."

The cost of conquest was regrettable, Aefbain said, *but you cannot change the past, Valis. That Which Dwells Beneath is a wild force of pure destruction. It will ruin the Kingdom of Winterwail for the people who live here* now, *in the present. People you are responsible for!*

"That includes the frost giants who live here, Aefbain," Valis said sharply, releasing Brynn's hand. "I cannot, in good conscience, keep one of their gods imprisoned." She narrowed her eyes at Aefbain's obsidian blade, which reflected the rainbows of light from above like rippling oil. "I will ask you directly: is That Which Dwells Beneath Hadronax or not?"

That Which Dwells Beneath is not something you can control, Valis! Your ancestors kept it sealed away for good reason, because to release it would bring ruin—

"Yes, yes, ruin. I heard you the first time. You didn't answer my question. A yes or no will do."

Your ancestors—

"Very well. Keep your bloody secrets, you wretched kitchen knife. Since you refuse to enlighten me, I have no choice but to discover the truth for myself." Valis sliced her palm, then sheathed Aefbain, refusing to use it as a focus. She had a feeling that releasing whatever dwelt beneath would take far less energy than keeping it contained.

"Don't you need my blood?" Brynn asked.

"The undoing of such an ancient spell should be far less taxing than re-energizing it. Besides, I've interacted with this web of spellwork many times. I know it by heart."

"Are you sure?" Brynn's brow furrowed. She took a cautious step closer to Valis. "I don't want you to get hurt... or magic drunk like last time."

Valis forced what she hoped was a reassuring smile. "I appreciate your concern, but I will be fine, I promise. Now, before I bleed all over the place..."

She stepped toward the pedestal of ice and the frozen orb that sat on top. The dark swirls of blood that floated within the orb became agitated as she approached, squirming like angry serpents. It was as though they sensed her intentions.

Please, I beg of you, Aefbain said, in a beseeching voice Valis had never heard before. It had never once begged her for anything since she'd bonded with it. Its usual emotions were limited to bossiness, resentment, wry amusement, and disdain. *What would your mother think of such recklessness? Your sister? You're releasing the enemy they spent their whole lives protecting the kingdom from!*

That almost gave Valis pause, but she continued, stopping in front of the orb. "I am thinking of my mother and sister." She stared down at the spiraling whorls of blood. As she placed her bloody hand upon the orb's surface, they wiggled toward her palm with what seemed to her like reluctance. "If they knew what I know now, I have no doubt they would have done the same."

"Unbelievable," Brynn muttered from the background. "Aefbain's bringing up your family now? Really? It's absolutely insufferable."

Valis snorted in agreement, then focused on her blood as it flowed into the orb. She closed her eyes, feeling the chill of ice beneath her palm, the heat of her blood as it wept from the cut, and the white-hot prickle of arcane power that crawled along her skin. She felt the heady rush of magic as it swelled within her, searching for an outlet. Her heart raced and a sharp, burnt smell filled her nose.

She opened her eyes. Silver ley lines of spell work shimmered all around her, a dome of gossamer netting that resembled a spider web. Fragile and delicate, yet ancient beyond any other magic she'd interacted with, its roots burrowed deep into the ice below. Inside the orb, the ribbonlike strands of blood floated into a perfectly identical design.

Valis couldn't help but pause to admire the geometric, crystalline pattern of the ley lines. When she looked closer, it resembled a snowflake. Undeniably beautiful, but like all snowflakes, there was a time to melt.

Apologies, Your Majesty. I cannot let you do this.

Valis blinked, breaking concentration. The ley lines flickered, turning dark scarlet. She gritted her teeth and gripped the orb tighter, refusing to dignify Aefbain with a response.

Very well... if you insist.

Pain exploded in Valis' head, so sudden and sharp that her vision went white. She staggered, releasing the orb and clutching her head in both hands. Another spike of pure agony drove through her skull, piercing her very mind.

Her legs gave out. She crumbled to her knees.

"Valis?!"

She barely recognized her name. The voice was dull, distant. All she knew was blinding torment. Her thoughts shattered, leaving everything twisted and warped, like peering through shards of glass. She could barely find the strength to see through the blinding white light—

No. Red. The light was red. The color of blood.

She groped blindly through the red, searching for a handhold, an anchor for the splintered pieces of her consciousness—and found the cold metal of Aefbain's hilt.

I did warn you, Majesty. Aefbain's voice boomed over the scattered remnants of her mind. *Fortunately, troublesome marriages have a loophole: 'til death do you part.*

* * * * *

Brynn rushed toward Valis, dropping to one knee and extending her hand. "Valis?!"

Valis ignored the offered hand. She remained on elbows and knees, breathing heavily. Her back rose and fell in a jagged, uneven motion. Choked sobs accompanied each one, soft at first, then growing louder—

—into high, cold laughter.

Brynn's blood ran cold. This was nothing like the silver bells she was used to hearing when Valis laughed. "Valis, can you hear me?"

Valis lifted her head. Her eyes glowed with piercing crimson light and her wide, unhinged smile showed the sharp points of her teeth. Strands of long white hair had escaped her crown of braids, clinging to the edge of her mouth. A sluggish trail of blood poured down her chin where she'd bitten through her bottom lip.

Brynn's stomach lurched. She grasped Valis' shoulder and shook. "Valis? What should I do? Answer me!"

With frightening speed, Valis threw off Brynn's hand and bounded to her feet. She tilted her head and stared at Brynn, dragging her dark purple tongue along the bloody split in her lip. The glittering rubies of her eyes had no whites or irises as she brandished Aefbain. There was nothing of her in them. Her silence was deafening.

"Shit." Grimacing, Brynn reached for her bow. Her hand faltered. She couldn't shoot Valis. She was clearly possessed or something—

A howling rush of wind swept Brynn off her feet. She flew through the air, slamming into the ground and skidding across the ice. She threw out her arms and kicked her feet, searching for some kind of purchase. She collided with a jutting stalagmite, shouting as it jarred her injured shoulder.

Pushing past the sudden shockwave of pain, she used the stalagmite to pull herself upright. "What are you doing?!" she panted, clinging to the stalagmite for support.

Valis stepped forward. The echo of her high-heeled boots clicked across the snow-dusted ice. The wind had vanished, leaving the cavern eerily silent but for the two of them. Valis' lips curled in a snarl, as though she were fighting the words that spat forth. "Removing the problem."

Brynn's eyes darted from Valis' crazed red eyes, which wept tears of blood down her pale periwinkle cheeks, to Aefbain. The dagger glowed like fire-forged metal in Valis' outstretched hand. Though Brynn's mind and heart raced with the pounding rush of her blood, she understood what had happened. Aefbain had taken control. She had to separate Valis from her dagger.

"Valis, I know you're in there," she called, reaching slowly over her shoulder for her bow. Miraculously, it had survived her crash landing. "You're the most powerful blood mage in centuries, right? That's what you told me. Fight it! Aefbain doesn't want what's best for you. It's corrupting you."

A bolt of crimson lightning streaked past Brynn's head, close enough to singe her hair. It smashed into the stalactite beside her, shattering it to pieces. Shards of ice pierced Brynn's flesh, embedding in her cheek and arm. She barely felt them as she stumbled away, struggling to keep her balance.

Brynn felt the faint flutter of hope. Her gut told her that Valis had caused the near miss on purpose. She was still in there somewhere, fighting.

Valis adopted a sideways stance. One arm hung loose behind her, while the other pointed Aefbain like a fencer's foil, aimed dead between Brynn's eyes. "Surrender, and I will make your death swift and painless," Valis said, but her voice wasn't her own. It was a terrifying chorus of voices, high and low, soft and loud, a cacophony of contradicting pitches and tones.

Brynn whipped an arrow from her quiver and nocked it to her bowstring. "Counteroffer: let her go, or I'll make sure she destroys you." For the first time since childhood, when she'd first learned the art of archery, her hands trembled, as though forgetting what to do. She didn't want to shoot Valis, but she knew no other way to fight. Her usual strategy of downing opponents with a single shot wouldn't work here.

Valis threw her head back and laughed with the crazed, overlapping sound of dozens of voices. She wiped her hair away from her mouth, smearing the trail of blood on her cheek and chin, then licked the remainder from her lips. "Very well. It's a shame to end you, Woodwarden. Your blood was positively delectable. Even she thinks so."

Brynn grimaced as she drew back her bowstring. "You don't speak for her." She chose her target, the hand which brandished Aefbain, and fired.

Valis gave the slightest nod of her head. A red dome sprung up around her, much like the one Galesha had made. Brynn's arrow splintered against its surface, falling to the floor in pieces.

Brynn winced. *Not this shit again!*

Valis raised Aefbain to her mouth, blowing across its point as though putting out a candle. Bright orange sparks sprang from the glowing metal, then converged into a gout of fire that blasted straight for Brynn.

Brynn dove behind another stalagmite and ducked. The top half of the stalagmite melted in a crackling hiss of steam. Once more, Brynn smelled singed hair. Stupidly, she wondered if the new hairdresser would be able to fix it—which would be the least of her problems if Aefbain killed her.

Get a grip, Woodwarden! Fight!

She popped up over the remnants of the stalagmite, fired an arrow through the cloud of steam, then ran, searching for a hiding place.

There was little cover to be found. Stalagmites were her only option, but they were few in number. She crouched behind one and waited for the steam to disperse, hoping against hope for a shot.

The steam rose.

Brynn spotted Valis' shadow and loosed another arrow. Valis swept it away like a troublesome fly, then blew across Aefbain's blade. Another dragon's breath of fire streaked toward Brynn's stalagmite.

Brynn ducked and rolled. Her shoulder screamed at the impact with the ground, but cold and fear had all but numbed her body. With little choice, she scurried for the next stalagmite as another cloud of steam billowed around her.

"Come out, come out, Brynn Woodwarden," Aefbain sang in a haunting chorus, as though they were playing a deadly game of hide-and-seek. "She's screaming for me to end this, but I'm dragging it out as a lesson. Hopefully she learns from this. She was always too stubborn for her own good."

While Aefbain monologued, Brynn crept silently from behind the stalagmite, bowstring drawn taut. She skirted to the edge of the steam cloud and fired at the distant red glow of Aefbain's blade. It streaked past the writhing serpents of blood in Valis' shield, but disintegrated the moment it touched Aefbain, falling to the floor in a pile of ash.

Valis whirled toward Brynn and threw out her empty hand. The whorls of blood flew toward Brynn, tangling around her limbs. She clung to her bow, but one slimy tentacle of blood ripped it from her hands. Another bound her wrists. Yet a third seized her ankles, while a fourth wrapped around her throat, yanking her into the air.

High, cold laughter filled the cavern again. "She loves you terribly, you know," Aefbain said with awful glee. "That's what she tells me as she begs for your life."

"Then fight it, Valis," Brynn shouted, staring down at Valis in wide-eyed desperation. "Fight for me!"

Valis licked more blood from her lips. She curled the fingers of her outstretched hand. The slimy tendrils of blood tightened around Brynn's limbs.

"You brought this on yourself," Aefbain said. "If you'd been the compliant bloodbag I needed, you would have lived a charmed life in exchange. I suppose it's too much to ask for a wood elf to recognize a beneficial exchange when they see one. Goodbye, Brynn Woodwarden. It hasn't been a pleasure."

The tendril around Brynn's throat began crushing her windpipe, cutting off her breath and blackening the edges of her vision. She kept staring at Valis as the dark tunnel narrowed, grieving more for her than herself. *She doesn't deserve to lose anyone else... This is all my fault...*

Mere moments before darkness overtook the scarlet glow, an enormous black shadow dove in front of Brynn. With a bellowing roar, the shadow collided with Valis.

The blood tendrils around Brynn's throat and limbs loosened. She coughed, sucked in a desperate gasp, and fought for freedom. She writhed and thrashed with all her strength until she finally managed to squirm out of their grip.

Brynn hit the floor with her hip, wincing as the jolt coursed through her bruised body. Her vision swam, but she made out the blurry sight of her bow—no, two bows—lying abandoned a few yards away. She dragged herself toward the bow and seized the one she hoped was real, heaving a sigh of relief when her fingers found polished wood. She shook her head to clear her vision and cast about for her quiver.

Another terrifying roar sounded nearby. Brynn whipped her head up to see Kraal's looming figure attempting to grapple Valis. Red blasts fired wildly into the air as Valis fended her off, sending several stalactites crashing to the ground in a glittering shower of ice.

"Stop pulling your punches, you foolish child!" Aefbain howled through Valis' mouth. *"Obey! Incinerate her!"*

The red light around Valis flared. Her body went rigid, floating into the air high above Kraal's grasping hands. Aefbain glowed forged orange again and sparks danced along its keen edge. Valis pursed her lips to blow.

Brynn grabbed her quiver. Most of the remaining arrows had snapped, but a single shaft looked promisingly strong. She nocked the arrow to her bow, squinted to steady her wavering sight, and aimed at Valis' clenched fist.

She loosed the arrow. It hissed as it streaked toward Aefbain. The arrow struck Valis' hand. She jerked, dropping Aefbain. Fire erupted from the dagger as it fell, blasting stalactites from the cavern ceiling. Valis swayed, then collapsed on the ground. A large stalactite snapped free, hurtling toward her.

Brynn scrabbled across the ice, struggling to stand. She had to reach Valis—protect her! The wound behind her shoulder protested. Her arm seized. She slipped, falling face first into the snow. She could only watch in horror as the stalactite fell.

A loud shout shook the cavern. Kraal charged Valis, gripping her staff in both hands. She collided with the stalactite, splintering her staff but sending it off course. It crashed less than a yard away from Valis, sending shards and debris everywhere. Kraal grunted, dropping to one knee and catching herself on her hand. She dropped the broken pieces of her staff, her broad back heaving with each breath.

Forgetting the pain behind her shoulder, Brynn used her other arm to regain her footing. She half jogged, half limped toward Valis and Kraal, reaching out for them well before she arrived. Valis lay still upon the ground, her white braid coiled above her head like a serpent. Dark crimson dots stained the white dusting of snow beneath her body.

"Is she..." Brynn stared helplessly at Kraal.

Kraal dropped her other knee. A pained shadow flickered across her face as she placed two fingers against the base of Valis' throat. "She has a pulse," Kraal rasped, "but it's faint." Her wide eyes shimmered, the black of her pupils nearly eclipsing the dark brown irises.

Brynn's heart clenched. She was no Druid, no healer, no Darrow. Nevertheless, she crouched on Valis' other side, brushing a bloodstained lock of hair from her forehead. Aside from the smears around her mouth and the scarlet tear streaks that cut across her pale cheeks, she wasn't bleeding heavily. Thank the seasons for small miracles.

"Valis," Brynn croaked, grasping Valis' hand in both of hers. She realized she was bleeding too when hot blood dripped between their palms. Valis' fingers were ice cold. Brynn clutched her hand tighter, blinking back tears. "I saw how hard you fought." Her tears fell, dripping onto Valis' cheek. "Don't stop now!"

Valis remained still and silent but for the shallow rise and fall of her chest.

"We need to move her." Kraal glanced toward the spiral staircase. "Her injuries seem minor. It's magic making her like this."

Brynn clutched Valis' hand tight. "What if moving her makes things worse?"

Kraal's frown was cut like a deep crevice in the side of a stone cliff. "What choice do we have? We aren't mages. Farthest thing from."

"No…" Brynn looked for Aefbain, which lay several yards away in the snow. It remained unbroken, but without Valis' blood flowing into it, the blade no longer glowed with unnatural light. "But if we destroy the dagger, Valis might wake up."

"Aefbain cannot be destroyed by natural means," Kraal said. "We need a blood mage, and who knows if one exists with enough power?"

"We need Valis." Brynn laid Valis' limp hand to rest in the center of her chest, then pulled a broken arrow from her quiver. She dragged the tip swiftly across her hand. A line of blood bloomed from the cut, flowing through the crevices of her palm. She cast the arrow aside and took Valis' hand again, lacing their fingers together.

"Come on," Brynn muttered, staring intently at Valis. More tears rolled down her cheeks, dripping from her chin. "You're so strong and brave and fierce, and I love you too fucking much to let it end like this. Use my blood and *fight.*"

* * * * *

Valis groped through an ocean of thick, congealed blood. Unlike the warm, fresh blood that pulsed through living arteries, this blood was ice cold. She clawed for the surface, but there was no surface. The sea surrounding her was too vast to feel her way up or down.

She wrenched her eyes open. Endless black stretched in all directions. Her desperate attempts to breathe caused only a weak stream of bubbles. She choked and sputtered as blood filled her mouth, thrashing in search of a handhold.

There were none to be found. Harsh currents tossed her about like a loose piece of driftwood in a storm. Deprived of sight, trapped in dead silence, unable to breathe without drawing blood into her lungs, she fought helplessly against the chilling tide.

Aefbain had trapped her here. There had to be an end to this bloody ocean, some way to regain control and reach Brynn.

The battering current of blood formed clotted coils that wrapped around Valis' calves and forearms. They jerked her violently through the slimy sea, wrenching her limbs into strange contortions. Aefbain was puppeteering her. *Using* her.

Valis! For a brief moment, Brynn's distant, pleading voice broke the barrier of silence. *I saw how hard you fought. Don't stop now!*

A spark lit in Valis' heart, sending a weak pulse of warmth through her frozen body. *No—no! I can't lose Brynn! I can't let Brynn lose me!* She clenched her fists and howled, releasing another stream of bubbles. It made no difference. The all-consuming darkness grew fuzzy and her eyes fluttered shut. Her trembling limbs slackened even as her mind screamed for her to resist.

Summoning the last of her strength, Valis writhed against the tendrils that bound her arms and legs, fighting with the strength of fear and fury. She almost tore her left arm free, but the coil around her wrist tightened until she could no longer feel her hand. She screamed, but there was no sound. The silence remained unbroken. Her body gave out and she went limp, surrendering to the current.

Come on, Brynn said from somewhere beyond the dark sea, her voice a pleading whisper. *You're so strong and brave and fierce, and I love you too fucking much to let it end like this. Use my blood and fight.*

Continuing to fight the cold, heavy blackness that bound her and weighed her down seemed an impossible task. Valis couldn't find the strength to move, but she managed to crack her eyes open. A wavy ribbon of red pushed through the cold black waters, reaching out for her. When it wrapped around her waist, Valis felt its warmth—and an unmistakable, intoxicating rush of power.

This was Brynn's blood, no doubt. Somehow, Brynn had reached through the darkness to save her.

Valis' sluggish heartbeat sped up, hammering against the cage of her ribs. Fresh, tingling energy surged through her limbs like lightning, filling her with new strength. She forced her frozen body into movement, ripping her arms free of Aefbain's coils and grabbing onto the ribbon of Brynn's blood with all her might.

A chorus of angry shrieks pierced the silence. The tendrils around Valis' legs curled tighter, winding up past her hips. She twisted and kicked, sloughing off the wet, slimy clots and diving headfirst into the current of Brynn's blood. It swept her away, its powerful roar drowning out the overlapping screams until they were no more.

As she glided through the cold black sea, Valis saw faint pinpricks of light. They grew larger as she sped along, shining brighter and brighter, like evening stars had sunk beneath the churning waves.

No. Bubbles. As the current pulled Valis along, she entered a field of glowing bubbles. They shimmered with an eerie red light, suspended weightlessly in the sea. Within each bubble was a shadow—shadows with a torso, arms, legs, and a head.

Valis realized at once what they were. These were the fragments of her ancestors' souls stored within Aefbain. More like imprisoned. Would this be her fate as well, to float forever in a sea of blood with a bubble for a cage? Never. She wouldn't allow it. Once she found freedom, this would end with her.

The shining field of bubbles vanished behind her and the current became a whirlpool, bearing her up, up, up toward a hazy light in the distance. She reached for the light with both hands, spiraling up toward the surface.

Valis slammed shoulder-first into a sheet of black ice. Its glassy obsidian surface, the same color as Aefbain's blade, allowed only the faintest traces of light to filter through. She clawed desperately at the barrier until her nails split and her fingers were shredded raw, but there was barely a scratch to be seen for her efforts.

Cease fighting, you impudent child, Aefbain shouted, causing the bloody waters to churn and the sheet of ice above to quake. *Do you know why they call you the most powerful blood mage in generations? Because I have always amplified your powers. Without me, you are nothing more than a novice playing parlor tricks.*

Valis snarled, beating upon the ice with both hands. *I am no novice! They were calling me a prodigy before I ever laid hands upon you, you useless piece of scrap metal! I have never needed you the way you need me!*

She rammed her shoulder into the ice. The whirlpool of Brynn's warm, living blood shot up like a geyser, shattering the obsidian barrier and breaking through to the surface.

* * * * *

Valis coughed. She flopped her head sideways, spitting blood onto the snow. Her entire body pounded painfully with each beat of her heart. She shivered, gasping for air, then became aware of squeezing warmth around her hand. She squinted, waiting for the blurry silhouette hovering above her to solidify. Brynn peered down at her with a grief-stricken expression, clutching her hand tight.

"Great Root," Brynn croaked, removing one of her hands and cupping Valis' bloodstained cheek. "I thought I'd lost you."

Valis tried to speak, but all that came out was a weak groan. She cleared her throat and tried again. "You... found me..." Brynn had reached through the darkness when her own strength hadn't been enough and, against all odds, had pulled her back to herself.

Another large shadow passed over Valis as Kraal stepped into view. She held the twisted, smoking remnants of Aefbain, little more than a lump of warped gold that had once been its hilt and a few splinters of jet-black stone. "Never liked this piece of junk anyway." Her voice was rough and choked, as though she'd been crying.

Valis tried to sit up, but the rush of dizziness that followed made it clear that moving was a mistake. She flopped back onto the snow, exhaling a long sigh. Despite remaining sprawled on the cavern floor, she felt lighter than she had in years. A great weight had been lifted, one she'd grown so accustomed to that being without it came as an unexpected relief.

Brynn's hand moved from Valis' face to her shoulder, attempting to keep her still. "Don't move. Just breathe. We almost... I almost..."

Valis lifted her free hand and rested it on top of Brynn's. Connected through both palms, warmth began seeping back into her body, filling her with new strength. "Almost is the key word there," she said.

Brynn laughed. Wet tears welled from her dark eyes, streaming down her face. "You ass."

Valis managed a weak smile. "You're all right, aren't you? Kraal?" She glanced between them. Kraal stood upright while Brynn kneeled, both alive and alert.

"Right enough to carry you." Kraal handed Brynn the broken pieces of Aefbain and bent down to scoop Valis into her arms.

Only then did Valis notice Kraal's torn, crimson-stained sleeve and the jagged gash beneath. Valis reached for the scabbard strapped to her thigh only to find it empty. That was a problem to solve later, when she wasn't one giant, bloody bruise. She groaned, resting her head on Kraal's shoulder. Her eyes fluttered shut, but she felt one of Brynn's hands find hers again.

Together, the three of them limped up the stairs toward the light above.

Chapter Twenty-One

BY THE TIME THE harried and haggard Bloodtender Horys was summoned for a third time, Valis felt more like a puddle of melted snow sludge than a person. She remained silent and compliant as he treated her, responding to his mumbled chastisements with short nods and soft noises of concurrence.

Brynn and Kraal remained by her side the whole time, equally subdued. No doubt they were still processing the battle that had taken place beneath the palace. Whenever the churning sensation of guilt threatened to boil over in Valis' stomach, she stared at Brynn's face—her warm, living face; her skin the proper, healthy shade of copper.

She's alive. I didn't kill her. Then why do I feel so terrible?

Too exhausted to probe those thoughts, she remained quiet until Horys left—to take a long and well-deserved nap, he claimed—and Lord-Adviser Naddox entered her suite. His pale face went ashen when he looked upon her bloody, bruised countenance.

"Your Majesty! What in the world—"

Valis held up her hand. "It is a very long story. Here is the short version. Unbeknownst to me, my ancestors have kept a sacred frost wyrm egg sealed beneath the palace. Brynn informed me of this, and when I tried to investigate, Aefbain... resisted." She chose not to describe the battle that had followed.

Naddox blinked rapidly. "Resisted?" His mouth fell open and his ears stood straight up.

Valis sighed, slumping her shoulders. "Aefbain is no more."

A long, tense moment of silence followed. Valis saw the wheels turning in Naddox's mind through his wide, startled blue eyes. In the end, he shrugged. "I have absolutely no idea what to say in light of that information."

"Our course is clear," Valis said. "Arrange for Gruush to be brought to the palace. She is one of the foremost frost giant leaders in the city of Winterwail, with ties throughout the kingdom. Most important of all, I trust her not to retaliate with violence when this information comes to light." Her heavy heart felt a bit lighter when she noticed Brynn's warm, encouraging smile.

"Are you sure you wish to do this right now?" Lord-Adviser Naddox asked. "You, Consort Woodwarden, and Kraal are injured. Shouldn't this wait until tomorrow, at least? Or even longer."

Valis chewed her inner cheek while she considered Naddox's advice. She didn't have the energy to put on her usual emotionless mask. Exhaustion soon won out. The egg had been kept in stasis for centuries. One more day wouldn't change anything. "Very well. For my peace of mind, please send the messenger tonight. I trust you can draft a suitable missive—one which conveys the appropriate urgency without revealing too much on paper."

Naddox bowed and offered his upturned palms. Though Valis couldn't reach them while lying in bed, she nodded in acceptance of the gesture. "Very well, Your Majesty." He held her gaze. For once, the title didn't sound condescending coming from his lips. Valis was certain she saw respect shining in his long, measured stare. "For what my opinion is worth, I believe your choice has the potential to change our entire kingdom for the better."

"The choice to return what was stolen is easy," Valis said. "The fallout, however... that may be more difficult to manage."

Naddox smiled, perhaps the first genuine smile Valis had ever seen him bestow upon her. "You need not manage the coming difficulties alone. Besides, two adviser positions have suddenly fallen vacant. Take some time to think about who will be most helpful to you in the coming months."

"Kraal." She looked to her loyal attendant, the woman who had saved not only her, but Brynn and the entire kingdom as well. According to Brynn's recounting of events, she'd intervened without hesitation.

Kraal coughed. She pointed at herself. "Me? I—"

Valis waved off her protests. "Promise you'll think about it. If that responsibility is too heavy for your shoulders, I understand. You have done more than enough for me and Winterwail already, but don't reject my offer because you doubt your own capabilities. I need someone who will advocate for the frost giants and put their needs first, but who doesn't want to kill me."

Kraal floundered, her mouth opening and closing. In the end, she placed her large hand on Valis' shoulder, with the gentlest possible pressure. "I don't need to think about it. You're my best friend. I'll do whatever you ask."

"But tell me when I misstep," Valis said.

Kraal smiled. "Isn't that what friends do?"

"Yes. Yes it is." Valis leaned over to hug Kraal, relaxing in her warm, comforting embrace.

"This is so sweet I might gag," Brynn said, more than a hint of laughter in her voice.

"I approve of your choice," Naddox said. "I have always thought we needed a frost giant adviser, and Kraal strikes me as a wise, measured person."

Kraal pulled away from Valis and smirked at Naddox. "Now I feel guilty for all the times I've badmouthed you in private, Lord-Adviser."

Naddox waved her away. "Never mind. Consider this a new beginning, colleague."

* * * * *

Gruush and Madge arrived at the palace shortly after sunrise the next morning. Brynn greeted them at the entrance with a firm clasp of hands and a friendly smile. "Good to see you again, Gruush. Madge. Though I didn't think it would be so soon."

"Likewise, Brynn Woodwarden." Gruush patted Brynn's hand. Gruush's enormous hands swallowed hers completely and she tried not to wince at the strong grip. "The message we received was unexpected, but not unwelcome."

"Unexpected indeed." Madge hobbled over to Brynn for her own greeting. Despite her age, her grip was even stronger than Gruush's. "I knew I liked you right away, Brynn, but you should have told me you were the royal consort!"

Brynn winked at Madge. "If I opened with that information right away, you wouldn't have liked me as much."

"True," Madge said. "Good morning, Kraal. A pleasure to see you as well."

Kraal took Madge's knobbled hands in hers, bending to touch their foreheads. "A good morning to you as well, Grandmother." Brynn suspected the term wasn't literal, but one of respect.

Gruush gave Kraal a friendly clap on the shoulder. "Well, to business. Why exactly has Aefbain summoned us here?" Brynn noted the lack of title with interest but said nothing. Did it mean Gruush didn't recognize Valis as the sovereign of Winterwail? If so, she was surprised Valis had spoken of her relationship with Gruush in such positive terms.

"To return something stolen long ago," Kraal said. "Before we show you, please understand that Valis did not know its true nature until yesterday evening, when Brynn discovered it."

Madge's drooping eyelids rose. "Does it have to do with the picture book?" She glanced around to make sure none of the posted guards were near enough to hear their conversation, but lowered her voice anyway. "With the Great Mother?"

Kraal nodded. "Yes, it does. I assure you, Valis only wishes to return what was taken. You may have an emotional reaction to this discovery, but please—for my sake, save your fury and insults for her ancestors."

"Understood," Gruush said.

"No promises," Madge muttered.

Gruush frowned. "Mother!"

Madge huffed. "All right. No sense standing about here jawing any longer. Lead on, Kraal. Brynn."

They spoke of other things as they made their way through the palace, toward the hidden staircase, and down toward the cavern. Brynn was content to listen to Gruush, Madge, and Kraal share the sort of community gossip she was used to overhearing back home. She found their chatter comforting, as they pooled information about recent illnesses, new babies, and other tidbits of drama from the temple.

As they descended the stairs, the conversation circled to Kraal's new job.

"A frost giant as adviser." Madge shook her head in happy disbelief. "Never thought I'd live to see that." She winked at Kraal. "You'll do us proud, child."

"I'll do my best." Kraal hesitated, then added, "I've always known Valis was searching for a way to leave the Aefbain legacy behind. I just didn't think it would happen so quickly."

"Only eight hundred years late," Madge grumbled.

Gruush clicked her tongue. "Mother...for Kraal's sake, don't blame the girl. She hasn't even been on the throne a year."

"So?" Madge said. "I'm old. Time is something I don't have much of, and I'd like to see our lot improve before I kick the bucket."

"Mother!"

"We're here," Kraal said.

Though Brynn had been to the cavern twice before, she joined Gruush and Madge in craning their necks to look around. The cavern maintained its wondrous natural beauty, despite the fight that had taken place the day before. Aside from the snapped crowns of several stalactites on the ceiling and the jagged bases of blasted stalagmites, it looked much the same—until Brynn noted dots of old blood in the snow.

Brynn looked away. The unpleasant reminder lodged in her throat, despite her efforts to swallow down the burning lump of emotion. It pained her to think of Valis under Aefbain's control. She reminded herself that they had overcome the worst, but a shadow of fear and sadness remained until she looked up.

Valis stood by the pedestal of ice and the orb it carried, gazing into its swirling depths. When the group approached, she lifted her head and smiled. "Ah. Prompt as ever, Gruush. Madge. Welcome." She inclined her head to them, then looked directly at Brynn.

The heat of Valis' stare sent a pleasant prickle down Brynn's spine. It was a relief to see Valis alive and well. Thanks to Horys' tireless work, her delicate features were no longer marred by the previous day's events. Still, Brynn couldn't help but remember the tears of blood that had marred Valis' cheeks. She forced those thoughts to the back of her mind.

"Thank you for the invitation." Gruush neither bowed nor offered her hands, but the low tones of her voice conveyed respect.

"Kraal says you wish to return something that was stolen long ago." Madge approached the pedestal, examining it with unconcealed interest.

"Yes," Valis said. "No doubt Kraal has already informed you I wasn't aware of its significance until yesterday."

Gruush nodded. "Indeed. For my part, I believe you. Despite what your ancestors have done, you have never been dishonest with me and mine."

Watching from a few yards away, Brynn noted the lowering of Valis' shoulders. A misty cloud exhaled slowly from her mouth. "It was Brynn who figured it out." Valis looked at her again. Brynn felt the uncomfortable urge to straighten like a soldier at attention as all eyes focused on her.

"We believe it's an egg." Valis pointed at the white glow beneath the ice. "A frost wyrm egg. Maybe even Hadronax herself."

Gruush and Madge appeared shaken, but not surprised. Their faces appeared quite similar, as they regarded the glow with wide, hopeful eyes and parted lips, the only difference being Madge's deep wrinkles.

"I had my suspicions, based on Brynn's questions and the way Kraal danced around the subject, but to consider the reality..." Gruush shook her head slowly, an open-mouthed smile stretching across her face. "I can scarcely allow myself to hope, yet my heart feels lighter than I can explain in words. Part of me is desperate to believe this."

"Only one way to find out," Madge said. "Can you unseal it, Aefbain?"

"I prefer that you call me Valis, and I believe I can."

Madge grinned, showing slightly crooked teeth. "We'll see about that afterward."

Valis nodded. "Fair enough. Brynn, would you be so kind?"

Brynn's ears perked at the sound of her name. She stepped forward, joining Valis beside the pedestal. Valis drew a silver dagger from a new, heavily bejeweled scabbard strapped to her thigh. "This is Starfall." Valis allowed Brynn to examine the blade. Though beautifully crafted, the blade was shining silver rather than obsidian.

"Please tell me Starfall isn't sentient," Brynn said.

"Not in the way Aefbain was," Valis said. "Its magical essence vibrates in tune with my emotions, but it is merely a focus. It possesses no will of its own. This is the dagger I bonded and studied with before my mother's death."

Brynn breathed a sigh of relief. "Thank the seasons for that."

Valis laughed softly, and Brynn's face flushed at the familiar sound of silver bells. It seemed Valis' beautiful laugh was back to normal. Another thing to be thankful for. "Hold out your hand, please."

Brynn offered her upturned palm. To her delight, Valis caressed the side of her hand with her thumb before slicing Starfall across the middle. Its edge was so sharp that Brynn hardly felt any pain before blood began pooling in her cupped hand. Quickly and efficiently, Valis sliced both of her hands, placing her right hand, with Starfall, upon the orb. She laced the fingers of her left with Brynn's.

"Prepare yourselves," Valis said to Kraal, Gruush, and Madge. "I believe, down to my bones, That Which Dwells Beneath is indeed Hadronax's egg, but in the unlikely event that I'm wrong, whatever is sealed beneath the ice may be dangerous when it awakens."

Brynn glanced at the giants. Kraal drew a large wooden staff from her back, similar to the one she had broken in the cavern the day before. Gruush pushed back the fur cape she wore to reveal the end of a sword, wrapping her hand around the hilt. Even Madge clutched her carved walking stick.

Feeling Valis' eyes upon her, Brynn turned back toward the pedestal. Valis offered a small smile, which Brynn couldn't help but return. "You've got this." She squeezed Valis' hand tighter. Sticky warmth pooled between their palms.

"I know." Valis gazed into the orb's clouded depths. Dark whorls of blood slithered toward her hand, as though trying to break through the orb's surface and seize Valis' wrist. Brynn ignored the unpleasant churning in her stomach that she had come to recognize as fear.

Valis opened her mouth and sang. The ringing soprano of her voice poured forth, filling the cavern. It was the same melody Brynn had heard before during the monthly ritual, but this time, the words were different.

> "I am Aefbain, daughter of Aefbain.
> Look upon my shining blade,
> That which dwells beneath the ice,
> Tis I shall see your blood price paid.
> Magic blood your thirst to slake,
> Magic blood for you to wake.
> I am Aefbain, daughter of Aefbain.
> Through my blood, the compact break."

A curious, tingling pull extended down Brynn's arm, warming her hand. She gripped Valis' fingers tighter, relaxing when Valis squeezed back. The whorls of blood within the orb stirred, forming crystalline patterns. The lines shone through its surface, painting bright crimson cracks upon the cavern ceiling.

Brynn craned her neck, looking up in awe. Though the lines of light shone a brilliant red, she felt no encroaching sense of foreboding. Not like when Valis used Aefbain for her blood magic. The warm, tingling feeling became a pleasant burn. Brynn's heart beat faster in her chest.

The crimson cracks extended down the walls, forming patterns that looked to her like snowflakes—each one unique and beautiful. When the cracks reached the bottom of the cavern walls, they spread across the floor like cracks in the surface of a glass mirror. The white glow beneath the ice pulsed, growing brighter and brighter until Brynn had to close her eyes.

A loud rumble shook the cavern, causing the ground beneath their feet to shudder and quake. Brynn felt Valis falter and turned toward her, placing a steadying hand on her hip. They were face to face, close enough that she felt Valis' warm breath upon her cheek.

Another blinding flash erupted through the cavern floor. Someone shouted, but Brynn couldn't make out the words above the loud *crrrack* of breaking ice. The light flared, then dimmed, leaving white spots behind Brynn's eyelids. After several moments of empty silence, she risked opening her eyes. She gasped and nearly stumbled back. A large, steaming canyon had formed in the middle of the room, less than a foot from where she and Valis stood.

"Great Root." Brynn stared, open mouthed, into the crevice until Valis released her hand. The light was gone, but she thought she saw an oval shape somewhere near the bottom. She only tore her eyes away when Valis released her hand. "Are you all right?" she asked, gazing worriedly at Valis. Brynn kept a hand on her waist just in case.

Valis squinted, then blinked, obviously recovering from the flash as well. When she opened her eyes, Brynn noted that her irises had returned to their usual soft, gray color. "That was easier than expected," she said. "The spell work was ancient and beautiful, but fragile after all these centuries. Even the strongest enchantments eventually show wear and tear." She removed her hand and Starfall from the orb, which lay upon the pedestal in pieces. "Give me your hand again."

Brynn offered her hand and Valis closed the cut with the flat of Starfall's blade. After a pleasant surge of warmth, no sign of the cut remained. The blood that had stained Brynn's palm and dripped from between her fingers was gone, having seeped into the dagger.

Valis sealed her own cuts, then stepped back and turned, regarding Kraal, Gruush, and Madge. Brynn turned as well. All three of them were staring down into the crevice, leaning forward and craning their necks. "Pull back a bit or you'll fall," Brynn said, walking over and nudging Kraal's hip with her elbow.

Kraal ignored her, continuing to stare down at the orb nestled below. Though it no longer glowed, its surface possessed a silvery, almost metallic sheen that reminded Brynn of the picture book. No doubt remained in her mind that this was indeed Hadronax's egg.

"Well?" Madge said, her voice brimming with excitement. "Get us down there, Valis!"

Brynn caught the flicker of Valis' smile from the corner of her eye. "Easily done." Valis ran her tongue along Starfall's edge, then made several horizontal sweeps, as though carving the air. The closest side of the crevice melted, releasing steam into the air. Once it cleared, a set of steps led down to the bottom.

Though Brynn fairly buzzed with curiosity, she resisted the impulse to run down the steps, allowing the frost giants to descend first. They did so in single file, surrounding the silver egg at the bottom. Brynn began to follow but stopped partway down. Madge—old, knobbly Madge—had dropped her staff with a clatter and fallen to her knees. She pressed her open palms against the egg, staring into its surface with wide-eyed wonder.

"A frost wyrm egg. A real frost wyrm egg!"

Gruush placed her hands upon the egg as well. As Brynn hopped down the final steps, she noticed tears glistening on Gruush's cheeks. "It's cold," Gruush murmured. A wide, toothy grin stretched from one side of her face to the other.

"Is that good news?" Valis asked, joining Brynn at the bottom of the crevice. They maintained a respectful distance as Gruush, Madge, and Kraal examined the egg.

"Better than good." Kraal didn't spare them a single glance as she too possessed the egg. "They need to maintain an extremely cold temperature to survive. Believe it or not, being buried beneath all those layers of ice kept it too warm to hatch."

"Do you think it will hatch?" Brynn asked, her voice rising with excitement. Though she felt like something of an interloper in this moment, she was overjoyed that this creature, long presumed extinct, had returned to the world. A sacred creature, no less!

"Only one way to find out," Madge said. Her grin looked almost exactly like her daughter's, though her teeth were more worn with age. "We'll need some ropes and pulleys to—yowch!" She yanked her hand away from the egg, swatting at her arm. "Ah, get them off!"

Brynn stepped closer, raising her hand to help—with what, she had no idea—but Gruush got to Madge first. "Hold still so I can get them," she said, brushing something from Madge's arm.

"Just get the blasted things off!" Madge did a hobbling little dance, while Gruush tried to pat her down, with mixed success.

"Ouch," Kraal said, retreating from the egg to stand on Valis' other side. "Looks like the egg wasn't the only thing sealed down here. Those are frost mites. Harmless, but they bite if their nests are disturbed."

"Where?" Brynn and Valis asked at the same time. Brynn checked her own arms while Valis brushed nervously at her robes.

"There," Kraal said, pointing at their feet.

Hundreds of tiny black dots scurried away from the egg in haphazard lines, reminding Brynn of ants marching along the forest floor. She shifted so one of the lines would stop crawling over the toe of her boot. "Well, they don't seem to be coming for us."

"Speak for yourself," Madge grumbled. She'd stopped hopping about, leaning on Gruush for support while Gruush bent down to retrieve the staff.

"You disturbed them," Gruush said. "I wager you'd bite with far less provocation than that, if you had any teeth left to bite with."

Madge huffed as she reclaimed her staff. "Point taken."

"Frost mites are very important to the ecosystem of the northern territories, you know," said Gruush. "We should save this nest if we can."

"Are they?" Valis asked, without looking up. "I've never heard of frost mites before."

Brynn watched the mites as they began burrowing into the ice. Their tiny tunnels looked like fracture-lines in a thick sheet of glass.

"Yes." Gruush wrinkled her nose. "They eat black fungus."

"I've never heard of black fungus either," Valis said.

"Neither have I," said Kraal, "although I've lived my whole life in the south."

"No?" Gruush sighed. "Black fungus is horrible. It only grows in the northernmost territories, so colonies are typically small. Frost mites help keep the numbers down."

"Horrible is underselling it," Madge whispered conspiratorially to Brynn and Valis. "It spends most of its life growing on trees without much harm, but in the final stage of its life cycle, its spores can infect higher mammals as well. Almost got eaten by a crazed, half-Rotted direwolf when I was a little girl."

Brynn's head spun toward Madge. "Wait. Rotted?"

"Sure." Madge's smile became more of a leer, like an elder regaling children with a scary story. "According to legend, mammals infected with black fungus can grow all kinds of mutated appendages. Extra arms, legs, eyes, even mouths...granted, I've only seen the one."

Brynn was scarcely listening. A muffled roar rose in her ears as her pounding heart sent blood rushing through her head. She looked at Valis, then Kraal, who gaped at her with matching expressions of bewilderment.

"Black Wolf," Valis gasped. "Did the frost giants have the answer all along? Right under our very noses?"

"Apparently so," Kraal mumbled, shaking her head.

"Answer to what?" Gruush asked.

Brynn tried to speak, but all that came out was an embarrassing croak. She cleared her throat. Happy tears welled in her eyes and threatened to roll down her cheeks. "A mysterious Rot has been infecting the southern forests for the past few years. Mutating our animals, injuring and even killing our people. We had no idea what was at the bottom of it, so... I married Valis. She promised her alchemists would find an answer."

Gruush's mouth fell open. She shook her head slowly but said nothing.

Madge rolled her eyes. "Pshh. Alchemists. What do they know?"

"Apparently not everything you do." Brynn dropped to her knees before Madge and Gruush, bowing her head. "Please. You've got no reason to help the wood elves, but my people are being driven from their villages. Some are dying. We need you."

"Get up, foolish girl." Madge grasped Brynn's elbow in a bony hand

and hauled her back to her feet. "We have every reason to help you. Don't you realize what you've done? You've returned the frost wyrms to us!"

"Of course we'll help," Gruush said. "I for one won't stand by while a large group of people are in need."

Brynn couldn't hold back her tears any longer. She threw her arms around Gruush's waist and hugged her, sobbing far too loudly into her shirt. "Thank you. Thank you!" After months of research by the brightest minds the snow elves had to offer, the answer had come in the smallest, humblest form of all.

Grandmother would call it destiny. A gift for a gift. Brynn could only call it a miracle.

Chapter Twenty-Two

VALIS STARED AT HER pale reflection in the bathroom mirror. As usual, the ghost of Ruith stared back at her. The fate of her mother's soul weighed heavily upon her shoulders. Had the soul-sliver imprisoned within Aefbain passed safely beyond the Veil? Had it joined the rest of Ruith's spirit?

She opened her eyes, avoiding her reflection as she uncapped a bottle of moisturizer and rubbed her face. Though Ivoss had healed her worst bruises, some tenderness remained, as did the dark crescent shadows under her eyes.

Valis let down her braid, sighing as it uncoiled from around her head and fell down her back. Her scalp ached with relief. Double-checking the knot on her purple silk robe, she left the bathroom and stepped into the bedroom.

Brynn sat in an armchair by the fireplace, bundled in a bearskin blanket with her legs curled on the seat. She smiled as Valis entered. "Washed off your face, have you?"

"Yes." Valis managed a small smile. "I see no reason to stand on ceremony with you after... well. You've seen me possessed and covered in blood—a slightly more horrifying sight than my face without makeup."

Brynn laughed. "Come sit with me." She patted the armchair.

Valis raised a brow. "Where am I supposed to sit?"

"It's a big chair. There's room for two."

Valis' heart fluttered as she approached Brynn. Her cold hands suddenly felt warm, as did the tips of her ears. Brynn scooted over, but Valis perched on the chair's arm so their thighs wouldn't touch.

Brynn turned back toward the fireplace, gazing into the dancing orange flames. Even after they broke eye contact, Valis felt the intensity of Brynn's stare upon her skin. It was a strange, pleasant tingling sensation.

"Thanks for letting me sleep in your suite, by the way," Brynn said. "Since mine is still, you know."

Valis nodded without looking, even though she longed to. "There was no need for you to sleep in the armchair last night. We could have shared the bed."

The corners of Brynn's mouth quirked upward. "I'll consider it."

Valis swallowed. There were enough words on the tip of her tongue to fill a book. One of the big, dusty tomes that made Brynn roll her eyes. Still, she fumbled before she could say any of them, allowing the conversation to lapse.

They stared at the flames a while. It wasn't an oppressive silence, as Valis had feared, but a peaceful one. Valis caught herself admiring the way the orange glow highlighted Brynn's bronze skin more than once.

Eventually, Brynn spoke. "I've been thinking about how black fungus could have infested the southern forests." She let the statement hang between them, gazing into the fire, or perhaps somewhere beyond it.

"No doubt the unicorn hunters my mother sent into your forest brought it in their food supplies or on their boots," Valis said. "You needn't dance around the subject. I am willing to accept responsibility—"

Brynn turned, looking up at Valis. Her shining brown eyes bordered on amber in the firelight. "Hey." She placed her hand on Valis' thigh. "You can't blame yourself for every single thing that goes wrong. You've quite literally severed yourself from the past now."

Valis' eyes darted down to Brynn's hand. Her thigh burned beneath Brynn's palm. "I know. It never feels like enough."

"Fixing something that's remained broken for centuries takes a long time and a great many people," Brynn said softly.

Valis sighed. "I suppose so."

"Forgiving yourself for your ancestors' sins will be a process, won't it?"

"It keeps me humble."

Brynn squeezed Valis' leg. "Save your energy to give the nobles who cling to the old ways what-for, then. Someone they're conditioned to respect has to do it. Who better than you?"

Valis swallowed again. Despite the somber topic, she couldn't concentrate as the rough archer's callus on the heel of Brynn's palm rubbed her skin.

"You're right. That is something I can do." She gathered her courage, then said, "How are you feeling about everything? What happened down in the cavern."

Brynn tilted her head. "Which time?"

Valis resisted the impulse to bite her lip. "The first time. When Aefbain possessed me."

Brynn's brow furrowed. Her full lips tugged into a frown. "To be honest, I can't stop thinking about it. About how close you came to..." She looked away, lowering her voice to a whisper. "How close I came to losing you. It made me realize I don't know what I'd do if I did."

Valis' breath hitched. There it was. The fear that had clung to her like a shadow ever since her family's death. The terror that gripped her tighter in its claws the longer she spent in Brynn's company. The fear that love would inevitably lead to loss. She wanted to look away, but forced herself to hold Brynn's eyes. "Sometimes, it feels as though we have no choice. Not in who we love, nor who we lose."

Brynn's other hand came up to caress Valis' shoulder. Her thumb stroked back and forth along Valis' collarbone. "No, we don't, but we get to choose whether to accept our feelings, the good and the bad—or bury them. I think you know my choice."

Valis held her breath. The hope and tenderness in Brynn's gaze were unmistakable. "This will make things complicated. Messy."

Brynn stared at Valis without blinking. "Even the best marriages are sometimes. It doesn't scare me." Her full lips parted, as though she were waiting for Valis to bridge the final gap.

Valis was more than scared. She was utterly terrified. *But what manner of life would I lead, ruled foremost by fear? Not the one my mother and sister would have wanted for me. Not the one I want for myself.*

Before she could change her mind, Valis dipped down and kissed Brynn. She froze when their lips met, still somewhat bewildered by her own choice, but once the warmth of Brynn's mouth met hers, she melted like a spring thaw. She slid her fingers through Brynn's curls, cupping the back of her neck.

She grew more certain of her choice when Brynn moaned, returning the kiss with enthusiasm. Brynn's tongue swept along her bottom lip, seeking entrance with a boldness that made her shudder. In a matter of moments, the silk of her smallclothes had soaked through.

Valis didn't resist when Brynn's hand moved up her leg, dipping beneath the hem of her robe to caress her hip. She curled her fingers tighter in Brynn's hair and whined, an embarrassing and undignified sound, but one she couldn't stifle. Heat pooled in her lower belly and she parted her thighs on instinct.

It should have been too fast, too much, but craving was a keen-edged knife in her belly, urging her to arch into Brynn's touch. Her flesh burned as Brynn's fingertips grazed her stomach, following the thin band of her smallclothes.

Valis broke away for breath, panting as she gazed into Brynn's wide brown eyes. She might have been able to resist, or at least slow down, if lust were all she saw reflected there, but the soft sheen spoke of much stronger emotions. Emotions that were easier for Valis to name now, but impossible to resist.

"I love you," Valis said.

A grin as wide and white as the moon broke across Brynn's face. "I know." She pulled Valis off the arm of the chair and into her lap, hooking an elbow behind her waist for support.

"You *know?*" Valis repeated, feeling especially naked and vulnerable. The fact that Brynn hadn't immediately returned the sentiment had her squirming with embarrassment.

Brynn dipped down for another kiss, swallowing any possible insults with the gentle warmth of her mouth. She withdrew only long enough to say, "I know, and I love you, too," before sliding the front of Valis' robe aside to palm her breast.

Valis' lashes fluttered. As much as she wanted to keep admiring Brynn, it became difficult to keep her eyes open. She arched within the circle of Brynn's strong arm, pushing her breast further into Brynn's hand. "Please," she whispered, her voice trembling. "Show me?"

Brynn's amusement was audible in her voice. "As you command, queen of my heart."

Valis opened her eyes and snorted with laughter. The tension was effectively broken when she saw Brynn's ridiculous grin. No longer the least bit afraid, she pulled Brynn toward her other breast. Her core clenched as the heat of Brynn's mouth closed around her nipple.

Soon, Valis was a whimpering, squirming mess in Brynn's lap. Brynn switched between her breasts, tormenting her with teeth and tongue. Her hand stroked soothing lines along the curve of Valis' side before hooking into her smallclothes and pulling them down. She lifted her hips to help, gasping when Brynn's hand returned to cup between her legs.

"I'd love it if you came fast and hard for me," Brynn murmured, kissing Valis' sternum. She bit the inner curve of Valis' breast, then soothed the sting with the warm, silky flat of her tongue. "But I'd love it even more if you let yourself relax and enjoy it for a while. We've got all night, if you want."

Valis gave a low moan of agreement. She spread her legs wider, rocking against Brynn's cupped hand. When two fingers grazed her entrance in wordless request, she planted one foot on the arm of the chair and slid down onto them, certain she was more than ready. She stiffened, adjusting to the sudden stretch, but also savoring it. There was no pain, only a rising burn that spread throughout her shaking body.

"When you're ready," Brynn said. Her fingers remained still as she latched onto one of Valis' nipples. She rolled her tongue around the stiff bud, then tugged it gently between her teeth.

A breathless gasp caught in Valis' chest. With Brynn's mouth on her, Brynn's fingers inside her, she felt... It was difficult to name the wonderful, weightless sensation. Free? Untethered? Her grief, her burdens, and all her fears floated away. Brynn wanted her, but not as others did. Brynn wanted the whole of her, but only her. No more and no less.

Love. The only word for it was love.

Valis relaxed her tense limbs, combing her fingers through Brynn's curls and rocking slowly against her hand.

Brynn groaned around Valis' nipple, tugging harder with her teeth. She curled her fingers forward and up, applying steady, gentle pressure. The motion sent ripples of white heat through Valis' core. She squeezed instinctively around Brynn's fingers, shivering as they moved inside her.

Part of her was sorely tempted to pull Brynn away, straddle her lap, and ride her hand to climax. A powerful peak was already building within her, rising higher every moment. Only Brynn's words stopped her: "I'd love it even more if you let yourself relax and enjoy it for a while."

Trusting that Brynn would guide her, she breathed deep and savored the slower pace. They didn't need words to communicate. When she wanted Brynn to curl harder, all she had to do was raise her hips. When she needed pressure on her clit, she rubbed herself against the heel of Brynn's hand until Brynn's thumb found her. It was a game of give and take as easy and natural as breathing.

The ball of heat in Valis' lower belly grew until she was panting and gritting her teeth to hold it off, an exquisite sort of torture. Each pass of Brynn's thumb and sweep of her tongue sent a little lightning bolt straight to Valis' core. Just when she thought she might come despite her efforts, Brynn stopped.

"Look at me," she said. Not a command, but a soft plea.

Valis hadn't realized she'd shut her eyes again. She opened them to see Brynn's face descending toward hers. She parted her lips and lifted her head to meet Brynn halfway. When they kissed, she came. She fluttered around Brynn's fingers despite their stillness, rocking once, twice onto them before releasing a muffled sob into Brynn's mouth.

The flutters became heavy pulses as Brynn resumed the steady curling motion, this time with more force. She spilled more cries into Brynn's mouth, but Brynn seemed all too happy to have them. She growled, nipping Valis' lower lip, and trapped her clit beneath a firm thumb.

Valis felt like she was falling. No, flying—riding her release with a freedom she'd never imagined. The rippling of her inner walls became sharp pangs and a sudden fullness swelled to bursting. When she spilled a gush of warmth into Brynn's hand, she kept rocking her hips and let it happen. No need to hold back any longer.

"That's it," Brynn gasped against Valis' lips. "I've got you."

Got you.

Valis clung to those words and to Brynn, holding onto her hair and clutching at the beautifully formed muscles of her back. She felt slightly guilty as her peak faded and she realized she'd left scratch marks—as well as a puddle on Brynn's leg and part of the armchair.

"Don't," Brynn said before Valis could even catch her breath. She pressed a tender kiss to Valis' forehead, then nuzzled the tips of their noses together. "That's a later problem."

"The only problem right now," Valis said, still panting lightly, "is that you didn't come with me." She chased Brynn's lips with hers, but Brynn remained tantalizingly out of reach.

"We can fix that, but I'm not one to keep score."

Valis smiled and dragged her nails lightly over the scratch marks she'd already left. "Don't think of it as keeping score. Think of it as making up for all the nights we wasted sleeping apart."

"They were necessary." Brynn ran her tongue over her bottom lip, a sight that sent another little shock through Valis' core. "But we do have a lot to catch up on, don't we?" She withdrew her fingers, then scooped Valis into her arms, rising from the chair and carrying her toward the bed.

Valis' robe slid the rest of the way off, but she didn't bother watching where it fell. She kicked away her ruined smallclothes, which had apparently been dangling from her ankle the entire time, as Brynn lowered her to the mattress. She fixed Brynn with a heated stare, leaning back onto her elbows and spreading her legs. The blue caveworm silk shirt and leggings she wore simply wouldn't do.

"No more pajamas," she said. "By royal decree, pajamas are hereby banned from our bedchamber forever. Unless it's terribly cold."

Brynn laughed and began unbuttoning her shirt. "Finally! An order I'm all too happy to obey."

THREE MONTHS LATER

Brynn smiled as she sat on the picnic blanket, leaning back on her hands and tilting her face up toward the night sky. Dark blue clouds hovered over the moon, allowing only a faint silver haze to peek through, but Grandmother had assured her it would clear up later on.

That was why she'd brought Valis here, to her favorite stargazing clearing. That, and the fact that early tomorrow morning, the frost giant shamans would release the first frost mite colonies into the fungus-infested trees. Tonight, Brynn wanted to put that task from her mind, at least for a few hours.

"Even with the clouds, it's beautiful," Valis said from beside her. The gentle warmth of her hand covered Brynn's. Their fingers laced together with comforting familiarity.

"I know." Brynn stole a glance at Valis, whose white hair had taken on faint silver highlights under the moon's glow. For once, she wore it loose about her shoulders, with only two small braids to keep her forelocks tied behind the nape of her neck. "But the northern stars are absolutely stunning. I want to show you mine, too."

Valis squeezed Brynn's hand. "It isn't a competition, you know."

"I know, but I grew up with these stars. My family taught me all about the constellations..."

Valis leaned over, silencing Brynn with a soft kiss. The impression of her lips lingered upon Brynn's for several seconds afterward. "Grandmother very much enjoyed informing me about each and every constellation we could expect to see tonight while you helped your parents with dinner."

Brynn sighed. "Of course she did." She had looked forward to introducing Valis to Grandmother, but Grandmother could talk anyone's ear off, given half the chance. Even a queen's. Brynn thanked her lucky stars—which still weren't visible, unfortunately—that they hadn't yet ventured into the territory of embarrassing childhood anecdotes.

"I used to stargaze like this with Shalana," Valis said. "We'd sneak out of bed and share a blanket on one of the palace balconies. We enjoyed making up our own stories about the constellations."

Brynn's ears perked for any traces of sadness in Valis' voice, but her tone sounded more bittersweet than broken. "Good memories, I hope."

Valis leaned sideways, resting her cheek on Brynn's shoulder. "Yes."

Brynn kissed the top of her head. "I did the same with Darrow. Except he told me if I focused on any one star for too long, my eyes would cross and they'd stick that way forever. Then I'd never convince anyone to marry me."

Valis gave a light gasp of laughter. "What an awful thing to say."

"I told him Grandmother could probably fix crossed eyes, but she couldn't fix stupid." They both laughed, then lapsed into comfortable silence. The quiet chirps of crickets and nighttime frogs replaced the conversation, interspersed by the rustle of leaves.

Brynn treasured moments like this, when she could share bits of Darrow and learn bits about Shalana without one of them breaking down in tears. It happened less often now. She recalled one of

Grandmother's teachings. *Pain never goes away, but it often finds a more comfortable place to live.*

The rustle of leaves grew louder as a nighttime breeze picked up, sweeping across the glade and sending a chill through Brynn's shirt. She'd been so eager to discard the heavy winter clothes necessary to life in Winterwail that she hadn't bothered to bundle up back home.

"Come here," Valis said, lifting her head from Brynn's shoulder and letting go of her hand. She lifted the purple cloak she wore with one arm, allowing Brynn to curl beneath it. Brynn sighed happily as the cloak and Valis' body heat banished the brief chill.

"Look," she said, turning her gaze upward. "The clouds are clearing."

The hazy clouds blanketing the sky dissolved into smaller shadows, which were borne away by the wind. One by one, the twinkling stars peeked out. Then small clusters stood out. Soon, shining rivers of stars dripped down toward the horizon on purple-yellow bands. The luminous swirls reminded Brynn of the vastness and constant movement of the ocean.

Valis huddled closer against Brynn's side. "It's easy to get lost up there, isn't it?" she asked in a whisper. "To feel small and insignificant in the face of such majesty. Even queens are nothing to the stars."

"I don't see it that way," Brynn said. "When I look at the stars, it makes me feel like I'm a part of something so enormous, wild, and beautiful that I can't even perceive it all. I feel... connected."

"Connected. Yes. Each star is part of the celestial dance." Valis' slender body relaxed further against Brynn's. "It's all so complex that we often fail to recognize the coming patterns until they've passed us by."

Brynn knew Valis was speaking about more than the stars. "Hey, I thought we had a deal? I don't worry about the frost mites, you don't worry about the egg."

If she were being honest with herself, Brynn was also concerned for the egg, but she knew it had found a safe home up north. A group of the wisest frost giants alive, summoned from all corners of Winterwail, had taken it into their care. Hopefully, it would hatch soon under their stewardship.

"I am not worrying about the egg," Valis protested. "But I am thinking about it. About how many little pieces had to line up just right in order for it to return to the world. In order for us to discover the frost mites. In order for the new legislative council to begin taking shape. In order for us to become... us."

"I'm glad they did. I'm glad *we* did."

Brynn turned to look at Valis. Her pale-gray eyes shone like twin moons themselves. The faint lavender freckles across the bridge of her nose were an equally wondrous constellation. Like the stars above, Brynn could have admired their pattern for hours. She settled for a long, lingering kiss. A smug smile spread across her face when she caught Valis' lashes fluttering afterward.

"Come on," Brynn said, raising her arms toward the sky and stretching out her spine. "Let's lie down." When she fell onto her back, Valis did the same. Their hands found each other again as they lifted their gazes back to the stars.

Valis was right. It was easy for Brynn to lose herself in the swirling vastness of the night sky. But in Valis, she had an anchor. A center. A partner.

A wife.

The End

About Rae D. Magdon

Rae D. Magdon is an author of queer speculative fiction. She believes everyone deserves to see themselves represented in the stories they read, especially lesbians, bisexual women, queer women, trans women, and nonbinary folks. She has published over 10 novels through Desert Palm Press. Her cyberpunk novel, *Lucky 7,* received a Golden Crown Literary Award for Sci-Fi/Fantasy (2019) as well as a Rainbow Award for Science Fiction (2019). Starless Nights, her 2017 space opera with co-author Michelle Magly, also received a Rainbow Award.

Connect with Rae online
Facebook: Rae D. Magdon
Tumblr: https://raedmagdon.tumblr.com/
Email: raedmagdon@gmail.com

Cover Design By : Rachel George
www.rachelgeorgeillustration.com

Note to Readers:

Thank you for reading a book from Desert Palm Press. We appreciate you as a reader and want to ensure you enjoy the reading process. We would like you to consider posting a review on your preferred media sites and/or your blog or website.

For more information on upcoming releases, author interviews, contests, giveaways and more, please sign up for our newsletter and visit us at Desert Palm Press: www.desertpalmpress.com and "Like" us on Facebook: Desert Palm Press.

Bright Blessings